BC

THE MALP[A] W9-BEP-051 62

Also by Sam Llewellyn

The Shadow in the Sands
The Sea Garden
Hell Bay

Dead Reckoning
Blood Orange
Death Roll
Deadeye
Blood Knot
Riptide
Clawhammer
Maelstrom
The Iron Hotel

for children

Pegleg
Pig in the Middle
The Rope School
Wonderdog
The Polecat Cafe
The Magic Boathouse

THE MALPAS LEGACY

Sam Llewellyn

HEADLINE
FEATURE

First Published in 2001
by HEADLINE BOOK PUBLISHING

A HEADLINE FEATURE hardback

10 9 8 7 6 5 4 3 2 1

British Library Cataloguing in Publication Data

Llewellyn, Sam
   The malpas legacy
   I.Title
   823.9'14[F]

ISBN 0 7472 7275 1

Typeset by
Letterpart Limited, Reigate, Surrey

Printed and bound in Great Britain by
Mackays of Chatham PLC, Chatham, Kent

HEADLINE BOOK PUBLISHING
A division of Hodder Headline
338 Euston Road
LONDON NW1 3BH

www.headline.co.uk
www.hodderheadline.com

stories told by Jesse Costelloe to his daughter are founded on myths current in Ireland in the years after the Second World War. All other incidents and all characters in this book are entirely fictitious. Any resemblance between them and events past or present and people living or dead is entirely coincidental.

A Note to the Reader

What follows is a piece of the past. In order to put it behind me, I have had to put it in front of you. Its purpose is to explain to posterity the lives of people now forgotten. And in the retelling of their stories, I hope that I will secure for some of them at least a sympathetic remembrance.

I have assembled the narrative from letters, casebooks and other material brought by David Walker from Ireland and elsewhere. David has raised no objection to the work, even though parts of the story are painful and worse than painful for him. He has even been good enough to read through the manuscript, going so far in some places as to edit and reposition sections. Any additions and reconstructions I have made have been with his consent and approval.

H.C.

Prologue

It started like this.

When I came on deck I saw Dave standing right up in the nose of the boat. He would have been fifty-five then – a tall man, but with a shell-backed stoop that diminished his height and increased his age. As I went forward, Jerry the hand rolled his eyes at me from behind the wheelhouse screen. Dave had insisted he knew the water. But his hand signals had stopped almost as soon as the estuary had narrowed into the serpent of the river proper: an Irish serpent, that seemed to have him mesmerised.

From the front end of the boat you could not hear the engine. The only sound was the rustle of the water parted by the stem, the *yarp* of a grey crow on the bank. When I arrived at Dave's side, he looked surprised to see me. He said, 'Sorry,' and raised his hand, straight on, steady as she goes. The bank slid by, the river curving to the right, broadening into a black sheet of water full of the smell of mud and trees.

Far ahead, a salmon jumped. The boat had turned into the tide and slowed. Chain roared. The anchor caught and held. Silence washed back from the shore, carrying the dusk song of a blackbird.

I heard myself say, 'Gosh.'

To the north the ground rose, clothed in a tangled rain-forest which might, by the faint mauve glow of *rhododendron ponticum*, once have been ornamental woodland. At the foot of the hills, on a piece of flat ground behind a sea wall, was a dark, hulking shape: a house. An enormous, half-ruined house, ponderous, late-Georgian. There was glass in some of the windows, but no light. I felt I was being watched.

1

Which was dumb, of course. It was just a huge house in a beautiful position. Without all that ivy, with a lick of paint and some new gutters, it could be absolutely wonderful.

'Dave?' I said.

He was sunk in a sort of reverie. I took his hand. I said, 'What is it?'

He turned to look at me. He would have seen a woman of twenty-three, tall, with a long, strong face, good skin, irritatingly freckled, lit up now with excitement. I learned later that the first sight of the place took people in this way.

A light had appeared on the dusky hill above the house. It was a dim light, as if it were a forty-watt bulb, and it came and went, as if the breeze might have been blowing branches between it and the viewer.

'That?' he said. 'Malpas.'

'Who lives there?'

'Nobody.'

'Why not? I mean it's so beautiful, how could someone own it and not be there all the time?'

No answer. The blackbird had stopped singing. A new moon floated into a starry gap in the clouds.

'So who does it belong to?'

He gave me a sideways look with his psychologist's eyes. There was something wrong with them. 'I would like to tell you I don't know,' he said.

It was not like him to give me all this portentous stuff. At the same time, I felt the chill in his voice; felt it enough to shiver. I said, impatiently, 'For God's sake, who?'

'You,' he said.

He turned away. And into the whirl of my head there came the knowledge of what was wrong with the eyes.

For the first time in the lifetime I had known him, Dave, cool, collected, Mr Rational, was almost certainly crying.

Hannah Costello

1910

It was a bright spring day, and the river came sliding out of the mountains like one of its own black eels looking for the sea. Here in the middle of the House Pool the air was soft and quiet, with that smell, half sea, half pond, half shite, that Mairi did not actually notice any more, because she had breathed it every day for the past fifteen years, and it was natural to her as the taste of her own spit.

Mairi Dugdale was a thick red girl with black hair and china blue eyes. Mairi was a girl who loved facts, particularly facts you could count.

This was the tale of today's counting. It was the eighth of May 1910, with the sun up and over the third oak on the Nun's Point, and herself in the little black cot, a rowing boat of two ends, five planks a side, painted with one and three sixteenths gallons of tar, poised at an angle of thirty-eight degrees to the main current on the black swirl of the second eddy downstream from the rock that in the English of the Irish translated as the Rock of the Gull.

Mairi's heavy face had a discontented cast. The numbers were not right.

On the east bank of the River, thirty-seven herons sat in the dead oak they had turned white as a holy altar candle. Mairi sent her eyes skibbling across the river, along the hooky dam of the Herring Weir, across the inch with the stone arch of the Abbey, into the park and up to the long, gold-stone front of the House. Flags fluttered behind the statues on the balustrade at the roof's edge and from the summits of the pyramid-shaped pavilions at the ends of the wings: green ones with harps for Ireland, gold ones for the Holy Father, Union Jacks for the King.

3

The wrong thing was above on the Stag's Hill.

At the hill's foot were a tulip and a red oak, bright with young leaves in the sun. Above them on the hill's grassy crown was a tall Wellingtonia, black-needled, droop-branched, like a class of a tombstone against the spring-green hills. Three trees was the right number for the hill.

What was wrong about the hill was the crows.

Sure there were always crows to balance the herons. But today the world was crow-heavy, the sky above the tree speckled black with them. There was never any shortage of crows at Malpas, just the reverse, but generally they were creatures that went in ones and twos, unless they were rooks, which these were not. There were too many of them to count. When something turned up that you could not count, the world had no shape at all.

Mairi sat solid as a stone in the boat. But beneath her mud-coloured skirt and jersey she felt yeasty with panic.

She put her thick fingers to the oar looms and gave a heave. The cot came out of the eddy and crabbed into the creek that led up towards the House's lawns and terraces. A couple of minutes later, her thick figure popped out of the reeds (spires, they called them on the River) and sidled across the grass towards the rhododendron flowering blood-red on the margins of the shrubbery.

Inside in the shrubbery, hundreds of tiny suns swam on the leaf mould. Mairi stumped past lawns shaved for a week now by Seamus at the head of an ass with big leather shoes, the way its feet would never mark the sward. On the lawns moved creatures she distantly recognised as human – twenty-three gentlemen in tight frock coats with great glowing buttonholes, and twenty-one women in flowing white muslin, and hats, Christmas! Wedding people. The House was ram jam full for the wedding, the Doctor had said.

She hurried on past the house and into the park. A deer cocked an eye at her, recognised a being as wild as itself, and went back to gnawing the bejesus out of a seedling oak. She crossed grass, still climbing, her eyes uphill, on the Wellingtonia under its tower of crows.

There was a bench in front of the Wellingtonia, stationed for those who wished to contemplate the view. But nobody on the bench was looking at the view today. Today the bench was a pile of crows, hopping, beak-jabbing, uncountable. As Mairi came into view, the birds rustled into the air, and she saw what it was that was on the bench.

She was sick, neatly, between her thick black boots. Then she turned and went slowly down the hill, counting eight hundred and sixty-one footsteps, and simultaneously two hundred and seventeen posts for the park railings, eighteen rungs of the shrubbery gates, six hundred and ten trees, twenty-one whitenappers on the West Lawn.

But no matter how she counted, she could not get out of her head the mass rustle of those crows.

She marched straight out onto the lawn. There were forty-three people on the Terrace now.

Mercifully, one of them was the Doctor.

Book 1

Chapter One

I remember with great precision the night in September 1972 that I met Helen Costelloe.

I parked the Zephyr. I pulled my pier rod out of the boot, cinching in the tackle-bag strap in anticipation of the obstacles ahead. I started down the pier that stretched board beyond board out of the promenade lights to the hulking pavilion at its end. My ammunition boots (unfashionable but practical) made a satisfactory clatter as I walked.

Helmstone West Pier had been in steady decline since about the time of the death of Queen Victoria. Now it was no better than derelict, dark, lonely, haunted by the ghosts of cheap fun. In those days I was a post-graduate student at the Department of Further Psychology, much attracted to darkness.

To tell the truth, as far as I was concerned the real lure of the West Pier was not ghosts but fish. The grounds at its closed-to-the-public, boarded-up end were undisturbed by Helmstone's legions of anglers. At some personal peril, I had contrived a means of access. Nowadays, the end of the West Pier was my own private and exclusive fishing hole.

I walked out of the lights. The night was dark but clear, with a small wind from the southwest. The sea made a heavy churning in the pier's pillars. It would be stirring rag and sand eels out of the bottom, food for big bass. I was dry-mouthed and excited. I was walking away from the land, from Doctor Gale (more about him later) and Mara (her too) and into that private place where I communed with night and fish.

The pavilion wall was dark, its windows boarded up. I went to its right-hand end. I heaved aside a KEEP OUT sign and squeezed through the gap behind it. Across a sagging ballroom full of sea-breeze and rot-spore was a little balcony once used by couples for heavy breathing and moon-survey. There was salty air here, a rotten lifebelt on a rack. Beside the lifebelt was a spiked gate, with beyond it a steel ladder heading downward to a platform six feet above the high water mark, once part of a gangway arrangement for pleasure steamers.

I clambered over the gate and down to the platform. I baited my hook from a Horlicks jar of ragworms I had dug that morning. I saw the dark flash of the lead as it swung over the sea. I held my breath.

Often, a fish will take on the first sinking of the bait. Not this time. I wound in slack and looked east at the curve of the bay twinkling in the slow heave of the sea, feeling the nag and fuss of the Department drift out of my bones.

The insulating-tape handle tugged hard in my hands. I yanked the rod upright. Down in the sea between my feet something heavy twisted and jerked, struggling. This was not the soggy wriggle of a dogfish. This was the lively throb of a bass, a big one. You could explain a bass even to Mara. She was due back from America tomorrow. This was excellent timing.

I put on strain, hauling the rod-point up, dropping it and winding in the slack, hauling up again.

The fish took line. I started sweating. This was a fish of ten, perhaps twelve pounds. A serious fish, capable of fixing up any relationship, no matter how dodgy—

Out in the night, beyond the place where my line cut the surface, there was a commotion in the water. At first I thought it was a dog. But what would a dog be doing half a mile off Helmstone beach? Something lifted from the water. Something that was unquestionably a human arm, unclad.

The bass yanked at the line. My first instinct was to yell at this fool and warn him away from my fish. But I did not want to give away my position, in case I got busted and they stopped me coming back. And actually, I knew perfectly well that this person could not be just swimming, all the way out here on a cool autumn night. This person was thrashing, possibly drowning.

There was no way up onto the pier from the sea. Sitting on my platform under the ballroom balcony I had often wondered what I would do if I fell in, without coming to any conclusion. I shouted 'I'm coming!' and jammed the fishing rod into the iron rungs. Then I went up to the balcony and unhooked the lifebelt.

The belt felt sodden and heavy. I threw it towards the commotion in the water. It travelled perhaps ten feet, not a fifth of the distance to the swimmer, and was brought up short by its rope. 'Over here!' I shouted. There was no reply. The struggles seemed to be getting weaker.

At this point I realised that I had done what I sensibly could. What came next happened because I was bored, unhappy, and twenty-six years old, and had for a long time been separated from the world by what some thought was cool, but felt to me like acute loneliness.

I took off my boots and my leather jacket. I hauled in the lifebelt, put it round my waist, and cut the rope attaching it to the pier. Then, if you can believe this, I climbed over the rail and jumped.

The lifebelt smacked me blindingly in the nose. The water was much rougher than it had looked from above, the pier much higher. I blinked the tears out of my eyes, coughed out the water I had inhaled, and kicked forwards. I thought I was making no progress at all. But when I looked round I saw the loom of the pavilion on the pier's end some distance behind me, like a great balloon tethered to the sea by its iron legs.

I now began to be rather frightened. I was not much of a swimmer, let alone a lifesaver. The sea seemed large and lonely. I seemed to have lost the person whose life I was meant to be saving. And somewhere in the more distant reaches of my mind was the thought that a man looking for a subject for a research degree was most unlikely to find one in the water off the end of Helmstone West Pier at ten thirty on an October evening.

In this, as it turned out, I was quite wrong.

A hand rose not too far in front of me. 'Coming,' I called, but my voice fell thin in the black waste of the night. From over the next wave but one came what I can only describe as a sleepy moan. I started to splash my way towards it.

There was definitely a head in the water. 'It's all right,' I said, through a mouthful. Then we were practically face to face, and I was wondering what to do next.

Some scoutmaster or other once told me that the only ambition of a drowning person was to grab you and drag you with them into the depths. I wriggled out of the lifebelt and pushed it gingerly forward, as if offering a Polo mint to à savage dog. Nothing happened.

'Hey,' I said. 'Grab hold.'

Beside the head, the hands made little thrashing movements.

I said, 'Lifebelt,' and pushed it closer. The hands made no attempt to grip. I reached out and grabbed an arm – a thin arm, limp, bare – and slapped it onto the canvas cover of the lifebelt. The hand moved. I jumped back, insofar as it is possible to jump in water, hearing the scoutmaster's camp squeaks of warning. But the hand grabbed the lifebelt, not me. A strange noise began.

Sobbing. A woman's sobbing.

There we floated, fifty yards off the pier in the dark, one each side of the life ring. Between inhalations of water I explained that we could not land on the pier, because all the steps stopped four feet above high water mark. So it was the beach or nothing. The woman on the far side of the life ring seemed tired. I myself did not lead the kind of life that prepared you for towing people ashore in lifebelts. I found myself thinking about what would happen when the bodies were washed up. It would merely be further evidence, if Mara needed any, of my unfitness for life in the glamorous 1970s. Not only does he go *fishing*, for God's sake, he falls in and *drowns*. So *uncool*.

The woman in the dark said, in a new, firm voice, 'What am I doing here?'

'Swimming,' I said. 'Kick.'

We kicked, splashily and to small avail. The tide washed us past the end of the pier. The lights of the Esplanade opened out. Shoulder to shoulder, we inched towards the beach.

After a while, she said, 'Rest.'

We rested. I had a theory I should keep her talking. I did not feel my normal acute shyness, but an original conversational opening seemed hard to find. I said, 'Funny time for a swim.'

'I don't know.'

'I mean, were you swimming? As in having a swim?'

'I suppose I must have been.' If she was a suicide, she was a very matter-of-fact one. 'Don't you think we'd better save our breath?'

I felt slightly resentful at this swiping of the therapeutic initiative. She said, 'What's your name?'

'Dave.'

'I'm Helen. What were you doing out there?'

I told her about the fish. 'I'm sorry,' she said, rather endearingly. 'What do you catch?'

I could not help thinking that if she had the breath to make conversation, she could have saved herself, and I could have landed that majestic bass. Though of course the lifebelt had helped. I kicked harder. So did she. Suddenly, the lights of the Esplanade were upon us. A white tumble of wave, shingle underfoot, and we were stumbling loose-kneed up the beach.

She was a tall girl, her body big and white and well-shaped, overflowing a small black bra and pants. She stood looking back at the sea as if she did not understand why it was there. Then she whimpered and fell to her knees, lowering her head to the gravel.

The breeze felt icy cold. I gave her my jersey, wet wool being better than no wool. I said, 'Do you need the hospital?'

'No.'

'Where do you live?'

'Saxon Lane.'

'I'll take you.'

We hobbled to the Zephyr. I put her into the passenger seat (not without a thought for the upholstery, real leather, of course. Getting the salt out would be murder). I started the engine and turned on the heater and the inside light.

She seemed to be about twenty-five. Her hair was shortish and spiky, dark red, her eyes a deep, slaty blue. She had a raw-boned, symmetrical face with an unfashionable eighteenth-century look, as if she belonged in a Gainsborough painting, not a mid-range Ford. I pulled a blanket out of the back seat and put it round her shoulders. 'Nice car,' she said.

Mara sneered at the walnut dash and called the leather seats bourgeois formalist bullshit (I noticed she would rather ride than walk, though). I said, 'Wait here.'

There were a few people scattered along the Esplanade benches, watching the night-black sea. As I went onto the pier to retrieve my boots and fishing tackle, an old man was leaning on the rails at its root, polo-neck jersey up to his chin, hands in his overcoat pockets, watching the lap of waves on the beach. He said, in a strange, over-precise voice, 'Was that a girl swimming?'

'Yes.'

'I thought she'd maybe drown.' He sounded as if he had been watching a play, not a real woman in real danger. 'Her clothes are there below.' His face was luminously pale, the eye-bags black.

I retrieved Helen's gear, then mine (the bass had gone, worse luck). Then I drove her to Saxon Lane. She lived in a two-room flat, superior to the usual student bedsit, decorated with shop-window mannequins painted paisley. There were books on art in alphabetical order by author, a smell of wet oil paint. 'You at the University?' I said.

'Yes. You're Dave Walker,' she said.

'How do you know?'

'I'm doing some classes in Further Psych. You're famous. Tall. Nocturnal. Mystery Dave, is it?'

I felt at a disadvantage. She was shivering again, goose-bumped, hunched in her wet blanket. 'Get in the bath,' I said.

She gave me a dressing gown and a bottle of Paddy. 'Boil a kettle,' she said. 'Put the hot water and sugar in first. Then the whiskey. All right?' She was gone for ten minutes, and came back pinkish and steamy. 'Your turn,' she said. The bathroom was painted with murals of Norman castles in a landscape. When I went back to the living room, she was asleep on the sofa. I could not wake her. I carried her into the bedroom, which contained a huge painting of a single bed with a cream counterpane decorated with blue forget-me-nots, and a similar real bed. I tucked her in, wrote her a note, and walked bare-legged into the night.

Next morning I brought her dressing gown back. The streets were flooded with bluish light from the sea. When I rang her bell, she opened the door quickly enough to have been waiting for me. She was wearing a grey-blue silk shirt that matched her eyes. We sat at the table and ate bacon and eggs. In trendy urban Helmstone, there was something pleasantly rural about her. We did not mention night swimming. Actually, now I come to think of it, we *chatted*, something until then virtually outside my experience.

It turned out that she was doing Fine Art, and was coming to Further Psych cognition lectures in a futile attempt to fathom the mind of the French symbolist painter Odilon Redon. I told her I was preparing to write a thesis, on what I did not yet know, but definitely something to do with psychiatry before 1914. She said she knew.

I was taken aback. 'How?'

'I checked.'

'Ah.'

She sat there in the morning sun, rawboned and wholesome, grinning with the pleasure of successful detection. She had thick, creamy skin, freckled on the cheekbones. Compared to Mara, she was like an open window in a stuffy room. No, that is too trite. She made me suspect that everything else in my life – Mara, Gale, the Zephyr and the way I had acquired it, even the fishing – were a lot of bad habits. Helen offered the chance of breaking them all at once, and moving on to something fresher and much better.

You will recall that I had only known her for twelve hours, during one of which I had been swimming, and during ten of which I had been asleep.

It was all very surprising.

Chapter Two

It got weirder.

After breakfast she stood up, stretched, and said, 'Come this way.' I followed her down the stairs, into the mews, and round to a little garage. She opened the door onto a square of blackness that smelled of oil and steel. Light filtered in, picking up chromed pipes, an industrial-sized oil cooler: a motorbike, huge and bestial. A Triumph Trident, a three-cylinder race-derived monster that was just about the last gasp of the British motorbike industry before the Japanese came in and blew it away. Not necessarily a lady's bike.

Helen bent and fiddled with the carburettors. Then she slung a leg over the saddle, stood up on the kick start, and came down with all her weight. A thunderstorm bust loose in the garage. She heaved the thing off its stand and rolled out into the lane, spewing noise down the housefronts. I can always see her like that – tall, elegant, with that hellish machine crouched between her thighs, grinning, because she knew that she was only in control by accident, that anything could happen at any moment . . .

'Hop on,' she said.

There were no helmets, and it seemed churlish to ask for one. So I shut the garage door and climbed onto the pillion and put my arms round her waist, which was nice. And off we went on the sharp end of a hard wedge of noise, into the main road, sixty by the time we got to the lights, then swooping hard right, seventy, eighty, the wind trying to tear the eyelids off the face, onto the Downs, taking the bike low enough on the bends to sandpaper the sides of my boots. Then we were up under the sky, and my heart was going like a train, and she was picking the midges out of her teeth, so I realised that she had been laughing all the way. And cautious academic Dave Walker was telling himself, watch out, madwoman. But not listening.

We sat up there on the Downs, talking, looking down at Helmstone and the sea through a veil of larks. We howled back into the town at lunchtime. I climbed off and said, weak-kneed, 'I should get to the Department.'

'Before lunch?'

The Department shimmered and vanished. I suggested the King's Head, a student pub. 'Ugh,' she said. 'Red Barrel.' She drove us to a place called Clancy's and left the bike outside. We sat in comfortable, fetid armchairs, and ate toasted cheese sandwiches which seemed to contain mashed potato. I said, 'What were you doing out there last night?'

'Absolutely no idea,' she said. She was watching her hands, large and narrow, stained with paint.

'Odd time for a swim. In the dark, and all that.'

She looked up at me. She said, 'Sometimes I do odd things.'

This was a pretty conventional thing to say, in the first half of the 1970s. 'What kind of things?'

'Things there's no reason for.' Like riding a Trident, for God's sake. Maybe midnight swims were just part of the picture.

'But it's odd,' she said. 'Normally I do things on purpose. But last night, one minute we were in the pub, the next I was in the water.' The way she looked at me she was worried, all right. 'I wasn't drunk.'

That was true, as far as I had been able to tell.

'So a blackout?'

She shrugged.

I said, 'Who were you with?'

'A friend. Steve.'

'Until closing time?'

She opened her mouth, but no sound came out.

I said, 'When did you leave?'

Her face became opaque. She frowned, as if she had lost the thread of her thoughts.

I said again, 'When did you leave?'

'Leave what?'

'The pub. Last night.'

She frowned. 'Don't know,' she said. 'Perhaps I did have some drinks, at that.' She shrugged, as if the subject was of no importance. 'All's well that ends well,' she said.

I said, 'You nearly drowned yourself. Don't you want to know why?' I certainly did.

Again the blank expression. She said, 'You're the headshrinker, not me.' We began to talk about the Department, which of course meant the famous George Gale. Professor Gale was my supervisor. He had a velvet suit and suspiciously good teeth, and a quote for every occasion. He was greatly committed to the female student body, with whom he liked to do research based on orgasm therapy. For me he felt a dislike based largely on jealousy of what he conceived to be my relationship with Mara.

'I met him at a party,' she said. 'He asked me out to dinner. He tried to screw me. I think it was the bike.' I was surprised at the intensity of the irritation this caused. 'I told him he was too old,' she said. Her grin was sudden, surprising, beautiful. It warmed up the smoky, sour-beer air of the pub. We had another pint, and talked about ourselves, increasingly confident that what we had to say would be interesting.

Her name was Helen Costelloe. Her father had been Irish, her mother English. She had been brought up in Droitwich, a place I associated with the brine baths of early nervous cures. She spoke of her home distantly, as if it was somewhere she had consigned to an archive. Her father had been a pianist. Her mother had died when she had been a child.

I usually avoided talking about my parents early in new relationships, the facts being grotesque enough to create a silence from which a new, fragile intimacy often failed to recover.

You may remember that around the end of the 1960s there were several air crashes, in which DC10s fell out of the sky after explosive depressurisation caused by the failure of a latch on a cargo door. My parents had gone skiing near Munich. I had been left at home in Cornwall. At breakfast on the last day of their holiday, the telephone rang. Both of them had been found in the wreckage of their aeroplane in a snowy clearing in the Black Forest.

My father had been a kind but unsuccessful daffodil grower. My mother had run an unprofitable gallery in Newlyn, and helped on the farm. Neither of them had life insurance. Once I had paid off the overdraft by selling up, my fortune amounted to a small sum of money at Barclay's Bank in Penzance and the white Ford Zephyr the parents had left in the car park at Heathrow. On my return from the giant refrigerator in Munich where I had been required to identify what was left of them, I picked up the Zephyr. I had no driving licence, but I was in the sort of griefstruck fury that made that irrelevant. The Zephyr was my only remaining family. I was – still am, will always be – an only child.

I had the presence of mind to send myself to Warwick, where I read history. I had fallen in love with Mara during my final year. She had been recruited by George Gale, talent spotting for Fur Psych at Helmstone. It was she who had suggested that I went there to do my MA. I pointed out that I was a historian, not a psychologist, and that my degree was no great shakes anyway. Mara had pointed out that Helmstone was a university famous for accepting students on the basis of looks, style and recreational drug of preference. Fur Psych was at the cutting edge of this tendency, which was how she had got in. In my case, I was six foot four, with a crew-cut, painfully thin and profoundly antisocial. I did not take drugs, and had the economical habit of dressing in army surplus gear. These two tendencies alone were so unfashionable as to be supremely avant-garde, which must have been the main attraction for Mara.

Well, I was reluctant. But I could not think of anything else to do, and also since the death of my parents I had been horribly lonely. Mara was the only person in the world to whom I was close. She introduced me to George Gale, who ran the department. I did not like Gale, who was a trendy fraud. But when the Adler Foundation offered to finance my studies, I caved in to the workings of Fate, moved to Helmstone and enrolled for a year, extendible if I converted my MA into a doctorate. Mara and I had begun to fall apart almost immediately. The process was still going on.

So here I was in Clancy's, the afternoon sun cutting a silver slice out of the Woodbine smoke, sitting with Helen.

Holding hands, actually, with Helen. Feeling that once again I had a companion. Telling her the story of my life, leaving out only the Mara bits.

When it tailed off, she said, 'That all sounds a bit rough.'

'There is always,' I said foolishly, 'the fishing.'

'And I have my swimming, of course.'

'Of course.'

A voice from behind me said, 'Damifitaint Mystery Dave Walker.'

I looked around. There was the hair over the ears, discreetly tinged with grey at the temples. There was the Turnbull and Asser shirt, the velvet jacket with the built-up shoulders, the granny glasses. I said, as near neutral as I could get it, 'How's things?'

'We never know, do we?' said Gale, darkly. His wet guru eyes landed on Helen. 'Hi,' he said, very cool.

'Who's this?' said Helen, one eyebrow up. He had forgotten her, and she was stringing him along, bless her dangerous heart.

'George Gale,' I said. 'My supervisor.'

'Far out,' said Gale. He ordered a Budweiser. 'Just been at Esalen,' he said. 'Sort of got the taste for it.'

'Incredible,' said Helen, straight-faced.

Gale's smile took on a slightly frozen quality. 'Aren't you in Further Psych?' he said.

'Only sometimes,' she said.

He lost interest. 'Mara's back,' he said. 'This afternoon. Did you know?' he turned to Helen. 'Sorry. Mara's Dave's old lady.'

Helen nodded, very casual. By the pinkness of her cheekbones it was obvious that she had not known. After our day together I was not pleased to be reminded. None of this would have escaped Gale.

'Well,' said Gale, draining his beer. 'I'd better split.'

Helen did not look at him, or at me. 'Me too,' she said. Gale went out with her, so I could not undo the damage he had done. A true creature of his age, Gale, idolised as a sage when any other era would have unhesitatingly spurned him as a twerp.

Outside the pub I stood for a moment blinking in the brightness of the day. Gale was walking off, pigeon-toed, stoop-shouldered, head on one side. I called after Helen, 'I've got to get a couple of things together. See you later?'

She knew I meant that I had to see Mara. I could feel a rawness about her, as if she had a layer of skin too few.

She fired up the bike and thundered away without looking back. But she raised a hand as she went. In a world turned suddenly bleak, I took that as a good sign.

You could hear the music in the road, an Allman Brothers solo noodling out of the open first-floor front bow window. The front door was open, too. Mara had papered the stairwell with a hoarding-size Marlboro poster. I climbed through Monument Valley towards the tinkle of laughter above.

Mara was sitting at the table in her room, long blonde hair hanging down on either side of her face. Opposite her was a man I did not recognise. 'Dave,' she said. 'Honey.' The smile came from an infinite distance that would have been construed by some as cosmic perspective, but that I immediately identified as Durban Poison. 'This is Don.' The man at the table had dark glasses, a large black moustache, and an even larger hat. 'Don roadies for the Bee Gees.'

'Sound engineer,' said Don.

'And actually, darling,' said Mara, 'Don's sort of staying for a bit.'

Mara had no spare bedroom. Mara's house guests got Mara too. It looked as if she and I were over. I collected a handful of books, trying not to look relieved. I said, 'George Gale was asking after you.'

'Really?' In Mara's book, telly dons were right up there with Bee Gees sound engineers. I thought I spotted unease behind Don's shrubbery. 'Will you call?' She gave me her famous little-girl pout, calculated to stop pigeons in flight.

I said, 'I will consult my diary,' and went down the stairs. Behind me

I heard the tap-tap of her cowboy boots descending through Marlboro country. Her hand gripped my shoulder. 'Don't get uptight,' she said. The problem about Mara was that she was incredibly beautiful. 'He's got nowhere to stay.' She had my other hand now. Her lips were soft as clouds. It was a promise of what could be waiting for me once she had fulfilled the sacred duties of hospitality. Somewhat to my surprise I found that my hands were on her hips.

But at that moment I saw Helen again, not pretty, like Mara, with her little nose and her heart-shaped face, but big and beautiful. Part of the sea and the night and solitude, not rooms full of smoke and mind games.

I dropped my hands, and said, 'I'll probably see you sometime.'

Her irises were a deep, hackneyed cornflower blue. She said, 'Sometime?'

'Small university,' I said, gaining strength now, Helen large in my mind.

'You're leaving me?'

'You've already left.'

Her face went blank. 'Bastard,' she said. '*Bourgeois* bastard.'

'Bye,' I said. Maybe I laughed.

Mara did not like being laughed at. I think it was the laugh that caused the trouble.

But I walked down the trim street of semis under the blue South Coast sky thinking I had handled things pretty well, meaning without throwing furniture, and that the direction in which I was walking led towards Helen.

It was late when I knocked on her door. Nobody answered, so I pushed. It was not locked. There were voices upstairs. Helen was behind a table covered in ashtrays and Guinness bottles. There were two other women and two men. One of the men was curly-haired, talking in a strong Irish accent about something political I had not been there at the beginning of. The women were listening to him. The other man had lank black hair over his ears and a mild, pale face. He was leaning back in his chair, watching Helen from under his long eyelids, drawing in a thick book with a blue cover. I said, 'Evening.' Nobody paid any attention, except Helen, who gave me a private smile, and said, 'Would you ever make some tea?'

I went into the kitchen. The voices next door sounded as if they had been drinking. As the kettle boiled, the man who had been drawing came in. He said, 'I'm Steve.'

I introduced myself, and put the water on the tealeaves. He radiated an awkwardness. I said, 'Could I see the drawing?'

He gave me an odd, sideways look, and handed me the book. Then he watched me with the beginnings of a smirk. The drawing was small, in the top-right hand corner of the page. It was Helen's head, poised at its noble angle over the world. He had made it the head of a Madonna, radiating love and kindness, but inaccessible. It was a very good drawing. An astonishing drawing. I said as much.

'Oh, well,' he said, with an inward grin. 'I sort of draw when I get nervous. I get nervous quite a lot because I am what they call a manic depressive.' He looked faintly smug. 'Helen was talking about you. About last night. You pulling her out of the water, and everything.' Again the inward grin. 'I wouldn't have been able to, if it had been me.'

'I was fishing,' I said. 'I saw her float by.' He gave off a strange, raw atmosphere of self-hatred. Mental illness was fashionable in the early 1970s, and many people laid claim to it. In Steve's case I believed the claim. It occurred to me that this man could perhaps fix my prurient curiosity. 'Do you know how she got there?'

'It was Smiffy,' said Steve.

'What?'

'We were in the pub,' he said. 'There was this old geezer. Irish. He looked like Smiffy in the Bash Street Kids. His jersey, you know. He was talking to her all evening. They left together.'

'Without you?'

He flushed. 'I tried to go. Actually she doesn't want me around, sometimes. Give her some space. She's sort of got a mind of her own. You've probably noticed.'

It was at this point that I realised two things about Steve. One, he was in love with Helen. And two, as well as being somewhere between manic and depressed, he was drunk.

I said, 'So who was this Smiffy?'

'He turned up a week ago. Old chap. Some sort of relation of Helen's, he said. She's got Irish relations. So have I. My mother comes from County Galway. She says that's why I've got all those brothers. I've got five brothers. And a sister—'

I said, 'Does she often go swimming?'

He tried to stuff the drawing book into his coat pocket. He was not wearing a coat. 'Not in the middle of the night before. But you never know what she'll do next. Christ, I wish she wouldn't.' His head rolled around his shoulders. 'She's all I've got,' he said, and fell off his chair.

I picked him up, made the tea and took it through. We argued incoherently about Northern Ireland, where things were going horribly wrong as usual. After twenty minutes of it, Helen said, 'I'm going to bed.' She turned to Steve with a dismissive wave of the hand. 'You get off home,' she said, with a sort of big-sisterly affection. She caught my eye and nodded. I found I was grinning at nothing. The others left.

Just before he lurched out of the door, Steve showed me a drawing of myself. The picture of Helen had not been a fluke. This one was the same size, underneath hers. He had put the light on the planes of my face and the stubble of my hair. The eyes were in darkness. I looked deep, violent, incomprehensible. A threat, poor bastard. He had dated the page at the bottom. He said, 'Would you like to buy it?'

'How much?'

'It's not for sale,' he said, with that weird, secretive almost-smirk again. 'I don't sell anything. I want it all there, in order. You can come to my retrospective, if you want.'

'When's that?'

'Fifty years,' he said. 'Who knows?' He giggled.

I wish he had been right.

Helen kissed him goodnight on the forehead. The front door finally closed. 'What's he all about?' I said.

'He's a mess,' said Helen. 'All he ever does is draw people and show them the drawings. So people can tell what he thinks of them, I suppose.'

'And all he's got is you.'

She gave me a coolish look. 'There is room in my life for more than one person,' she said.

Well, I had deserved it. I said, 'Who was Smiffy?'

'Smiffy?'

'Steve said he was a relation you met in a pub.'

'Oh.' Her face cleared. 'Him. No relation. Just someone who was at the next table.'

'But you went off with him, Steve said.'

She shook her head and laughed. 'Steve's very possessive. And he's a terrible lush. He went to sleep. I left on my own.'

We opened the windows to let the smoke out. I had the feeling that there was a lot I was not being allowed to know. I said, 'Is Steve supposed to be your boyfriend?'

She gave me a mind-your-own-business look. She said, 'What about you and this Mara?'

I had been thinking about this. I said, 'Not any more.'

'Since when?'

'Last night, twenty to eleven, off the end of the West Pier.'

She stood up. The curtains heaved in the cold night breeze, wild and bracing as her. She said, 'Do I believe you?'

'Yes.'

'She's beautiful.'

'Not as beautiful as you.'

The slate-blue eyes held mine nervously. She looked raw and unsure of herself. 'If you see her again, Steve's my boyfriend. All or nothing. Right?'

I shrugged. 'All right.'

Pause. Then she said, 'It stinks of smoke here. What size of a bed have you got?'

All or nothing. That was Helen.

Chapter Three

My room was only a room, but it was big, having once been half of a button factory. There was a bath behind a canvas screen, a Leak stereo with eighteen-inch Goodmans, and a sleeping platform raised seven feet from the ground on scaffolding poles. We went straight to bed.

The next day and the days after, we evolved a sort of routine. She scared the daylights out of me on the Trident. Then we went for walks on the Downs. On our return to the bike, she tickled the carburettors, using for the middle one the quarter-inch sable brush she kept lashed to the handlebars. Then we descended on Helmstone, swooping down the long hairpins at a speed that left me weak-kneed and her grinning that wild grin. After that, we made love. It was love and sex, but most of all it was togetherness. I liked it all, particularly the togetherness, something I was not used to.

We talked a lot about her French symbolist painters. To dispose of the subject for good, one rainy morning I took her into the Fur Psych library (she was not enthusiastic about libraries) and requested a lot of material on Charcot, the great French alienist of the nineteenth century. We took the pile into an empty seminar room. I explained. Our heads were close, down in a book. When I raised mine, I saw her watching me with her cool eyes. Behind her, George Gale's blue-goggled face hung in the glass porthole of the door. She took my hand and pulled me towards her and gave me a long, open-mouthed kiss. Sneakily, she had opened her leather jacket. Her breasts were under it, nude and hard-pointed. When we disengaged, she said, 'I love it when you teach me. Can we go home?'

Gale's face was gone from the porthole. I felt sort of smug.

Idiot.

By the end of our first fortnight, I had seen no sign of Steve. Helen seemed to have moved in, Mara's roadie Don had moved on, and Mara was reported to be refusing to admit that she and I had broken up, rejection being something that happened to other people. Reading between the lines, I realised that she was angry with me.

So was Professor Gale.

I found out like this.

It was a Monday morning, in what must have been mid-November, at quarter to eleven, coffee time in the blacked-out anechoic chamber that did duty as the Department common room. In the past, I had always avoided the group of coffee-drinkers that gathered here to swap gossip and hallucinogens; perhaps this had contributed to the Mystery Dave nonsense. Since Helen, that was changing. Not that I had become the life and soul of the party, but certainly through her I had found the confidence to sit with people and have a bit of a laugh, particularly if the group included Helen.

And today, thanks to the *Sunday Times*, there was plenty to laugh at, right there on the front page of the *Review*. *You can plumb my depths any time*, said the headline. The byline was Fanny Wheelwright, a popular romantic novelist. Sprawled on a sofa below the headline was George Gale, velvet suit, cowboy boots, hair, blue granny glasses and all.

'Oscar Wilde?' said Helen.

'Plus a bit of Abby Hoffman,' I said.

'With powerful elements of complete prat.'

She was right, as usual.

You can always tell a don. The egg on the Old Wykehamist tie, the strange stains on the lap of the cavalry twills, the tweed jacket with leather elbows and pens in the outside breast pocket. So that was what I was ready for as I got off the 10.30 at Helmstone the other day. I was wearing woolly tights, skirt to the knees. Hermes scarf, doing my lipstick (burnt bramble, might as well not be there at all, but mustn't frighten the horses, the Editor had told me. This is a significant experimental psychologist so no showing off darling.)

So there I was outside the station looking for a Morris 1000. Nothing. No Hush Puppies, no hornrimmed glasses. All I could see was this beautiful car, British Racing Green, with a divine Serge Gainsbourg in the driver's seat, flipping away the butt of a Gitane with the grace of Solomon tossing a canapé to the Queen of Sheba. Reader, I wanted some.

At this point he pushed the shades back on his Byronic brow, revealing eyes like chips of sapphire. His mouth, wry, clever, opened. 'Hey, babe,' he said. 'Are you Fanny Wheelwright?'

'Yes,' I said. 'Yes, yes, yes!'

'Hop in,' he said, casting open the door like Raleigh flinging down his cloak for Queen Elizabeth. 'We'll have lunch.'

'Yes,' I breathed, editors and grim boffins vanishing from my head. 'But who are you?'

'The name's Gale,' he said. 'George Gale.'

Reader, I have lunched with one of the most brilliant men of the last half of the twentieth century. His conversation touches on Timothy Leary, Esalen, Janov, R.D. Laing, Wilhelm Reich, William Burroughs – the people who in a hundred years will be seen as the defining intelligences of our era. He knows them. In a very real sense he is them. I have been blown away by the future, and its name is Gale. The waiter . . .[1]

I was reading this drivel aloud, doing the voices, making too much noise, probably, the way you do if you are a solitary suddenly the centre of attention. As I embarked on the final paragraph, I noticed that a silence had descended on the group, and felt Helen squeeze my knee, hard. I looked up.

Professor Gale was standing beside me. Mara was with him, her hand tucked into his arm (for protection only: Gale was someone she admired, but for some reason did not fancy). She looked outraged.

---

[1]   From the *Sunday Times*, 1972

Gale was smiling, but only to show that he was in touch with his feelings.

I smiled back. 'Nice piece,' I said.

Someone giggled. I was getting carried away. I said, 'I mean, she was obviously really impressed.'

'Nice photo,' said someone.

'Sapphires,' said someone else. 'Peacocks. Far out.'

'Glad you liked it,' said Gale, with a pissed-off twist to his mouth, wry, clever. 'We will speak soon.'

'Handy for him,' said someone, when they had left. 'He wants to teach summer school at Berkeley. They'll love it over there.'

Someone lit a fire with the newspaper. I thought no more about it.

A week later I was in the library when someone sat down next to me. It was Gale. He said, 'So what are we working on at the moment, Mr Mystery?'

'Charcot,' I said, non-committal.

Gale made a face. 'Not a little *vieux chapeau?*'

'I don't think so.'

'Perhaps I'd better have a look at your notes.'

'When they're ready.'

He said, 'Do they exist at all?'

'I beg your pardon?'

He said, 'This is a popular Department on the cutting edge of research, in a state-of-the-art university. Our seminar rooms are for study, not foreplay. No passengers, Dave.'

I felt the blood rise in my face. 'Who's a passenger?'

'You are an Adler Foundation beneficiary. Dabbling. We don't do dabbling at Helmstone.'

I said, 'Precisely what are you getting at?'

He pulled out a Gitane, stuck it in his famous mouth, did not, this being the library, light it. 'I think you are a disruptive influence on the Department. It is your sense of inadequacy that leads you to cultivate all this . . . psychic turbulence. Dave, we must all work through our traumas, or risk being abusive to others.'

'Quite.'

'Mockery is a symptom of insecurity. Relax, and let yourself be helped.' He took the cigarette out of his mouth and tapped it on the desk, slowly, once a heartbeat. He said, 'And I know that Mara is really unhappy.'

The library was hushed and sleepy, overlapping pools of light sliding away into infinite space.

'You walked away from her when she came back from the States. She was vulnerable.'

Like a Sherman tank.

'She's a great chick,' said the Professor. 'Where you're at now is too far out. You have to ask yourself, is this me? Come back inside. I want to see that great work I know you can do. Be kind to her, Dave.' His cigarette was the size of a fluorescent light tube. Perhaps he was right. For a moment I could almost feel her lips, that unbelievable California Girl softness.

Then through the drowsiness there shot a thread of something sharp. Someone had said something about Gale teaching summer school at Berkeley. Mara's father was Dean of something or other at Berkeley. I said, 'Why?'

'It's dangerous out there where you are,' he said.

I was not sleepy any more. 'What are you suggesting?' I said.

The cigarette jumped away from the table and into his mouth. 'Nobody's suggesting anything,' he said. He looked alarmed. Suggestion was a technical term in Fur Psych. It meant what people in the outside world called hypnosis.

'Only I get the idea,' I said, clear-headed now, 'that you are saying I should be nice to Mara so her pride will be mended and she will be nice to her father who will be nice to you and make sure you get your summer school job at Berkeley.'

For a moment, his eyes were hot and angry. Then he took the blue glasses from his breast pocket and shut himself away behind them. He said, 'You have got a really primitive little mind. I will put it to you in a way you may be able to understand. You have to stop hurting Mara with this Helen woman and concentrate on work that I as your supervisor approve. Helen, I would remind you, is an undergraduate, while you are a graduate with teaching responsibilities. She is *de facto* if not *de jure* your pupil. Ethically—'

'What in the name of hell would you know about ethics?'

He ignored me. 'If this state of affairs continues, I shall have no option but to recommend that your Adler grant be terminated forthwith,' he said. 'You should go and see Mara. Get that stuff between you sorted. Straight away. Do you understand?'

I understood. I could feel my hands turning into fists, ready to give him a really primitive little answer.

'Think about it,' he said, getting up. 'Don't do anything hasty.' And before I could wrap a chair round his haircut he was out of range, a fashionable back view bopping to the inner Miles Davis.

When I calmed down, I began to think straight. My Adler grant depended on Gale. Gale's summer school depended on Mara. My staying in Helmstone near Helen depended on my Adler grant. All I had to do was go round to Mara and tell her what a great guy George was. Which would fix up George's Berkeley job, and Mara's pride. I could not believe that anything more than some simple diplomacy was needed. Mara was a much-courted woman, and she could definitely get along without me. I would go and tell her so.

Just as long as Helen did not find out. I knew Helen well enough now to realise that when she had said all or nothing, that was exactly what she meant.

But she would not find out. Not if I went for ten minutes.

So later that evening I parked the Zephyr and walked slowly down Mara's street. I would drop in and tell her, using simple and irresistible logic, that there was nothing between us any more. Then I could get over to my flat. Helen and I had agreed to meet at eight. It was our three-week anniversary.

The door was on the latch. In the hall, I said, 'It's me.'

Mara's voice said, 'Dave!' sounding pleased and surprised. Despite myself, I found that warming. I climbed through Marlboro country and into her room.

She was at the table, foolscap pad in front of her, pile of books open one on another. She was wearing a kimono wrapped close under her chin, so the perfect oval of her face was pale and clear against the dark blue silk. Her mouth and eyes stood out blood-red and sky-blue. Her hair was in a loose knot on the back of her head. I had to admit that she looked incredibly beautiful. And incredibly pleased to see me. As I have already said, I was not at all used to togetherness.

I said, 'Am I interrupting?'

She raised her hands to her hair. I could see the heavy rise of her breasts under the silk. 'No way,' she said. 'Essay crisis. I'm sick of it.' She came and kissed me hello, that Mara kiss, very soft, on the lips. 'Time for a little drink of something.' I was about to say no, and deliver my message, but she was already past me and in the kitchen, and the top was coming out of a bottle of . . . *champagne*, already? No. Leave. Now.

'Here,' she said, handing me a couple of glasses. I took them. There was nowhere to sit except on the bed, unless I wanted to sit at the table and glare at her over her essay. We sat on the bed. She poured. 'I was wondering when you'd come.'

'I saw Gale in the library.' Say your piece. Leave.

'He's got his knickers in an awful twist. Thinks he's defending me.' I could feel her breath on my ear, with a small, Californian smell of toothpaste and champagne. A faint voice was telling me that promiscuity and insecurity were indivisible. I tuned it out, and said, 'The thing is . . .'

'You don't want me any more.'

There on the bed, drinking champagne and so close to her warmth, I had to admit that at that precise moment this was actually not true.

'I can take it,' she said, in a voice so small I could hardly hear it. Against reason, I began to feel a total heel. She moved so that my hand landed on her breast instead of her upper arm. She gave a small, contented sigh. Her nails sank gently into the nape of my neck, and those lips came down my jawbone until they found my mouth.

Needless to say, she was wearing nothing under the kimono. We were already, you will remember, on the bed. Well, one thing led to another. And in the fullness of time, the clocks all struck at once.

I lay there and watched the sweat glimmer on her cherry-pink nipples. 'That was pretty cool,' she said, as if she was talking about a cheeseburger she had eaten in the company of a stranger. Natural Mara, this was. Detached. Junk sex.

But if this was natural Mara, what had the other Mara been, the kind and loving one who had met me this evening?

I said, 'Oh, Christ.'

The clock on the wall said eight forty-five. I had been meeting Helen at eight.

'Problem?' said Mara

'I've got to go.'

Her mouth began to walk down my ribs like a red-hot snail. I sat up and pulled on my T-shirt. She said, 'Off to see the new bird, is it?'

I had my jeans back on. I was struggling with a boot. I had betrayed Helen, given the wrong signals to Mara, been untrue to the tangle of feelings and desires I thought of as myself. There was no need to answer. 'I'll see you,' I said.

'Whenever,' she said. I stared at her. Hands folded under her head, breasts high and round, narrow ankles crossed, cool smile.

Horribly cool smile.

'What is it?' I said.

She yawned. 'I think someone might have told her where you were,' she said.

'What?'

'George Gale rang,' she said. 'I think he was going to. He thinks it's wrong, you and her.'

'He *what?*'

She smiled, a small, distant smile. Gale would get his Berkeley job, no worries, because he had helped her reel me in. And he had had his own personal revenge. Tease Gale, and watch him wreck your life. One arm into my leather jacket, one boot half on, I stumbled down the stairs.

I was home by five past nine. Helen was not at my flat. But there was a piece of paper pinned to the door with a commando dagger I used as a poker for the fire. It was Helen's writing, small and precise. *I hear you're with Mara*, it said. *Don't bother to look for me*. There was no signature.

I loved her. I fell down most of the stairs and into the Zephyr. Too late. Her flat was locked up. Her landlady was there, sour-faced in floral overalls. 'Gone,' she said, with gloomy satisfaction.

'When's she coming back?'

'She's not,' said the woman, and started on an explanation of the sum Helen had paid in lieu of notice, which would barely cover repainting the bathroom walls.

'Where did she go?'

She sniffed. 'Off with her boyfriend. In his car.'

'Boyfriend?'

'Some hippie took her off. Steve, she called him. They've all got boyfriends now. Scrubbers. Is something the matter?'

I shook my head, numb-lipped.

'Oh I see,' she said. 'Stringing you along, was she? Big Irish tart. Are you Dave? She said you'd take her motorbike away. Now would be fine.'

I said, numb-lipped, 'Tomorrow.'

She was still whining her poison into the night as I slammed the car door and drove away.

I was angry with Mara. I was angry with Gale. I was angry with Steve, and with Helen.

But when I came right down to it, the only person there was to be angry with was me. It was the seventies, remember. People were falling in and out of bed with each other just about non-stop. But I had let that screw up the first time I had ever been in love with someone I liked as well. The only time.

I had excuses. It is not a warm feeling, to go to Germany and bury your family, and to spend the next four years in bedsits and libraries with a Ford Zephyr as your only friend. You develop a sort of horror of loneliness. You will do just about anything to fix it.

And when you have fixed it, you feel so damn pleased with yourself that you just can't stop. And all of a sudden, there you are, more alone than you have ever been.

I have very little memory of what happened after Helen disappeared. I collected the bike, and found a shed for it in an army camp on
the edge of the Downs. I looked for Helen everywhere. Nobody knew
where she was. I did a lot of fishing, and cooked what I caught under
the net of shadows thrown by the button factory's steel rafters. I stayed
well clear of everybody, particularly Mara.

Gale remained my supervisor, out of a spirit I suppose of *Schaden-
freude*, and conceded to the Adler Foundation that I was just about
earning my grant. For everyday purposes he passed me on to Greta
Wertheim, a large, dim Californian, who in view of my historical bent
and my talent for paper-mining set me to reviewing a lot of
nineteenth-century manuscript material. Among these great piles of
stuff were the results of the *Statistical Enquiry into the Efficacy of Prayer*,
made by the erratic Victorian genius Francis Galton. It is a measure of
my state of mind at the time that I found nothing absurd in such a
study.

Actually (and I suppose this is interesting in the light of what
happened later) I developed a sort of passing enthusiasm for Galton.
You have to remember that we were still in the psychedelic era. Uri
Geller was bending his first spoons, and parapsychology was becoming
the rage. Galton had been one of the early proponents of the idea that
the mind could be trained in new and exciting directions. Through a
form of self-hypnosis, he had trained himself to be terrified of cab
horses. He had taught himself to make breathing an act of conscious
will, and nearly killed himself in the process. This kind of auto-
suggestion led naturally to a curiosity about hypnosis. I took some
lessons from a man in Lewes with Pringle socks and a white goatee. I
was pretty good at it. But after a couple of sessions in which I
convinced pub acquaintances that they were weightlifters and poached
eggs, I lost interest, the way I was losing interest in just about
everything, those days.

I passed a dour Christmas with an aunt and uncle in Lincolnshire,
potting up polyanthus seedlings in a vast greenhouse while the wind
razored in from the North Sea. It was a relief to return to Helmstone
and my breath-clouded midnight perch on the West Pier. I spent a lot of

time in the pub, anaesthetising myself against memories of Helen and promoting quick, grubby one-night stands.

Spring and summer came and went. I converted my MA to a doctorate, and spent the next winter doing mechanical work for the benefit of Greta Wertheim's career, lacking the energy to protest. Having had her revenge, Mara had decided that she and I were back on speaking terms. She was still a close Platonic friend of Gale, who post *Deep Throat* had metamorphosed into a lifelong advocate of self-realisation through pornography. One morning in February he said, 'Well, Dave. What about the thesis?'

I said, 'Statistical method in psi experiments. Greta thinks it's fine.'

He steepled his fingers and smiled at something six inches to the right of my head. 'She would,' he said. 'But . . .'

I waited. This was his famous method of telling his students that their work was not interesting at all.

'The thing is, I've been doing my best for you with the Foundation. They want to know, what are you doing? And if I tell them statistical method, well . . . Frankly, they're looking for something with a little more, like, profile. I mean statistics doesn't break much new ground, does it?'

'Actually it does.'

He ignored me. 'So it's like, could you get together a list of possible other subjects for approval as soon as you can?'

'How soon?'

'Like, yesterday.'

I scrabbled for a grip on reality. I said, 'Give me till the beginning of next term.'

He scowled at me. 'Six weeks,' he said. 'Without fail.'

Well, I had no ideas. During the week that followed the interview, I began to see myself as a man falling out of a window – perfectly comfortable, but with a crisis approaching at ever-increasing speed.

That was when the letter arrived.

It was a rainy last Saturday in February. I was groping my way down the raw-brick hall, unshaven, unwashed, heading for the pub. The perfectly nice blonde art student who had spent the night had just left without coffee. I was hostile with last night's booze, ready for today's, sick of the world, which is to say myself, alone, in a cul-de-sac off a dead end, nowhere to go, going nowhere.

And there on the dirty doormat with the red gas bill was the envelope. Even at a range of eighteen months I recognised Helen's writing straight away.

I took it upstairs and threw it into the fire with a tragic flourish. I saw the flames heading towards my name, and in my booze-rancid head there rose a picture of her face. It was a weirdly vivid picture. Mostly, it was of the eyes, cool, slate-blue, watching me as if I was something in a zoo. They were saying, with that complete frankness of hers, what will be the point of throwing this away?

Face it. After all this time, I loved her. Still.

I fished the envelope out of the fire. I stamped out the flames. I tore it open.

The paper was pale blue, thick, old-looking. There was a sort of letterhead, done with an old-fashioned embossing machine. Malpas, County Waterford, it said. Tel: Kildonan 6.

When I had read it I ran outside to the call box. Five minutes later, an Irish voice was saying, 'Kildonan 6, the pole's down with a week and it won't be up again till God knows when.'

'Where is this place?' I said.

'Here,' said the operator. 'Bye now.' She hung up.

For the first morning in a year, I did not go to the pub. I went to the shed where the bike was living, and embarked on a week of frenzied titivation. I had it steam cleaned. I polished the chrome with Dura-glit and the paintwork with Simoniz. I saddle-soaped the saddle, fitted new plugs, tickled the carburettors, using Helen's paint brush for the middle one. Then I advanced the timing to the mark, rose in the air above the kickstart, and came down like a thunderbolt. The engine roared alive. And so, I told myself, did my life again.

I sold it for £450 in a transport café near Box Hill. I went to the bank and extracted money to the limit of my overdraft. Then I put a duffle-bag in the Zephyr and headed west.

Chapter Four

Walker Archive, Transcript, 1973 – 1
There does be nothing at all. There does be nothing to see nor to count nor to smell nor feel. Then there does be a light growing and in the light five bars in front of me, and the chairs of the fire. When the fire blows up big and red I can see the two men in the chairs, the one with a short pipe the other with a curly pipe, and I can smell the smoke that is in it. The smoke makes me cough. And Mary that is crouching by the fire turns at me the way I can see the little flame shiny orange in the sweat of her face, and says, silence, you eejit, you Dugdale, and she coughs herself. And I am fierce angry, and I make a great clashing of my five bars, and Mary comes over and gives me the skelp of a sod of turf across the fingers, and oh it hurts, Doctor it hurts terrible, and her coughing all the while.

So it is night after night: what I tell you is what I see anny night, anny night at all. But now it is all changing and different because I can see over the crossbar on the top of the five bars, and Mary is coughing worse, much worse, and the men in the chairs are looking at her, the way they are frightened. My hands still hurt but now it is because of the work I am doing, a scrubbing of floors now, a washing of crocks, and always the soda that burns the hands stinks in my nose like a drawers you didn't wash for six months. And they let me out, but at night they put me back again.

But then there is the morning it changed.

Because Mary is inside in the house, and it is light now, the way I can count the five stones in from the door, and make the sums of the spaces they use, and the beam of the sun is moving back to the door on the third space when hello! the door from the room of the beds opens up, and there is a fierce racket and men roaring and bawling and crying, and they are taking off the bars and I am

away to the place of the buckets for to begin on the stones, and they say, never mind never mind you'll come and see her now. And there was Mary on the bed, all white she was and grey except for the great swatch of blood she was after coughing out of her, and her not breathing any more. So they have told me I am to make her tidy and suitable, and I am after doing it, standing by the bed, and the men are after giving me a clean apron, white, with a hundred and ninety-one stitches up the one side of it and a hundred and ninety-two up the other. And the bigger man, him that taught me to count, says, you'll be here and help, and we'll go to the church after. And I went to the church, the first time then, and there was two hundred and eleven people inside, and I am starting to cry, because I do not know, I do not know . . .
[Q: Calm yourself, please, calm yourself.]
And they go, and I am looking for Mary to put me inside in the little bars. But something has happened and I am in the room itself and away on the wall is a small little hole in the wall with some wood bars in front of it, the way you would make a kennel for a dog. And your man with the short pipe is saying, you don't have to go there anny more. So I don't have to, I don't, and I can sleep by the fire and he will teach me how to row on the river and it is all right that that whore Bridie Dugdale came here and dropped me the way you would whelp a puppy, and then died on us. It is all right it is all right, and I will live here for ever and Johnny Cosgrave is older than me but he is great gas and he doesn't mind me counting, except when he gives me a clout. And there are the right number of clouds and river and pans above in the kitchen, and it is all right it is all right.

The low pink cottage where the Cosgraves had always lived was on the far side of the river from the House. Now as in the time of Mairi Dugdale, it was from there that you could first see things happening. It was sixty-eight years since the terrible day when Mairi had counted her way across to the crow-clotted Wellingtonia, and run from there to the Doctor. Trees had grown. Buildings had crumbled. Otherwise, very little had changed.

Paddy Cosgrave sat with his netting needle in his hand and the salmon net on his knee, on the elm bench that ran along the river wall of the cottage. The bench stood on sandstone slabs split out of the cliffs that came down to the water here; slabs polished to a leathery shine by the brush of two hundred years of net mending.

Being a Cosgrave meant that Paddy's life centred on the seining of the salmon from the House Pool and the maintenance of the Herring Weir, and when the fishing was done, lopping and digging in the woods and garden. It was possible that long-ago Cosgraves had built the Herring Weir. Without the River there would be no Malpas. Without the Cosgraves, there would as far as use and custom were concerned be no River.

From the net bench you could see the avenue all the way from the Top Lodge, down a seam in the trees, round its double hairpin in the park, and across the inch to the far side of the House. Paddy's large, sandy eyebrow moved north a fraction. Onto the topmost hairpin there had crept a minute white beetle; a beetle never before seen by Paddy.

'There's someone new beyond,' he said.

His mother came out of the house with a pair of German U-boat binoculars, swapped for drink with a fella by the name of Otto in 1943. She screwed the eyepieces into her hollow eye-sockets. 'Ford Zephyr 1965,' she said. 'English.'

'Grand car,' said Paddy, fingers moving steady in the net.

'Give me the Cortina anny day,' said his mother. 'Let's hope it's something dacent for the one beyond.'

Paddy nodded, working on. His mother was always right. Little puffs of dried-mud dust rose from his jersey and floated away down the breeze, obeying natural laws.

Cosgraves recognised no others.

Malpas, County Waterford[1]

An enormous late-eighteenth-century block of 2 storeys over a basement and 9 bays, with a symmetrical pedimented front, the basement heavily rusticated, with niches. The central block is connected by colonnades in the Moorish taste to a pair of Egyptian pavilions with roofs of pyramid form. The house's

---

[1]   From Jack Spencer-Smith, *Great Houses of Ireland*, Burke, 1976

situation in a great complex of nineteenth-century parks and terraces at the confluence of the River with the Owenafisk can give it a formidably romantic air, and its gardens were once the wonder of Munster. It must however be said that at all times of tide except high water, Malpas presents a clumsy, muddy look. House and park are now sadly decayed, having been partly burned in 1919 and much neglected since.

I remember my arrival at Malpas with the distinctness you would expect of the start of a new life.

I had taken the night boat to Rosslare and driven west, heavy-eyed under a roof of crows that rose from the road into the last stars of dawn. There had been a bridge over a river. After the bridge I had turned south, towards the coast. The woods had set in.

I was accustomed to polite British woods. These were nothing short of ferocious. Oaks and ashes and sycamores jostled each other, falling down, rotted, regenerating, bound together by insoluble lashings of ponticum. On the higher parts of the trees grew ferns, polypody and hound's tongue, and other epiphytes. This jungle crowded in on the road, which was in a state that suggested recent carpet bombing.

After ten miles or so, no more than three miles from the sea by my calculation, I crawled up a hill. On top was a lodge, limewashed shocking-pink. I turned between crumbling gate-pillars sprouting grass, and into another world.

Oh, yes. The letter.

Malpas, 24 February
Dear Dave,
This is probably a stupid letter and I hope you won't mind my writing, because I treated you really badly, and you would have every right to burn this without reading it. But I hope you haven't burnt it. I hope so a lot.

Okay, first an explanation. You remember Steve? Well, I was engaged to him. I should have told you, but somehow it never seemed to be the right moment. But he had told me Professor Gale had told him you had a date with your friend Mara. I was jealous, you know that. You were late, and I knew where you were. I was angry. Well, furious. I can get like that. I took off. Here, with Steve. We got married at Fishguard registry office. In case you're interested. Even while we were doing it I wished it was you. But by the time it stopped being exciting it was done, done, too late, too late.

I don't think I told you I had a house in Ireland. In fact I know I didn't because I never told anyone. Anyway I have, and it was over here that we came.

I see I have hardly mentioned Steve. Well, an awful thing happened. One of the things about this place is that it's by a river. And after we'd been here a year, he was drowned.

So I have been a widow for six months. There are some quite nice people here. But I often think about you and Helmstone. I know it is stupid because we were only together for less than a month, and even if you can remember who I am you are probably still furious at the way I just ran off. But I was happy then, I wanted to tell you that. And I wanted to say that if you did have a moment, and you wanted some peace and quiet and somewhere to stay, it would be lovely to see you. There's a load of room. Come and work, or hang out. Please.

Helen

p.s. if you have time, could you sell the bike and bring out the cash?

The world beyond the shocking-pink lodge and gateposts would have been an amazement (in the phrase of Paddy Cosgrave, whom I met later) to God himself, who made all things.

There was a watercourse of a drive. There was a sun-splashed tunnel of trees. And at the end of the tunnel, spread out below like an eighteenth-century painting, Malpas.

There was a green slope of park, dark shrubberies blood-splashed with early rhododendrons. There were lawns, the house, embracing in its colonnaded arms a parterre; then terraces, more lawns, reedbeds. And beyond the reedbeds, silver between low-water banks of black mud, the River.

I drove across a ha-ha overflowing with brambles on a bridge with a

---

wrought-iron gate, rusted to needles, hanging off a crumbling pillar. There was a pavilion with what looked liked a camellia growing out of a hole in its roof. There was a portico, held up by six huge columns. I pulled up the Zephyr bang in the geometric centre of the sweep, and opened the door.

She had watched him coming down the avenue. She had meant a lot of what she had said in the letter. He had saved her life, for goodness' sake. And he was big, and quiet, and sort of soothing. She needed soothing now. Everything felt so wild. Had felt wild, for just about ever. Not nice wild, either. Just wild.

She went and pulled down her jersey in front of the poxy gilt mirror. She was bigger than when she had last seen him. She was suddenly full of trepidation. Perhaps this was a bad idea. People you met in bedsits were not necessarily useful at Malpas. So much had changed. People who had loved you eighteen months ago did not necessarily even find your company tolerable now. And they could change themselves.

She slapped herself sharply on the cheeks. Her eyes glowed angrily out of the age-specked Venetian glass. Stiff-legged with fear, she walked the forty echoing steps across the hall to the front door.

And there was Dave, uncoiling from the driver's seat, running his eyes over the North Front. The eyes landed on her. There were dark bags under them. He looked thin. He had been unhappy. Because of her? Not after all this time, surely. Now here he came, leather jacket, drainpipe jeans, crunching across the moss and weeds in his army boots. The grin, diffident, the legs joined to the body only loosely. There were moths in her stomach, soft-winged. He raised an eyebrow. He said, 'Is this all?'

She had forgotten these things about him. She was feeling better already. She tried a smile. She said, 'Come in.'

The Zephyr stood between the huge sky and the enormous river, fridge-white, bourgeois, utterly insignificant. One leaf of the front door groaned shut.

It was done. She just hoped it was the right thing.

* * *

44

There is no respectable way of describing the House at Malpas. A cliff of windows, a massif of roofs, a city of chimneys spouting jackdaws. Ivy-riven, moss-green, slump-cracked, damp-stained, age-bulged, mould-reeking. But above all, gigantic, Brobdingnagian, absolutely bloody enormous.

And there under that beetle-browed portico stood Helen.

She was wearing a blue scarf round her head. It took up the colour of her eyes, gave them an exotic slant over her high, freckled cheek-bones as they watched me. She was wearing a blue jersey and jeans and cowboy boots. I had just about time to take her in. Then she came and took my hand and kissed me on the lips, so quickly she was gone almost before she arrived. 'Dave,' she said. Then I was left with the print of her breasts on my chest, and she was heading away across the chequer of the hall, leaving muddy footprints as she went. She had always been quick. But there was something extra quick about her now. Impetuous, was the word.

The hall had beaten-leather wallpaper, a smell of rats, and a lyre-shaped staircase, one side of which had been fallen through by a cow. Chunks of plaster were off the walls. Beyond the jammed sash windows, grass-clumped terraces fell away to the river. A plastic duck lay on a window seat. The blood had mostly been driven out of my brain. I said, 'All this belongs to you?'

'Correct,' said Helen.

'How?'

'My father was born here. But he went away to school and never came back. He never even talked about it. Can you believe, I didn't know it existed till he died?' Again that sense of haste. Perhaps she was nervous. Well, so was I. 'Let's have lunch.'

We sat at a fifteen-foot table in a kitchen with a sticky linoleum floor. The walls were covered in paintings. Most of them were romantic landscapes, some populated with fey girls in muslin dancing round trees. 'Oh,' said Helen, when I asked. 'I rounded them up from all over the house. Most of them had water running down them. That's an AE' – she pointed to the girls in muslin – 'and that's a Jack Butler Yeats, and so's that. Brother of WB, you know? What about some food, then?'

Lunch was cold salmon and potatoes, vast and waxy. 'Spuds from the garden,' she said. 'Fish from the river. Very economical.'

I said, 'You must be a millionaire.'

'Hah!' she said. 'You know what entailed means?'

'No.'

'Can't sell a thing. I get to live here for my lifetime, and pass it onto some other poor dear. Mister Walker, do not get no inferiority feelings, because round here we is stony broke.'

I said, 'I sold the bike,' and handed over the envelope of money.

She stuffed it into her jeans without counting it. I found myself worrying less. Palace Malpas might be, but here she was, back in reach of the things that had to be got out of the way.

I said, 'Why did you marry Steve?'

'It's hard to think straight at times like that.'

There had been confusion, certainly, terrible behaviour by me, jealous fury from her. But I still did not see how it added up to a sudden marriage. 'Times like what?' I said.

'I never told you, did I?' The skin between the freckles on her cheekbones had turned a clear, lovely red.

'Tell me what?'

'We were going to have a baby,' she said. 'She's above in the nursery now.'

The child in the nursery of Malpas – a bright room, painted yellow and white over the cracks, with vast damp-stained bunny rabbits above the picture rail – was about two foot six inches long, dark-haired, with grey-blue eyes like its mother. It was sitting in a playpen, studying a wooden block with the concentration of a safecracker planning a job. 'Hello,' I said. I was disappointed. More than disappointed. Excluded. Jealous.

'She's called Hannah.'

I said, 'Ah.' My pity for Steve had blown away. He remained in my mind only as a drunken weirdo who had got my girlfriend pregnant before I had even met her.

I watched the new Helen move around the room. She gave the baby

46

her lunch with one hand, and wrote a list of some kind with the other. We talked about the boat journey; small talk. Eventually, we began to laugh a little. She said, 'It's great that you came.' Our eyes held. There was a long, thick silence. Eventually she said, 'Everyone does things they regret.'

'Yes.'

We understood.

My sulk began to blow away. I could feel the rubbish of the past year and a half going with it. We could almost have started again where we had left off.

Then Steve's child started to yell.

'I'll show you round,' said Helen. She loaded the infant into a yacht-sized Victorian pram. We toiled off across tussocky lawns, past balustrades broken to show rusty metal cores. We passed through a fence separating a thicket of ponticum that had once been a shrub-bery from a desert of thistles that had once been a park. Rabbits bounced away as we passed, and a stag cantered into the oak wood above us. It was a battlefield where man had fought nature and long ago lost.

We hauled the pram up a hill. On a flat patch of summit, like a terrace or viewing platform, grew a huge black Wellingtonia. There was a bench, ancient and mossy. 'This is the Stag's Hill,' she said. We sat down, looking over the derelict park, the huge decayed mass of the woods.

I said, 'What happened to Steve?'

She looked at me out of the side of her eyes. For a moment I thought she was going to tell me to mind my own business. Then she seemed to swallow her pride. 'He went off drinking all day at Brady's, that's the pub down the river. He started home in the evening. Next morning Paddy Cosgrave found him below in the Herring Weir.'

'Where's the Herring Weir?'

She pointed down the river. 'The Guards reckon he was drunk, walking back from the pub, and he fell in.' She was very pale now. 'Ireland's a Catholic country. Nobody likes to say suicide.'

I said, 'And what do you think?'

She said, 'He was wearing sort of army trousers. There was a dirty great stone in each pocket.'

I remembered Steve, wet-eyed, sly, telling me about his manic depression. It would not have been a giant step for him in a depressive phase, out of life and into this Herring Weir.

Helen said, 'I mean it. I'm glad you came.'

Pause. I said, 'Why did you ask me?'

'Money for the bike.'

'And that's all?'

Her jaw came out. For a moment, I thought she would tell me to go to hell. Then she said, 'All right. I wanted to see you again.'

'Is that all?'

She looked away. 'I love it here,' she said. 'But it can get lonely.'

'Who do you see?'

'Only the neighbours. There's Finbarr Durcan. His family has lived here for a hundred years, at least. My father rented them the place until my twenty-third birthday. Now Finbarr works for me. Manages the farm. Angela Devereux has a sort of grace and favour house. Emily Durcan too, she's Finbarr's mother. So they've all got reasons to be nice to me.' She grinned, a real grin now. 'You haven't.' The grin went. 'But don't get me wrong. They're all really nice people.'

As I pushed the pram back to the house, she put her hand in my arm.

We were not exactly picking up where we had left off. That would have been too much to expect. But at least it looked as if we might both want to qualify for a second chance.

Good enough.

Chapter Five

From the Visitor's Book, June 1892.

Sonnet 'Dear Old Malpas'
Here lay the Viking. Here the Norman's chain
Plunged bubble-silvered to the oozy bed.
Here noble salmon, lamprey suck-em-dead
Flick to the shadows, and lie still again.
Here in the park, a proud stag sniffs the rain,
A fifteen pointer – what a splendid head!
While pheasant rockets at the beater's tread
And is in London by the morning train!
Malpas! You bestride the rivers' meet,
The clouds wreathe your great head, the flood your inch.
Your tenants are all loyal, breasts in heat
With fervent fires no Fenian foe can 'quinch'!
Oh! My soul. Yes! What a splendid dream –
Autumn at Malpas, by the river's stream!

Splendid shoot! 'Bonkers' Crichton-Aggs, 1874

The Park at Malpas was laid out in the eighteenth-century landscape taste.
Later improvements included the building of a Pompeiian Temple of the
Graces on the River Cliff, the construction of three balustraded terraces
descending from the River Front to the rustic boathouse on the House Creek,
and the planting of many rhododendron species and specimen trees on the
slopes behind the house. Cottages Ornés were constructed at several points of

vantage, including a Banqueting House in the Venetian taste in the middle of
Tivoli Wood.

To these conventional ornaments were added at the turn of the century a
gasworks, supplied with Welsh coal by freighter, the cargoes being unloaded at
the Gas Quay; and later (1915) a hydro-electric plant, supplying the house
with 24-volt DC current and driven by a reservoir on the upper Owenafisk.
These ornaments are now sadly decayed, most to the point of total invisibility.
But the evidence is still discernible by the keen eye, and bears lively witness to
the fact that in the last half of the C19 and the first fifth of the C20, Malpas
was one of the wonders not only of Ireland, but of the world.[1]

Dinny and Jer the garden boys came with the Doctor to the Wellingtonia. The noise of the crows was continuous, their shadows black as
the Doctor's coat on the sunlit ground. 'Shoo!' cried the doctor, waving
his hat. The birds lifted in a great rustling heap.

Behind the Doctor, Jer said, 'Mother of God.'

Under the crows was a man. The birds had taken his eyes, his eyelids,
and the flesh of his face. They had tugged his shirt out of his low-cut
grey waistcoat the better to excavate his bowels.

'Jesus,' said Jer, and looked away. He looked away not only from the
horror of the corpse, but from a worse horror: the unholy horror of
the big revolver held in the corpse's right hand, of the thumb locked in
the trigger guard, broken teeth stuck to the muzzle with dry blood. But
against his will, his eyes crept back. He stared at the head, the awful
grinning head, gazing with bloody sockets into the branches of the
tree, and through the branches into the Hell of suicides.

The Doctor had moved around the bench. He was examining the
top of the head, where a crater the size of a breakfast saucer had
replaced the gold-red curls touched for tidiness' sake with Trumpers'
Milk of Flowers.

'Get a hurdle,' said the Doctor, very pale. 'And a blanket. We won't
let Miss Dulcie see him just now.'

---

[1]   Denis Gielgud, 'Ozymandias In Munster', *Country Life*, 2 March 1981

'Gods no,' said Dinny, green-faced. The men started down the hill at a run.

The Doctor picked up the morning coat that was hanging from a branch nearby. The gardenia in the buttonhole spread its heavy smell over the raw stink of blood. Deliberately, he went through the pockets.

There were white gloves, a Morocco cigar case containing three Montecristo no. 2s, a clean linen handkerchief, and a red ring-box in whose cream satin there nestled a plain gold wedding band. The equipment of a bridegroom on his wedding morning.

And below in the house, the bride, waiting.

The Doctor put the coat over the terrible face. Then, heavily, he began to plod back down the hill.

A small man, the Doctor. Dark, clean-shaven, with hair that started a long way back on his head, more (people tended to assume) from intellect than from incipient baldness. But what you really noticed about the Doctor was not the compact face, or the nose, small and sharp and birdlike. What you noticed were the eyes, which were narrow, lustrous, and (here the more susceptible ladies were overtaken by a delicious shivering) oddly *deep*.

On the face of it, the Doctor was a Costelloe cousin of no great significance, a scholar and a general practitioner living the life of fashion and formaldehyde in far-off London. But during the month since he had arrived as one of the vanguard of the rabble of Costelloes just now filling every house worth the name between Lismore and the sea, the Doctor had established himself as a Presence. He seemed ready to talk to anybody, from the Duke of Devonshire (at Lismore for the fishing) to Mairi Dugdale, the scullion-girl from Cosgraves' over the river. In fact, by a process nobody understood, the Doctor had become the pivot round which the Malpas household turned.

So now he bustled under the floral inscription on the pediment of the house (GOD BLESS MR DESMOND AND HIS BRIDE). He strode across the mirror-polished chequer of the hall floor, and up the right-hand sweep of the lyre-shaped stairs. Outside the bride's room he paused, collecting himself.

A woman of about thirty-five watched him up the stairs. She was thickset, dressed in dove grey, with a ruddy face that would have been more at home under a hunting bowler than its present cartwheel of tea roses. The door was opened by a maid. Behind the maid was a slim woman in white, with a cloud of auburn hair and eyes of a startling cat green, open very wide at the sight of the Doctor. The Doctor went in.

The door closed. The thicket woman under the tea roses folded her lips and waited.

After ten minutes the Doctor came out. His hair was disarranged, as if he had been running his hands through it. The woman in the tea roses caught him on the bottom step, and said, 'How is the darling?'

'Poorly, Mrs Caroe, I thank you,' said the Doctor. 'I have given her a sedative.' The eyes sharpened. Mrs Caroe met them with her own, which were hard and stupid, like blue glass. 'It is to be expected. We must ask ourselves what has produced this catastrophe. Eh, Mrs Caroe?'

'I have been, without cease.'

The Doctor rotated his hat in his hands. 'Well, I must find the Best Man and cancel the . . . arrangements.'

'Indeed,' said Mrs Caroe, as if the death of a bridegroom on his wedding morning was only to be expected. 'I shall tell Cook, if you like. Oh, how dreadful. How *incomprehensible!*'

'Indeed,' said the Doctor. The woman's composure was false. She was sweating, her lips trembling. There was the pink of weeping in the blue-glass eyes. She flushed under his scrutiny, turned and hurried away.

By eleven o'clock, the nuptial hour, the last of the wedding carriages had rolled away through the rain (the weather had soured at ten) to the station. A short man with greased-down black hair and a sharp nose reddened by whiskey came fussing up against the Doctor, who was sitting in a chair, watching the flames of the hall fire as if trying to read them. 'Mrs Caroe,' said the man. 'Have you seen her, Doctor?'

'She is outside on the terrace, Mr Caroe,' said the Doctor.

'But it's raining.'

'So it is,' said the Doctor. The red-nosed man vanished, and came back with his wife, whose dove-grey dress now bore great dark patches of wet. 'You will catch a chill,' said the Doctor.

Mrs Caroe's eyes were even pinker now, and there was sherry on her breath. 'Mind your own bloody business,' she said. 'She doesn't love him. Didn't.'

'I *say*,' said Caroe. 'Look here . . . sorry, Doctor.' And he shunted her away.

The Doctor picked himself out of the chair. He walked through the empty house and up the stairs, and knocked on Miss Dulcie's door. The maid opened up. Miss Dulcie was quiet on the bed. From her window, the Doctor could see the Caroes' trap rolling away into the grey afternoon. Husband and wife seemed to be arguing. Caroe was too poor for a motor, too proud for an outside car. Mrs Caroe had not made a brilliant match.

The Doctor thought he would be seeing more of Mrs Caroe.

From the Letters of D.W.

Oh, Lord, what is to become of me? I am a stranger in a strange land, set about with snares. I am a sinner, in whose sin is her only salvation. My poor Desmond, that was so proud and fine, has not been able to bear the knowledge of my shame. He has taken himself away to a better place. And I am left behind. Horror!

Thank Heaven for the Doctor, who is my help and my succour now that I am beyond all other. I cannot ask God for strength, for I am that which he will not see. Instead, I ask the Doctor: and he giveth it a hundredfold.

From the Casebooks of Peter Costelloe

An induction into hypnosis I have always used, based on the observations of James Braid:

Take a bright silver pencil in the left hand. The subject must be made to understand, by direct instruction or implication, that he is to keep the eyes and indeed the whole attention steadily fixed on the object. Adjust the tone of the voice to one low and soothing. It will be observed that the pupils of the subject's eyes will be at first contracted. They will shortly begin to dilate. If the fore and middle fingers of the right hand be darted towards the eyes, most probably the eyes will close involuntarily. After ten or fifteen seconds, gently elevate an arm or a leg. If it is found that the patient leaves the limb where it has been put, one can assume that he is deeply affected, and proceed into a phase producing a deep waking sleep, in which the work of suggestion can begin.

This work may simply be an application of soothing counsel in a violent emotional disturbance. Or it may be work of a deeper, more lasting nature. Think of the system of servants' bells found running in ducts through any house. In the waking sleep, or 'trance', the patient is like the bell-system with the covers removed, so that the wires and levers are exposed, and may be modified at will by the practitioner . . .

The funeral of Desmond Costelloe took place at the Protestant Church of St Cormac, Malpas, on 23 May, 1910. There was what the Dunquin *Leader* called a large and representative attendance. A good suicide (the obituarist confided later to the snug bar at Murphy's) will always lash on an extra thirty to fifty per cent to your public participation.

Naturally, the death of poor Desmond was represented as an accident, which for all anyone knew it might well have been. The obsequies were conducted as per the special instructions in the Will, which made it clear that the deceased had had a horror of premature burial. Not that there was any question, after the revolver and the crows. But still, as Mr Deasy the undertaker observed, a will was a will.

Desmond was therefore laid in his coffin on a new shelf in the long, low Costelloe vault by the gate of Malpas churchyard. The lid was not screwed down. On the slab next to it were left a key to the vault and a bottle of Jameson's whiskey, the cork drawn and loosely replaced. The deceased's fiancée, Miss Dulcibella White of Dungarvan, attended the funeral supported by Dr Peter Costelloe, her medical advisor. As the vault doors were closed, she was removed in a collapsed state and was said to be dangerously ill, the brain being affected.

There was naturally a great deal of talk after the funeral. It was generally agreed that it was just as well Miss White collapsed, God love her, since she was thus spared the knowledge that when the vault was checked the morning after the funeral, the whiskey was found drunk, the coffin lid screwed firmly down, and the key back on its hook inside the church. Sure a will like that was a terrible thing to make, since it came from vanity and would cause only suffering.

But when the full contents of the will were finally known, it was generally acknowledged that, when all was said and done, the stuff about the funeral was the least of it.

*   *   *

It is a curious sensation to pick up the threads of a relationship after eighteen months of separation – particularly if the relationship was cut off by violence, and has to swallow a birth, a marriage and a death. As my first evening at Malpas drew to its close, I found my eyes meeting Helen's across the fire, and began to wonder about the sleeping arrangements.

At eleven o'clock, she stood up. 'Right,' she said, briskly. 'Hannah wakes up at six, and God knows if you've been on the ferry you'll need longer. So you can have the Green room, and see how you like it.' She watched me with a faint, ironic smile. If we got through this, there would be a next stage.

The carpet of the Green Room squelched faintly underfoot. 'It used to be the Blue Room,' she said. 'I changed the name to suit the mould on the curtains.' Next morning, I awoke to an eighteenth-century prospect of woods and river, through a window whose panes had been patched with cardboard onto which Helen (she told me with pride when she brought up the tea) had drawn the blanked-out portions of the view. I cleaned my teeth in soft brown water and drank coffee in the kitchen. Then Helen, wearing a cowboy hat and black gumboots, took me and Hannah's pram to meet the neighbours.

A light drizzle wafted onto a ruined Protestant church on the hill. There was a grey Georgian dower house with a shell over the front door. Here an Angela Devereux, with springy blonde hair and ironic eyes in a broad, hefty face, gave me a plump hand and accepted an invitation to lunch the next day. A sort of yarring howl came from within. Angela's smile did not flicker. 'Mummy,' she said. As we turned to go I saw at a first-floor window a grey face framed in lank, colourless hair.

'Angela looks after her mother,' said Helen, as we left. 'Her father was the richest man in Cork, until the railways came to Paraguay. Now they're flat broke. God knows we've got enough houses here.'

Further across the hill we strayed into a tangle of ugly sheds, some with roofs, most without. There was a great baying of dogs. We rounded a tumbledown wall.

In front of a row of barred kennel runs stood a man with curly hair and a foxy face. He was wearing a stained tweed suit of horsey cut. Helen removed her hand from the crook of my arm. She said, 'This is Finbarr Durcan. He's in charge.'

Another hand, a hard one this time, with pale-blue eyes that had not missed the hand on my arm. 'Sure we all know who's the boss,' said the ex-tenant. 'I just have a stab at managing the farm, God help me. You're welcome here.' He smiled at me, twinkling the eyes. There hung about him a slight whiff of horse manure. In three sentences, he had managed to give me the idea that he was the owner and Helen a guest.

Helen handed him an envelope. 'Dave sold my motorbike,' she said. The envelope was the one I had brought her the money in. It still looked fat. Finbarr pocketed it. 'You wouldn't believe the price of fence posts,' he said. 'Only fifty grand to go.'

Helen asked him to lunch as well. 'We're opening up the dining room,' she said. Again, the eyes took note of the 'we'. They chatted about someone called Cosgrave who had just caught a thirty-pound salmon in the draught net, whatever that was. (I felt a tug of interest. It would be possible for me to be something other than an outsider, if there was fishing involved.)

'So,' said Finbarr. 'Did you show him it all, Helen?'

'Just about. Emily's away in Cork.'

As we walked away, I said, 'Who's Emily?'

'Finbarr's mother. Old cow. Come on, I'll show you the Herring Weir.'

We walked over the flat green inch onto the river bank. A hooked bank of rounded stones curved out across the low-water mud in front of us. On top of the bank was a fence of stakes connected by rusting chainlink of the kind used for tennis court enclosures. The river bed inside the hook was dry except for a stranded puddle perhaps eight feet long by six wide. She said, 'Christ, that Steve. Such an eejit, he was.' She shook her head. 'You catch anything in it but herrings, really. The fish try to go out to sea on the tide. They hit the mesh and turn around. But then the water's going from them at a hell of a rate, and they're looking for the deep stuff, and it's in the middle of the weir. So next thing they know, they're in that puddle, and you can fish them out with a class of a shrimping net.'

I stood there, slightly stunned. Steve got passed by with a mention. Fishing techniques got a lecture of their own. Then I saw her looking at me sideways, one eyebrow up, and realised it was for my benefit. She knew I was a lot less interested in Steve than in fish.

I rolled up my trousers, picked up the big net and walked down the slimy stone steps. The water in the puddle was soup-black against my snow-white legs, suddenly full of swirls. I dismissed a vision of Steve, face-down, bluish-grey. I shovelled the net through the water and lifted it out. There were three fish in it, a foot long, twisting and thrashing.

'No good!' shouted Helen from the bank.

They were like herrings, but not herrings. Shad, maybe. I tossed them into the river, dredged around a bit more, found a two-pound bass, and went up the bank, the complete hunter-gatherer, ludicrously smug.

We put the fish in the pram. On the way back to the house, Hannah prodded at it, making cheerful noises. Steve's or not, it was hard not to like her. She was a civil baby, with whom it seemed I shared an interest. I said to Helen, 'Have you got any fish books?'

'The library's under the same bit of roof as the Green Room. All the books are soaking. I'd say there might be some in the Laboratory, though.'

'Where's that?'

'It's what they call the East Pavilion. The one with the roof on it.' We walked behind a screen of laurels hiding a mossy disc she said was the gasometer, that dated from the days when the house was lit by coal gas brewed on the premises. The house loomed above us like a sea-cliff. She pointed down a colonnade. 'At the end there. I'll cook the fish.'

There were young ash trees in the paving cracks, and by the door of the pavilion a gunnera had seeded itself like a giant rhubarb. If the outside was pure eighteenth-century, the inside was pure Edwardian. Three of the walls were lined with laboratory benches. The marble tops were covered in a blanket of ceiling plaster and bat dung. The label on a bottle of chemicals said *BORAX – John Bell & Croyden, Wimpole St, W. – January 1911*. The fourth wall was made of bookshelves.

There was indeed a fish book, a manuscript volume, illustrated with pedantic line drawings. On its title page it bore in large, clear copper-plate the words *The Fishes of the Malpas River – described and drawn by Peter Costelloe, M.D.* The fish I had caught in the weir were Allis shad, it seemed, a remote and unpopular cousin of a herring. But as my eye travelled across the shelves, I realised that there were more interesting things about this library than fish. There was much physiology and medicine, and a lot of early psychology: Charcot, Stoddart, Maudsley, Freud *On the Interpretation of Dreams*, Jung; even, oddly enough, Francis Galton. It was an interesting hodge-podge, spanning the change from the Victorian alienists, through psychoanalysis, to the drug therapies of early biological psychiatry. I dived in, and read until the clock in the ruined stables on the side of the hill struck sixteen, signifying lunch-time.

As I returned the books to their places I spotted a shelf above and to the right a run of leather-spined quarto volumes blocked in gold with the words CASEBOOKS, dated from 1910–19. They were all together, in a shelf that looked custom-built for them. There was a gap at the right hand end, as if some were missing.

I locked the door carefully and picked my way under the colonnade back to Helen and the bass. She had cooked it with lemon and fennel. The flesh came away from the bone in perfect white flakes. I made enthusiastic noises. She said, 'You'll get sick of it soon enough, it's all there is.'

I said, 'Whose is the laboratory?'

'Peter Costelloe, I think. My grandfather.' She looked vaguely guilty. 'I've been so busy stopping things falling down that I've hardly been in there. If it's who I think, there are all these legends about him. He had Russian ballerinas here for drug cures, prize greyhounds with complexes, you name it. A rackety life, a bad end, but nobody knows what. My father never talked about him.' She looked at her watch. 'Hell, I've got a farm meeting with Finbarr this minute. Would you be okay with Hannah until four or so? Just park the pram. She'll sleep.'

I said, 'Do you mind if I have a look round in the laboratory?'

'Be my guest. And tell me what you find. It's so long since I used the mind, I can hardly boil an egg without counting on me fingers.'

I parked Hannah in the colonnade and unlocked the laboratory. The casebooks were dated on the spine. I started at the earliest.

The casebooks I was used to were a collection of spare descriptions of cases and accounts of treatment. This was different. There was enough science to make them interesting. But the writer seemed to have used it as a journal, too. I sank into the book. Outside the laboratory was Malpas present, wild, vast, beautiful, with Helen at the helm. Inside the laboratory was Malpas past, a story unread since it had been written. And by fair means or foul, that morning I had caught a bass.

Life was good. Life was absolutely terrific.

Chapter Six

From the Casebooks of Peter Costelloe

It is extraordinary to reflect that it has now been a month since the tragedy at the wedding; a difficult month, poor Miss White in a state of collapse, brain fever a constant threat. She is well provided for, Desmond having in his Will left her the house and estate of Malpas. But the matter first of the death and then of the Will has made a great scandal in this most talkative of countries. The Will, it seems, was drawn up and duly witnessed – no fear of matters being otherwise, Probus the solicitor presiding – on the night before the wedding was to take place. Naturally this has not pleased Maurice Devereux, Desmond's first cousin, to whom failing this Will Malpas would have passed. For perhaps three hours, Maurice presumed himself in possession. He lacks the character to hide his disappointment, I think. Though sometimes I feel that that is an unworthy analysis, and that he feels a genuine grief for his cousin. I have advised the Police – the RIC, as I must learn to call them – who have at my suggestion taken fingermarks from the revolver according to the scheme of Sir Francis Galton, and compared them with those of the deceased. The pattern of whorl within loop is unmistakable, to my mind. The inquest is tomorrow, and we shall see if the RIC is of the same opinion.

Miss White has hovered between madness and sanity for four weeks, and I have charged myself with her care. It has been a task requiring constant attendance. Which is why it was not until this afternoon that I urged my bicycle up the avenue at Slaughterbridge, home of the Caroes. The RIC have been very discreet – scandal is a favourite local occupation, and God knows poor Desmond was a prominent figure in

61

the area. Curiosity has always been part of me – a weakness in the eyes of some, but an indispensable weapon in the scientist's armoury. As always when I felt the whole truth was lacking, I set about making enquiries.

The Slaughterbridge avenue is a poor, weedy thing, ringing today with the alarm calls of blackbirds. Grass grows in the sweep before the house, a pebble-dashed cheese-box some sixty years old. Having handed my bicycle to a groom I stood in a hideous porch of coloured glass, with a desiccated Crown of Thorns for company. Finally, a slovenly maid answered the bell.

The hall was dark. The maid showed me into a drawing room without pictures, in which Mrs Caroe was sitting over a wheezing fire. She greeted me (her voice, I find, somewhat flat, uninflected. Is lack of vocal modulation a symptom of low intelligence?) 'Maria!' she cried. 'Bring tea!' She began to talk haltingly about the weather. I formed the idea that she was not much called on. Of course, she knew why I was here, even if she did not like to admit it to herself.

'Now,' I said, taking out my silver pencil. 'About the death of my poor cousin Desmond. I know how close you were.'

Her chin went up. 'We were children together.'

Tea arrived, lukewarm and sooty. I moved my chair slightly, so the light reflected from the pencil caught her eye. 'You played in the woods,' I said. 'The high woods of beautiful Malpas.' I continued in this vein for some ten minutes, keeping my voice low and singing. She found it soothing, I know – beneath that bovine exterior she was an anxious woman, full of nerves. In the end, I saw her eyes unfocus. 'She took him from you,' I said. 'Is that it?'

More silence. I could feel her yield. Her voice came low and sleepy: 'Yes.'

'So he deserved to die, for letting himself be taken.'

'No. Of course not.'

'Why would he have killed himself?'

'Goodness knows. Goodness knows.' Her voice was a murmur, as if she did not know she was speaking aloud. 'He is, was, a very high-strung man. A man of the most aristocratic blood.'

A silence. Her face was becoming restless. She was conscious of herself again, slipping from my grasp.

'You and he were close,' I said, flattering her. 'None closer. You of all people would know if there was any reason he would have wanted to destroy himself.'

A change had come over her. Her face was pale except for the scarlet blotches of *acne rosacea* on her cheeks. She stood up.

'You were in the house the night before the wedding,' I said. 'You talked to him on the terrace.'

The spell was broken, the trance finished. All that remained were the normal methods of persuasion. 'Nonsense,' she said.

She was lying.

I had seen them from the bedroom window by the light of the moon. Desmond had been sitting on the raised lip of the pond in his shirt sleeves, smoking, watching the silver river winding towards the sea. Mrs Caroe had stumped across the flags to him, threading her way among the potted palms that the gardeners had wheeled out of the orangery for the wedding. I had heard the distant quack of her voice. Desmond had said nothing. But at a certain point in their discourse he had dropped the cigar he had been smoking into the pond. It had struck me as odd at the time. He was a tidy, even finicky man, proud of his pond as of everything else at Malpas. The cigar had been a Montecristo, a bridegroom's cigar. It had not been like Desmond to cast such a treasure half-consumed into a pond of prized *nymphea* hybrids.

Just as it had not been like Desmond to blow the top off his own head with a service revolver.

'I saw you,' I said. 'Of what did you speak?'

She chewed a thick finger. 'She was not fit for him,' she said.

'Tell me why not?'

'It is a known thing,' she said. 'She is from the wrong part of society. A milliner's daughter, coarse-grained, vulgar. She does not hunt, has no accomplishments. Her morals are . . . well. She has bad blood. The worst of blood. Poor Desmond was the purest, noblest creature. She is not fit for him.'

'You told him all this?'

'It was my duty.'

'And you did not want him for yourself.'

'Of course I did,' she said. Her voice was cracking. 'Once. But he told me it could not be. So I was married to Mr Caroe, and of course then I could never have him.'

'So you wanted to be sure that nobody else would.'

She started to cry.

'But Mrs Caroe,' I said, gently. 'Why should he listen to a disappointed woman pointing out the faults of a successful rival? With the best will in the world, it would be an easy thing to disbelieve.'

'He could not disbelieve it,' she said. 'It was true. There was more.'

'What more?'

She was crying properly now, her red face in her stubby hands.

I said, 'I think you should tell me. You would feel better.'

She said, 'I will never . . . feel . . . better . . . again.'

'Does your husband know of your feelings for poor Desmond?'

She stared at me with blood-red eyes. 'No,' she said in a vehement whisper.

'Perhaps he should know.'

'*No!*' Terror. I knew then that he beat her, poor woman.

'Then tell me, do.'

'Never.'

I said, 'You should give it some thought, Mrs Caroe. You must understand that anything you tell me will go no further.' Then I left her in the cold, dirty room.

Her husband was in the stable yard, hands in trouser pockets, rocking from heel to toe of his yellowish elastic-sided boots. He showed me his bad teeth and tried to bring my attention to a brown horse with a groom at its head. But even he could tell I was not interested in buying horses that afternoon. He said, 'Tell me, Doctor, how d'you find Mrs Caroe?'

'Shaken,' I said. 'Low.'

He wagged his greasy hand. 'Terrible thing, a suicide,' he said. 'She feels it deeply.' He did not look sorry at all, himself. 'I expect she talked to you about it, did she?'

'She told me nothing,' I said.

He looked slightly more cheerful. His wife was not the woman to hide from him the fact that she thought him a poor second best to Desmond. I had salved his grubby pride. I felt suddenly grubby myself. I had gone to make some discreet suggestions to Mrs Caroe. I had ended by bullying a disappointed woman, and soothing her jealous husband.

The sooner I got to the bottom of Mrs Caroe, the happier we would all be.

From the Letters of D.W.

How will I remember poor Desmond? Already his face is fading. There was the fineness of it: deep temples, a narrow nose, a chiselled jaw, the bones light as a bird's. The hair palest red, eyebrows and lashes the same, so that when the sun shone he looked dusted with gold. I do not remember him touching me, though at first I used to long for it. I remember someone saying, when we were in love, that he looked too good to be true. Perhaps he was.

For he came from another world. He would have made the supreme knight of King Arthur. Ordinary men (and women) were entirely beneath his notice. Me he put on a pedestal. He and I could communicate, he thought, in the high language of the spirit. I was dazzled by him.

Perhaps in time he would have driven me mad.

I am not a poet, so I cannot properly explain the miracle of the day I first came up from Dunguin to see Malpas. Instead of dirty red brick, golden stone. Instead of the fumes of whiskey and tobacco, hot bracken and the rose garden. Instead of Jerh the butcher's boy on his bicycle, a golden angel on a great bay mare.

But angels are creatures of no sex.

He was too high to live up to. He could not live up to himself, so what chance had I? People do not live by dreams alone. We have appetites and desires. I am afraid it was the realisation of this that brought about his end.

But I must not let the horrors sour my life: or so the Doctor says, and I believe him. He and I talk about it often, and he has given me exercises to perform, which I think are banishing the worst of the horror. Now when I try to picture Desmond, all I can see is a golden glow, without features or attributes.

Already he is fading.

From the Casebooks of Peter Costelloe

Well, the inquest is done. The Coroner was kind enough to direct the jury to return a verdict of accidental death. But this has been a terrible time for poor Dulcie, in a place larger than she is used to, with strange people – and people worse than strange. So I have stayed, and am keeping her company, and continuing my work in the East Pavilion, an empty building with a good light, which Dulcie has said I may use as a laboratory.

We were taking tea in the drawing room. I had stepped into the library next door, to find a reference for a point in our conversation, when the maid announced Desmond's cousin Maurice Devereux.

This was Devereux' first call since the wedding day. He knows that but for Dulcie he would have inherited Malpas entire. But now he has lost it and it is out of his line, and this gnaws at him. So I thought it politic to remain unseen in the library, and hear what he had to say.

'Well?' said Devereux, in a voice like the bark of a dog.

I heard Dulcie offer him tea, very civil. She is indeed the soul of consideration, all the more so towards Maurice because in the kindness of her nature she feels a genuine compunction that she has deprived him and his descendants of Malpas and its beauties.

'Damn your tea,' said Devereux. 'Why would I drink tea that is rightfully mine with the woman who has by stealth and guile snatched it from my mouth?'

I heard Dulcie draw in her breath. She was low in herself, having only recently risen from her sickbed. Where in health she would have felled him with a phrase, a treacherous sob now intervened.

'Crocodile!' said Devereux. 'I know you, you and that damned doctor with his knees under your table. If you ask me—'

It was at this moment that I grasped a volume of the *Oxford English Dictionary* and stepped into the room.

Devereux is a florid man with grizzled curly hair of which he is overproud, bloodshot blue eyes, and features creased by rage and tobacco, to both of which he is a slave. Poor Dulcie was on the sofa, and Devereux was standing over her, too close for her to be able to rise. I said, 'If you have objections to my conduct, it would be more gentlemanly to address them to me in person.'

He turned upon me a face dark and suffused. I saw to my astonishment that he had been weeping. 'I do, sir,' he said. 'I say that you are a damned impertinent quack, presuming to take the part of those who deprive law-abiding subjects of His Majesty of what is rightfully theirs.'

'I fear you are letting a natural disappointment betray you into slander.'

'Disappointment? After the death of my dear friend Desmond? By God you are a cold fish, Doctor whatever-your-name-is from wherever-you-come-from. We shall bloody well see who is disappointed around here. Sir, I shall be talking to Inspector Carson. I think you will find your life pretty uncomfortable; pretty uncomfortable indeed.' He turned to Dulcie. 'I address these remarks to the pair of you,' he said, and marched out of the room.

If this were a book, I would say the face Dulcie turned to me was beautiful. Since it is a mere journal, I must admit that her hair was disordered, her eyes red and shrunken, the skin of their orbits oedematous with weeping. 'Poor man,' she said.

She was wrong, of course. Devereux is rich, with a large house at Kiltane upstream from Malpas, and several excellent farms on the good land by Mallow, besides which he owns to my certain knowledge eleven streets in the city of Cork. But like many rich men he is greedy, and has long been accustomed to the gratification of his every wish.

'What do you think he will do?' she said. She was frightened.

'Anything he can to get his hands on Malpas.'

'But how?'

I said something soothing, and her face cleared. But to tell the truth I was somewhat uneasy myself. It was probable that Maurice was merely blustering. But it was possible – barely possible – that he knew something he should not.

Dulcie coughed slightly. It was only then that I realised that during all these reflections, we had been holding hands. I released her, feeling my face grow hot. What if the maid had come in? 'I'm sorry,' I said. She smiled at me under her lashes. We laughed; it was her way.

But really there was nothing to laugh at at all.

From the Casebooks of Peter Costelloe

This morning James Durcan appeared while I was preparing a Bittern skin in my laboratory in the East Pavilion – of which, I may say, I grow daily more proud. James works in the stables. He is the son of a past steward at Malpas – a young man of considerable natural intelligence, though he suffers from the provincial isolation in which he has spent his life. His manners are rustic, his views unsubtle, and his critical apparatus unformed. But he is a fine strong lad, eager to learn. He visits me often now, and seems interested in the work I am doing, the books I have begun to have sent here, &c. He mentioned this morning that he had seen Maurice Devereux. I know he admires Maurice, as a man of low station will admire a greater. But such a meeting was not unusual; so I was curious as to why he would think it worthy of remark. I prompted him discreetly.

'He was asking did I see you the night before the wedding,' he said. 'With a long face on him as if he was a class of a policeman.'

I waited. James is a strange mixture. He has been brought up as a true Durcan, which is to say as one of the Protestant steward class at Malpas. His father (dead now) was apparently a good, improving farm manager, and absolved poor Desmond of the necessity of contact with his tenants and the outside world. So the friendships and alliances customary between neighbours were made in his case not with Malpas' proprietor, but with its steward. I myself have been since arriving at Malpas entirely preoccupied with my scientific endeavours. But one cannot live in complete isolation. I have found in Jamesy an excellent source of information on the politics of the neighbourhood. And he seems to find in me the gratification of a scientific curiosity unsatisfied by his education. He is twenty-two now, old and hard in the ways of horses, but young and credulous in the subtler workings of the mind. I think he would himself make a good steward. I shall tell Dulcie.

In any case, I was much interested in what he had to say, and let things come out at their own speed, without encouragement.

'I got the idea that he's fierce keen to prove that Desmond went on his way other than by accident.'

'By suicide?'

'Not that.'

'Good Lord!'

'And he was asking other questions,' said James. 'About you and Miss Dulcie.'

'Namely what?'

James' pink face turned a shade pinker under the scarlet hair. 'Ah, ye know,' he said.

'So what do you think he was driving at?'

He shrugged. His eyes would not meet mine.

I moved my silver pencil into the light. I said, 'Jamesy.' His eyes came up. 'James, you can trust me. You know that.' I spoke on. The pupils dilated. The features took on the vulnerable, childlike look. When he was ready, I said, 'So tell me, what did Maurice mean, do you think?'

His voice came natural and easy. 'He was asking was you and Miss Dulcie having a love affair, the way you might have killed Mr Desmond after he made his will, so you could get her and the place all at the one time.'

'And is he the only person who thinks this way?'

'He was saying there's an Inspector Carson he knows, and he's interested.'

'Thank you, Jamesy,' I said. Then, returning to my normal voice, 'That's all for now.'

I saw his face cloud, as with something half-remembered. The cloud passed. I said, 'Don't worry about Maurice.'

He smiled, and nodded, and left.

Naturally, my first task was to prepare Dulcie for what was to come. At luncheon, we found on the table a pair of white trout (the Herring

Weir, Johnny Cosgrave, vigilant as always) with a glass of Chablis from poor Desmond's cellar. I said to Dulcie, 'So how's the patient?'

She smiled at me over her glass, a sad smile, distant.

I could have shifted into the light, and taken out my pencil, and suggested that she tell me more. But I some time ago began to feel a strong compunction against bending her will to my purposes – rather, perhaps, as a sportsman would feel about Johnny Cosgrave's shovelling of white trout out of the Herring Weir. And now I have resolved that our dealings will be as between equals, without the apparatus of hypnosis or suggestion. So instead, I said, 'Perhaps it is time I was going back to England.' Once it was said, I could not unsay it. And I must admit that I was surprised by the difficulty of saying it, and the sullen weight of the words as they hung in the air between us.

She gave me a long, silent look from her cool green eyes, thickened, unless I am much mistaken, with the beginning of tears. She said, 'It's only that dirty little Maurice and his jealousy. I was left alone on my wedding morning with nobody to trust. I would have landed in a bed of spikes, but you caught me. You can't go now.'

I gave her my handkerchief. When she was herself again, I said, 'You must prepare yourself for a great deal of trouble. I shall be here to face it with you.' She stood up, smiling. I took her hands. I should have liked to kiss her, but the maid was at the door. Now was not the time for kissing. Now was the time to be surprised leading a normal life.

Back at my laboratory I found Mairi Dugdale, a thickset, ill-favoured girl with a mat of black hair and a complexion studded with moles like black nails stuck in dough. I have discovered in our conversations that she has elements of the *idiot savant*. Her chief talent is a knack of seeing the physical world as patterns of numbers. I welcomed her presence as a relief from the complications of the luncheon table, and was soon quite absorbed in her case.

I had asked her here to explain to me her systems of calculation – she has many, founded not on tens and units, but on (for example) numbers of oar strokes required to travel across given speeds of current. We had a diverting hour at it. She is used to being treated on the estate as an idiot, and was overjoyed to find someone who would consent to share in her singular world, even if they were not equipped to understand it. We passed from mathematics to birds. As with everything else, Mairi had a system of classification of her own devising, based on observation. Thus a cormorant and a grebe were Axefisher and Needlefisher respectively; and we were discussing the relationship between the Common and the Goldcrested Wren (Switch-arse and Yellowhat) when there came a thunderous knocking at the door.

Mairi leaped to her feet and went out of the window, her habit when alarmed. I opened up.

There was a policeman outside. Above the dark-green tunic were a hostile brown eye, a black moustache and the fleshless jaws of an Inquisitor. He said, 'You are Doctor Costelloe?'

I bowed, and said, 'Won't you come in?'

'Carson,' he said. 'Inspector Carson, RIC.' He entered the laboratory with a back like a ruler, frowning about him as if my books and collections were evidence of my criminal propensities. I asked him to be seated, but he did not seem to hear. His uniform was beautifully brushed, his Sam Browne gleaming, his lip curled in disgust at this evidence of intellectual activity – the very model, in short, of an Imperial oaf. He said, 'I am not entirely happy about the death of Desmond Costelloe.'

'You have this in common with his other friends, among whom I am proud to number myself.'

He bared his teeth. 'I hear you assisted the local force with their enquiries,' he said.

'Only in that I showed them the correspondence of various signs, including finger-marks taken from the corpse and those on the revolver. I have made a study of the classification of finger-marks, along the lines proposed by Sir Francis—'

'I am familiar with your evidence. Gathered by you. Interpreted by you. In the matter of the finger-marks understood only by you.' I sat there, motionless, chilled by his eye. 'And you have no idea why Mr Desmond Costelloe should have done this terrible thing?'

'The Coroner's verdict was accidental death.'

'A kindly verdict at a nasty inquest. In your opinion, would marriage to Miss White have been a desirable outcome for Mr Costelloe?'

I felt the heat rising to my cheeks. 'Indeed. And in the view of any man, I expect.'

'We are not interested in any man. We are interested in you, Dr Costelloe.'

'I beg your pardon?'

'We would like you to account for your movements between midnight on the fourth of May and eight o'clock on the morning of the fifth.'

'With a view to what?'

'With a view to eliminating you from our enquiries in the matter of the murder of Desmond Costelloe.'

I stared at him, entirely discomposed. 'But I have demonstrated to the satisfaction of the Coroner that it was an accidental death.'

'Not to mine,' said Carson. 'Not to mine.' He has a smile like a pike. Lord, I dislike that smile.

I said, 'As to my movements, they were much like anyone else's. I was asleep, in bed, in the house. I am sorry to tell you that there were no witnesses.'

'Convenient,' he said, picking up a skull from the bench.

I found my composure weakened to breaking point. I said, 'The fact that I was innocently asleep does not point to the fact that I am guilty of murder. Or have I missed something?'

'Nothing at all.' He placed the skull carefully on the bench. 'It is just that you seem to have made yourself remarkably at home here. Now that Miss White is a rich woman.'

I felt the blood leave my face – the adrenal gland, of course, but that was a matter of purely academic interest, since the gland in question was my own and I was shivering in the grip of its secretions. I said, 'Damn you, sir, Miss White is a dear friend.'

Carson bared his teeth in a grin that implied a shocking intimacy with the foul crannies of the human spirit. 'A dear friend but a new friend, eh, Doctor? You may count on it that I am looking into you.' And he left.

I sat in my laboratory, much unnerved. He was right, of course. If Maurice had decided to fight, I did need to consider my position. I did indeed. And so, of course, did Dulcie.

Walker Archive, Transcript, 1973 – 2

The cage is still there inside in the house, but it is not for people nor for dogs. I am after scrubbing it with a great lash of soda and now I use it as a press for the good things I have found, the feather of a peacock from the House, a redhat[1] that was caught and dried in the glasshouses, a stone with a writing on it that is in no language but that you can understand when you look at it. And there is a class of a pretty straw hat that Johnny Murphy bought at Dunquin Fair and put on my head, saying, this is yours, this is yours from me, and you're the great girl yourself. And Johnny so wide and tall, a great lad altogether, he will never take anny nonsense from nobody. He is fifteen now and I would say I am thirteen but nobody can ever be certain. The lads are round most nights now and sometimes Johnny is here and sometimes he is away on the mountain and he is come back this morning in a motor car, and him with a big ulster on him, and when he opens the coat there are flowers inside, such beautiful flowers, and I am laughing and counting them over and over again and the little shoots that is on them have such a beautiful pattern, a growing in the numbers that goes one, then two, then three, then five, then eight, and so on, you understand. And Johnny laughs too and tells me I have the great noggin on me if only annyone could understand what was happening inside in it. So I have put the flowers to dry by the fire when Johnny was away again, and now they are inside the little press. And every time I think of Johnny coming home I think of the flowers, the way I will not see the strange red stain on the cuff of his ulster, nor smell the smell of burning house that is on it, nor hear the talk about Parkinstown, which was a place full of bad people that was burned and the agent shot at close range, nobody knows who by; but I only think of the flowers, and the kind fierce face and great shoulders of my beautiful Johnny.

They are fishing now. They are all fishing in the boat, and I am with them,

---

[1]   Goldfinch

---

because I have the shoulders to pull an oar and haul the net, and I can tell by the count of the water when the silvermen[1] are up from the sea. So I am fishing and doing the house now, me and the other girls, and the happiness that is in it, with the wedding coming at the House and all.

There is a little man comes across one day, rowing in a strange way, like a child that does not know how. He is the Doctor, he says. He has showed me the silver pencil he has, and he is asking questions. I like answering the questions, now, I always have, there was Padraig of the hedge school that told me my figuring and it's a grand feeling when you answer a question, and you're right, or maybe better than right, and you get a sweetie. So the Doctor is asking me questions, and I am showing him spotslippers,[2] steelbars,[3] bluemen,[4] axefishers,[5] needlefishers,[6] switcharse,[7] yellowhat,[8] orangemen,[9] slabberdegullions,[10] suckheads,[11] – such a list! and he never laughs at me, not once.

But I can feel his life, my little Doctor. Even when I am with him and playing. I can feel that only a little piece of his life is here with me, the kind piece, that is a game and has been with him when his mother was there and him a child. His mother is long dead, he has told me. So most of him is off and away somewhere else where I can't go, in his own places of the world, hard places with engines inside in them, nothing with anny slime or a feather in it. They are frightening places, they frighten me.

We are talking, me and the Doctor, all nice and funny, and I am hearing the crunch of boots on the stones outside, and I hold my breath and sure enough! In there comes a class of a man that by his stony face and cold eye and black-green coat you can tell is a Polis. So I am away out of the window. Later

---

[1]   Grilse
[2]   Orchids
[3]   Sea trout
[4]   Kingfishers
[5]   Cormorants
[6]   Great crested grebes
[7]   Wren
[8]   Goldcrest
[9]   Cock blackbird
[10]   Eels
[11]   Lampreys

I ask Johnny what is it that would make a Polis so hard so cold. And Johnny laughs at me, laughing down at me, like, and he said it is a hard cold world and yer man is an Our Eyes See polis, Join the Army and see the world, Join the Our Eyes See and see the next.

I laugh too, though it hurts my stomach to do it because I can see that Johnny thinks I am stupid. But what does he mean?

It means that when I ask Johnny he stops laughing and looks very bad, and I can see he is frightened. And that might be why he says, ya ignorant ya eejit, Mairi. Ya eejit ya lunatic.

At first I still don't know what he means. Then I know, and I say, don't make me cry just because you are frightened, and he starts roaring out of him, ya hole or it's the bars again.

Well, it's just his talk. Or maybe he means it, how would you tell?

I cry annyway. By the fire, all down among the sods of turf, I cry. But I don't make anny noise. Not anny.

Chapter Seven

When I went back to the kitchen at the end of the afternoon, Hannah waved and babbled in the pram, trying to attract my attention. She had no luck. My mind was back sixty years. I was treading paving stones uncracked, and the crows were piled black over the rhododendrons.

I found Helen in the kitchen, stuffing turf into the range from a great earthy box by the door. She looked up and smiled. 'Hello, darlings,' she said, grasping Hannah. 'What's wrong with you?'

'Me?'

'You look as if you've been hit by a truck. Did the ceiling fall in?' Mysteriously, Hannah was changed and in the high chair with a mug of milk.

I said, 'Do you know how your grandfather got here?'

'No.' She poured tea.

I told her: no technical stuff, only family history. Beyond the window a little group of men was hauling a net on the muddy beach of the House Pool. I thought I could see the white kick of fish in the bight. Helen's face had a pale, distant look. She chewed her lips. 'Jesus Murphy,' she said, when I was finished. The sleeves of her jersey were rolled up. I actually saw goose pimples on the bare skin of her arms, the short blonde hairs standing on end. 'All this fecking death. If Grandpa hadn't been staying they would have eased Granny out for sure. That little horror Maurice Devereux, he was Alice's husband, Angela's father, did you know that? If he thought it was him that was next in line for Malpas, he'd have just as much motive for killing Desmond as she did. Nobody mentions that, though, not the RIC, not anyone. He's above suspicion. Nasty little Ascendancy animal.'

This was a new Helen, defending her ancestral home against those living or dead who wanted to take it away. I was only a researcher. 'There is something,' I said. 'What do you think Peter Costelloe meant when he wondered whether Maurice knew something he shouldn't?'

She laughed. 'They've been dead fifty years,' she said. 'You can't exactly ask them, can you? Oh. Hey. Come on. Actually you can.'

She took my hand and pulled me across the chequer of the hall, through a half-collapsed doorway and down a passage hung with blackened landscapes. I stubbed my toe on a pile of chairs, dislodging a cloud of woodworm dust. She hauled open a door whose bottom hinge had come out of the jamb. 'Careful of the floor,' she said. 'Dry rot. This is the Gallery.'

It was a long room, facing north. A light of sorts crawled in at the dirty windows. 'Your friend Dulcie,' she said, pointing. 'By Sargent. Painted in 1909, for her engagement.'

And there she was, full length on the end wall in a silk ball gown, her hair Helen's Titian red, her eyes large and green, the chin round and imperious. Even Sargent, the great flatterer, had not managed to hide the blunt practicality of her hands.

'Keep close to the wall,' she said. 'The boards are better.' She showed me Desmond, pale-haired and fey with close-set eyes, holding a shotgun as if he was not sure what it was for. There was Maurice Devereux, smug and blocky next to his wife Alice, whose mouth wore a conventional smile, but whose eyes the painter had not managed to render as anything better than calculating. 'Jamesy Durcan,' she said. 'Finbarr's father. Married to Emily. You'll meet Emily.' And there he was, sleek as a seal in three-piece heather mixture and spats, fingertips joined, sprawled in an armchair. He had a heavy auctioneer's face, the chin already becoming a jowl. The eyes were clever, the hands enormous. Between the fingers was a silver pencil that caught the light.

Next to Jamesy was a smaller portrait, in very bad condition. The face of the sitter loomed out of a background of paint decayed to the consistency of tar. It was a small face with a broad brow. There was something faintly Napoleonic about it, except for the eyes. The eyes were deep and black and followed you around the room in conventional style. But there was something separate about them, as if they would rather observe than participate.

'Who's that?' I said.

'My grandfather. Peter Costelloe.'

As we turned to go, I saw that on the end wall, facing Dulcie down the length of the gallery, there was another picture. It was a woman in a ball gown, the chin up, the fan in the lap, the attitude imperious. The style was Sargent's. The face was Helen's.

'Who did that?' I said.

'Steve. It was his idea of a joke. He rearranged all these people in here.' She said 'people' as if they were still alive. 'He painted that one of me to go with them. He said there was too much history, he felt like an ant on a carwash and one of these days a great broom was going to come and sweep him down the drain, so there was nothing to do but take the piss.'

'You never feel like that?'

'It's just a farm,' she said. The words came out too quickly. There was darkness in these faces. We had chased it back towards the walls. It would return as soon as we were gone.

We tiptoed back to civilisation over the rotten floorboards. I held her hand, and she held mine.

Tight.

From the Casebooks of Peter Costelloe

Last week I went once more to call on the Caroes, at Mrs Caroe's request. I found her in the cheerless drawing room, crouched over her sooty tea. I said, 'Have you reflected on what I asked you last week?'

She drew breath, I think to defy me. Mr Caroe was standing outside the window, talking to a gardener. His eyes met mine. He grinned, and bowed slightly. Mrs Caroe caught the movement, and frowned, remembering the consequences of silence. She lowered her head on its thick puce neck. 'Yes,' she said. 'You must go to Cork, and see a woman called Beatrice Mulligan.' She wrote the address on a sheet of cheap writing paper.

I said, 'You will not regret this.'

She said, 'I already do, Doctor. I already do.'

Beatrice Mulligan lived in a great staring villa in Montenotte. A priest scuttled out of the door as I walked up the path between the privet bushes. Mrs Mulligan was a red-haired widow, heavily but inaccurately painted, dressed in a great deal of glittering black, and wrapped in the fumes of sherry. She invited me in, and had more sherry, to keep me company, as she put it (I took none). Under the influence, she told me that Mrs Caroe had warned her of my impending visit, and its reason. 'You must read this,' she said, tottering to a cupboard and getting the key into the lock at the third attempt. 'It is entirely shocking of course but I will make a bit of a guess and say there will be few surprises in life for a medical gentleman.' She tacked back across the room with a brown leather notebook. I took it from her, thanked her, and promised to return it within the week. 'Oh, no, I could never let it out of these four walls,' she said. 'You must read it here.' She hiccuped. 'My poor, poor brother.'

I opened the book at the place she had marked. At first I did not know what she meant. But as I read on under Mrs Mulligan's watery eye, it became plain enough. 'Where is your brother now?' I said.

'Dead, dead,' cried Mrs Mulligan, raking tragic fingers through her hair.

I cannot bring myself to paraphrase what was in that notebook. So I here reproduce the copy I made in that cluttered Montenotte parlour with its reek of face-powder and alcohol.

And may God have mercy on all therein!

From the Game Book of Major Ridley O'Dowd, May 1885

Last Tuesday, the weather being pretty fair, I went down to Waterford to see my old friend Henry Costelloe at lovely Malpas. Henry's wife Betty was in England; she never went much on ould Ireland, silly prim thing. So what does Henry decide but that we should have a *parti à l'ancienne*, according to the principles established by old Barrington the diarist.

My readers will remember – those of 'em sober enough – the peculiar festivities beloved of 'old Barrington'. The necessary ingredients are a pile of sheep and chickens trussed for roasting, a hogshead of claret, a blind fiddler, a cook, and some sort of cottage. After a turn in the park, we repaired at about dusk to the Alpine Bower in Kelly's Wood. Here we found the supplies assembled and the masons standing by, grinning behind their blindfolds—

Blindfolds?

I asked what the D—l this could mean. At the sound of my voice, there came from an inner room of the cottage *not only* a burst of Drowsy Maggie on the fiddle, *but also* the charming sound of female voices. I stared at Henry with a wild surmise. He nodded and winked. 'Couple of things old Barrington left out of his version,' quoth he. 'Now, then, in we go. And—' (to the masons) 'Work away, boys, work away.'

With this the masons set to with a will to brick up the doors, while the fair charmers hid inside and we pledged the setting sun in beakers of Chateau Lafite.

By the Gods, what a night that was – night? day? week? – How to tell, how to tell? The wine was the right Hippocrene, the cook a mistress of her art. And old Shamus the fiddler tore his native lays from his fingerboard in a style to make Toscanini wink.

And the girls! Charming companions, as witty as you like, Sirens in the candlelight. Some time – the D—l knows when – Shamus fell off his stool into the fire, and we rolled him into a corner to sleep. I remember little, as my readers will understand! But I do remember being upstairs in the room with two beds, big 'uns, and on each bed a girl, and on each girl a man. Mine was called Peggy, a fine big black-haired specimen. You may well imagine that once I had tumbled her and teased her and found the target of old John Thomas' aspiration, I lost no time in climbing aboard, much to her delight! She started a shoving, roundabout sort of wriggle, and soon we were bucking away as if we were in the last three furlongs of the National, though never rider had smoother saddle than your servant that night!

Well, soon enough she starts going bellows-to-mend, and I can tell the moment is at hand, so I give her a slack rein, and she comes to meet me, not being able to contain herself. Just then there comes a view-halloa from the other bed, and when I look across there is old Henry, scrawny beggar, kneeling up behind his piece, and she chucking herself back at him as if she wanted to screw it right off him. So, 'Race you home for fifty pound!' was the cry, and you may pretty much guess the rest. Result, a dead heat.

That was not the last ride we had in the Alpine Bower, no, nor the last glass of wine neither. When the meat was bones and the claret lees, we took up the hammer and broke our way out into the light, and damned bright it seemed too. My Peggy went off with fifty of my guineas tucked who knows where. Henry seemed to have developed a *tendre* for his Bridget. Apparently she had been a lady's maid at Malpas; but now he set her up as a milliner in Dunquin, and of course she turned into a shrew, and in the fullness of time presented him (to his disgust) with a daughter.

But what matter? The game's the thing. I think this was probably the last *parti à l'ancienne* to be held in Ireland, and we shall not see its like again, more's the pity! I shall always be grateful to my dear friend Henry for laying it on.

From Cork I rode to the priest at Dunquin, who showed me his registers, and then straight to Slaughterbridge, where I burst in unannounced. Mrs Caroe was turning the collar of a shirt. I took the envelope out of my pocket and shook its contents under her nose – a copy of a baptism record for one Dulcibella White, born 1880. The mother's name was Bridget White. The father's name was blank. Mrs Caroe's eyes rose to mine.

I said, 'You saw him the night before the wedding. You told him Dulcie was his half-sister.'

The eyes dropped. She picked with her needle at the hard skin on the end of her finger. 'I couldn't let him go through with it,' she said. 'She is a whore, daughter of a whore. He—'

'Not true,' I said, perhaps too sharply.

'I was just right for him,' she said. 'I had been keeping myself for him. But he said he didn't want me. Dulcie was prettier than me, of course.'

'How did you find out?'

Her face had taken on a terrier-like grimness. 'You must understand that I love Malpas,' she said. 'So I talked to a lot of people. I found out all about Dulcie's mother. Rose Murphy, that worked in the house, she died three years ago, was cook at the . . . orgy. She remembered, all right. I went to all the churches and looked at the registers. It's not difficult, once you start. As you know yourself.'

And I had thought she was stupid.

'So you told Desmond.'

'He could not be allowed to marry his sister, could he?'

'What were you hoping he would do instead?'

I saw her eyes turn inward. Her life was already lashed to Caroe's. Desmond had already rejected her. If she could not have her happiness, nobody else was to be allowed theirs. 'He did the right thing,' she said, finally. 'He was a truly honourable man. You knew him.'

I could see Desmond in my mind, sprawled in an armchair, ludicrously handsome, a half-calf Ovid under his aesthetic hand. A pattern gentleman, his word his bond, expecting nothing of others that he would not expect from himself.

'So you can see that he had no alternative.' She folded her lips. 'Just as well.' She had had her revenge on the world, and on herself. Suddenly I could not be in the same room as her any more.

I got up. I bicycled to the barracks and demanded an interview with Inspector Carson.

He was in a bare room, painted pea-green to shoulder level. He did not get up as the constable showed me in.

I said, 'I have some information for you.' And I laid before him the results of my conversation with Mrs Caroe.

His face remained stiff, British, Imperial. But I saw a muscle jump under his eye as he read my transcript of Ridley O'Dowd's orgy. When I had finished, there was a silence. Somewhere in the cells, a voice howled without words. 'Yes,' he said, finally. 'I see.'

'A motive,' I said.

'Our enquiries continue.' But the conviction had gone from his voice. Policeman he might be, but first and foremost he was an English gentleman, with an Englishman's squeamishness. Faced with the evidence I had brought him, he would admit that Desmond had taken the decent way out, and bury the whole ghastly business. He would still dislike me, of course; I was a nasty little nobody from nobody knew where, and he was a friend of Maurice Devereux.

But for the sake of Malpas, I could live with that.

Chapter Eight

The evening before the lunch party Helen and I were in the dining room cleaning ceiling-plaster and birdshit off the sixteen-seater mahogany table. Hannah was upstairs, asleep among her damp yellow bunnies. I was explaining the day's research, according to developing custom. 'So there they were on the terrace,' I said. 'She gives him the bad news, and he drops his Montecristo in the pond, and whatever it was she told him, from then on he was as good as dead.'

Helen had hauled a cardboard box of tarnished silver up from a rusty safe in the lamp room. She said, 'How do you know they met by the pond?'

'The Doctor saw them from his bedroom.'

She stood a sugar-dredger on the table where it would hide a knife-wound in the French polish. She said, 'You can't see the pond from the bedrooms. All the bedrooms look straight over the river. The pond's round the corner. Let's go and open a bottle of wine.' We had been to Venice McGrath's in Dunquin, and spent some of the Trident money on burgundy, old stock, cheap to clear.

'He saw it, all right. I checked. There is a bedroom. Windows on two sides. A nice one.'

'The Pink Room. But it doesn't really count.'

'Why not?'

'It was Dulcie's room apparently,' said Helen. Then her hand went to her mouth. 'Oh, my goodness me.'

'What?' I said.

She gave me a strange smile. Her eyes narrowed into cattish slits. She took my hand and led me out of the dining room, across the hall, and up the side of the lyre-shaped double stair the cow had not fallen through. At the top, she opened a door. 'The Pink Room,' she said.

The Pink Room was huge. It smelt of her perfume. Her clothes lay on the chair.

'The view from the window,' she said.

There were windows on two adjacent walls. One side looked over the terrace and the park to the river. The other looked at right angles to it, over the little arm of the terrace with the raised pond, now cracked and empty. As she had said, it was the only window on the bedroom floor with this view.

We stood side by side, looking down. Our fingers were still locked. I turned to face her. 'See what I mean?' she said, and laughed. 'The things that Maurice might know that he should not have known. What do you think?'

Then somehow we were kissing each other, in a sort of fury, and there were clothes going everywhere. And then nobody had any clothes on any more, and we were on her bed.

Probably, actually, the same bed.

Her father, offstage after the concert, somewhere in Central Europe. Prague, it could have been, she had been too young to take it in properly. All she remembered was that it had been very cold and dry, with a thick mat of snow on the window sill that fell in at the window when you opened it. And a little girl who lived down the corridor in the hotel. The little girl had a big doll called Emilie, who had got on very well with Helen's bear Edouard. The girl's mother had been kind and tall and very beautiful, with very very red lips. Helen, having no mother, was keen to get one. The little girl who had Emilie would have made a good sister, too. She hoped desperately that Daddy would notice she was thinking this.

But then on the Sunday morning there had been Daddy with the newspapers all over the bed, open at the Notices, with a picture of him in. And the flowers coming in and the telephone off the hook otherwise it would ring and ring and not a moment's peace. But that was not what made her heart sink and her mouth open and her eyes fill up with horrible stinging tears. What did that was the pesky awful suitcases, out on the bed for packing.

'Off we go,' said Daddy, with the big smile he only used when he was going to be moving across the world on boring boring boring trains planes and limousanes.

'I want to stay somewhere,' she said. 'Here.'

'No you don't,' he said. 'We're us. Wherever we are is somewhere.'

And off they went, goodbye Emilie and the little girl and her mother and stop that horrible screaming and yelling and get in the taxi, to wherever it had been next.

But now it was different. Now it was the Pink Bedroom, and her holding Dave's head so she could kiss his mouth just how she wanted it, and that amazing feeling of having and holding and bodies humming with the same sweet delight, and all in the middle of this fantastic wild horse of a place that was hers and hers alone, permanent, if she could hold onto it.

Malpas.

As the waves rolled in her, she was going to shout it. But she shouted, 'Dave,' instead. Out of politeness.

And afterwards, thought about Dulcie.

The night before the wedding. Dulcie in that bed in the Pink Room, laid away by her maid like a beautiful dress in tissue paper. Looking at the shadows in the room's corners, put there by the glow and wane of the gas in the mantles. A little scent, something musky, chypre, perhaps, whatever that was. Thinking about what would happen tomorrow in this new life, and every day after that, so long as she and Desmond should live . . .

The creak of the door. The long split of passage-light opening and closing. The clocks of the house striking a ragged midnight. The voice: *And how are we this evening, Miss Dulcie?* All the better for seeing you, Doctor. And in her body that secret melting, while the Doctor turns the key gently in the door and lowers the gas; and goes to the curtains, peering out, seeing Desmond pitch his cigar away as he listens to stubby Mrs Caroe by the moonlit pond. And all the time the doctor watches he is undressing, until he is standing there small, pale, hard in the silver light from the windows. Dulcie sitting up in bed, fingers fumbling at the front of the nightdress into which her maid not half an hour ago buttoned her. Her body glowing under the patient hands that knew just where, for just how long. He was in her arms now, his body economical, no softness at all. They were moving, both of them, his hand by her cheek where she could turn to bite it when she had to cry out.

And all this while down there on the terrace, Desmond looking into the flat glint of Mrs Caroe's eyes, and hearing his death sentence.

All this with the wedding in ten hours.

All this as part of Dulcie's farewell to the single life, its friends and lovers, before she buckled her marriage about her. That would have been the intention, anyway . . .

The front door clattered. 'Hello?' said a voice, echoing in the hall. 'Anyone inside?'

The dining room was a double cube with a Carrara fireplace and three quarters of an Italian plaster ceiling. Besides Helen and me there were Finbarr and Angela, and four more distant neighbours. Helen distributed us round the table with the authority I recognised from Steve's satirical portrait. I landed up next to Angela, who was looking practical and efficient in not-too-tight jeans and a black cashmere jersey weighted by a string of pearls between her breasts. I found her watching as my glance clashed with Helen's, knocking off little sparks that lit up the huge, ruinous room. She smiled knowledgeably as she caught my eye, and said, to change the subject, 'So what have you been up to in the Pavilion?'

'In the Pavilion?'

'This is Malpas. Your every move is watched.'

'Tidying up,' I said evasively. I started to talk about the Allis shad in the weir, moving onto fishing, a subject about which I did not have to fake an obsession. The light in Angela's eyes curdled, poor woman. She said, vaguely, 'Paddy Cosgrave's your man, then. Mr Fish in person.'

Finbarr turned a hot pink eye upon me. There were at least two bottles of wine inside him. He said with a sort of concentrated savagery, 'You'd want to be careful in the river, though.' I was shocked. Surely he was not talking about Steve? He drained a bottle into his glass and drank the contents. 'Well,' he said. 'Thank you Helen, that was grand. See you, Angela.' He gave me a bare nod, and left.

Helen rocked in her chair at the Steve reference, too. She took Finbarr out, came back and said, 'He doesn't mean any of it. He's had a shock in life, giving in the tenancy. He takes it very well really. He'll be off on a horse somewhere and when he comes in he'll be right as rain.'

Angela said, 'Poor Finbarr. He used to be a hell of an amateur rider. Then he kept the hounds above at the Kennels. Then he couldn't afford to feed them any more, so they've gone, all but a couple. And now he just races himself round and round the park, for Christ's sake.'

Helen gave me another connecting sort of look. Poor Angela, it said; looking after her demented mother, in the middle of nowhere, nice person, no hardship to the eye but no raving beauty either. She's making excuses for Finbarr. But she's talking about herself as well. You and me, said the look, we have each other, we're so lucky.

At teatime, Helen said she was going to play with Hannah for an hour or two. As it was raining I took Angela home in the Zephyr. I stopped outside her door. 'Cup of tea?' she said.

'Better not.'

She laughed as if she could see into my head. She said, 'Thanks.' Then she leaned over and kissed me. By the look of her wide, outdoor face, it should have been merely a sociable kiss. It was more than that. Her lips were soft, her perfume a fragrant cloud mixed with fumes of wine. It was a kiss that suggested hidden depths.

As you will have guessed from the ease with which Mara wound me round her fingers, I am not made of stone. But I was suddenly, violently back in love with Helen. As if to emphasise this, in the window above the front door there appeared the grey face and vacant eyes of Alice. A doleful wail floated into the rain.

'Feck off, you owd lunatic,' said Angela brightly, and slid out of the car.

As I jounced back down the drive, Finbarr was coming down the road on a tall white horse. He waved an arm, beckoning regally. Helen would still be with the baby. Malpas was a small place. I might have a future here. I needed to get on a footing with this man. I followed him into the kennel yard. He handed the horse to a small, bandy man. He seemed to have forgotten his cataclysmic rudeness. 'Fancy a jar?' he said. He scooped a bunch of keys off a ledge above the door and led me into a spartan kitchen, with two armchairs facing a cold range. He sloshed Paddy into two glasses and watered it out of a green-crusted tap over a Belfast sink. I felt completely out of my element. 'Nice horse,' I said, though of course I knew nothing about horses.

'She is,' he said. 'Did you know your aura's going muddy?'

'My what?' Auras were undergoing a brief vogue in parapsychological circles, and naturally I had read about them. But I was surprised that they had reached as far as Finbarr.

'Sort of halo class of a thing,' he said. 'It clouds up when you're telling a fib. You're not all that interested in the horses, am I right?'

I acknowledged this, while privately discounting the demonstration of second sight. Helmstone had been full of Finbarrs, ready to talk any mystagogic claptrap to make themselves feel important. Feigning respect, I asked him how he had got into such matters.

'It's not a full-time job, running the farm here,' he said. 'So I have time to do a bit in the vet line. Not your sheep drench, more like bonesetting, I suppose you'd call it, it's always been in the family. The mare outside, when I got her she was lame as a milking stool and your man had her brought to the kennels. For the hounds' dinner, you know.' He did not mention that the hounds were now departed. 'But I got her inside in the stable and there she was, right as rain. So what are you by profession?'

'Student,' I said.

'Of what?'

'Psychology.'

'Plenty of that round here,' he said, with a wag of his head. He looked at a yellowish watch. 'Let's go to Brady's.'

He drove his Land Rover with an astonishing lack of skill. At the shocking-pink lodge he jumped out of the cab, hauled the carcass of a deer out of the back, and carried it to a car parked up the road. A bundle of notes changed hands. 'Hit it with the car,' he said, climbing back in. 'Waste not, want not. You'd need every penny you can get on a place like this, good work with the motorbike by the way. Brave girl, that Helen.' He wagged his head, the professional assessing the talented amateur, and hauled the vehicle off the road and onto a small, muddy track. We jounced along for five minutes, emerging finally on a bluff round which the river flowed black and sinuous. On the spine of the bluff stood Brady's, a long white house with a roof of mossy thatch. There was no outward sign that it was a pub. But inside there was a dark room with a barrel of Guinness, lit mostly by the red-hot glow of a stove at the inner end.

The man behind the bar said, 'Finbarr,' with no great enthusiasm.

'Paddy,' said Finbarr. He ordered pints, and told Paddy to put them on the slate. The man's enthusiasm diminished further. 'Well,' said Finbarr, drinking. 'Beats home, eh?'

I nodded. Finbarr's home, anyway.

'Steve thought it did,' he said. 'Poor Steve, now. You were in the same place in England. You knew him, did you?' He did not wait for an answer. 'What Helen saw in him, fine big girl like her, little tick like him, I will never know. We were in here his last day, him and me. Jesus, but he was down that night. Isn't that right, Paddy?'

'It is,' said the man behind the counter. 'I said would I give him a spin home. But he said, go away to hell, and he would walk and get some air in his head.'

'Only it wasn't air he landed up with,' said Finbarr.

Paddy gave a large, crass laugh.

'Pity,' said Finbarr. 'Talented man, talented man. God the drawings he'd do not that you'd get one out of him for love or money.'

'Did he ever show you his drawing book?'

Finbarr looked at me with a curiously wooden expression. 'He did,' he said. 'Not bad. Not bad . . . at . . . all.'

'A bit sharp.'

'What do you mean?'

'He used to draw people to piss them off.'

91

Finbarr laid his eyes upon me as if he had just noticed my existence. 'So you did know him, then.'

'Did they find the book after he died?' I could see Steve vividly, smirking at me about his retrospective. Fifty years, he had said, who knows?

'They did not,' said Paddy, with the authority of an Official Source.

'It'll be in the river I'd say,' said Finbarr. 'He was never without it, God knows.'

'Not that night,' said Paddy. 'I remember thinking that night, that's odd, where is it? But he was that far gone he was maybe after leaving it somewhere.'

'Well,' said Finbarr, finishing his pint. 'Another one, so?'

Helen would be through with Hannah soon. 'I'll walk home,' I said.

'Mind how you go,' said crass Paddy, and roared with laughter.

I set off uphill, on a path they pointed out. If you had to have a last walk, this was a beautiful one. The evening sun carved golden slabs out of the darkness under the trees, and the ground was lit by constellations of pale-blue anemones. Beyond the trees the river slid, rumpled with eddies.

The path snaked up a cliff. At the top was a flat area of paving, walled with a broken balustrade. Cylindrical stones lay tumbled in the briars. Presumably this was the Temple of the Graces. Malpas lay spread below, the house red-windowed in the evening sun, the Herring Weir a little question mark dragging a wake in the ebb.

I tried to identify with Steve, walking back from the pub, lonely, drunk, depressed. But all I could manage was to think: what was he doing without his sketchbook?

Like Paddy said, he had been drunk. He must have left it behind.

I walked down the hill and into the house.

Chapter Nine

One of the most ambitious (which is not to say the most successful) gas plants was the one at Malpas, County Waterford. Here, in an enclave of the grounds tastefully screened by a tall hedge of cypress, Henry Costelloe caused to be erected a gasworks in miniature. It was a closed-retort system, in which rough Welsh coal was heated. The resulting gas was cleaned and detoxified in the usual processes, and stored in a very perfect miniature gasometer, this being a drum some forty feet in diameter and twenty feet high, rising and falling as usual over a tank of water.

The Malpas gas plant served to light and heat not only the gigantic house of the same name, but also the estate's legendary greenhouse. Its heyday was short, however, lasting only until 1915, at which point it was replaced by a hydro-electric scheme.

It is perhaps worth pointing out that this substitution was effected purely on the basis that the gasworks was smelly, and in no way because of the risk it posed to its operators, the difficulty of acquiring Welsh coal during the War, or the residues of tar and cyanide constantly in need of disposal. The proprietors of Malpas had a tendency – marked in their kind, it must be said – to value their own convenience at the expense of their employees' health and safety, let alone that of the men who navigated the treacherous estuary of the river to bring them their fuel . . . [1]

Next morning I woke early, in a state of extreme happiness. This was the moment I had been waiting for all my life, but never expected to

[1]   Cadwallader Clyro Strang, *The Newport Colliers – A History* (unpublished Ms, National Library of Wales, Aberystwyth, 1978)

see. I turned to Helen on the pillow beside me, watched the delicate poise of her eyelids over her eyes, felt the warmth of her breath. Then the lids rose, and the eyes were looking straight into mine, and she smiled and put out her hand and pulled me towards her and kissed me with her sweet morning mouth.

She went to sleep in my arms. I waited till her breathing steadied. It was five o'clock, early even for Hannah. I pulled on some clothes, put up my fly rod in the hall, and walked outside.

The rain had stopped. The eastern sky was duck-egg blue, the air soft and wild-smelling. I walked across what had once been the South Drive, winding away towards the ruins of the bridge that had carried it over the Owenafisk. The river was marked by a strip of reeds (spires, they called them) marching into the forest. The tide was nearly covering the banks of ink-black mud on either side of the water. On the bank was drawn up one of the boats they call cots, a primitive thing, double-ended, heavily tarred. Footprints led out of the mud and away into the reeds.

I found a narrow path that burrowed its way through the reeds, crossing sallows fallen and re-rooted. Duck leaped into the air at the sound of my passing.

Then I was out of the spires, and the ground was sloping up in front of me. The river itself had ceased to be a heavy thing crawling through mud, and had become young and muscular, sliding among rocks and over gravel. I made a couple of false casts, and landed the fly gently in a riffle. I saw in my head the fly with tail and hackles quivering, the fish rising piston-smooth from its slot in the river floor, my heartbeat rising to meet it—

Something took hold of my line and tried to yank it off the reel. From the black moil under the rock leaped a bar of silver as long as my arm, shaking its head. It hit the water and dived away downstream, clattering my knuckles with the reel. There was a great jagging as the line sawed against stone. I let if float downstream in a great loop. When I raised the rod again the line was slack, and my heart with it.

'He's after spitting out yer fly,' said a voice, irritatingly. 'You'd be crazy mad not to use a double hook.'

He was a short man, very wide in the growing light, with a mat of black hair that grew down to within an inch of his eyebrows. He grinned at me from above a jersey crusted grey with dried mud. 'You're Dave Walker,' he said with mystifying enthusiasm. 'You're staying with Miss Helen and Miss Hannah.'

I grinned back at him. His accent was thick as mud. I could only just distinguish the words, let alone understand what they meant. He was carrying a fishing rod himself, an ancient, corkscrewy greenheart. I said, 'Any luck?'

'Just a bit of breakfast for Mam,' he said. 'She likes a bit of trout. Then it's hey ho haul the net.'

I remembered Angela's remark at lunch yesterday. I said, 'You'll be Paddy Cosgrave.'

'That's right,' he said, apparently delighted. 'And you'll be fishing above under the Dam, I'd say. Am I right? Am I right?'

We talked fishing for ten minutes. There was a hell of a run of spring fish now, and it was early for white trout, but they were there all right. He showed me his fly box, prodding with his great pork-sausage fingers at infinitesimal size-eighteen midges tied on double hooks from black hackle and button thread. He told me about the draught net, and how to fish the River when the tide was off it, and the Owenafisk when the sun was off it, and later in the year at night. I began to sweat with the possibilities of the fishing, and he noticed, one fisherman to another. We got on like a house on fire. So at the end of the fishing conversation, it seemed perfectly natural to say, 'I heard it was you found Stephen Brennan.'

An immediate coolness fell over us. 'That's it,' he said, after a pause. His face was in shadow.

'Did you find a little book anywhere on him? A book of drawings?'

He moved. A shaft of sun fell on his face. All the animation was gone from it. He could have been a well-coloured clay mask of himself. 'I did not.'

'His pockets were empty?'

'They were.'

'Except the stones.'

A sort of twitch agitated the mask. 'We used to talk, we used to talk, all the time.' He shook his head, giving off embarrassment and discomfort. 'Terrible,' he said. 'It was a terrible thing altogether, no sense to it at all, I can't tell you anything except what you know, you'd have to ask Mammy.' He would not meet my eye. He said, 'I'll be off,' and marched splay-footed into the reeds.

I hitched the fly to the rod and walked on up the right bank, unsettled by the change in his mood. The morning's happiness was congealing. A line of poles joined the river, cableless, crusted with green lichen. They ended in a small shed at the foot of a steep hillside. From round a bluff of rock came a roaring. I followed the path along the river bank, and found myself standing on the margin of a wide black pool into which there plunged from the mouth of a vast pipe a fair-sized waterfall.

I caught two trout and lost another two before the sun came on the pool and the fish went down. As I walked downstream I passed once again the hut from which the poles came. Propping my rod against a rock, I went to have a look.

The door was padlocked shut. Through the dirty window I saw two rust-red steel housings connected to pipes. Next to them were the finned cases of generators. The back wall was earthed up. Above the wall two thick pipes snaked up a bank.

When I climbed the bank I found myself looking at a lake. It was perhaps fifty acres, its steep margins dense with willows. The bank on which I was standing was a dam, built of squared-off black stones that bulged through weeping rents in a coat of turf. The pipe making the waterfall was an overflow; I could see machinery that must have been a sluice.

At the far end of the dam, something splashed into the water, sending a wave across the inky surface. A head came up, spluttering. The head of Finbarr Durcan. It went down, and started surging powerfully across the lake, round a post and back to the shore, then out again. The whole business had the look of a daily routine.

The sun had not yet reached the kitchen by the time I got back to the house. Helen was still in her dressing gown, painting with Hannah, who greeted me with a gratifying cheer.

I slapped the fish on the table. 'Thank God,' said Helen. 'Not a bit of mate in the house, it's good to have a provider, so.'

I said, 'Finbarr was saying nobody ever found Steve's sketchbook.'

She said, 'I know. Funny, isn't it? He never went more than two feet away from it in his life. He was in a terrible state, though, poor man. I'd say he took it into the river with him – look *out!*'

Hannah was hauling the fish towards her. The milk jug went over. The morning dissolved into the usual chaos.

After breakfast I went to the laboratory and started on the casebooks again.

From the Dunquin Examiner, *June, 1911*

A pigeon flutters in from Malpas bringing word of a great improvement (say some) or deterioration (say others) in the administration of this palace. Be it known that in this abode of peace and harmony (tho' recently smirched by Tragedy itself) there was a pump through which water was conveyed to the tanks in the roof, from which the gentry drew their baths. This pump was a clever contrivance, based on one in Edgworthstown, and works by this principle, much to the benefit (!) of the mendicant community. For every two hundred and fifty strokes of the handle, the mechanism delivers 1d to the pumper – a glowing example of automatic charity. Now, though, Miss Dulcibella White of Malpas has caused the pump to be removed, and installed an electric device in its place. Who can stand in the way of progress? Not the mendicant, who will now be at our door, dirty hand out, more even than before . . .

'Quillsman – Behind the Curtain'

From the Casebooks of Peter Costelloe

It is now a year since the inquest; three months since that man Carson read O'Dowd's filth in the barracks, his face twitching with disgust. I have made myself a set of bachelor apartments in the West Bedrooms, where I live in a state of perfect propriety, treating whatever patients present themselves. My laboratory is in the East Pavilion.

There are two things that keep me here. The first is Dulcie, the woman I love, who has for fourteen months now been my daily companion. The second is Malpas itself. To the outsider, it is a great estate in a country with a dark past and a doubtful future. To me and to Dulcie, it is a blank canvas on which we will paint the picture of our lives together – a picture based on fairness and equity, stripped of corrosive jealousies founded on religion and culture.

Yesterday, though.

We were out on the constitutional we take daily after luncheon, rain or shine. We had paused at the gasworks, a nasty smelly place. Dulcie has in mind a conversion to electricity, powered by a reservoir she is having built – dear practical Dulcie! The Cardiff ship was tied up at the coal quay. On the bridge, arguing with the Welsh captain, was Jamesy Durcan, whom Dulcie has appointed Steward, and who takes his duties very seriously.

I see Jamesy every morning in the Laboratory. He has attached himself to me as a pupil, and very considerable strides he is making in his understanding of that elusive creature, the mind. But I have little to do with his business on the estate. The Durcans know Malpas and its people well. They make the home farm work profitably, and even in these times when rents are almost universally withheld, manage in some mysterious way to exact a contribution from the tenantry.

But this morning, as Jamesy came towards us through the coal bags, he had a preoccupied look.

We walked all three of us in silence through the Abbey Meadow, that is coming ready for haymaking. Finally, he said, 'We have trouble with the Whites above.'

'Ah?' The Whites are a family with strong Fenian sympathies, tenants of Bundore, an inordinately sour and boggy farm on the high western fringes of the estate.

'They will pay no more rent, they say.'

'Then we should offer to sell it to them,' said Dulcie.

'I have. I am after telling them they can have it under the Act.' (He referred of course to the Wyndham Act, put in place to reduce the evils of landlordism. The Act would have meant a capital sum for the estate, and a repayment for the Whites at three per cent over sixty-eight and a half years – a bargain for the Whites, being eighteen per cent less than the rent.) 'But they told me . . . well.' Jamesy is the kind of crimson-haired youth who blushes easily. He said, 'I'll give them notice to quit, so, if it's all the same to you.'

I said, 'No.'

'I beg your pardon?'

In the winter I had been called to Edmund, the father of the family, and diagnosed rheumatic fever. The labour of the farm is now beyond him, and his two sons are too young yet to take their full part, even if their father would countenance their absence from school, which to his credit he will not. All in all, the Whites run counter to the slothful Malpas tendency. This I explained to Jamesy.

'They're troublemakers,' said Jamesy, looking at Dulcie, not me.

Jamesy knows that Dulcie's liberality towards her tenants is largely due to my influence. I think he despises me for it – he has been brought up to landlordism, and is ruthless in pursuit of good order. Dulcie looked at me, then at him, and I sensed that she was torn between love and duty. 'Take no action for the moment,' she said. I managed to steer the conversation back to the gasworks, and we parted without further argument.

Dulcie said, 'You know why he wants the Whites out?'

'They're Shinners.'

'And Mrs White's a Cosgrave. He hates the lot of them, you know.'

She put her hand in mine. 'Jamesy is a treasure,' she said. 'But how would I stand up to him on my own?'

We went and sat on the bench in the Temple of the Graces, looking down over Malpas emerald green among the sour hills of Munster. At the end of our tête-a-tête, we returned to the house not arm in arm like strollers, but with Dulcie's arm around my waist and mine around hers, not caring who saw; from which it may be guessed what the matter of the discourse had been!

We arrived back at the house as the stable clock struck half past four. Too late, we saw the Rolls Royce motor car in the drive. There was the crest of a bull's head on the door, and Joseph Sullivan the stable boy staring at the whole, chewing a straw. 'Grand motor, Joe,' said Dulcie.

Joe was eleven, deeply conscious of the dignity of the stables. 'Sure give me a horse anny day. Mr Maurice is inside in the house.' He wagged his head, as if to say we had been warned, and strolled off, groomlike, whistling. But even on so glorious a day there is very little to whistle about in a visit from Maurice Devereux.

He was on the hall sofa, boots planted, gnawing the knob of his walking stick. Dulcie greeted him pleasantly. He stood up, not out of politeness but in order to tower over her. He glowered down upon her and said, 'What d'ye mean by it?'

'By what in particular?' said Dulcie.

'I am told that you are refusing to evict that damned Shinner Patrick White.'

'He's a good man. It's bad land he's on.'

'I do not care if he is the Archangel Gabriel in the Gobi Desert, if you refuse your duty as a landlord you are opening the floodgates for every vagabond and inebriate in creation to lie around all day stealing what is rightfully someone else's. Now you will send for White and you will tell him where he can take himself.'

Dulcie had turned somewhat pale about the mouth. She said with great sweetness, 'Will I send for his family too?'

'Obviously.'

'Ah.' Had Devereux been looking at her, he would have noticed that her smile had taken on a rigidity. Experience had taught me the danger of this smile.

I said, quickly, 'Excuse me, but what business is this of yours?'

Devereux kept his eyes out of the window. 'I am addressing my remarks to Miss Costelloe, who is for better or worse the owner of Malpas.'

'Oh, well,' said Dulcie, brightly. 'You may address yourself to Dr Costelloe as well, in that case, because I am sure you will be pleased to be the first to know that he has done me the honour of asking me to become his wife, and I have accepted. And of course he is right, the Whites are none of your damn business.' There was a short but bottomless silence. Then she said, 'Would you care for a cup of tea?'

But Devereux had gone.

And it is easy to forget him, now Dulcie has consented to be mine, and our love, which has for so long had to grow in the dark, can now burgeon in the fair light of day. This evening, we have asked our friends to a party, to announce our news.

From the Letters of D.W.

What can I say about my Doctor? I am no great hand with a pen. But I do not have to be a poet to say that I love him. First of all, I loved him in guilt. But he was there when poor Desmond ceased to be: and a goodbye became a new morning (how pompous that sounds!)

Why do I love him? He is small, and quiet, and horribly stubborn. In politics, he can see the logic of all causes. In dealings with his fellow man his will always prevails, because he has given his view ten times as much thought as the people he is dealing with. In manner, he is persuasive to the last degree, as I was the first at Malpas to find out.

It was six weeks before my wedding to Desmond. We were in the Temple of the Graces on the River Cliff. I told him my feelings for Desmond: a respect and admiration that I though might in time ripen into love. He sat across from me with that dark gaze of his that seems to fill the world, intent on what I was saying, tapping his palm with that silver pencil of his. Then he began to speak. And it was as if Desmond grew smaller and smaller as he grew bigger and bigger.

One of my great difficulties as a woman is that, like it or not, I understand a great deal about how things are made and done. Unlady-like, people call it, but it cannot be helped. That is one of the reasons I wanted to marry Desmond. I wanted to look after him, poor thing, so hopelessly impractical. But the Doctor is different. He understands the deep things of the mind. You can never know what is happening behind those bright, dark eyes. I find it so terribly – sinfully – exciting. There came a time when even though I was to marry Desmond, I simply could not forbear from touching Peter. Yes, it was I who went over to him and took his face in my hands and made him kiss me. And then I gave myself to him. Of my own free will.

There is no excuse, and I do not know why I did it. Except that I wanted to be his, then: to possess him, and be possessed. It would have stopped after the wedding. I know it would.

There was no wedding, though.

But now there may be two.

There is a nice girl called Emily Gumbleton, whom I met in Kinsale a fortnight ago. She is I think quite pretty, and would do awfully well for Jamesy Durcan, who is of an age, but like all Durcans seldom turns his attention beyond the demesne wall. As it turns out, Emily is second cousin to Maurice Devereux. It has been pointed out that any connexion of this kind would be a great diplomatic advantage, since Maurice is in such a passion that I inherited Malpas instead of him. (Though I am not sure that he will take kindly to being a connexion of the farm manager, rather than the proprietor!!)

I have talked to my dear Doctor, and he thinks an introduction a capital idea. Indeed, he has met Emily, and finds her kind and practical, not without attractions, and with an amusing frankness of expression that would make an excellent foil for Jamesy's great silences. So we are taking to the river for a picnic, and we shall see what we shall see!

From the Casebooks of Peter Costelloe

The announcement is made. Dulcie is wearing on the third finger of her left hand the diamond I have had sent from Messrs Asprey in a box marked PILLS, and we are betrothed in the sight of all.

I must say that I was nervous before the gathering. It would be foolish to pretend that in a year of our living in the same house – even a house the size of Malpas – there has been no gossip. I made a short speech, and Dulcie, in a green dress that threw her beautiful hair into relief like a burning rick against a grassy hill, made one too. Everyone clapped, except Alice Devereux (Maurice had not come, but sent her as his spy) and Mrs Caroe. After the applause had died away, I heard Alice mutter something. I saw Dulcie flush up. 'I beg your pardon?' she said, aloud.

'The decline of a great house,' said Alice in a penetrating voice. She was flushed herself, but with drink, not anger. 'Into the hands of bastards and bog-trotters.'

There was a large and deadly silence. Then Dulcie said, 'I do understand how upset you must be.'

Alice looked at her out of her black poisoner's eyes. 'You understand far less than you think,' she said.

Dulcie stood there as if paralysed. If she smiled it would have been to swallow the insult. If she threw Alice off the place, if would have been a declaration of war between neighbours. If I intervened, it would have been a declaration of her weakness, and would have made matters worse – no doubt of that.

Then from out of the blue salvation came. A voice from the throng said, 'Oh, for God's *sake*, Alice.' It was a young woman, pretty rather than beautiful, wholesome of face, in a dove-grey dress and pearls – Emily, the new friend of Jamesy since our river picnic of Tuesday, a woman of no fortune but great forthrightness. Jamesy seems much struck, and Dulcie is confident of a match.

Well, Alice raked Emily from sole to crown, taking in the worn shoes, the not-new dress, the small pearls. Emily was not at all put out. 'Dulcie's on the place,' she said. 'You and Maurice are off it. That's about all there is to understand, am I right?'

'How dare you!' said Alice, in hot retreat.

'Or would there be something else?'

Alice looked at me with those venomous eyes. I knew she was thinking of the policeman Carson, and the accusations made against me. But now we are in possession, there would be no difficulty in making a counter-accusation. This is the kind of thing Alice finds easy to understand.

I returned her stare. I could almost see the thoughts grinding nose to tail through her head. Finally, she said, 'I believe it is a free country, in which one may express an opinion.'

'Sure it is,' said Emily. 'So tell me, Alice, how are the rhododendrons this year?'

The hum of conversation rose again. Emily had lanced the boil. I felt a great warmth towards her. There have not been many close friends in my life, and those I have I treasure. I feel that in Emily I may have found another.

This morning, the first of our life as an engaged couple, I went out to the Laboratory. Mairi was already there. She was labouring under an access of romantic happiness that was actually interfering with her breathing. 'Wish you joy, Doctor,' she said, repeatedly. 'Wish you joy and happiness, God love you, and we're all safe now,' referring, I imagine, to her cousins the Whites.

'Yes, Mairi,' I said. 'We're all safe now.'

Walker Archive, Transcript, 1973 – 3

There have been people, people, people inside in the house. The Whites from Bundore has been down, the old chap walking with a stick, but him very strong the way he can walk out of the mountain and over the bridge and through the bad places to our house, all in only six hours. When I am talking about my little Doctor I can see that they are laughing at him for being soft and not evicting, some of them, but I can feel that the laughing is mixed up with liking. And they are still on the farm above and they will not have to go away, and this may look to some like the work of Miss Dulcibella but all here know that this is because of himself and himself alone.

Johnny is in the chair by the fire. He is wearing a big coat now, and you can smell him far off, a wild smell like an animal with crushed grass and trees. Like an angry animal. And tonight there is a new thing about the smell of him, a sharp parafeeny smell, like in the lamp room at the House where Bridie asked me. There is a thing in his lap that he is wiping with a bit of a cloth, and I can go closer to Johnny because I like to feel him big and near, and I can see that the thing is a class of a gun.

He can feel me stand so still so still. He looks up at me the way I can see the fire jump in his eyes. He says, 'There's a great day coming, my own Mairi.' And I know it is true, because the Doctor has told me that it will happen one day and when it does happen he will be looking after Miss Dulcibella and she will be looking after him, and there will be no bad secrets because of them all being tucked away inside in the marriage bed. And we are all happy fellas, because everything is working out lovely and it is all happening right, the numbers are right, everything.

And Johnny is looking up at me from the gun, holding it in his hand the way he will shoot the bad people, and talking about something. But I cannot hear a word of it because I am looking at the gun and I can feel the fierce shout of it, the way it will spit and kill. I say to him, Johnny why have you got that thing with you inside in the house?

And he looks up at me with his eyes narrow and angry, polecat eyes, and says to me, to keep us safe, Mairi.

But I would rather have the bed.

Chapter Ten

After breakfast on my tenth day at Malpas, I gave Helen a Peter Costelloe update. Afterwards she took me to the West Bedrooms. It was raining. We passed regions of green slime, and others where the plaster had come away from the rotting lath, and lay over the passages like drifts of feta cheese. Finally, after a ten-minute walk, we pushed through coils of damp-unglued wallpaper and into a long, straight passage with a balustrade at its end. She stopped, prodding with a finger at a sort of white mushroom bulging from the wall, silent. There was a powerful smell of fungus. At last she said. 'When you get up here you realise there isn't a hope in hell.'

I dredged around for something encouraging to say, but found nothing. 'There,' she said, pointing. I pushed open a door. There was an iron bedstead, grand but rusty, a desk, clean of papers, an ancient engraving of Charcot the hypnotist. Helen walked across to the window and rubbed a pane clean of grime. Beyond it, the savannahs and jungles of Malpas stretched into grey drifts of rain. She took my hand. Hers was cold. 'Poor bloody Trident,' she said. 'A drop in the ocean.'

'What happened?'

'My father never came here. It's a landlord's job to improve, and he didn't. Finbarr kept it going, just. But it's too late. Poor man, he's half frantic. The Cosgraves cut spires for thatch and net fish. There's four acres of roof on the house, and a leak every square foot. Finbarr says we need big money, and he's right. It's the same as with Grandpa. You're always in a state of siege. If it isn't Alice Devereux telling Dulcie she doesn't understand, it's the bloody bank manager refusing me an overdraft. Everyone fights everybody. Always has. And I love it. Oh, *fuck.*'

I put my arms around her. She put hers around me. Far away in the house, something heavy fell onto something solid. The tide of history receded, and there we were, cast up, safe together.

For the moment.

I was now working my way steadily through the casebooks. What they held was something really exceptional – the complete records of a pre-Freudian psychiatrist and hypnotherapist, working along lines of his own, uninfluenced by any thought except a sort of superstitious reverence for Francis Galton. I had written to Gale to tell him that I had found a subject for my thesis. Needless to say, Gale had not replied. But I had Helen, and I had work. Sorry to go on about it, but I was happy.

On Wednesday night we had dinner with Angela. Finbarr was there, and a couple of neighbours from upriver, not the same ones as last time. On Thursday morning I met Finbarr by the Herring Weir. His eyes were bloodshot. 'How are you?' he said.

I admitted to a slight hangover. He nodded, with something more like professional interest than sympathy. 'I'll heal yez,' he said. Next thing I knew I was sitting on a tree stump, and he was crouching in front of me. 'Think of nothing,' he was saying. His face was close to mine. There were yellow crusts of sleep in his eyes. He held his hands close to my temples, and murmured something about energy. 'Can you feel it?' he said. 'The heat?'

'A bit,' I said. 'Maybe.' All I actually felt was embarrassed.

'That'd be yer chakras firing up,' he said, as if I was a tractor. 'It's like I'm channelling it all into you, your aura's going a lovely gold now, and I'm getting a class of a glow—'

'Stick yer tongue out and say om,' said a woman's voice. Angela was standing there, her mother nodding on her arm. Finbarr scowled at me and stumbled off towards the stables. Angela stood with an eyebrow cocked a significant millimetre.

'He was trying to faith-heal my hangover,' I said, somewhat shamefaced.

'Sure he was,' said Angela. She looked brisk and blonde and matily ironic, as usual.

Alice turned on me the empty old eyes that according to the Doctor had once spewed death rays. 'Oh, dear,' she said, about something only she could see.

'Do be quiet,' said Angela. 'We're off to see Emily. Biscuits, Mummy.' She walked off. She had a great walk; a racehorse stalk, really, not at all in keeping with her worn black gumboots and patched jeans.

I went with them. It would be interesting to meet in the flesh another figure I had met in the casebooks. Behind a neat fuchsia hedge was a pleasant pink Regency villa. As we walked up the path to the navy-blue front door, several dogs started barking somewhere behind the house. It was only then that I realised the house we were approaching was the back – front, rather – of Finbarr's den.

A woman opened the door. She had a soft, powdery face and white hair neatly permed. She must have been well over eighty, but her eyes were brilliant blue in her head, and her voice was a funky, uncracked alto. 'Angela!' she hollered zestfully. 'Alice!'

'This is Dave,' said Angela.

'I know!' cried Emily, beaming from behind perfect lipstick. 'Come in come *in*!'

The air in the house smelt of roses, turf smoke and coffee. Amazingly for Malpas, nothing was falling down. The coffee itself was in the drawing room, which had Persian rugs and carefully arranged white camellias. Emily lit a Senior Service from the packet on the marble mantelpiece and said, 'How are you finding it?'

'Every prospect pleases,' I said, remembering too late that the next line was 'only man is vile', and noticing that Emily's eyes were shrewd as well as bright.

'And Helen?'

I was being dug into. I said, noncommittally, 'She loves it here, who can blame her?'

'The baby must have been a surprise.'

'She was.'

'And poor Steve, of course. I do so hate suicide.'

The Doctor had described her as outspoken and honest. That sounded about right. 'Wife, baby,' I said, keeping it conventional. 'Horrible.'

Emily put her cup carefully on its saucer. Then she said with a bright smile, 'He was what they call a manic depressive of course. But what baby?'

'His daughter.'

'Daughter?'

'Hannah.'

'*His* daughter? Oh, no,' said Emily. 'Not *his*. Goodness, is that the time? Lunch will be burning to bits. Goodbye, goodbye.'

Angela and I found ourselves outside. I think my mouth was hanging open.

Angela said, 'Take a look in the mirror. Then take a look at Hannah. She's *so* handsome.'

'Bastard,' said Alice.

Somehow, I navigated the potholes back to the House.

Put yourself in Steve's boots. Imagine you are delighted to find yourself a husband and father. Then imagine someone telling you you are nothing of the kind. And you go down like a depth charge, and put stones in your pockets, and walk into the weir.

I was not happy any more.

In the kitchen, I scrutinised Hannah's small, bean-puree-smeared face. She did not look like Steve, it was true. But then she did not look like anyone much. After lunch I pushed her into the colonnade for a nap, and went back to the kitchen. Helen said, 'What's wrong?'

No chance of keeping anything from Helen. 'Everyone seems to think that Hannah isn't Steve's child.'

Silence. Then she said, 'Ah.'

I said, 'Why did you suddenly agree to marry Steve?'

More silence.

'Because I had got you pregnant and you thought I was back with Mara and you wanted the child but you didn't want me?'

She raised her eyes. They were glassy with tears. 'You shouldn't listen,' she said.

I said, 'Did Steve find out?'

'There was nothing to find out.'

'Why did you ask me to stay?'

'Because I love you.' She would not look at me.

'So who's Hannah's father?'

'Steve. These people,' she said. 'They're bored. They'll say any-thing to make their lives interesting.' There was a silence. 'That's one side of things. There's another. When Steve died everyone just accepted it, you know, that's the way it is at Malpas. Even the Guards. Everyone seemed to think it was just part of history, as if history was something on its own, independent of people. But I don't know. I really just don't know if he killed himself or if it was an accident. And I don't know how to find out. They don't care about the truth.'

I said, 'I do.' I was horribly disappointed.

She held her arms above the elbows, as if she was cold. 'Could you find out?'

All around us, the great wreck ticked and moaned. 'I'm not a detective,' I said.

She took my face in her hands and kissed me. I would not believe that Hannah was Steve's daughter. She had lied to me so I would not feel guilty about Steve's death.

The lie was a shadow between us.

But we were not alone. That was the main thing: not to be alone.

When he was not on tour or in the studio, Helen's father spent time on his boat. She was a little ketch called *St Cecilia*, thirty-seven feet long. Her father always used to claim that ketches were a good idea for pianists because there were more smaller sails, which made sailing lighter, which meant you were in less danger of destroying your hands. Helen loved going with him on the boat, because it was the nearest thing to a permanent home she had. They spent the summers in Brittany and Cornwall and the Baltic and on the West Coast of Scotland (never in Ireland, though) – not sailing great distances, but cruising gently from anchorage to anchorage. When they were anchored in Dinard or Crinan, her father wrote music on the chart table, while she dredged around for people her own age. She often found them. After a day or a week her father would want to move on, of course. But sometimes the other kids moved on in the same direction, and you could have something approaching a friend.

In the evenings after work, her father would break out the cigarettes and the wine, and drink and smoke (weather permitting) in the cockpit. The wine, or perhaps the cigarettes, tended to make him gloomy. It was the only time he ever talked about Ireland, and even then never about Malpas.

One night in July, in Acairsead Mhor on Rona, he was watching a pig rooting in the seaweed on the shore. 'There is a house called Ballynatray,' he said. 'On the Blackwater in Country Cork, forty-odd miles from bloody Malpas. A beautiful house, grand, elegant, not a monster, nothing like Malpas. Anyway there was a salmon weir there that left a puddle when the tide went out, and you'd go and scoop up whatever was inside in the way of fish. So one day the man I knew who lived there found a monkfish in the puddle, a horrid great thing the size of a table, but very good to eat in the tail regions. He told me about it. 'I put it in the barrow,' he said. 'hell of a job it was, just me and this great snapping class of a shark. So I wheel it up to the house and across the sweep and into the hall. And just then the telephone starts to ring, far away down in the butler's pantry. So I left the barrow stand in the hall and went to answer it, and it was a man I knew, something about the farm, and we talked about it for ten or fifteen minutes. Then I rang off and went back to the hall to look after the wheelbarrow. And do you know while I'd been on the telephone the pigs had eaten the fish?'

Helen's father poured himself another mug of wine and drank deeply. 'In the hall of that great beautiful house a barrow with a shark in it, torn apart by pigs,' he said. '*Ghastly.*'

Helen, twelve years old, had nodded earnestly, making her eyes big and innocent, the way Daddy liked them when he told his stories of gloom and despair. But what she really thought was this.

A great square monster of a house, where people had lived for ever with their animals and their fish and their friends, living there all the time, not all neat and tidy, but a great friendly funny filthy shambles on the edge of chaos.

Absolutely *super*!

Book 2

Chapter Eleven

One of the many remarkable features of the Malpas demesne was the walled garden. This is a five-acre oblong of ground with a gentle south slope and twenty-foot walls. The walls are built of marble shipped direct from Carrara – an act of extravagance aimed only at producing peaches two week earlier than at Kiltane, seat of the Devereux (q.v.), the next great house up the river, rivals in horticulture as in much else. In the late 19th century, two boys were employed to keep these walls scrubbed to an icy glare. In winter, the greenhouses were heated by gas piped from the nearby Works. In 1911 the gasworks was abolished by Dulcibella Costelloe, a determined woman with a keen sense of smell and a strong mechanical sense. After that date, the greenhouses were fired by turf furnaces of Mrs Costelloe's design.

As if heating the greenhouses was not enough, the early vegetables of Malpas were assisted in their growth by steam led in cast-iron conduits through the garden's open ground. Needless to say, the vegetables would have been cheaper if they had been brought severally by motor-car from Covent Garden. Equally needless to say, the Walled Garden is now a white elephant, its stoves in ruin, its pipework shattered, its Carrara walls green with moss and black with fungus. It is instructive to sit on a decayed potting bench, eat one's sandwiches and perhaps a blackberry from the brambles that now choke the place, and contemplate the vanity of human aspiration.[1]

From the Casebooks of Peter Costelloe

Well, we are married! Such has been the happiness of it all, that I have

---

[1]   Anthony Magdalen-Small, *Perambulations in Ireland*, 1964

not even contrived to write my journal or my casebooks these past two weeks – an omission I have not made since those far-off days with Galton, when my mind was also in a ferment, but of how different a kind!

First, the wedding.

We were sensible that a great throng would present too gaudy a picture for dignity. So we went to the other extreme, and were married by Father Hefernan in the presence of Attracta Dowd, Dulcie's confidential friend from Dunquin days, and Jamesy Durcan, my stalwart companion and helper. Dulcie looked entirely charming in a dress of sky-blue silk and a matching silk beret, she having decided these six months and more that rational dress is to be preferred to corseting. Jamesy conquered his objections to Rome, for the morning. We had a breakfast, very nice, in the dining room, and saw off a bucket of peaches from the White Wall, and some of the champagne laid down by poor Desmond. Then we went honeymooning to Chamonix, where we walked a great deal, and Dulcie admired the funicular railway; after a month of which, we were both (wordlessly, but there is a sympathy between myself and my dear wife amounting almost to telepathy) – we were both, I say, pining for dear Malpas.

Of course, Malpas punished us for being away.

We arrived late on a Tuesday, and found the house in perfect order, Dulcie having telegraphed ahead. Next morning I set off on my daily tour.

It was low tide, and the salmon boat was fishing. There is above the beach the downcurved branch of an oak that makes a capital bench. On this I sat, and through the leaves watched the men working the draught net. The sun came up red over the river. The netsmen were so clagged with black mud as to resemble Golems (animated, I regret to say, by the name of God continually in their mouths). They had a poor morning of it. As the tide rose they loaded the net back into the boat, with one basket of fish and that barely half-full. The oarsmen climbed aboard. The helmsman stood thigh-deep in water, ready to push off.

At that moment there came a hail from the shore, and a man slid down the black rocks onto the beach. He was wearing a dirty Norfolk jacket and corduroy trousers bound with string below the knees. He said something to the men in the boat. The helmsman said something back, waving him away with a contemptuous movement of the arm. The man on the beach started to scream threats. I recognised him as Jeremiah Walsh, a sullen entity from the hothouses, a member of what I have come to perceive as the Durcan or anti-Cosgrave faction on the estate – indeed, the Norfolk jacket would be a Durcan reach-me-down. 'I'll split on yez,' he was saying, or rather bellowing. 'Five fish. Give me five fish or by the Cross I'll send ye public.'

The helmsman's shoulders dropped. I saw him tilt the basket and sort through its contents.

'And none of yer bloody shprats or slob neither,' yelled Walsh. 'What we want is great lepping bastards of springers.'

It was at this point that I came out of the oaks and onto the beach and stood leaning on my stick. The helmsman was Johnny Cosgrave. I saw his eyes move onto me, white against the black mud on his face. I said, 'What is the trouble?'

Walsh turned. When he saw me his face became bland and obsequious. He said, 'Johnny is just after agreeing to give me some fish, sir.'

'Not a fish will I give this man,' said Johnny. 'Not if you was to carve if off of my body with the shteel of the boat's hook.'

The smell of hatred was nearly as strong as the mud. I turned to Walsh and said, 'Why would Cosgrave be giving you fish?'

'Sure it's . . . usual,' said Walsh.

'But they're the boat's fish. My fish, with the boat's share for the crew. Forgive me, but what exactly do you conceive to be your part in this transaction?'

Walsh scowled at his boots. 'I had a fancy for a bit of salmon to me dinner,' he said, eventually. 'That's all.'

'Five salmon?' I said. 'Great lepping bastards of springers, fifteen pounds or so? You must have a very considerable appetite.'

A snigger from the boat greeted this sally. Walsh looked at me out of his flat-planed red face. He said, 'There are some things you should leave alone, Doctor.'

'Such as?'

But he turned, and marched away into the oak woods at the top of the beach.

'Now there,' said Johnny, the sun blazing scarlet through the great ear on either side of his mud-black face, 'is a man having a bad day.'

'And what is the meaning of all this nonsense?'

Johnny turned towards me, but his eyes were not meeting mine. 'Little matter of right and wrong and basic principle, perhaps,' he said.

'Ah.' Johnny was generally suspected of Sinn Fein connections. 'So that's me in trouble, then.'

'Oh, I don't know,' said Johnny. 'Not if what we hear from Bundore's right.'

Bundore, you will remember, is the farm inhabited by the Whites, whom I had refused to evict. I said, 'I am in favour of no political party. I believe in fair shares for all. Including me.'

'Well, now,' said Johnny, blank as a minstrel behind his coating of silt. He gave the boat a shove, hoisted his buttocks on the gunwale, and swung in his legs. The oars churned water. I watched the boat dwindle on the metal sheet of the river, me with the flood lapping at my boots. Then I went back to the house, and thought no more about the incident.

My views on the Irish Question are simple, and exactly as I had expressed them to Johnny. This makes them not so much simple as simple-minded, according to Jamesy. But Jamesy has been brought up to collect rents from the Malpas tenantry, and I have always been engaged upon the preservation of human life and health in the wider world. I have the occasional patient visit me in the Laboratory, and if I fail to charge them, it drives Jamesy half mad. 'It's all very well you looking out for the poor, or whatever the hell you do,' he said the other day, as I shooed out a newly set radius and ulna. 'But if you do that, you'll be one of the poor yourself.' When I told him that this attitude was a guarantee of barbarism, he said, 'It's every man for himself in this world, Doctor, and never forget it.' This remark, made by a man of twenty-three to a man of thirty-five, is indeed not easy to forget.

I found Dulcie later that day by the generator shed as she supervised the installation of a bank of knife switches – she has taken command of the hydro-electric scheme, and very good it seems. I told her that I had interfered between Cosgrave and Walsh. She dutifully approved, of course. But she did not look happy. She said, 'You'll start a war.'

'Not at all.'

'Mairi worships you. The Cosgraves put up with you, so. But what about Jamesy? Walsh is one of his men.'

'Jamesy's a fine fellow,' I said. But she was right to ask, and I was conscious of a sort of inner cooling. All the time Jamesy can spare from the farm he spends with me in the Laboratory. Once we were occupied with science, and science alone. But I must admit that our discussions of late have been coloured by the difference of our politics, so that sometimes he becomes impatient and bad-tempered. And I have observed in him a competitive streak that must be watched.

'You leave Jamesy to me,' I said.

Dulcie said nothing, tightening the last screw and pulling off her hide work gloves. When she believes something, she is a hard woman to reassure. I tried to take her in my arms, but she pulled away. So I know she worries that I am wrong. Well, time will tell.

From the Diaries of D.W.

Today was the last of the gasworks, thank God. I was nervous about the Electric Scheme, but it has worked better than I could have hoped. We burned off the gas in a *feu de joie*, and left the gasometer drum to sink down, and that is that. No more terrible stinks, no more smoke nor brass turning green when the wind blows onto the house.

Once we had finished there, we went up to the machine shed under the Dam for a small opening ceremony. We had Emily with us, the men of course, and Maurice Devereux, whom I had asked because we are neighbours and must learn to put up with each other, there is no doubt of that. I cut a ribbon, and Maurice looked most interested by the turbines and the generators. Really he can be quite warm, but of course it is too much to expect that he will speak to Peter.

So while he was cross-examining me about switchgear and battery stacks, Peter was talking to Jamesy, with Emily left on the sidelines. As

I watched him, I could not help comparing Jamesy with Maurice – yes, and Peter! Jamesy has grown from a gawky carrot-headed thing into a man of presence – a greater presence than Maurice. He lacks the calm that gives Peter his poise. There is sometimes in Jamesy's eye a roll like a horse that is about to kick the manger into the hayloft. For Jamesy is a Durcan, and Durcans will never be easy when they are not in charge – in the Laboratory as on the farm. Once Jamesy begins to feel that he has extracted all possible advantage from Peter, I fear he may be less loyal. I must watch him. Yes, I must watch him closely.

From the Casebooks of Peter Costelloe

O, strange and terrible day!

I was in the Laboratory, working on my description of the River's fish, when there was a great beating at the window, and there was Mairi making faces through the glass. She said, 'Bring your bag, Doctor! Bring your bag!' what must have been fifteen times. So I collected my bag and suffered her to lead me at a dead run down to the House Creek, she counting as she ran, multiplying footsteps by cormorants, clouds by branches, all those games of obsession that since I have been treating her she plays only when her emotions are out of balance.

She made me sit in the cot, and rowed me across the River, still counting, darting the boat from eddy to eddy. Then she dragged me up the steps to the pink cottage of all Cosgraves; and there, sitting on the bench at its front under a sort of verandah, was poor Johnny.

I say poor Johnny, because the right hand side of his face was laid open, and the ball of the eye was hanging on his cheek. It was a terrible wound. There was, I was led to believe, no question of the hospital. So I laid him on the elm bench, applied the ether there and then, and spent two hours in a light drizzle (I have learned during my years in Ireland that conditions inside the cabins make sepsis inevitable) removing the injured organ, setting the bones, and stitching the facial tissues as best I could. I sat with him until consciousness returned. His remaining eye opened and fixed upon me, clouded and bleary. 'How did it happen?' I said.

He mumbled that he did not know.

'Walsh?' I said.

The eye closed. I went into the house and spoke to his cousin Eileen, who was in charge of the house, about the care of the invalid. She listened, I think. But she was in a white, icy rage at those that had done this thing to her kinsman. When I had finished giving her my instructions she said, 'I hope you've plenty time, Doctor.'

'I beg your pardon?'

'You'll need it to sew up those that have done this to my poor Johnny when Oweneen is after getting through with them.'

On the way out of the house I saw that my patient was not alone. Standing by the bench on which he lay was a small man in a golfing cap. Under the cap was a pug face with an outdoor complexion and eyes of a blue so pale as to be almost colourless. On seeing me, he slid away into the woods with the ease of a wild animal. 'Who's that?' I said to Mairi.

She put a big finger to her lips. 'Oweneen Watereye,' she said. 'Shh, Doctor.' And with sixty-seven strokes of her massive shoulders she rowed me back across the river.

Immediately I was back in the house, I sent Jerry the stable boy for Walsh. But Jerry came back shaking his head. 'Gone,' he said. 'There was a crowd below at his house. They're after finding this.' He waved a Norfolk jacket at me.

I recognised it immediately as the Norfolk jacket Walsh had been wearing on the beach of the House Pool, except that now it was horribly spattered with blood.

So far, we have stayed out of the terrible events now loose in the world. But Johnny mentioned politics, and Dulcie mentioned war. I fear we can stay out no longer.

God send I am wrong.

From the Casebooks 5 days later

Jamesy found me in the Laboratory today. He had a strange, wooden expression. I bade him good morning. He nodded distantly; this Jamesy, my friend and apprentice. I said, 'Is something amiss?'

He said, 'You'd better come and see,' with the air of a parent who wanted to show a child the consequences of a foolish action.

The pony trap was waiting outside. Jamesy took the reins. He would answer none of my questions. We passed out of the gates into a maze of lanes I had never before penetrated, but which Jamsey negotiated with confidence. Finally we turned onto a road no bigger than a boreen, with a thick hedge on either side. Jamesy said, 'Wouldn't you worry that some Shinner would put a bullet in you from beyond in the ditch?'

I said, 'No.'

'Then you're a fool.'

I said, 'You know that I treat people as I expect to be treated myself.'

He gave a cold sort of laugh. I confess I found the laugh irritating, and I was going to ask him what he found so amusing. But at this point he pulled the horse's head round and through a gate.

There was a crowd of people in the field – the usual mob that will appear out of thin air in Ireland, the men in working rags, the women in shawls. There were two tall figures in dark-green RIC uniforms, separate from the people. Ignoring the crowd, Jamesy strode through the rushy grass straight towards the RIC men, who (I now saw) were standing by the tumbled circular wall of a well.

They saluted Jamesy, and made a half-touch of the cap to me. Refusing to take sides was no way to endear yourself to the RIC. I said, 'What's all this about?'

The shorter of the RIC men, a sergeant, said, 'We have a fatality.' He bent and twitched the tarpaulin from the long, narrow thing on the ground beside him.

It was a man, of course; a man with soaking clothes, and dark hair plastered over a marble-white face. The eyes were open. I should rather say 'the eye'; for the corpse had been savagely beaten while still alive, and where the right eye should have been was only an empty socket, revoltingly mangled. But battered or not, the face was definitely the face of Jeremiah Walsh.

'He was below in the well,' said the sergeant, wooden with irony. 'He will have maybe drowned.'

I peered over the parapet. The well was sheer-sided. The water reflected my white face ten feet below.

'I heard,' said the sergeant, 'that there was a class of a row between the deceased and Johnny Cosgrave, would it have been a week ago?'

'So I believe. About fish.'

'We'll ask Johnny, so.'

'I haven't seen Johnny this last little while.' A terrible thought hung dark and loud in my mind. I saw Eileen Cosgrave white with fury, pug-faced Oweneen with the colourless eyes fading into the wood behind the Cosgraves' pink cottage. In my ears I could hear a harsh and ancient voice. *An eye for an eye*, it roared like a war-gong.

There were several women nearby, gathered in a huddle. At the centre of the huddle was a tall figure, shawl cast over her head. The eyes came at me like snakes. I recognised her as Dervla, Walsh's wife. I was being noted, my part in all this assessed.

At my side, Jamesy was hissing like a kettle. 'By the Christ, this is war,' he said, echoing Dulcie.

'Not a war that we're in.'

He looked at me, scornful. 'We were born in it,' he said.

Him, perhaps. Not me. My task is to do my duty to Science and my fellow man. And there, I would like to think, the matter rests. But I fear it may be too late. I can feel the rift between Jamesy and myself widening into a chasm, and there is nothing I can do to stop it. Nothing.

I came home, away from the corpse and Mrs Walsh's terrible eyes. Now I am in the Laboratory, and I will frankly admit that I am frightened. If they discover that I helped Johnny Cosgrave, they will take it as a partisan act, and nothing I can say will dissuade them. I can feel myself being drawn into something savage and uncontrollable.

Earlier this evening I looked out of the Laboratory window on a valley cement-grey with rain, and smelt in the air a thick breath of fungus and decay. I resolved to tell Dulcie to pack, leave by the first train, go anywhere where there is not this claustrophobic burden. I even started to pack my books. Then I heard footsteps in the colonnade, and there was Dulcie herself. But tonight, there was something special in the flush of her face and the sparkle of her eye. She came and stood by me and said, 'Will you look at that?'

Outside the window, beyond the rain, the sun was on the Sugarloaf. Between our eyes and the brilliant purple of the mountains was a rainbow.

'So beautiful,' said Dulcie. I gave her a dismal sort of nod. Dulcie has in common with all these people a capacity to ignore the horrors of the hour. For me, the glory of Malpas was a painted lid on a boxful of corpses.

She took my hand and put it on her belly. She said, 'Do you feel anything?'

Well, I felt the belly, that warm and charming curve of flesh. But even that was a mockery now.

She said, 'I'm after seeing Doctor Rainbird. I'm going to have a baby.'

I stared at her. 'But the war,' I said. 'We must go away. Immediately—'

'Hell no,' she said. 'This is our home. Here we are and here we stay, and if we have to fight for it, it's all the more worth fighting for if there's a child in it. Do you not think?'

She stood shining in the buttery sun that had walked up the river and in at the window. I took her hand. I was back in the world, in which was this beautiful woman who was carrying our child. Life triumphs over death. Whatever will happen at Malpas, I decided, I must stay here and take my part in it.

From the Diaries of D.W.

It's a strange thing, to be carrying a child. I understand the machinery of it, because I am not a fool, and what I don't understand I can read, all right. But this feeling I have: a feeling that the world is moving fast and artificial, and that I am in a slow place in it, slow but real, almost as if it was a separate stream of time, the main stream, and everyone around me is swirling madly in an eddy, swimming for dear life.

Mrs Walsh came to see me: the mother of Jeremiah Walsh, not the wife. I gave her some money, poor woman, God knows what she must feel. She is full of stuff against the Cosgraves, that they are Shinners, behind God knows how many burnings and robberies. But frankly (and I told her this) Walsh was a bandit and an extortionist, and it was he who flung the first stone by beating poor Johnny so dreadfully; not that it matters now.

But the Cosgraves are seen as being under Peter's protection, and that will sit badly with Maurice and his friends. It is all very well to speak brave words about fighting for what is ours. But I want my baby to be born in peace, and to live in peace thereafter. God knows there was enough trouble at the beginning of our time together. Now it is time for things to be quiet.

In a way, they are quiet. We are not invited about much, any more. I must rely on Jamesy for knowledge of what is happening in the world. He sees the Caroes, Maurice and Alice Devereux, the whole notability of the River. They have always been suspicious of everything about Peter. Jamesy has asked me to persuade him to sever himself from the Cosgraves, to see reason . . .

But Jamesy knows already, and I told him again. Nobody can persuade the Doctor.

Chapter Twelve

Pursuant to Helen's instructions, a couple of days later I borrowed the dinghy pulled up by the House Creek and rowed across the river to the pink cottage that belonged to the Cosgraves. There was a blue-and-black salmon boat tied up to a landing stage. I tied up alongside it, and climbed the eleven steps that led to a gap in the tall fuchsia hedge lining the top of the bank. 'Hello!' I called.

A face appeared in the gap, flanked on either side by green fuchsia. It was a leathery face, gaunt and seamed, the skin pulled back over the high cheekbones so it looked like a Peruvian mask. 'Mrs Cosgrave?' I said.

'And you'll be Mr Walker from the House beyond,' she said. 'You're welcome here.' She opened the gate, and held it while I went through. She was tall and wide and fleshless, wearing a flowered overall and black gumboots, the right-hand boot sewn up with baler twine. She and the cottage gave off the same strong, earthy smell. 'Sit down sit down,' she said.

We sat on the long elm bench under the overhang of the roof. There was a pile of nets on the flagged floor, which was covered in a soft grey dust of dried river-mud. We talked about the weather, looking for an opening. I got the conversation round to fishing, and then to Paddy. 'He's inside, he's inside,' she said. 'Paddy!'

Paddy came shuffling round the end of the house in carpet slippers, his eyes points of light under his great eyebrow. 'I'm sorry to disturb you,' I said (not a bit, not a bit of it, they muttered), 'but last time we met, by the river, we were talking about Steve Brennan,' (may he rest in peace, may he rest in peace, they murmured) 'and Steve was a friend of mine, and I am trying to work out how he felt, what he did his last week, the week before he fell into the river.'

'By God but you've come to the right place now,' said Paddy. 'Mammy's an encyclopaedia on two legs aren't you Mammy?'

'Ah give over,' said Mrs Cosgrave with a sternness that did not entirely mask her pleasure. 'It was a Thursday you found the poor man, so, Paddy. Start a week before. Thursday and Friday he was above on the dam, painting away, a class of a picture of the house and the river with the net on it. Saturday morning he came over here and we sat just where you were sitting. He was after finishing the picture, he said. Then we talked about the old times.'

'The old times?'

'The Troubles, the Tans' time, all that. There was a lot of work done out of this house in them days by the ones that were here before,' she said. 'He was always asking what happened where when, but nobody remembers those times now, nor wants to either.' This delicacy was for my English benefit. 'Annyway here he was with his little book, drawing away. Then he went away and the next day Sunday they had a lunch beyond at the house, and that took all day, and on Monday morning he was back here, not so good then.'

'What do you mean, not so good?'

Mrs Cosgrave averted her eyes politely from mine. 'Well you would not say he was exactly the full shilling,' she said. 'But he was an artist of course, up and down, up and down. He talked a fierce lot that day. I do not exactly recall what about.'

'You wouldn't know and you God himself,' said Paddy.

'We sent him home, so,' said Mrs Cosgrave. 'And in the evening he went to Finbarr Durcan's and then to the Dower House and he stayed there with the one inside till after dark. Then the next day Tuesday he went to Finbarr Durcan's in the morning and up to the Dower House after his lunch, but he came out of there shouting and roaring out of him, the way he had had a disagreement with herself, Angela I mean. Then I heard he went back to the House. And the next morning he was at Brady's when Patrick Brady opened the door, and he stayed there all day, they say. And the morning after, Paddy found him in the weir. Isn't that right, Paddy?'

Paddy nodded, his face blank with upset. 'I was after telling Mr Walker,' he said.

'And on the Monday,' I said. 'Did he have his little drawing book with him?'

Mrs Cosgrave reflected a second. 'He did not,' she said. 'He had it on the Saturday. He didn't have it on the Monday. Paddy?'

'He did not,' said Paddy. 'He was fierce unhappy, and he did not have it.'

'And that was unusual.'

'It was.'

Soon after that, I rowed back across the river.

I am ashamed to say that I felt no need to give much time to Steve, then. In the morning, I worked on Peter Costelloe. In the afternoon Helen went and painted in the Morning Room – she had an exhibition coming up in Fermoy – while I looked after Hannah. Faced with the magic of Hannah's personality, it was sometimes possible to forget my worries about her paternity. She had several teeth, a large vocabulary of animal noises, and fair skills on four legs. Her table manners were not up to much, and she had her mother's temper. But she was highly intelligent and handsome when clean. For the first half of April we were a very happy family.

Nothing lasts for ever.

The three of us were sitting at the kitchen table one Tuesday. The windows were open, spring was pouring in, and the bees were working on the honeysuckle outside. One flew onto the tray of Hannah's high chair and stuck its nose into a patch of jam. 'Bee,' I said, educationally. Helen, more practical, flapped her hand to drive it away.

'Bee,' said Hannah, who had not yet learned to talk.

There was a stunned silence.

'Bee,' said Hannah again. 'Beeeee.'

'Darling!' cried Helen. There was a colossal celebration. Helen sang an aria she claimed came from *La Bohème*. Hannah joined in, then fell asleep, exhausted. When she awoke at teatime she was hot, and sprinkled with yellow-headed spots. I researched them in Doctor

Costelloe's library. It seemed to be chickenpox.

'Poor darling,' said Helen, looking up from the horse's head she was framing. 'Could you ever take her in and get her looked at? The number's in the kitchen book under "doctor".'

So I called the doctor, bundled Hannah into the Zephyr and took her into Dunquin.

Dr Moriarty lived in a grim late-Victorian villa in the grey cement outskirts of the town. He looked the same age as his house. He was tall and stooped, with yellow-white hair, an axe of a nose, and dull blue eyes over bags of wrinkles. He smiled with a vast set of false teeth. 'Mr Walker what a pleasure to see you after hearing so much, so much.' I had no idea where he could have heard anything, so I assumed it was a form of words. 'Hello, little fella,' he said to Hannah, who was slumped gloomily in the crook of my arm.

'She's a girl,' I said.

'Same thing, same thing,' said Moriarty, projecting a gust of halitosis through the teeth. 'And poor you, you've got the chickenpox. Anny headache?'

Hannah decided this was enough clinical stuff for the day, and began to squirm. Moriarty's sister, a white-faced woman in her seventies, materialised from the cabbage-smelling dark that cloaked the back regions. 'Who's calling for ice cream?' she said. 'We'll get some, so. Would you come to me, spotty girl?' They left, concluding the medical part of the interview. I got the feeling that Moriarty was short of company. He gave me brown tea in a sitting room foul with pipe smoke. He said, 'So you've come from England to see your daughter.'

'Helen Costelloe's daughter.'

'Of course, of course.' Pause. 'She's very like you,' he said.

I said, non-committally, 'So I have been told.'

'And there – forgive me, Mr Walker, I speak as a doctor under the er seal of the consulting room – I did hear it mentioned that, well, yer man who died, he wasn't the father.'

I said, 'She's a great girl, that's all that matters.' A lie, of course. Hannah's paternity was frankly the last obstacle between me and complete happiness. It may sound stupid, but as long as Steve might live in Hannah, we were not a family but a triangle.

'Only we could find out,' said Moriarty. 'For sure. Once and for all. Unless you'd rather not.'

'How's that?'

He leaned towards me, so I could smell the grave-reek of his breath. 'A little blood,' he said.

It struck me that such enthusiasm was not natural. He seemed to guess this. 'In great old age the execution fails, but the understanding increases,' he said, and I immediately assumed he was talking about my overwhelming solitariness. 'Not that it is anny consolation, God knows.'

I heard myself say, 'All right.'

'Now,' he said. 'Roll up your sleeve.'

He took blood. His daughter brought Hannah back. He took her blood too. Then we went home.

Later, I sat in the bathroom while she swam to and from in the seven-foot tub. Helen was there, glass of wine in hand, running an eye over her daughter's pocky white flesh. Hannah had been scratching, so the blood-test scar blended in with the other craters. 'Disgusting,' said Helen. 'Poor darling.'

Hannah launched a duck at the plughole. 'Moriarty said she'd be fine,' I said.

'Who?'

'Moriarty.'

'Who's Moriarty?'

'The doctor.'

She said, 'You went to Moriarty? What's wrong with Collins?'

'Moriarty was in your book—'

She said. 'Jesus. You're lucky to be alive. I went to him once, when I knew no better. I must have forgotten to cross him out. He thinks he's a bloody psychiatrist, but all he is is the biggest Nosey Parker in Waterford. And he's a dreadful gossip. He looks after Alice and Emily and that lot. The dead taking care of the dead. We go to Collins. He may not be Christiaan Barnard but at least he's still alive. Poor darling girl.'

'Sorry.'

'You weren't to know.' But there was a stiffness in her voice.

After the bath I went up the river with my fishing rod. The green line snaked over the black water and came round fishless. Helen would take the blood test as evidence that I had gone behind her back, something I had the best evidence to know she hated.

But the test was done. It could not be undone.

I wound in and started back for the house. But as I rounded the corner I saw Finbarr's Land Rover in the drive. My heart sank. He would be at the kitchen table, sucking up whiskey, talking Tantric farming. My job would be to nod intelligently and agree with every-thing everyone said, no matter how bloody stupid.

Headlights glowed behind me. A car stopped. The driver's window wound down.

'You look like the Wandering Jew,' said Angela. 'Come and have a drink.'

Her voice was warm and uncomplicated. I went round to the passenger seat and climbed in.

The Dower House drawing room was big and shabby, with battered chairs and a whiff of smoke, no books. I lit a fire and opened a bottle. We sat on adjacent sofas and drank wine quickly. Angela said, 'So how are you getting on?'

I began talking about Steve, and my visit to the Cosgraves. 'Mrs Cosgrave said he was here the Monday and Tuesday before he died.'

Angela made a face. 'That bloody woman and her binoculars,' she said.

'What was he saying that day?'

'He just barged in and started talking drivel.'

'Can you remember what?'

'As I remember he said he was the Salvation of Ireland and he would shortly be elected to the head of the IRA and Malpas was Bethlehem. Also he had a hotline on a vast buried treasure and he was the reincarnation of Gainsborough or was it Sickert. Just slightly manic, if you take my meaning. He got Mummy in a terrible state. It took me till ten o'clock to get rid of him. Then the next day he came and apologised. I finished up pushing him out of the front door. Then there he was, dead, and I thought, Oh, God, maybe I should have made a big effort and listened. But I didn't. So there it is and it can't be helped.'

And she was away on to the next thing already. She talked to make you laugh, and herself. I could understand why Steve had come to see her. The responsibilities of Malpas were always with Helen, and I could not see him having much to say to Finbarr.

'What do you think?' she was saying.

'I'm sorry?'

'Do you want some dinner?' she said.

'I'd better ring Helen.'

'Tell her to come too.'

But as I had expected, Helen was farming with Finbarr. So Angela and I ate cheese omelettes and salad and drank a lot of wine.

After supper, I helped her do the washing-up. We talked about uncomplicated matters, Malpas mostly, who was who round about. She never talked about herself, and had a way of deflecting questions that would have meant awkward discussions of her life or her relationships. I found myself wondering why she consented to be trapped in this strange place.

'Help!' cried an ancient voice from the direction of the stairs. There was the crash of breaking china. 'Ow!' said the voice.

'Oh, *mummy*,' said Angela.

And of course, Alice was the answer.

The old woman had fallen down a short flight of stairs onto a fortuitously placed armchair. She did not seem to have broken anything, but a vase she had grabbed at had made some shallow but impressive cuts on her arms. I carried her to the bathroom and in the cold yellow light helped Angela clean up the cuts. She said, 'I'll put her to bed.' But Alice sat on the cork-topped bathside cabinet with her arms folded tight, and refused to budge.

'Who's that man?' she said. 'Who's that new man?'

'Oh, be quiet,' said Angela. 'Get up and come back to bed.'

'No,' said Alice, and folded her arms.

'You can't stay here all night,' said Angela.

Alice made settling-in movements on the cabinet. A look of desperation crossed Angela's face. 'Mummy,' she said. 'Please.'

'You'll have to carry me. And you can't.'

'I can,' I said.

Alice looked at me, bright and empty as a bird. 'All right,' she said.

I picked her up. She was a bundle of skin and bone and disinfectant. 'Where to?' I said.

'No, really,' said Angela, who now looked oddly apprehensive.

'Quick,' said Alice, wriggling slightly.

So I carried her to the room Angela pointed out, and put her on her bed. As I turned to leave, I saw the painting.

It was on the wall at the foot of the bed: an oil painting of a nude woman sprawled among rumpled sheets. The wide, good-humoured face looked drowsy and sensual as a Gaugin vahine. The body gleamed with post-coital sweat. There was no doubt who the painter was, and the signature confirmed it. Stephen Brennan, it said, in vermilion capitals. It was a strong painting, with Steve's usual powerful eye for a likeness. But this was not one of his satirical squibs. This was a technically brilliant picture, executed with soul and passion. It was indubitably a portrait of Angela, and it looked as if it had been done from life.

'That'll fix you,' said Angela to her mother, with a final vicious shove of sheet under mattress. 'Let's have coffee.'

We sat at the kitchen table. I said, 'I thought you hardly knew Steve.'

She blushed. 'You are referring to the painting,' she said. 'Well, it wasn't my idea. He just turned up with it one evening.'

'Odd picture to hang in your mother's room.'

'Mummy thinks it's nice and bright. Not many people go into her room. Steve was married to Helen. My friend. And landlady. Do you think she would have liked it?'

I found my loyalties unpleasantly stretched. I did not like conniving at going behind Helen's back. But I liked Angela. And she needed a life that contained something beyond going for walks with her mother, and in the end, who she had affairs with was her business. To change the subject, I said, 'I've been looking for his sketchbook. Did he have it when you were all at lunch at the house on his last Sunday?'

'He did,' she said. 'He was too drunk to draw, though. He was giving his celebrated lecture on the glory of the IRA.'

'What about Monday and Tuesday?'

'No book.'

'Pity.'

'What do you mean, pity?'

'I saw it once, in England. I thought it was a good way of telling what he was thinking.'

She blushed again. I said, 'What is it?'

'He showed me some drawings he did. For the painting upstairs. That was what he did, draw you, then show you, then keep the drawings.' I remembered. 'What is all this?'

'Helen wants to know whether it was suicide or accident.'

'In Steve's case,' she said, 'there is just about no difference at all.'

'What?'

'Steve hated Steve,' she said. 'That was about the only thing he had in common with the rest of the human race.' Again the blush. 'What a dreadful thing to say.'

'What do you mean?'

'Nothing. Look, there was nobody near him when he died. The Guards checked up on that. But as for the sketchbook, there are those who will be extremely glad it's gone.'

Chapter Thirteen

The Dunquin barracks comes on you suddenly, in the middle of a wood. It is a roofless ruin now, a shell of dirty render over engineering brick, torn apart by an ivy that appears to be trying to match in ruthlessness the RIC men and irregulars whose base of operations this once was. One might unroll one's sleeping bag under the remaining patch of roof, commune with crows and rats and brambles. But a strange reluctance comes over the wanderer. It is a place of evil memory, the Barracks – one of those dishonourable ruins that owe their dereliction to the cruelties once harboured by their walls. Better to leave it to its vermin, and walk five miles on to the beautiful Abbey transept upstream from Malpas, itself a ruin, but one mellowed by prayer and pilgrimage . . .[1]

From the Casebooks of Peter Costelloe

There are times when I think that on arriving at Malpas, I was putting myself into one of those contrivances of steel with incurved teeth in which the struggles of the victim result only in a more secure captivity. I did not mean to fall in love with Dulcie. I did not mean to stay here, in a place where I am accepted neither by the native population nor the Ascendancy. But I have made my bed, and now I suppose I must lie in it.

On the face of it, I am the happiest man in the world, with a beautiful wife and a bouncing six-month-old son. But over this happiness there hangs a cloud I can see no way of dispelling.

Well.

I had hoped that after the awful events culminating in the murder of

---

[1] Harvey Pocock, *Walks in Munster*, Blackwater Press 1962

Jeremiah Walsh, a truce might be declared. Certainly, it was quiet for a while. I continued our experiments in the nature of the intellectual faculty, as outlined in my casebooks. It has been because of my absorption in this, and the first months of the life of our dear son Jesse, that I allowed my attention to stray from certain important features of my existence at Malpas.

Matters came to a head one day when Jamesy and I were dissecting the cranium of a salmon, examining each of the bones with a magnetometer in an attempt to determine the source of the fish's homing instinct. I had observed that James, never loquacious nowadays, was especially taciturn this morning. But I presumed that his attention was fully occupied by the dissection, a tricky one, using glass scalpels to exclude any possibility of magnetic contamination of the subject.

At eleven o'clock I straightened my back, and (my lungs being full of fish smell) walked away from the bench to breathe by the open window. It was at this point that I noticed on the lawn a flock of men in uniforms, like peewits on the green. At my exclamation, Jamesy raised his eyes from the salmon's head. 'Oh,' he said. 'That'll be looking for Oweneen that murdered poor Jeremiah Walsh.'

Immediately my mind went back to the day I had dissected away Johnny Cosgrave's smashed eye, and the pug-faced man in the golfing cap who had slid away into the trees. 'Oweneen?' I said.

'He's a bloody Shinner,' said James. 'Calls himself a Brigadier, the murdering fecking animal.'

I said, 'How long have you suspected this?'

Jamesy gave me a face like a strongroom door. 'Sure they're making enquiries with a year now,' he said.

'Why did you not tell me?'

'I thought you'd know already.'

I put my hands in the pockets of my frock-coat so he would not see them shake. I had thought the Walsh affair safely dead and buried. I had given aid and comfort to Johnny Cosgrave, as was my duty as a doctor and a fellow human. But the RIC would not see it like that. Oweneen had killed Walsh. The police would maintain that the murder had been in revenge for the mutilation of Johnny. In the judicial atmosphere now prevailing in Ireland, that would make Johnny an accessory, and me an accessory through my assistance of Johnny.

It would have been a comfort to have someone to confide in, if only to help me share the burden, and help me think. But there is no-one to whom I can speak frankly. Of course not Jamesy. Not Dulcie either. Everything is politics now, and to tell her would be to distress her unduly and to involve her in the war. So I must keep my knowledge to myself.

I have a feeling that Maurice Devereux will spare no effort, through his creature Carson, to get me into prison and out of the way. With me away, Dulcie will be no match for him. For the sake of Dulcie and Malpas, I shall have to tread with great caution.

I went out and introduced myself to the RIC sergeant. He was respectful, of course, but his eyes were stony under the peak of his cap, and I could see he had been warned about me.

That afternoon, Jamesy was off about farm business, and I remained in the Laboratory. I locked the door, as is nowadays my wont, and made drawings of the salmon's head – very bad drawings, as my mind was far away. At four o'clock there was a rap on the window, and Mairi lumbered in.

Mairi and I have appointments most days at about this time, for tea and treatment. But on this afternoon she seemed in no mood for either. Her doughy face was greenish-white, and her great lips trembled. She sat in her hard varnished chair and said nothing. I took out my silver pencil. 'No,' she said, eyeing it as if it were a gun. 'Not that.'

I said, 'What is it?'

'They are after coming. Five polis come to the house with sixty-six bootsteps on the stair from the river's landing. They pulled Johnny off of the bed and they took him away to the barracks three on one side and two the other, with the silver hat man his own self saying not a thing at all.'

'They arrested Johnny?'

'They did. Because of Oweneen Watereye. But if they was to get Oweneen for murder it'd be Johnny too. The lads that came to the house say this.' Part of her condition is an extraordinary power of recall – not only can she remember verbatim what she hears, she can remember it sound for sound. So that now her voice changed, until it was a high Cork city whine. 'It was Dick Driscoll from Kilmacthomas turned tout on them. Tell the Doctor Oweneen was with him inside in his Laboratory on the twelfth of May last year, have you got that?' She frowned. 'What does it mean?'

I sat there, feeling gravity drag at my bones. 'Who said this?'

'Oweneen himself. What does it mean?'

Silence.

'Doctor?' Her face was creased with anxiety.

To agree was to take sides in the war. To refuse was . . . well, to refuse was to invite consequences worse than taking sides. 'It means nobody's going to hang,' I said.

So there I was, six weeks later, in court, with a red judge above me on a pyramid of oak, and twelve good men and true shivering like rabbits at the prospect of giving a verdict that would hang one of Ireland's own. As for Counsel for the Prosecution, I could smell the drink on him from ten yards away. He was watching Counsel for the Defence, a Jesuit-pale Dubliner with round black-rimmed glasses. So was Oweneen, in the dock. Counsel for the Defence had prevailed upon Oweneen to recognise the court, on the grounds that if he did not they would hang him, but if he did he stood a good chance of living to maim another day.

There has been too much murder already, and it sickens me. But what can I do?

So Counsel for the Defence says, 'What is your name?'

I give him my name.

'And your place of residence?'

Malpas, of course.

'And the size of the estate at Malpas?'

I tell him twenty thousand acres.

'So you are a landlord.'

'My wife and I have that good fortune.'

The jury are watching us now. There are not many landlords called as witnesses by the defence lawyers of the political brethren of the likes of Oweneen.

'And do you see Owen Driscoll in this court?'

I see him, and point him out, as requested.

'And did you see him on the twelfth of May last year?'

I feel my adrenal gland squirt into my blood. I take out my casebooks, and refer. 'Yes,' I say.

'At what time?'

'From eight o'clock in the morning until two o'clock on the morning of the next day.'

'He left then?'

'No. He went to sleep in the Laboratory.'

'But he could have left after you had shown him the bed.'

'It is most unlikely.'

'Why is that?'

'Because I was engaged with him in experiments that compare the effects of Veronal with those of hypnosis. The culmination of the experiments was the administration of fifteen drops of Veronal, then ten drops three hours later, and a further ten three hours after that.'

'This is a large dose?'

'Very large. Sufficient to induce unconsciousness for' – here I consult my notes again – 'fourteen hours and a quarter.'

'So there is no question of his being able to cause harm to Mr Walsh between eight a.m. on the 12th November 1907 and six p.m. on 13th November.'

'None at all.'

In the jury box, there is a murmur and a release of tension as the good men and true wake up from the bad dream in which a conviction will make them targets for Sinn Fein, and a closely argued acquittal will make them targets for the RIC. Counsel for the Prosecution gapes about him. On his oak pyramid, the red judge goes purple as a thundercloud. For a long time, nobody says anything.

But they will be thinking. Back in the public benches, Devereux will be thinking, and Inspector Carson.

Carson will be thinking very hard indeed.

The judge directs the jury to acquit, which it does, as judiciously as its relief permits. The prisoners Owen Driscoll and John Cosgrave are released. We go our ways. And I wait.

Carson came a week later. He was shaved as close as a billiard-ball, the jaw of him gleaming with a sort of grey light. I was in my Laboratory, of course. This visit was what I had been waiting for, but now it was actually upon me, I found myself weak with fear. He looked at the books and apparatus, wrinkling his nose at these instruments of untrammelled thought. He said, 'Mr . . . *Doctor* Costelloe, I should very much like a sight of your casebooks.'

'With what purpose?'

'To determine whether you spoke the truth in court, when you established an alibi for Owen Driscoll.'

'I fear that I do not have those volumes by me.' I felt a dryness in my mouth. The adrenal gland again. 'Mr Driscoll has been acquitted. He cannot be retried for this crime.'

Carson's eyes lay on me like cold pebbles. 'Perjury is also an offence,' he said. 'A very serious offence.'

I felt the blood go from my face. Why can I not control this? The adrenal gland, the adrenal gland. 'I beg your pardon?'

'The investigations of some murders were bungled,' he said.

'Some murders?' I felt the blood leave my face.

'I must say that I still have reservations about the investigation into the death of Desmond Costelloe,' he said. 'My . . . shock at the sordid nature of the evidence you produced perhaps led me to a too hasty conclusion. I think I must now follow up some lines of enquiry that I let fall out of, well, discretion. In the case of Owen Driscoll, I feel that the court accepted your words as a gentleman . . . too easily. Counsel for the Prosecution is a poor wineskin of a man, incapable of asking directions to the nearest public house, let alone cross-examining or viewing evidence. And the judge believed the label rather than the man, if you take my meaning.' His smile was a dreadful thing, confected of ice and vinegar. 'Whereas I have the impression that the man is not as loyal to the label as one might wish. I am sure you will desire to prove otherwise. So what I ask, Doctor, is that you will be so good as privately and in confidence to show me the casebooks relating to the experiments you were conducting with the assistance of our friend Owen.'

I said, through lips numb with lack of blood, 'As a matter of professional ethics that is impossible.'

He smiled again, colder than before, if possible. 'Then I shall have to insist.'

'I think you will need a warrant.' I needed time. I could manufacture something. Something not convincing, perhaps; but open to reasonable doubt. Reasonable doubt might be enough ... But for immediate purposes, anything was better than immediate arrest, and what would undoubtedly follow.

'I am lunching with Mr Devereux and the Resident Magistrate. I feel sure that once the R.M. becomes acquainted with our conversation, he will make no difficulty about issuing one. I know that Maurice Devereux will be anxious to know more about the death of Mr Costelloe.'

The glands were filling my brain with an odd, buzzing static. 'Then we can continue this discussion later in the day,' I said.

He nodded. 'I am sure you will understand that the worst possible construction will be placed upon any sudden fires or losses.' He frowned. 'And I am very sorry that you have not found it in yourself to settle this as between gentlemen. You will not find your life pleasant, once it becomes official.' Stiff-backed, he marched from the room.

I remained staring at my hands, which were shaking. I had put off the evil hour, but only by half a day. None of my evidence would stand up, of course. My world was at an end. My world, and Dulcie's.

I started for the door. Then I heard the sound outside the window, and turned. Mairi was staring at me, her wet mouth ajar. For a second she held my eye. Then she was off, blobbing across the lawns at a dead run. Poor devoted Mairi, author of my troubles. No. Mot Mairi. Malpas.

Once, I thought I could control it. Now I know that it controls me.

I took the casebook in question from the shelf. I wrote a set of spurious case notes and glued them into the binding. Then I walked slowly down the colonnade to the house. Dulcie was in the drawing room. Her face was pale and stunned. I was sure then that Carson had questioned her. Perhaps she had told him something that had undone the careful tissue I had woven . . .

I was wrong.

What had stunned her was this.

Carson had left my laboratory and climbed onto his pony trap in the stables. The RIC sergeant eating his luncheon in the tack room offered him an escort. Carson might have been a skilful policeman, but he was a vain man when it came to impressing his inferiors. He rejected the sergeant's offer with contempt. Kiltane was a mere five miles up the river. Carson was perfectly capable of doing his travelling by himself; had ridden to summon relief during the Siege of Mafeking, and begged leave to doubt that a job botched by the brave Boer could be done by some bogwog with a blunderbuss. He flicked the reins at the pony, and was gone.

A mile north of the Malpas gate, the road winds round a left-hand bend, following the line of the river cliff. Between the road and the river is a small copse of willows growing on a muddy island. One of the willows had shed a branch into the road. This is a common habit of willows, so Carson thought nothing of it. He jumped down from the trap to drag the branch aside.

It was at this point that two men stepped out of the copse. They wore golfing caps. Handkerchiefs hid their features. They carried rifles. One of them said, 'So perish all the enemies of Ireland.' The other fired, and missed. The man who had spoken shot Carson in the chest. Carson slammed back against the trap's wheel. He seemed to be trying to say something. Before he could get it out, the second man dropped to one knee and fired again. The bullet went through Carson's mouth and took the back of his head off, blowing his cap ten feet up the cliff, where it lodged at the summit of a red streak of brains. Here he was found at two o'clock by Murphy the carrier, who brought the news to Malpas.

It is not known how Carson's last moments came to be recorded in such detail. It is generally assumed in the district that it is a legitimate embroidery of facts; though it was noticeable that what is omitted from the story is the fact that the second gunman, like Johnny Cosgrave, had only one eye. (At the time of the assassination, Johnny Cosgrave had been at home with a toothache and four witnesses).

I listened to Dulcie's relaying of this tale with emotions that passed from despair, through dawning relief, to a state of mind that I dimly recognised as hysterical. And when Dulcie had finished, I laughed.

She turned upon me a face blank with horror. 'What do you find so amusing?' she said.

'Nothing.' In that face, I saw that some bond of understanding between us had ruptured. But the laughter came up from inside me until I had to rush from the room and scream my mirth out in the downstairs lavatory. I gave myself a little bromine as a sedative, and by evening was myself again, I think. But there remains with me a curious sensation, as if I have woken out of one nightmare into another.

And, as in a nightmare, there is nothing I can do.

But Carson is dead, and the things he knew with him. I can put my casebooks back on the shelves, and greet the world with a bright smile. Nobody else will want to see them now. We are back to normal, now.

Whatever that means.

Walker Archive, Transcript, 1973 – 4

There is no light at all. I am inside on the turf stack and there is no light at all. But there is a racket, a hell of a racket and even before I have got my eyelids apart I can tell that something is happening, and I give out with a class of a yell. It is six hundred and sixty boot-tips on the stairs from the landing place, there being thirty-three stairs so that is ten men with two legs each, and I am out of the fireplace and I can hear Johnny going ump, ump in the next room and a yellow light under the door and I get in there and he is in his shirt with a candle and the yellow flame is on the gun and the gun is in his hand and it is howling out of me and I clump him a great skelp and he falls on the bed over backwards and I put my teeth in the wrist of his hand, his poor wrist, and he gives a yell and down goes the gun into the dark by the bed and me on top of it so it is under my front. And the door is down and the room is full of boots and me lying on the gun that would have hung him, my darling Johnny.

There is an English voice that buzzes like a hive of sweetmen, arresting, in the name of the King, for the murder of Jeremiah Walsh. Someone gives me a kick in the broad of my back and roars roll over get up, but I am staying there on the earth the way they will not find the gun and hang my Johnny. He has shut up now, and the polis are pulling and tugging at me, and there's Johnny saying, leave her alone, she is a one that is fat and touched in the head into . . . the . . . bargain . . .

[Q: Don't cry, Mairi. Don't cry, tell me what next.]

They have gone, with Johnny. There are men in the house, and women like after a funeral, and they have their heads together and they are saying will Oweneen recognise the court if he won't he'll hang, and Mairi the great thing she is always with that little Costelloe . . .

So they are all round me now and Eileen Cosgrave the cousin is pinching my arm and telling me what I must say. She is saying the Doctor will do it because he knows that I have power over him because of what I have seen the morning of the wedding.

[Q: What does she mean by this?]

Later, later. And anyway, I am saying what Eileen has told me to my little Doctor and I can see his eyes that were once (I remember from the time I do not remember) so bright and tight, now dull and baggy, and I can see I have asked him to do a thing that he does not want to do. And in the Court he does it, he does it.

[Q: But why would the Doctor shield Johnny and Oweneen from the police, at the risk of his own safety?]

He had his reasons as you will find later.

[Q: What was it you saw the morning of the wedding?]

I can't o Gods I can't I can't.

[Q: Calm yourself, calm yourself, please.]

So now later I must guard my little Doctor. I sit under his window and I can hear him writing, the sound of his pen scritch scratch, the sound of glass clinking when he does his work, the sound of him breathing, heavy, a sigh, a belch, a fart. Unhappy sounds.

And the sounds of the great raw-faced Polis that said he was a liar, and my little Doctor's voice, giving up, giving up for good and all. I know the Doctor *will not like me telling Johnny, because that will be to overhear him, and overhearing a man's thoughts is bad, Johnny says. But he has overheard my thoughts, and fair is fair.*

So I have gone across the river and told Johnny, and Johnny has got his new gun and gone off with Oweneen after that fecking polis Carson he says.

It will be better for the Doctor; everything will be better for him now. I know it will.

From the Diaries of D.W.

He laughed. When the news came in that poor Inspector Carson had had his brains blown all over the River Cliff by the Shinners, he *laughed*. How can he do this? I know him as a compassionate man, a kind man – detached from landowning, but enthusiastic for all my schemes for developing Malpas. Now, it seems, something in him has turned.

After I left him I went up to the Dam, and I looked at the Plant, and I went through it in my mind until it was clear as my beautiful circuits. I had thought he was even-handed, a neutral in this war. He speaks of the importance of the individual over the mass. But he cannot be speaking the truth, not when he can laugh like that. His talk of love and humanity is a mask. In this war, he has taken sides with the enemy.

As I closed the Plant door I saw a man toiling up the valley towards me. It was Jamesy; Jamesy, who has a great talent for appearing where he is needed. He waved. We went to sit by the sluice, the water rushing away under our feet. He said, 'Should you be up here on your own?'

'Why not?'

'It might not be entirely safe.'

'Who would hurt me?'

He let his eyes rest upon me: deep eyes, I realised for the first time, steady, without self-doubt. 'Those damn Shinners'd skin their grand-mothers,' he said.

I said, 'I can't believe it.'

He shook his head. 'You don't believe it till you've seen it for yourself. Like Carson, lying there with no back to his head. Not a pretty picture, I can tell you.'

I said, 'Terrible, terrible.' How could Peter have *laughed*?

'We must just hang on,' said Jamesy, and put his hand on mine, warm and dry. 'We'll get through.' His eyes had a true, heavy gleam. I knew at that moment, of all the people at Malpas, this is the one I can trust.

And it is a curious thing. While I was with him I felt a great lightness, a lifting of the gloom that (I now realise) has hung over me for months. We walked back to the house chatting and laughing, and I was sorry to see him turn off back towards the Kennels. And for hours afterwards, I could feel on my fingers the pressure of his hand, so warm and firm.

Peter came to bed after an evening in the Laboratory. He sat down, and put his legs in, as usual. His pyjama jacket was unbuttoned, which means he has the intention of making love. But – terrible to relate – tonight I saw him not as my life's other half, the father of our child, but as a hard man, small, opinionated, stubborn: a stranger. And when he came across the bed to take me in his arms, I could think only of Inspector Carson with half his head blown away, and the comfort of Jamesy's hand.

I turned away from him. I told him some lie or other. I lay feeling that all my worries of late have come to a crisis – that we are on opposite sides. In the middle of the night, I got up, and took myself to another bedroom.

What is happening?

Chapter Fourteen

The Battery House

As you walk through Malpas, you can feel the pressure of a life now gone. There are layers of technology, one on another, showing like the edges of rock-strata still distinct above the beach they will soon become. Take the lighting plant. There is a cellarful of rat-gnawed candle boxes. Alongside that cellar is the Glass Room, containing the huge stone tank known as the Glass Bath, in which a mixture of caustic soda and water was used to clean the soot from the chimneys of nineteenth-century lamps filled from the great brass paraffin-tank set in the wall. On the walls of the Glass Room are the copper pipes that brought from the gasworks the coal-gas that supplanted the paraffin. And above and outside, hemmed in by coalholes and sculleries in a yard the sun never reaches, is the Battery House.

The Battery House is full of glass cases like small, opaque aquaria. Once, these held hydrochloric acid and lead electrodes to make batteries charged by the current generated in the Malpas hydro-electric plant. After gas, this was a marvel – safe, clean, odourless, inexpensive.

And more besides.

Early this century in the Munster wilds, electricity was a little-known phenomenon. The Malpas diaries that have survived speak of Fridays, when the arthritic of the region came to grasp the bus bars and receive the Shock, famously therapeutic . . .

But the batteries and their cranky, perished wiring gave way to the electricity mains. And now even the mains have gone, and Malpas is lit only by the sun, and the moon, and the occasional bonfire of the tramps who wade the

---

slush of broken glass in the Battery House . . .[1]

A couple of days after my meeting with Angela, I went fishing among the shingle banks that came out of the river below the House Pool when the tide was off it. I caught two sea trout, three and five pounds respectively, in the pitch dark, heart hammering, reel shrieking. I was looking forward to an evening with Helen, during which she would be deeply impressed by my hunter-gathering skills. We would drink some wine, play a game of chess, and make love. Well, she did not play chess, and nor did I, but I knew she would like the rest of it.

This cheery anticipation did not survive the sight of a strange Land Rover looming against the bulk of the house, and the hoarse bray of Finbarr's laughter from the kitchen. And there at the end of the table was bloody Finbarr himself, wreathed in cigarette smoke and gazing upon Helen through a three-quarters empty bottle of my Paddy.

'Sorry to interrupt,' I said. 'Whose is the car?'

'Mine,' said Finbarr. 'Converted from a Triumph Trident.'

'Meeting's over,' said Helen, smiling happily. 'Have a drink.'

I poured whiskey. Helen was flat broke. Her own car had run a big end. I said, 'I thought the money was for fence posts.'

'Priorities,' said Finbarr airily.

'Pretty bloody strange priorities,' I said. It came out sharper than I had meant.

'Have you fifty grand to lend us, so?' said Finbarr. I did not like the 'us'. They giggled, with an irritating complicity. Finbarr gathered up his cigarettes and his matches. 'Well Helen it's the road for me,' he said. 'I have a dun in the morning I'd say. I'll let meself out.' He did not say goodnight to me, nor I to him. I had put considerable effort into selling the Trident, and I did not like the idea of Finbarr appropriating the money for his own use. I told Helen so.

---

[1]   James Le Doux, *Where Raleigh met Spenser*, London 1982

'He knows what he's doing,' she said. 'Everything's entailed. We can't borrow from the bank. Finbarr knows how it works. He has to have the final say.'

I said, 'It's crazy.'

'It's Malpas.' She frowned. 'Dave, are you jealous?'

'Should I be?' I grinned at her. I could feel the grin cracking.

'Oh, for God's sake.' She put her hands on her knees, changing the subject. 'Still no drawing book?'

'He had it on the Sunday. Nobody saw it after that.'

At least, nobody admitted to having seen it. I believed Helen, and Angela, and the Cosgraves. The only one I did not necessarily believe was Finbarr. But to be fair, that was hardly a reasoned judgement.

Helen had a point. I was jealous, all right.

Helen yawned. I took her in my arms, warm and smelling faintly of whiskey. She put her arms around my neck and kissed me. Then we went to bed and turned off the lights, and the moon poured in at the window and onto her body as she stalked me across the bed. We took hold of each other in the tick and groan of the house. The only human sounds were Helen's small moans, and our loud, fierce breathing. From outside came the yell of courting owls, and the hiss of the small breeze in the oak-jungles, and a huge, wild silence. Nobody thought about Finbarr for a good eight hours.

Next day at lunchtime I left aside an attempted cure of schizophrenia by hypnotherapy, went into the house and told Helen about the Doctor's account of the trial of Oweneen and the murder of Carson. She listened, playing planes and hangars with Hannah, using spoonfuls of mashed carrot.

At the end she said, 'That can't be right. Why would he cover up for the Cosgraves and Oweneen? He would have known that would have put him under the Cosgraves' thumb for ever.'

'The Hippocratic oath.'

'The Hippocratic oath says he's got to heal the sick, not perjure himself to get a patient off the hook.'

'Also, he had a wife and child,' I said. 'And the example of what the

Shinners did to Walsh and Carson. Maybe he worked out who was going to win.'

She nodded. I saw her look out of the window at that ancient battle ground, and shiver. Then she got up. 'I'd better do some painting. Oh, by the way, letter for you.' She tossed it across the table. 'From Dunquin.'

'Bill,' I said.

It was not a bill. It was a white envelope, addressed in a shuddering copperplate. The letterhead said 'Denis Moriarty, M.D.'

Dear Mr Walker,

With reference to the blood tests conducted on your goodself and child on 4th inst. The results are now returned and I am pleased to tell you that it is fifty to one that the girl is your own daughter, odds at which I would have no hesitation in staking my small savings confident of a profitable outcome. Trusting this finds you in the bloom of health, as it leaves yours truly (age taken into consideration).

Denis Moriarty.

I put the letter on the table. I picked it up and read it again. I wanted to take Helen and Hannah in my arms and tell them how happy I was that the doubt was over and that we were all linked together in the most basic way it was possible to be linked, a real family at last.

But that would expose what Helen would see as my grubby little trick, which would be a bad idea. So I limited myself to shaking Hannah's small, sticky hand. 'Welcome aboard,' I said, and she grinned peg-toothed back.

Then I put her in the pram and wheeled her joyfully down the colonnade to the Laboratory. She had her nap in the fresh air. I went in, and burned Moriarty's letter. Then I started the review of the shelves that I had been promising myself. And found myself on this day of discoveries making yet another.

I have already mentioned that, where the last five volumes of Peter Costelloe's casebooks should have stood on the shelves, there was empty space. That afternoon, delving in a box of papers stored in the cupboards at the base of the bookcase, I found a thin volume bound in mouldy leather and stamped on the outside with the word CATALOGUE.

I started immediately to compare it with the actual contents of the shelves. It seemed comprehensive – there were omissions, of course, but only of the kind easily explicable over sixty years of use. And the mystery of the incomplete run of casebooks was solved. On the shelves as I had found them, there were nineteen fat brown volumes. The catalogue listed another five. A pencilled note in the Catalogue read *Borrowed by James Durcan, June 1917*. There was no record of the books ever having been returned.

From the Casebooks of Peter Costelloe

The events of last year have now faded, so they seem like a terrible dream. To count my blessings: our son Jesse is growing like a young tree. My work continues apace. And – joy and honour! – we have been privileged to welcome as a distinguished visitor no less a personage than Sir Francis Galton himself!

I had the great man's rooms prepared as he would like them: which is to say, simple furniture, bare floorboards without carpets – he has a horror of dust, being susceptible to asthma. I collected him from a first-class carriage at Dunquin, a tall and distinguished figure, densely whiskered, with a keen and probing eye despite his great age. Dulcie went forward to greet him, holding Jesse by the hand. Sir F. glanced at her and at the little boy, and scarcely seemed to register their presence.

Dulcie (to whom I had spoken at length about this colossus of science) was I think at first disappointed. Sir F. is famous for his indifference to women, and seemed reluctant to give her credit for her work on the electrical system. He was, however, intrigued when at teatime Liam O'Rourke arrived, cap twisting in his gnarled fingers, and requested the Shock. He watched with close attention as Liam gripped the electrodes and Dulcie threw the switch.

He listened closely as Liam (the convulsions abating) delivered a speech on the beneficial effect of electricity on his rheumatics. He then proposed a statistical investigation, statistics being an obsession of his. Dulcie at this point sighed noisily, and left.

We then returned to my Laboratory, where Mairi was waiting. It was of course she who was the pretext for Sir Francis' visit. The key to her mind is her private system of classification – her reclassification of the natural world is one example, and another her classification of numbers as *developing shapes*. This latter observation in particular confirms (to his intense gratification) earlier work by Sir F. But it is as if her remarkable ability to calculate and observe has displaced the ability to combine, to make *ideas* of individual phenomena in combination. Sir Francis is less interested in curing her affliction than in its pathology. I ask myself, as a physician, *can she be cured?*

I therefore outlined the course of therapeutic exercises in which we have been engaged, only to have the great honour of an interruption from him, in which he expatiated *in full* on some of his mental experiments.

For instance: on one occasion he convinced himself that all policemen were disguised agents of a foreign power. The trust of policemen lies (for Sir Francis, at least) deeply woven into his idea of a society of which he is a member; but he found it can be undone – reversed, even – in the course of a five-mile walk across London, at the end of which the mere sight of a policeman inspired absolute terror – how well I know the feeling!

I explained to him that I had used these techniques – induced terrors, the summoning to the conscious mind of unconscious mental processes – in conjunction with hypnosis, to alter the unconscious roots of thought. We agreed that I shall make further use of these techniques, and send him reports. He in his turn promises that should my work continue to progress, he will secure me an invitation to speak on the subject at the Royal Society. This would mark a crucial step forward in my career.

Not only my career. If I can show Dulcie that in my own field I, too, am to be reckoned with, perhaps she will think of me more fondly. So, to work with Mairi, hardly daring to hope!

From the Diaries of D.W.

It was Jess's birthday last week. He was very excited, the darling boy. We do not spoil him, of course, and Frau Bildt is strict but fair. But there was to be a cake, and a tea party in the Temple of the Graces, of all the places on the Estate his favourite. Peter and I met at luncheon, when I reminded him to be in the Temple at teatime. In the early years of our marriage we would have had this discussion over our tea, warm in bed in the morning. But now we have taken to sleeping in separate rooms we scarcely meet till lunchtime, and briefly then. At any rate, Peter announced that, tea party or no tea party, we must all go that afternoon to Dunquin station, to meet some notability he had asked to stay. When I demurred, he flew into a great passion and cried that there were many birthdays but only one Sir Francis Galton. And dear Jesse, who loves his father devotedly and wishes him to be forgiven at all times, said that he could put off his party from a four o'clock tea to a six o'clock supper; but with the tears standing in his eyes, poor brave little soldier.

So off we trailed to the station, where a fat old man struggled from a first-class compartment and into the trap with never an acknowledgement of Jess nor me. So gross was he that he greatly slowed the trap, and his wheezing frightened the horse. Then he could not climb to the Temple, and we had to arrange for him to be carried up, and all the children were fractious with hunger and of course it began to rain and the day was quite spoilt. But this seems to be of no interest to Peter, who dances round the old brute like a spaniel, while he smokes haschisch cigarettes to ease his rotten lungs and snarls at Jack, the terrier puppy I have given Jess for his birthday, in a manner rude and cruel.

But the worst of it is Jamesy. I know that he was eager to meet this Galton, who has had such an effect on Peter, who has after all been Jamesy's teacher. We were in the trap, passing down the avenue. Jamesy had stationed himself to one side, and waved us down. We stopped alongside him, and I know that he wished passionately to be recognised. He stepped forward, hand out. Peter looked surprised. 'Who is this?' says Galton. 'An employee,' says Peter, and was not going so much as to introduce him. So I did the job myself, earning a scowl for my pains. He is so jealous, so petty!

The old man is gone now, thank goodness. But the confusion of his visit is still with us, and Jamesy is sorely worried. He has sent me a letter, and insists I present it – for the same reason I write this. He needs to put his worries in writing, because they are of a nature that cannot be communicated as speech. It concerns the 'cure' of Mairi Dugdale – the final 'session'.

Narrative of James Durcan

Mairi came to the Laboratory at her usual time, 11 a.m. – her punctuality has improved steadily over the course of treatment. Doctor Costelloe seated her as normal in the patient's chair, stationed himself in front of her, and commenced the Braid induction that (out of ritual rather than therapeutic need, in my view) he always uses.

The hypnotic state supervened quickly. Mairi's voice became low and slow, the way it is during these sessions. She replied to his promptings not (as in earlier years she would have) with a string of irrelevant numerals and quantities; but with a pleasant conversational exchange, that they were after washing the curtains, and the grilse run was after starting, and Johnny's sister Dervla had brought home her third, the little doat.

The Doctor took her through all this, kind and forbearing as always with a patient, his fingertips steepled against his lips. 'So,' he said, and I thought I saw the small shine of sweat on his forehead. 'Jamesy, you may go.'

He often said that, when he was going to tread on ground that he felt was too delicate for what he considers the non-medical foot – I am still non-medical, despite my degrees, my work with him these six years! I got up to leave. As was my own habit, I went out of the Laboratory door and turned right, so the way took me towards the open window. During the Doctor's séances, he was almost as absorbed as his patient. He never noticed when I, anxious to increase my knowledge of the full procedure – not merely those parts he deemed suitable – listened outside the window.

This time, I closed the door and waited. The voice above droned on. The Doctor was saying, 'And the crows.'

'There are plenty of crows.'

He said, 'It is a spring morning. There are flags on the house: red, white and blue for the Queen, green for Ireland.'

'A grand morning,' she said. 'A grand morning for a wedding.'

'Are you going to the wedding?'

'All wrong,' she said. 'All wrong, the numbers.'

'Do you know why they're wrong?'

Silence.

'What is it that makes the numbers wrong?'

A whimpering, most unpleasant to the ear.

'Is it something that you've seen?'

Her voice again. 'I don't remember.'

'Try.'

Whimpering. 'I can't remember. It's all . . . bits.'

'From before the time you can remember?'

'Yes.'

An odd sound, now. The Doctor's voice; a sigh.

'Well,' he said. 'Leave it there. Forget it. You have dug the great hole. There is a pile of earth, look. Use your shovel, the shovel we have brought. Load the bits into the hole. Bury them. Never bring them back.'

There was a silence. Then Mairi's voice. 'Too much,' she said. 'It won't bury. It won't go in the hole. I am shovelling onto it but it won't be in there, it won't be quiet, it's wriggling about, too much, too much!' Then, suddenly, she started a harsh, wild screaming. I heard a chair falling over, the slam of a door. I saw her running huge and ungainly towards the river.

And the Doctor standing in the doorway, looking after her, white-faced, hair disarranged into short black spikes.

Then his eye fell on me. 'What are you doing here?' he said, sharp as sharp.

'Tying my lace. What happened?'

'An hysterical episode,' he said. 'Nothing to worry about. In fact,' he said, 'I think we can regard Mairi as cured.'

And no more was said about it.

Since these events nobody at Malpas has seen Mairi. My reason for setting them down is that I fear some evil may have befallen the poor woman, and I wish to make a record of these events while they are yet clear in my mind, for the assistance of those who in the future may wish to make enquiries into the matter.

Chapter Fifteen

The Mairi case was remarkable. If the Doctor was to be believed, he had with his 'Galtonian' techniques successfully treated something closely resembling autism. I spent the best part of a week preparing a digest, which I sent to George Gale at Helmstone, with notes culled from the Doctor's more technical papers, proposing a detailed account of the case as a foundation for my doctoral thesis. I finished as the stable clock struck fifteen, drove it to the post office in the Zephyr, and went into the house to lunch with an unusually strong sense of achievement. Hannah beat her tray with her spoon. We sat down to a salad of the year's first new potatoes, grown by Paddy Cosgrave in an unruined fragment of greenhouse, and were soon deep in Peter Costelloe. 'She's gone off him,' said Helen. 'So weird.'

'What?'

'I don't know if I like knowing this much about my grandparents.'

I must confess that, in the excitement of the chase, I sometimes lost sight of the fact that the people coming to life in the notes I gave her were her close relations. I said, 'I could stop telling you what's going on.'

She laughed. 'Don't you bloody dare,' she said. 'I want to know everything. *Everything.*'

And she had barely finished speaking before there rolled through the house the hollow thunder of the knocker on the front door.

The man standing on the step was a stranger wearing a cheap grey suit and a couple of pints of Old Spice.

'Sergeant Rourke, Garda Siochana,' he said. 'Investigating the death of Mr Stephen Brennan.'

'How can I help?'

He squinted his little black eyes at me. 'I'd like to speak to a Mr David Walker.'

'That's me.' I took him in and introduced him.

'We've met,' said Helen. She looked pale. 'Do you want some lunch?'

Rourke's eyes were scuttling round the room, seeing my coat on a hook, the table laid for two, little signs that said these two people are living together. 'No, thank you,' he said. 'Mr Walker, would you ever show me some identification?' I went upstairs and dug out my passport. 'Ah, yes,' he said, having frowned at it. 'And what would be the purpose of your visit?'

'To see my friend Mrs Brennan. What is all this about?'

'We have information received.'

Helen said, 'What are you talking about?'

The Guard put his hands in his cheap grey pockets. 'It's not much at all,' he said. 'But put yourself in my boots, now. You have a man found drowned. You have a friend of that man's wife from England takes that woman's child to Dunquin to have a blood test done. And that blood test shows that the child isn't the husband's, but yer man's from England.'

My stomach turned cold and swooped away. A tide of blood swept into Helen's face. 'I *beg* your pardon?' she said.

The policeman said, 'You didn't know?'

Helen said, '*Blood* tests?'

Rourke took a step backwards, with the air of a man who had opened a cupboard for a biscuit and found a rattlesnake. Carefully not looking at Helen, he said to me, 'When did you arrive in Ireland, Mr Walker?'

I gave him the date.

'And how would you describe your relationship with Mrs Brennan?'

Helen said in a thin, neutral voice, 'Mr Walker is staying in my house while he does some historical research.' She had picked Hannah out of the high chair and was holding her against her blue jersey like a breastplate. I could feel her eyes on me, hurt and angry. Walker, you bloody fool.

Rourke started asking questions. He found out about Helmstone. He nodded. 'Yer man Brennan, now, would he have taken your place in Mrs Brennan's affections, like?'

'Yes,' said Helen, in a voice like an escape of liquid nitrogen.

'Mr Walker?'

'I suppose so.'

'So in a manner of speaking you might have had something to gain from Mr Brennan's death?'

'What do you mean?'

'Yes, yes,' said Rourke, soothingly. 'But you'll understand that just as a matter of form, now, I have to ask you what would you have been doing on the night of August 19th last?'

'What day of the week was that?'

'Wednesday.'

In that faraway world, Wednesday had been darts night. 'I would have been in the public bar of the Goat and Compasses in Helmstone. The landlord knows me. I don't have the telephone number.'

He made a note.

I said, 'Where did you get your information?'

'Quite so,' said Rourke, smiling an enigmatic smile. 'That's all, Mr Walker, Mrs Brennan. For now, annyway. Goodbye now.'

He left. Helen sat down. She said to the table, 'So you got that old corpse Moriarty to suck her blood.' She did not sound angry any more, only exasperated. She said, 'The reason for not going to Moriarty besides the dirty needles is that yer man is about as discreet as a megaphone. You might as well tell the polis direct.' Pause. 'Dave, I need to trust somebody, and you're all I've got. So be trustworthy, would you ever?'

Her hand came across the table, long, tapered, smeared with crimson lake and indigo.

And I thought, we all needed to trust somebody.

Including ourselves.

Helen had the idea that there was a link between her father's music and his enthusiasm for tides. He had been brought up by the estuary.

Sometimes she thought that in his music she could hear themes running against each other, tearing up rips and spinning whirlpools of sound. He never talked about it, of course. But certainly, tides were something that got him excited.

She was watching him closely as he steered *St Cecilia* up the east coast of Jura. He looked at his watch often. Down on the chart table, the music paper was put away and had been replaced by a spiral-bound notebook, bearing calculations based on a difference on high water Oban. She could see from the movements of his neck – a good neck still, no jowls or extra chins – that he was swallowing. She was excited herself, a little jump in the stomach. This was a big day.

St Cecilia was motoring up a mirror-green sea, following the shore as it trended north and west towards the narrows between the two islands. There were odd seams and creases in the water. Otherwise everything was quiet, as in a great, breathless room where the Paps of Jura held up the blue roof. But she had read the pilot book. This gap between the islands was called the Corryvreckan, and it was the most dangerous place round all the shores of Britain, except for four twenty-minute periods every day. And here they were, Helen and her father and dear *St Cecilia*, heading for one of those twenty-minute periods, chugging gently down this green satin road. A green satin road that at this speed would take half an hour to ride.

They were three-quarters of the way through now. Her father looked at his watch and said, 'Any minute.' He grinned at her, and she grinned back, her mouth dry, but with a sweet tension in the pit of her stomach, knowing Daddy could do no wrong.

And suddenly all that flat water began to move. It moved at different speeds, becoming plates, with little eddies at their junctions. Where *St Cecilia*'s wake hit them it caused a confusion that spread and amplified itself until the whole sheet had become rumpled and opaque. And suddenly over the thump of the engine there came a huge and savage roar, and out in the middle of the channel a gigantic smooth wave rose and stood and bellowed like a jet. There were whirlpools everywhere now, and the boat was twitching, caught in a violent eddy, heeled over thirty degrees, so a coffee cup whizzed down the after end of the cockpit and shattered on the side. Then suddenly they were in still water, while astern the tide shot a tongue of racing water between the two islands and licked deep into the broad, smooth sea.

Helen clapped. Her father bowed, as she had seen him do at the Purcell Room. She felt free and happy and close to him.

It did not last.

They went down Jura and into West Loch Tarbet, wafting through the maze of rock channels on the flood, arriving finally on the grey sheet of water that lies quiet at the heart of the island. *Georges Sand* lay under the blue ten o'clock Highland sky, no stars yet. Her father poured his first whisky. A curlew let rip a long, bubbling yell. 'Loneliest place ever,' she said.

'Not as lonely as Malpas.'

It was the third time in her life she had heard him mention the name. She saw his hand go out, those long, precise fingers close round the bottle and pour till the whisky was most of the way up the glass. 'This is wild,' he said. 'Malpas is lonely. And cold. People have made it cold.' He drank some of the whisky, a lot of it, and missed the cigarette with the lighter. The warmth of the Corryvreckan foolishness had gone. She held her breath, in case he carried on talking and she missed something.

'There's a castle on the Blackwater,' he said. 'Dozens of them, actually, all just out of cannon shot of each other. But this one, won't tell you which one.' She let out her breath, disappointed. 'There was an old chap lived there, a widower with his two spinster daughters. He was horribly lonely. His daughters were useless, not a patch on you. So he advertised in the matrimonial advertisements of the Cork *Examiner*, wife wanted by Lepping Henry who has good farm of land, reply box number, you know. He got two replies.' Pause. '*One from each of his daughters.*' Another flame to another cigarette. He shivered. 'Ghastly.'

Helen shivered too. But not with the chill of it. She shivered with the bitterness of it, the idea of people pushed as far as they could go and further, into desperate actions with even more desperate consequences . . .

Delicious.

BOOK 3

Chapter Sixteen

From the Casebooks of Peter Costelloe

It is hard to think of Jamesy as the crimson-headed youth of seven years ago. Now he is tall, red-headed certainly but of a dark Titian colour, with a fine commanding presence and a broad, pale brow. Here is the tally of his achievements since our first meeting:

— he has achieved full mastery of the Malpas economy, with particular reference to the farm;

— he has taken an extramural degree in physiology and alienism at Cork;

— he has done a twelve-month apprenticeship with a Thomas Major of Fethard, Co. Tipperary – by all accounts a wonderful practitioner on the muscular and skeletal ills of horses and greyhounds;

— and last but not least, he has married the clever and beautiful Emily.

It is less to his credit that he has used what I can only describe as hedge-doctoring on some of my patients. Here I think particularly of an incident before the Mairi cure – that of Mrs Font-Lennox of Clonmel.

Mrs Font-Lennox suffered from excruciating migraines, which I had for some years been treating with suggestion, supplemented where necessary with cocaine as an analgesic. When she arrived in her motor car three months ago, I was laid low with the *grippe*. It was therefore James who met her. He conducted her to the Laboratory and sat her in the chair. He then subjected her skull and nape to what he describes as a series of *manipulations*, the object of which was apparently to realign the plates of her skull – this regardless of the fact that she is a woman of some fifty years, and her skull-plates have been fused for the past forty-five at least. Having done this, he proceeded to *file her back teeth* in the veterinary manner, on the pretext that the misalignment of the skull proceeded from a fault in her jaw posture caused by irregular growth of her molars; displacing, in the process, much expensive dental work by Mr Attlee of Cheltenham. Mrs Font-Lennox's migraines returned with redoubled violence *sur-le-champ*, and I was compelled to pay for a further course of restorative dentistry in Cork.

When I remonstrated with him, he would have none of it. He described Mrs Font-Lennox as a scheming Papist (and Catholic she is, though more injured than scheming). So arrogant was his approach to the question that I intemperately accused him of seeking to redress the wrongs of the Inquisition by causing pain to those who dig with what he sees as the wrong foot. We then entered in on an argument that concentrated all the slights of the past seven years; slights that on a day-to-day basis have been hugely outweighed by the harmonious aspects of our life and research, but which, concentrated into a half-hour discourse, represented a positive catalogue of turpitude. By the end, I was to his satisfaction a Fenian quack, and he was to mine a half-educated Prod bigot, racked with rustic superstition. He sat there with dead-white face and wild red hair, staring at me with his pale, furious eyes.

'Here you sit,' he said. 'In this dirty great house that you have come to from God knows where, behaving what way you like. What gives you the right?'

I felt the blood leaving my face. I told myself that anger would not help. But the wish to crush, to humiliate, was too strong. I said, 'I and Mrs Costelloe are here as guardians of the heritage of Ireland.'

'A big house,' he said. 'A farm you couldn't run if you tried.'

I bowed. It was true, Jamesy knows the ins and outs of the Malpas land as nobody else could. I said, 'But there is what is in the house.'

He raised his eyebrows. 'Such as?'

'The pictures,' I said. 'Great treasures of Irish art. The sculptures, the treasure chest of Walter Raleigh. The Crown of Tara.' And as I said it, I knew it was a mistake.

'The *what?*'

'Nothing.' I pulled paper towards me. I must be rid of him, before I committed any other indiscretions. 'It is none of your business, I am afraid. It must not be spoken of. It was a mistake. It does not exist.'

This conversation took place shortly before the completion of my cure of Mairi and her departure from Malpas. Since that time, he has seemed worried and even hostile. I catch him looking at me with . . . well, dislike. His appearances in the Laboratory grow less frequent, our meetings more guarded. And this morning, he put his meaty hands flat on the bench top and said, 'Costelloe, what was it with Mairi Dugdale?'

'She is cured,' I said. 'She has flown the nest into the wide, wide world.' Though to be truthful, I do not know where she has gone, at all.

'And what is it that she does not remember?'

I felt the blood in my face. 'I cannot discuss a patient,' I said.

'What have you done?' he said.

I should have sent him away. Instead, I laughed in his face.

He lifted his hands from the marble bench top, and the light fell on twin prints etched in angry palm-sweat. 'I don't like to hear a patient scream,' he said. 'I can't be part of such things, not at all.' Then he left.

I had thought this incident forgotten. On the day of our last row, I did not see Dulcie till the evening, when she looked distant – even sullen – and would not talk to me while the nurserymaid brought Jess down for his tea. Afterwards, she said, 'Jamesy came to see me today.'

'Indeed?'

'He wants to set up in practice on his own. I have said he may have the Kennels on a ninety-nine-year lease, to do with as he will.'

This was a surprise. She and I are no longer as close as once we were, it is true. But she has always consulted me before – particularly now, when she has as good as passed the advantage to Jamesy. When all is said and done, though, the estate is hers to control. So I confined myself to a bow. 'This is very sudden,' I said.

'He tells me he wishes to start a hospital for people with nervous diseases,' she said.

'And how is he qualified?'

'By apprenticeship to you,' she said. 'And by his degree, and his other training.'

'As a horse doctor.'

She looked at me very cool. 'One would think you were jealous.'

'I am merely solicitous of the welfare of his patients.'

But of course she was right.

So now Jamesy and I are estranged, and in his estimation competitors. He has rechristened the Kennels the Malpas Refuge for the Nervous. Here he provides a broad – some would say quixotic – system of treatment, including Deep Sleep, the Rest Cure with milk diet, Hydrotherapy, Hypnosis, spinal manipulation, what he imagines to be Psychoanalysis, and any other fad or quackery he can dig up in the literature. His brochure is a splendid thing, splattered with gorgeous pictures, printed on the finest paper and endorsed by four professors and a duke.

The Durcan circle is a landowning, Ascendancy sort, who since the Oweneen trial and the death of Carson frankly do not trust Dulcie and me. They tell little stories – Dulcie and her electrical installations and her riding astride, me with my charity cases and my hypnotism, and of course my famous Fenian sympathies. Ah well, Jamesy has gone, and taken much trouble with him (and also, I regret to say, several volumes of my case notes. But the time is not right to recover them, just now).

Yesterday, Johnny Cosgrave came in: a lean Johnny, with his eyepatch, and the complexion of one who spends much time in the open air. I had the sense that he was leading up to something. Finally, he leaned towards me.

'I hear you have the Crown of Tara beyond in the house,' he said.

'Good God!' I cried, much taken aback. 'Who told you that?'

'They were talking about it above at Durcan's Asylum.' (This is the name the people on the estate give to Jamesy's Refuge for the Nervous.)

'What about it?'

'Only that it was a priceless thing, a beautiful thing, one of the great things of Ireland.'

'Mr James has never seen it.' Ach, Jamesy!

'Sure it was only a class of a rumour, the one that was serving at the table did say.' Johnny's single eye became narrow. 'But if there is a crown of Ireland, why would it be in Malpas?'

'Well,' I said, downcast and angry that Jamesy should make of our secrets an item of gossip. 'It is a curious story, and may not be true.'

'What is it?' he said, eagerly. Johnny is a practical Republican, but he is also a fierce romantic, and loves a story.

'A plain circlet of massy gold set with tourmaline,' I said.

'Tourmaline,' he breathed. There was a rapt look on his face. He could see the syrupy gleam of gold, the sparkle of tourmaline, whatever he imagined that to be.

'The Crown was kept by the O'Briens, descendants of the High Kings, you remember, until it was given in the strictest secrecy to the Parliament in Dublin, to the Speaker in person, in the year 1756, by the hand itself of the last descendant of the High Kings.'

'The last descendant,' breathed Johnny. 'God love us all.'

I nodded. 'Then in 1800 the Dublin Parliament was abolished, and the Government went to London.'

'And the Crown as well?'

'Now,' said I, leaning close towards him, and he towards me. 'Now!' In the silence I could hear the weight of his breathing. 'At that same Parliament soon to be flung to the winds was a certain Patrick Costelloe. He was a true man and a loyal Irishman. So the Speaker of the Parliament came to Cormac Durcan, who was my ancestor's steward, in Dublin on business, and he said to him, to the devil with this treachery, but there is nothing we can do about it and the politics that is in it. But I am damned (said the Speaker) double damned and in perdition if as a true-born Irishman I will let the Saxon get his dirty fingers on the Crown itself of Ireland. So Cormac (says the Speaker) I hereby solemnly charge you to take this (and here he gives him a box, a box I have seen myself) and take it to the new house they are building at Malpas, and convey it to Patrick Costelloe and there in that strong place to guard and keep it without telling a soul or entering it in any record nor inventory, until Ireland shall once again be free. It is a thing of incalculable value in money, but more by far in the power it carries.'

'By the living Christ,' breathed Johnny. 'You have it still.'

'In a place that no man may know of,' I said.

'Inside in the House.'

There was a long silence. 'Now,' I said at last, to break it. 'Do you have any news from Mairi?'

He came to himself like a man rising from a trance – which, of course, was exactly what he was. He said, 'Sure she's in America. She does be fine.'

'Thank God,' I said, and I was truly pleased. 'Married, yet?'

Here Johnny's face became oddly motionless, as if I had stepped too close to something he did not wish to discuss. 'Not just yet,' he said, and directed his one eye at the Laboratory clock. 'Great God, is that the time already?' And he was gone.

I remained in the Laboratory and finished my work, a statistical analysis of salmon caught in the weir and the draught nets. The trend was upward. I asked myself, was it the War sparing the fish at sea? But this question occupied only half my mind. The other half toyed with the Crown of Tara. I knew why I had revealed to Johnny that great secret. My disagreement with Jamesy rankles still. Always I want – childishly – to have the credit for possessing fuller information than him on any subject. Jamesy's knowledge would be wholly derived from speculation, based on my unguarded remarks. My own is based on a more intimate acquaintance with this priceless thing . . .

But it is all vanity. Now Jamesy is gone, and I have dismissed the affair from my mind.

Walker Archive, Transcript, 1973 – 5

It is a strange place that I am in, all this time since I am off the boat. There are no trees, no river, no fish, no birds. There is a roar of racket from outside the window, a huge boiling roar that comes up seven storeys from the road below, and opposite there are nine windows I can see from the chair where I sit, and a different family inside in each one like ferrets in a house of ferrets. It is a bad room all right, a bad room for noise, I can hear your man on the left that is called Dinny belting his young fellas with a strap now he has drink taken again, and on the other side Kathleen whose man was killed pinned by a bull three weeks and four days ago not counting today, and her crying and weeping what will become of her now.

But it is time for off and out, into my coat that is too thin for this terrible winter and my shoes that have a hole and out out down all ninety-one stairs and out into the road. It is raining a cold thin rain and the automobiles go past whish, whish, and the water is getting through my feet and my coat so I will be wet all right. But we are strong nowadays Mairi aren't we, and onto the El and you can hear the stockyards before you get there, a great low and stamp of beasts and a bank of cattle-breath like fog that rolls down the wind on you. I am a checker in the office. I have a desk far from the stove. Mr Tkatchenko is a little fella with a little moustache. I am good at my work because I am a great counter with a real head for figures and one hell of a memory, Mr Calhoun says, who is Mr Tkatchenko's boss, if you was half as good as her Tkatchenko you would be real good you Bohunk dummy. So Mr Tkatchenko puts me far from the stove and o my poor feet, and it is dark outside because of being on nights, and I must go out into the awful clash and screech of the place with the trains in it, and count the beasts that can already smell the blood, the blood.

There is a lot of us from home inside in the stockyards, more every day, and tonight I am in the middle of a crowd of beasts when I hear a voice say my name and it is Dessie Bruton from Cappoquin, and he tells me his news and says, And now long are you here?

Well Dessie is a grand fella so we arrange to meet and it is in the drugstore and I am having a sarsaparilla soda and it is only great, so great to see him that I tell him everything, about lovely Johnny Cosgrave and my little Doctor and the things the Doctor did that lifted up the fog of numbers I lived in, and how he took me back to a thing . . . a bad thing . . . a thing that once I saw, and I could not go on with it.

And Dessie said, not listening but only waiting his turn to speak, yes, yes, it was the same for him, and we must earn our wages and there is a great day coming, and how helluva pretty I was looking, which is not true but I am thinner now because of the bad food and having my teeth all out and new ones in. And he told me that talking about pretty, Johnny Cosgrave had told him he was coming out this way and to tell me if he saw me, and Dessie said he reckoned your man had plans for me, and all of a sudden I felt my face so hot I thought I would burn right up, and Dessie laughed and told me I was the grand girl and a lucky one, too, because Johnny was a high man with the Lads, and he was mine for the taking.

And I am so happy. So happy. So, so happy now.

From the Letters of D.W.

Peter has treated Jamesy shamefully. Of course a man of Jamesy's power of mind would diverge from him in view and resent humiliation. It is only surprising that Jamesy stayed with him as long as he did. Well, James has set up his own establishment, and very successful it has become, offering much of what is ultra-modern in science, and patronised by *the right kind of people*. It is strange for me to think how once I admired P. for taking in his hobbledehoys and freaks into the West Bedrooms. He was never systematic. And of course he never charged them a suitable fee. Not indeed that many of them would have been able to pay. Many did not even show gratitude – take fat Mairi Dugdale, whom P. claims to have cured of her simpleness, but nobody can tell because she vanished straight after, to America it is thought. And of course the paper on Mairi, that would make his reputation when sent to the disgusting old Galton, never materialised. Something went wrong with her treatment, apparently – or that is the excuse. The result is that while Jamesy's reputation grows daily higher, P. sinks deeper into his grubby privacies . . .

It is now two years since I moved out of his bed. And I ask myself daily, do I still love him? Now he is no longer the pivot of my life – now there is Jess, and there is—

No. I can't write the name.

Do I still love him?

Do I?

From the Casebooks of Peter Costelloe

Today I took myself to the stables, where dear Jess is to meet his new pony.

And there he was, our angel! There was Joey the groom, and the pony, which rejoices in the name of the Badger, an elegant gelding, balletic of step, a neat fourteen two. There was Dulcie, today in navy blue, upright, pale and proud, with no attention to spare from Jesse, putting the Badger at a jump in the yard as if he were the Master of the Galway Blazers.

Dulcie barely glanced at me as I came into the yard. I watched as Jess belted the pony round the little paddock, balanced in his stirrups like a professional, and him seven years old next birthday. It was prettiness itself, speaking of a domestic intimacy from which I felt excluded. I thought I would go back to the Laboratory and talk to Jamesy. Then I remembered that since a year now there has been no more Jamesy. I have no patients just at the moment – have had none for some little while, actually. So I found myself in the drawing room, contemplating from one of the window seats the fall of the terraces to the river. Noting that the lawns are not as good as formerly, that there are elders peering above the rhododendrons. Hoping, perhaps, to see Mairi in her cot, hurrying over to Cosgraves'?

But of course there was no Mairi either.

So I went to the tray and mixed myself a firm whiskey and water, to cure the megrims. Now that my wife and my assistant and my chief patient are all distant from me, I shall have to find some means to occupy myself.

Not that I am bored. Oh, no; certainly not that. It is just that now there is nobody to discuss things with, I fall into the grip of a little . . . maggot of whimsy, really. Telling Jamesy and Johnny about the Crown is but one of these episodes. It is loneliness that makes me do it, I think.

But this is an old theme. Yes, yes, very well. I should admit that before luncheon today I took not one but three glasses of whiskey. These have produced in me not the gaiety I see in drinkers at dinner parties, but a sort of fixed melancholy. Look on the bright side. I have striven to achieve Malpas, and now I have it safe. And when a man possesses such a place, what does he need beyond it?

I shall stop now. I am away to the Laboratory. There is so much to do!

Chapter Seventeen

The week after the visit of Guard Rourke was a peculiar one. After her first shock, Helen seemed much less upset than I had feared. Indeed, it seemed that for her as well as me, the outcome of the blood test had made us a family in a way we never were before. The thing that had changed most with me was that my jealousy of dead Steve – pathetic, but there – had gone. In its place had come a sort of guilt about the small amount I had found out about the circumstances leading up to his suicide.

I must confess, though, that more important than Steve was Peter Costelloe. I had come to know him as confident, happy in his researches and his improvements. The vision of that steady, clever man friendless, aimless, bitter, sucking down the lunchtime whiskey, was deeply shocking. His life was falling apart, and I could not bring myself to believe it was his fault. There seemed something emotionally inert about the talented, efficient Dulcie. Jamesy was by all accounts a quack, determined to knock a profit out of his education the way he knocked it out of the Malpas farms. And beneath it all there was the small, nagging question about Mairi's flight. Something was wrong there.

I thought about this as I put my daughter to bed. Helen was in the library, sprawled in a swampy armchair. In her lap was a thick, leather-bound book. She said, 'It's not here.'

'What isn't?'

'The Crown of Tara.' She held up the book. 'This is the inventory. Every bloody thing on the estate, down to the last doorknob and azalea. Entailed. Unsellable.'

'So?'

'If it isn't here, we can sell it.'

'If we can find it.'

'We'll find it,' she said. 'By the way, Angela rang, said do we want a jar at Brady's about now?'

I said, 'Do you?'

'God, I'd love to, but Finbarr's spent the Trident and I've got to get this exhibition on the road so we can eat.' She was working a lot, nowadays; I was not seeing as much of her as when I had first arrived. So off I went, into the Zephyr, out of the park, to Brady's.

The bar was empty except for dust, shadows and crass Paddy. I bought a pint and sat on the bench outside the west wall, and wished Helen was there.

The sun appeared from behind a cloud, touched the trees on the top of the hill. There was a scrunch of tyres on wet gravel. And there was Angela in a short skirt and a Guernsey, trim and blonde.

'No Helen?' she said.

'She's working.'

We agreed that the evening was too beautiful for sitting in pubs. We set off up the path through the riverside woods, chatting about this and that.

At the top of the path was the balustrade of what had once been the Temple of the Graces. Below us, the river was spread out, the great sprawling building by the black sheet of the House Pool. We watched the shadow of the hill creep up the park, snuffing out the trees one by one. At the bottom of the long slope of trees a salmon jumped, sending dark rings of ripple across the rivers' meet. The valley filled with darkness. 'What a place,' I said.

'Too much of it,' she said. Her face was still and blank, without its normal ironic spark. I felt shallow as a tourist. Of course it was more than just a beautiful assembly of river and wilderness. I could feel it working on me, as it had worked on Angela and her parents and all the other lives it had changed and bent and terminated.

Far below, a light came on in the house. I thought of Helen's hand on the switch, putting that tiny yellow pin-glow into the smothering ocean of dark. For a moment I was full of unease for her.

'Come on,' said Angela, brisk and jolly again.

We went back down to the pub.

It was dark. There were a couple more cars now. One of them was Finbarr's Land Rover. He was leaning on the dirty elm counter, laughing, with the light picking out the high bones of his face. When he saw Angela and me, the laugh went. 'So what have you been doing this beautiful evening?' he said.

'Walking on the River Cliff,' said Angela. 'It was lovely.'

Finbarr's eyes were resting on me. 'Right, so,' he said. 'Where's Helen?'

'She's working,' I said.

'Sure she is,' said Finbarr, nodding, the eyes flat and blue and full of drink.

And angry.

I could not be bothered with his neuroses. To change the subject, I said, 'How's business?'

Angela was talking to a man down the bar. Finbarr said, 'You know you are a man who sticks his nose in a hell of a lot of places.'

He was going to start throwing his weight about, and I could not be bothered to listen. I said, 'Helen asked me to.'

'You act more like a polis than a writer.'

Then something odd happened.

There was a crush of people in the place. We were close together – too close for comfort, frankly. He said, 'Let it go.' The pub felt warm and dark, with a growing warmth, a deepening dark. Against the roar of the voices his voice droned on, brown and soothing. I cannot directly report that insidious murmur, for the individual words were lost between the bitterness of the Guinness on my tongue and the warmth of the air. But it went something like this. 'Give it a rest. Stop thinking about Helen. She's not so important. She called you from England, but what you're here for is the work, not the women. It's not that they want you, it's that they haven't enough to do, any port in a storm. Stop thinking about it . . . when I say now, now, *now*.' On the third 'Now' something clicked like a switch in my head, and for a second my mind . . . *went out*. There is no other way of describing it. I was in a state of complete peace, not interested in anything, floating—

What the fuck is this? I came to with a crash. I am a lousy hypnotic subject, but for a moment he had me under, no doubt about it. At least I hoped it was only a moment. He had been trying to warn me off Helen. I decided to see how far it went.

He could see I was no longer under the influence. So I shook my head and tried to look dazed, as if I had woken up by accident. The noise of the pub washed around me. 'What was all that about?' I said.

'You were a bit anxious,' said Finbarr. 'You looked like you could do with a bit of calming down. It's only a party trick, now.' I meant to ask him what kind of party trick. But somehow, I just said goodbye to Angela and walked outside.

The night was clear, and there was a moon flying among the stars above the river. I had intended to go straight home along the river cliff. Instead I found myself walking to the point of the headland, standing with my hands in my pockets, watching the dark swirl of the moonlit water forty feet below. I was not thinking about anything in particular. Indeed, I had no very clear idea what I was doing at all.

A hand clamped on my arm. 'Dave,' said the voice of Finbarr. 'Now how did I know you'd be here?'

I meant to say, 'Post-hypnotic suggestion.' But suddenly I was too frightened to speak. And at the same time I realised that I was very close to the edge of the cliff, so my feet had lost touch with the ground, and had it not been for Finbarr's hand clamped on my arm I would have fallen. I managed to ask him what he was doing.

'You'd need to be careful,' he said. I saw his foxy face touched with moonlight. It wore an expression of judicious gravity. 'Not to upset things.'

'What things?'

'Sure you know yourself,' he said, and moved backwards, so my feet were in firm touch with the ground. 'We have our own ways here, and there's trouble in store for any who go against them.'

I said, 'Who the hell do you think you are?'

'You know that too,' he said. 'Or ask Helen.' Then, somehow, he was gone.

I stood there and rubbed the place where his hand had gripped me. I was shaking. I was still shaking when I got back to the house.

I should have talked to Helen, I suppose – told her what Finbarr had done, and what he had said. But I was shaken and tired. Perhaps it would all be fine in the morning.

But this was a great dark place in which Steve had landed up in a river, dead. It might not be fine at all.

From the Casebooks of Peter Costelloe

We sit in a country lurching towards civil war, at the western extremity of a continent whose children have been sliced to ribbons and drowned in mud.

But inside the walls of Malpas, all seems peace and plenty. In the shrubberies, the azaleas have finished a season acknowledged by all beholders as perfection itself. The kitchen garden is also a marvel, the glass giving a succession of what is required in the way of peaches and nectarines, the beds salads, chicory, the best of beans, and *artichouts* from stock sent back from France with dear little Jess, who now it is peace has been in Poitiers, to learn the language. The farm is doing awfully well – Dulcie and James between them make sure of that. The War poured out on us great profits in beef and barley. On the face of it, all things should be bright and beautiful.

But this is not the old, happy Malpas of seven years ago. There are gaps among the people, since 1916 and the brave follies at the Post Office in Dublin. Johnny Cosgrave has after frequent absences entirely disappeared. Jamesy Durcan and his little son Timsy are to be seen strutting around weirdly accoutred in Norfolk jackets and Martini-Henry rifles. Jamesy's human patients still flood to the Kennels, but his veterinary practice has fallen off amazingly – it is a measure of the gravity of the situation that people are now more attached to their politics than their horses.

I love Dulcie. I love Jess. Jess loves me. As for Dulcie, I do not know. She complains of my drinking, of my research. Certainly I have few patients. All right, I am lonely, while she has mended fences with the neighbours, and hunts and dines and sails while I do not. We do not sleep together. But the river still flows, and the tides still run, and the House still stands, golden and eternal at the eye of the tumult.

Why am I telling this to my casebook? Because of the whiskey, perhaps. Because of Lieutenant Carruthers, certainly. Carruthers is a living symbol of the madness of this world. My feelings about him are too strong for scientific detachment.

He was sent by his mother, a woman I had known in the old London days. In August 1917 he had been in a dugout near Ypres that had received a direct hit from a German howitzer. He was buried far underground, packed among the corpses of his comrades. He escaped his tomb after three days by wriggling out of the earth of a fox which had made its home close to this fine source of food. He was found staggering in no-man's-land, naked and filthy, his only method of communication being frequent bouts of screaming. At home his father refused to have him admitted to a shell-shock hospital on the grounds that this would taint with insanity the family wholesale grocery business. His mother, as I say, thought that I could be of some help in curing or at any rate alleviating his condition. And of course, packing him off to Ireland had (for the father) the merit of discretion. So in due course Carruthers arrived, in a motor-car with the blinds drawn down.

At first, he sat completely withdrawn in the corner of one of the West Bedrooms. I took it upon myself to sit with him. To begin with, the mere presence of a fellow-human brought on fits of screaming abated only by the exhaustion of the vocal chords. But he at length consented to drink water. Into this water I insinuated graduated doses of bromine, talking to him the while. After four months, the bromine had altogether ceased, and I could talk to him without his becoming agitated. After six months, I had achieved a certain rapport, and was able to undertake some formal sessions of hypnosis, reinforced with my Galtonian suggestions. I suggested to him that whenever the hallucinations came upon him – for hallucinations there were, of blackness and deliquescent corpses – he would instantly be transported to a flowering meadow, much like the inch at Malpas. This of course was merely to substitute one hallucination for another. But it did to an extent decrease his agitation. I was able in time to populate the meadow with the people of Malpas, so he became accustomed to speaking – but only, at first, with figures that I presented to his inner eye. Soon we were able to allow the light into his room, and set him moving about the house, then the garden and beyond.

He now began to be much better. His general level of agitation had decreased markedly, and he was capable of objective discussion of his condition. There was, however, a difficulty. He resolutely refused to attribute any therapeutic value to my own interventions. I must confess that having spent many a month coaxing him out of the shadows, I found this more than a little irritating. My only consolation came from the fact that he had at least stayed out of the clutches of Jamesy.

As I say, under my ministrations Tom Carruthers began to improve at an astonishing rate. But one factor marred an otherwise rosy picture: that the personality of the Carruthers now receiving his cure was not, it seemed, the personality that had existed before the burial alive.

In pre-war days he had by all accounts been a boy of great personal sweetness. The Carruthers now emerging from the shadows was dark-browed and passionate, subject to frequent changes of mood. His mother, on a visit to Ireland, suggested going for a walk at the time of the evening milking. Carruthers is much addicted to dairy work, and the company of Pegeen Murphy, one of the dairymaids, a large girl of soothing disposition. Well, Carruthers used foul language to his mother, climbed out of the drawing-room window, and fled. I did my best to soothe Mrs Carruthers. These tendencies, I assured her, must have been present before her son's illness, and would in time settle into the general matrix of his personality.

'No,' she said, lifting her chin. 'This is not the Tommy I once knew. I want my Tommy *back*, Doctor.' And she swept like a battleship from the room and back to England.

I was for some time at a loss as to how she could be placated. Then one morning there was a double-knock at the door of my Laboratory, just the double-knock Jamesy used to give, and Jamesy himself came in.

We shook hands, and watched each other stiffly. We had not been alone together for two years. We talked about the weather and the state of the crops. Finally, he said, 'And your patient.'

'Mr Carruthers?'

'Lieutenant Carruthers,' he said. 'Tell me. How do you find him?' This, mark you, as if he was the physician in charge of the case, and I the bystander.

'And might I ask what you have to do with him?' I said.

Jamesy's lips tightened. 'His mother writes to me. She asks when your treatment will start moving towards a cure.'

Well, I was not obliged to utter any view of the matter. But by God I resented his impertinence, gossiping with my patients' friends behind my back. My irritation got the better of me.

I said, 'He is cured.'

'I beg to differ,' said Jamesy.

The anger nearly drowned me. I wanted to grip his neck and knock his stupid red head against the wall. But I mastered myself. 'Do pray vouchsafe me the fruit of your wisdom,' I said.

He gave me a glance of his sharp blue eyes. He knew what I was thinking. 'Your patient is in a neurotic state entirely,' he said. 'You have been treating him with your suggestions, I believe. I am much afraid that these scenes you present to his inner eye, to divert his attention from his inner horrors, do nothing but mask the horrors, without solving them. The behaviours that we now observe are neurotic entirely, a product of the tensions set up in him by superimposed hallucinations, no more.'

I made myself stay calm. 'I am grateful for these observations,' I said. 'Now I am sure you are busy.'

'For God's sake,' said Jamesy, apparently exasperated. 'You hold that he has completed the ascent from the abyss. I tell you that he is on a ledge with miles to go, and the smallest thing could knock him back into the depths.'

I heard this pompous nonsense only dimly, through the roar of blood in my ears. I hated Jamesy. I hated Malpas, Dulcie, the life that kept me confined and friendless. That had it not been for Jesse I would have left, for . . .

For somewhere.

I said, 'What do you mean, neurotic?'

'You are acquainted with the work of Doctor Freud of Vienna?'

'I have read the weird drivellings of a quack of that name. You are a disciple, I suppose.'

'He has much that is interesting to say about cases of mental disequilibrium.'

'Not to me.' I found I was standing up, my fingers clenched painfully on the laboratory bench. 'I will show you, sir,' I said. 'I will show you that this is not a man who is ill, but a man whose character has been changed by the flow of the natural tides of his existence, and whose personality is now stable, damn you! Stable!'

Jamesy just stood there, one eyebrow cocked in a way I found frankly objectionable.

'You will see tomorrow morning,' I said.

He shrugged his shoulders and left. I sat down and poured myself a drink from the bottle I nowadays keep in the Laboratory to steady my nerves. He would not come to watch a demonstration, of course. But there would be eyes. There are eyes everywhere at Malpas nowadays. From outside the walls and within. The ones within are worst. But now Dulcie has come into the Laboratory. She says I am drunk. Well, she may be right, right she may be. I am coming, damn you, woman. I am coming . . .

Chapter Eighteen

From the Casebooks of Peter Costelloe
Well, well. Or rather, not well. Not well at all. Neither I nor . . . well. Perhaps I should tell you everything, whoever you may be, reading this, hovering over these pages in the piece of space I now occupy. If you are lucky, you will not have my headache, or my queasiness of stomach, or live in a house of strong women. And of course Dulcie has taken my bottle. Or perhaps I took it myself. I don't remember.

At any rate, here is how the day started. I rose, took some liver salts and an aspirin, and made a bad breakfast of soda bread and black coffee. The boy Carruthers was there, eating eggs (noisily, the pig), very ill-natured across the table. Afterwards we went to the laboratory, where I set about a hypnotic session. But when I put my face close to his, he said, 'Your breath smells of corpses.'

'I am sorry,' I said, turning my silver pencil to catch the light.

He glanced at the pencil and looked away. 'I don't think we'll do any mumbo jumbo today,' he said.

'Not mumbo jumbo,' I said, reproachfully. 'Let us—'

'Call it what you like,' he said. He has very black eyes, which just now were snapping alarmingly; but that is their characteristic mode, and there is nothing pathological about it. He has followed the course, and is cured. 'I have had ebloodynough of you,' he said. 'The sun is out. I am going to read a book on the terrace.'

'But—'

'Oh, bugger off, quacky boy,' he said. And while I stood there mute with offence, the door slammed and he was gone.

I found some whiskey for my nerves. It did not take me long to realise that this aggression in one previously so timid was a splendid earnest of my success. I began to bethink me of a test that would demonstrate my remarkable therapeutic achievement. Very soon I found (to my satisfaction, then at least) the solution. It was not a complicated idea. Some, indeed, would have branded it childishly simple.

Curious, how many people's lives can be changed by one injudicious decision. Curious, if not tragic.

I waited my moment. Yes, indeed. I waited till Carruthers was on the stone bench on the south terrace, absorbed in a shilling shocker called, if I remember, *The Golden Web* by Anthony Partridge. Possessing myself of a brown-paper bag from a drawer in the kitchen, I crept silently out of the French door and onto the terrace.

I kept low, feeling (I must confess) a little foolish. I made my way across the flagstones between the beds of the *parterre*. It was hot; I sweated. Pausing in the shelter of an urn, I blew up the bag. I then advanced swiftly but furtively until I was close enough to hear his breathing and see the nervous jig of his foot on the ground. Then, raising the bag with my left hand, I struck it a sharp blow with my right.

The explosion was really most satisfactory. I am afraid that Carruthers' reaction was quite the opposite. He let out a piercing scream and leaped to his feet. Before I could blink he had vaulted the balustrade and was running across the lawn and into the shrubbery. Dimly I could hear his screams, and the crash of breaking branches. There was a little whirlwind of skirts, and Dulcie was by my side. She said, 'What is all this?'

'Poor Carruthers has had a relapse,' I said, with what dignity I could muster. 'He has run away.' I was sorry for the child, of course. But most of all I felt the binoculars of Jamesy, who I knew would be stationed on the River Cliff, having watched my failure with the deepest satisfaction. And Dulcie has witnessed it too, and I feel something is broken that can never be mended.

What have I done? What in God's name have I done?

A week later

I have been feeling very strange. Things that seemed to be solid are not. What is life but a story that tells itself, becomes incoherent, lapses into silence . . .

Control.

The facts, now.

After luncheon on the day I did . . . that absurdity with the paper bag, I took to my bed. I woke later, with a headache. Carruthers had vanished, and could not be found. Next day I made enquiries on the estate, and pieced together this alarming story.

Carruthers had taken refuge in the Temple of the Graces on the River Cliff, where he had lain in a state approaching his old catatonia. But not identical with it. For now he was capable of an odd, extreme sort of functioning. He had chased away several people who had gone to reason with him. He had perched in the temple dome, flinging slates at all comers, gibbering with rage. Finally, he had asked for Pegeen Murphy the milkmaid. Pegeen, brave girl (kind and motherly, beautiful too, in her pink-and-brown fashion) had gone in and soothed him. Soothed him indeed to such effect that he had come out of his eyrie, and they had vanished together nobody knew where for some days. The sequel seems to have been as follows.

When they reappeared, the first person they met as they walked arm in arm down the road was Jamesy, with his walking stick and his Norfolk jacket. Carruthers hunched his shoulders and tried to push past him. But Jamesy halted him with his big, soft hand.

'I just wanted to say,' said Jamesy, the hound, 'that I heard what the Doctor is after doing, and I am sorry for it, very sorry indeed.' His voice was quiet, by all accounts, full of that authority he can put on like a thief's mask. 'And if you need anywhere to stay, you can stay with me.'

'Oh, no,' says the young man, and him one tic and twitch all over his face and body. 'Peggy and I are to be married. We're on the way to ask her father.'

Jamesy's face went still as anything. He said, 'Well, the best of luck with it. Any trouble, my offer stands.'

The young man nodded, and Pegeen dropped Jamesy a curtsey, and away they went, the British officer and the milkmaid, to tell her father the old Shinner how they planned to live happily ever after.

The Murphy house is on the mountain, long and low and white, with a thatched roof in good repair and barns flung like arms round a yard still half-full of muck from last winter. Patrick Murphy, Pegeen's father, was sitting by the door of the house with a few of Pegeen's brothers when the young lovers came into the yard. So up goes Carruthers, twitching like a bag of rabbits, and says, 'Mr Murphy?'

Paddy looked at Carruthers from under the one thick eyebrow that ran from his left temple to his right. He did not tell Carruthers he was welcome, as custom demanded. Being a foreigner, Carruthers did not notice. Peggy did, though. She reined back as if her father had slapped her. She was going to say something, but Carruthers got in first. 'Mr Murphy,' says he, in a voice like a circular saw in a thick log, 'I love your daughter, and she loves me, and I have the honour to request her hand in marriage.'

Paddy gave him a look, and then his daughter. He said, 'Never.'

'But Mr Murphy—'

'This is the way of it,' said Paddy, looking at his feet. 'I have no doubt that you are a grand fella in your own country, and all that, and no offence to you. But no daughter of mine will marry a British officer.'

Carruthers now apparently went a silvery white colour. His mouth was hanging open. He said, 'You can't do this.'

Paddy said, 'I am after doing it.'

'Daddy!' screams Pegeen, and would have said a lot more, but two of her brothers, Danny the roadmender and Joe from the smithy, took her one by the arms and the other by the legs, and they carried her away and they locked her in the house.

When the Lieutenant saw this beginning to happen, he jumped on Danny to stop him. But Patrick gave him a great clout on the ear that sent him sprawling in the muck. Pegeen was yelling blue murder as they carted her round the corner. The Lieutenant tried to get up. But Paddy put his great boot on his neck, and there was nothing the

Lieutenant could do about it, him having been ill, not to mention Victor and Dessie Murphy, the other two boys, holding one his arms and the other his legs.

'Now,' said Patrick. 'I'm sorry it has come to this. But you stay away from Pegeen, is that clear? Because if you do not, I know men who will take it amiss.' At that moment, the door of the house opened and a man came out wearing a motoring cap and a handkerchief over his face. He carried a Lee-Enfield in his hands, all gleaming with oil and in perfect shooting trim, as the Lieutenant would certainly have recognised. The man worked the rifle's bolt. He pressed the muzzle into the Lieutenant's leg, just above the knee, until it ground against the long bone. Then he pulled the trigger.

The Lieutenant screamed. But instead of there being an explosion, the gun said only, '*Click.*'

'Next time you come around Pegeen, there's a bullet inside,' said Paddy. 'All right?'

Carruthers lay there with the muck in his thick dark hair. He was crying. They put him on the back of a cart, and took him back down the mountain and rolled him into the ditch by the Malpas gate lodge.

After a while, he felt able to crawl down the avenue. But he did not come to me. He dragged himself to the Kennels to see Jamesy, and Jamesy got him cleaned up and able to speak, a gift he used (I heard) to issue vile and unreasonable threats against me, as the man who had put him in this state. A month later, there was a rumour that he was staying with Maurice Devereux above at Tourtane. A month or two after that, there was a story that he had taken employment with a group of Special Constables sent over by the British Parliament, known in the vernacular as the Black and Tans. I know that Dulcie has tried to write to him. But I saw yesterday morning her letter to him on the hall table, marked Return to Sender – Fenian scum.

I think now that Jamesy was right. Carruthers is not cured – perhaps he never will be. Perhaps there is no such thing as a cure. Perhaps madness is the only sane response to a world that is itself mad. Perhaps I am mad to love Dulcie.

But at the bottom of everything I do, I do.

Letter from Dave Walker to Professor George Gale, Dept. of Further Psychology, Helmstone University.

Dear George,

I hope that all is well at Helmstone. Did you get my recent letter with enclosures? You may have noticed that I have not been around for a while. This is because I have been deeply involved in the work of Peter Costelloe, a pre-Freudian with those journals and casebooks I am currently pressing ahead. I sent you an account of his treatment of a case presenting autistic features.

Please tell me if you received the material. I know you are going to find this very interesting.

Yours

Dave.

Actually, it was not true that I was pressing ahead. The truth of the matter was that I had come to the end of the volumes in the Laboratory. I needed the last five, borrowed by Jamesy in 1917 and apparently never returned. Finbarr would have them, if anyone would.

But Finbarr had hypnotised me and threatened me with death. When he passed me on the avenue in his nice new Land Rover, he grinned and waved, affable as the parish priest. But I stood there with two handfuls of cold sweat, telling myself it could not have happened, but thinking always of Steve, blue, drowned, and dreading the big, blank Malpas nights.

It did not help that Helen was silent and preoccupied. When I asked her what the trouble was, she said, 'Money.'

'Sell Finbarr's Land Rover.'

She said, 'Shut up about Finbarr.'

'One question.'

Her eyebrows went up. It was not a good sign.

'Where was Finbarr the morning Steve's body was found?'

'Oh, for God's *sake.*' Pause. 'He got up and went swimming in the Lake, which he always does. There was no-one within two miles of the Herring Weir, and Steve had been in the water not more than half an hour when Paddy found him. Are you happy now?'

'Delighted.'

'So stop being such an old misery and come and see what I've found.'

She led me along the terrace to a room I had never visited before. Its French windows were heavily whitewashed. Inside were a diesel concrete mixer, half a horsedrawn lawn mower, and a Canadian canoe, painted red. 'Grab an end,' she said.

As we lifted the canoe, powdery woodworm dust floated in a shaft of sun. We parked Hannah with Angela, dragged the canoe to the House Creek, and set off downriver.

The tide was ebbing fast, the banks showing all around. Helen reclined in the front of the canoe, wielding a small, ragged parasol she had dug up from somewhere, making Edwardian conversation, one knee up, the skin of her ankle blue-white between the cuff of her jeans and her tennis shoe. We slid through the channels the river had plaited in the shingle banks.

After a couple of miles the banks drew apart. We were off Malpas land now. There seemed to be a lightening of the atmosphere, though it might only have been that the river was getting wider. Then we turned a corner.

Suddenly the sky was no longer a roof on a trench of woods, but a blue bowl, mountainous with clouds. And there across the estuary, low and clear behind its quays, dragged by distance out of squalor and into a Canaletto, was Dunquin.

Helen said, with a sort of sigh, 'I'd forgotten about daylight.'

We took the canoe to the quay, and went to Power's for crab claws and thick black pints of Murphy. We sat there for a long time, forgetting about Malpas, and everything except each other. It felt to me as if we were playing truant. I think to her too, though Helen being Helen, she never would have admitted it. 'We'll do it again,' she said.

The tide would have turned. I put my head out of the door. The sky had blackened over, and an evil wind was coming down the estuary in white-frosted squalls. The canoe itself was half full of water. As I came back from my inspection, Helen met me. 'I've rung Finbarr,' she said. 'I told him to come and get us.'

'Ah.' I did not want to see Finbarr.

'He said he was busy,' she said. 'I told him to do as he was damn well bid. Power,' she said, grinning. 'I love it.' She kissed my mouth. 'And you.'

Finbarr showed up one and a half pints later, with a lower lip like a church doorstep. He refused a drink without looking at me. We loaded the canoe onto his nice new Land Rover, and he drove us sulkily home while we sang rebel songs in the passenger seat, holding hands.

When we unloaded the canoe in front of the house, its main spar broke in half, perished with woodworm. We stood in the thin rain that had started to fall, and looked at the wreckage. 'Won't be doing that again,' said Finbarr, more cheerful now.

'We'll find a way,' I said, whistling in the dark. Helen took my hand. We went into the house.

Next morning I was unsettled and worried, with not enough work to do in the absence of the casebook volumes. I had to make something happen. I guessed that Finbarr would not be well disposed to a request for books in his possession, if it came from me. So at eleven o'clock one morning I waded up the avenue and hammered on Emily's door.

In her drawing room, she poured doses of Paddy and lit a Senior Service, while I wondered where to start. She said, 'How lovely that you're still here. What have you been up to?'

'Reading,' I said. 'About your husband and Peter Costelloe.'

'And Finbarr tells me you're looking for the Crown of Tara.'

'Does he?'

'He tells me just about everything.'

I wondered whether that included threats against my person. I said, 'Did you ever hear of it?'

'It was always the thing that was going to turn up to save Malpas. Even when Peter Costelloe was alive.'

I came forward in my chair and said, 'Really?'

She said, 'You know it's wonderful to find someone who's actually interested in all this.' She lit a new cigarette. 'One didn't need any crowns with Jamesy here, of course,' she said. 'He was terribly talented at helping people. We made an absolute packet out of it. Syphilis, a lot of them. Paresis. They'd say brain fever, dementia, anything not to have to confess that they'd jumped into bed with a tart. But you could always tell. They had pupils different sizes, couldn't stand up with their eyes closed without toppling over. In a good week it was like having a houseful of ninepins. And shell shock, of course, and oh my God melancholics and neurasthenics and you name it. He was awfully good with them. Much better than the Doctor. The Doctor was the one who needed things like crowns or football pools or something. He may have been a great scientist, I don't know, but he was a very strange little man.'

I said, 'He and your husband didn't get on.'

Emily pulled the corners of her mouth down. Through pressure of memories or whiskey, her bright mood was curdling. 'Faults on both sides,' she said. 'What you might not have worked out is that the Doctor had more spikes on him than a hedgehog. I won't say that Jamesy was perfect, sure. But the Doctor taught him his hobby horses and then expected him to stay his assistant for ever after. Jamesy was in awe of him, too, at the beginning.'

I said, 'But I've been reading that they couldn't be in the same room together.'

She put her head back against the sofa, and let the smoke trickle out of her nostrils and into her white meringue of hair. She said, 'That was partly me.'

'I'm sorry?'

The eyelids were like grey paper. Her mood had gone altogether. 'You know what really went wrong, don't you?'

'No.'

'He tried to rape me,' she said.

'*What?*'

'He had a go. He wanted to get back at James because the Refuge was doing so well. You don't believe me, do you?'

The Doctor had been a man of powerful mind, betrayed by circumstances. Rape? Not him.

I said, as non-committally as I could, 'That's terrible.'

Her eyes would not meet mine. 'And Jamesy found out.'

'And Dulcie?'

She looked up at me. 'Dulcie was a prostitute,' she hissed.

I was shocked by her vehemence. 'What do you mean?'

'It doesn't matter,' she said. 'It doesn't at all. James died in 1930, you know. Heart.'

I nodded, trying to keep track of her thoughts, which were skidding under the influence of anger and Paddy.

She nodded. 'You would never have guessed he had one,' she said. 'Except when he was with the boy. My elder son. Tim. Timsy, we called him. Jamesy and Timsy. Finbarr came later. Much later. An accident, posthumous, poor darling. Tim was Jamesy's assistant, for a while. But it all closed down after Jamesy died. He went away. Nothing was the same, you know. He worked in England, Ireland, everywhere. In variety theatre, can you believe it? On the halls. Theatre Royal Norwich. The Great Mentalini. Thank God Jamesy never saw it. You'd be terrifically interested.'

'So what's become of Tim?' I said.

'He died,' she said. 'Last year. Heart. Like his father.' She looked up at me. 'I do so love my boys,' she said. 'You don't get on with Finbarr, do you?'

I shrugged, I think. There was no polite answer.

'Quarrels over women,' she said.

'Women?'

She shook her head. I had no idea what she was talking about. There was a distant look in her eye, as if she wanted to float off elsewhere on the Paddy. I said, 'Actually, I'm looking for some books missing from the Laboratory. Your husband borrowed them and never gave them back.'

'Not here,' she said. 'Definitely not. Ask Finbarr. Oh, talk of the devil.'

The door opened. Finbarr came in. 'Mummy,' he said, and took her hand and kissed it, an odd, old-fashioned gesture. Then he turned his foxy face on me. 'Detecting, is it?' he said. 'What is it you're after this time?'

I said, 'Helen's probably told you, I'm doing a bit of research into the time when this was all a rest home. I had an idea that maybe some of Peter Costelloe's records are still in your house somewhere?'

The eyes slid away. He said, 'That owd stuff.'

'You've got it?'

'We took it out,' he said. 'Burned it, I'd say. As my mother well knows. Forgetful in her old age, you know?' The eyes still did not meet mine. 'Sorry about that,' he said.

'Oh, well,' I said. 'Can't be helped.'

'Not by you,' he said, with a small, unnecessary flash of malice.

As I walked down the path, my spirits were high. The malicious flash had done it. I did not believe that Finbarr had burned his grandfather's records any more than I believed Emily's rape story. He was not frightening any more. He was just a mean-minded twerp whom I had caught in a lie.

A beam of sun slanted out of the west. It lit up the windows of the house and turned its cliffs of mouldy ashlar to ramparts of gold. The darkness of the week rolled away with the clouds. I walked into the kitchen and the golden present of Hannah in her high chair and Helen's powerful alto ringing among the damp cobwebs of the vaulting. I kissed everyone in sight, and got kissed back. It was no hardship not to mention Finbarr. After lunch, Hannah went to bed, and Helen and I talked about the casebooks. She said, 'Why didn't Grandpa leave?'

'He loved his family.'

'Grandma was in love with Jamesy. Plain as the nose on your face. Warm hands, giving him the Kennels, all that. You can trust her to go where the power is. She did it with Grandpa.'

I stared at her. Now she came to mention it, it was obvious. 'But why would Peter Costelloe sit around and put up with it?'

'There's something Grandpa's not talking about. The things Mairi knows that nobody else seems to. Don't you get the idea that Grandpa's protecting Granny from something?'

'Or she's got some sort of hold over him.'

She said, 'Well, they're dead, and we shall never know. Now for the benefit of the living I should do some framing. I've got the show next weekend.'

'Do you want me to come?'

'Would you ever be here and look after Hannah?'

'Of course.'

She kissed me, and put her arms around me. She said, 'I don't have to go back to work straight away. And there's something upstairs I'd like some help with.'

'Oh?'

'In the bedroom.'

'Ah.'

Like I said. A normal, happy family.

Give or take a secret or two.

Chapter Nineteen

Malpas Church[1]

Descend through the woods. Gleams of water lie across the land ahead – dark, sinister, ruffled with strange winds that come from nowhere and moan in the trees. In front of you is a low wall. Beyond it, a field of brambles, in which teeth of stone stand at vexed and sinister angles. In the middle of the brambles, a church rises. It is one of those churches that were regulation issue to the Church of Ireland in the nineteenth century – a crenellated tower, slatted Gothic windows hiding a belfry never at the best of times tenanted by ringers, now the home of owls and bats and great dark moths that make the night tremulous with their whirrings.

This is Malpas church.

Like all churches – even Protestant ones – it has seen its share of baptisms and weddings. And funerals. Of course, funerals.

Now, the church is in ruins, the tombstones higgledy-piggledy in the ground. The only thing in good repair is a long, low building with a roof of massy copper, sunk eaves-deep in the ground by the churchyard's eastern wall. A path leads to it through the brambles. It is hard to see what use this path can be. For it leads only to the locked bronze doors of a family vault. The Costelloe family vault. And hereabouts the name of Costelloe, that once resounded in the valley, has died away until it is nothing but the tiny ghost of an echo in this huge, quiet land.

Only the vault remains. And the . . . presences . . . therein.

From the Casebooks of Peter Costelloe

I remember well how cross Dulcie was when Sir Francis arrived on

---

[1]   *Haunted Munster*, Abraham le Poer Hill, Pan Books, 1973

Jesse's birthday two years ago. Since that frightful business of Carruthers, I do not want to vex her again, and I am determined to be a good father in every respect. Today was his birthday, and we went together to the Temple of the Graces. There is a simple delight in his company that I have long found missing in the company of others.

Jack the terrier came too, of course. Both of them very much like a picnic, so Dulcie being busy I asked Cook to put up some things in a basket. We scuffled about for twigs, took wood from the iron-doored log press under the floor, and made a great fire in the range. Jess fried some kidneys and bacon, which we ate at the Roman marble table Desmond's grandfather brought back from the Grand Tour. Jack had a kidney of his own, smuggled to him by Jess – a shocking crime but one forgivable, I thought, on a birthday.

As always, we talked. I make it my business to inform Jess of things strange to Frau Bildt. He now seems more interested in the world beyond the demesne wall than in what takes place inside it – an excellent tendency, and one I shall encourage.

I shall set down for posterity a pen-portrait of my son in his ninth year. He is a tall lad, with dark hair, introspective grey eyes and a cream-coloured skin much freckled. He is more inclined to the pursuits of the mind than to the outdoor life. His hands are long and narrow, unusually clean for a boy of his age, well adapted to his favourite pursuit of playing the piano. He takes after neither of his parents.

But this is by nature of a digression. Perhaps I have been describing the dear child at such length in order to delay recounting the horrors of the day. Actually, it was he who drew my attention to their first signs.

We had just finished washing the dishes at the spring that comes from the little carved dolphin under the gazebo, and were stowing them in the cupboard. We had piled all the remaining wood on the fire, according to custom. Malpas lay spread below, a doll's house in a green map blotched blood-red by clumps of rhododendron.

'Papa,' said Jesse. 'What's that?'

From the green canopy of trees to the east there rose a strand of black smoke. Even as we watched, the strand became a plume, the plume a long, rolling cloud. 'Slaughterbridge,' I said. We ran down the hill to Malpas.

In the house, no-one had yet heard the news. I took up my medical bag and threw it into the dickey of the Ford. The boy said, 'Can I come, papa?'

'No.'

I saw his face fall; it was his birthday, after all. 'Please.'

But my eye had been caught by something else. High on the green river-cliff was a bright orange point of flame. 'Did we put out the fire?' said I.

'No.'

Our Temple of the Graces was burning. We gazed upon it for a moment. It was too late to do anything, of course. There was no-one in danger, and the woods around were wet enough not to take fire, God knows. But the knowledge that our eyrie was ruined left something ashy in my heart. I trod on the self-starter. Only when we were on the road did I notice that Jess was still in the car. Perhaps part of his innocence had gone with the Temple. In this fearful country, the rest would not be long following. Well, I thought: so be it.

The Drumquin fire brigade was screeching into the Slaughterbridge avenue as we came round the corner under the trees. The air was filled with a steady crackling roar. Black motes whirled in the sky above the trees. The avenue was the same old weedy strip. In place of the blackbirds were men in clothes bagged at seat and knee with continual wear. They stood on the verges in their thick boots, staring down towards the end of the avenue. I pulled the car off the gravel, and stared myself. There was nothing more constructive to be done.

The house had been blackish-grey, with blank unmullioned windows and that hideous coloured-glass porch. Now, probably for the first time ever, the windows were bright and merry, twinkling red and yellow and orange with the fire inside.

Beside me I heard Jess make a strange, high noise. Then the cymbals of a great orchestra all clashed together at once, and the glass fell in. Fed by the new air, the flames roared out of the windows and up the walls, lighting the Virginia creeper and sending little tongues and jags of fire to dance among the slates.

'Hell of a thing,' said a voice at my side.

I looked round. The speaker was a man in a filthy pinstripe suit. The cap was pulled low on the brow. Beneath it, the flames struck sparks in the single eye of Johnny Cosgrave, of Malpas and (according to rumour) America.

Behind my surprise at seeing him I found a heavy anger. I said, 'Is this something to do with you?'

The flames in his eye went out, then kindled again. He was winking. I felt Jess's small hand grip mine, damp with fear. I should never have allowed him to come. 'There'll be more of it before there's less of it,' said Johnny. 'But I'd say you'd be all right yourself, Doctor.'

I was furious. I said, 'What the hell does that mean?'

Again the flames in the eye-socket came and went.

'Hoy!' said a heavy voice down the avenue. It was Maurice Devereux, bulging out of a suit of thornproof tweed, dragging a hosepipe. 'Lend a hand, there!' he cried. Then he recognised me.

'What needs doing?' I said.

'They all need shooting. And will be shot. Who was that you were talking to?'

'Talking?' I said. In the shadows of the laurel where Johnny had stood was now vacancy.

'Johnny,' piped Jess, at my side.

Devereux' eyes settled on me like cold iron. 'Johnny,' he said, and I could sense him filing it away in my docket with Oweneen and dead Carson. 'And what did Johnny say?'

'He said we'd be—'

I said, 'I'd better go and make myself useful.'

'I shall remember you to Lieutenant Carstairs,' said Devereux, with an odious leer.

I took Jess by the hand, and dragged him down to the sweep in front of the house, before he could hammer any more innocent nails into my coffin.

There are in these times informal categories of arson. In the case of landlords who have friends among the people but who are deemed through possessions or attitude to have earned a burning, warnings may be issued. These may vary in length from the minutes required to pack a bag of clothes and jewels, to the days required to take out pictures and furniture and even marble fireplaces.

But nobody cared about the Caroes, now standing among the debris of their lives. There had been no warning. Mrs Caroe's frumpish gowns and greasy furniture were even now ashes. What had been saved from the blaze stood outside the front door – two hall chairs, and a hatstand still bearing Mr Caroe's macassar-stained bowler.

When he saw me, Caroe waved the bottle in his hand. 'To hell with you!' he cried. 'To hell with you, coming to gloat on innocent people. To fecking hell with you.'

I was taken aback. I said, 'But—'

'Hey!' he roared. 'Agnes! Look who it is!'

His wife still affected the piled hair and long skirts of ten years ago. Now her hair was over one eye, and the hem of her skirt was charred. She glanced at me from a lumpy and soot-smeared face. 'You,' she said. She looked partially mad. I started to say something about my sorrow, shouting against the deafening clatter of the fire engine pumps. I saw the blood mount to her face. 'Why not you?' she screamed. 'Why not *you?*'

A voice from the fire brigade roared, 'Back, lads! She's going!' And back we reeled as the roof fell in. I found I was holding Mrs Caroe's arm. She shook it free, and gave me something half-way between a shove and a clout. I said, 'Where will you go?'

'I have a sister in Hove,' she said. 'We will go to Hove. Coutts' Bank, Hove, will find me. Now trot back to your whore, Doctor Costelloe.'

'And our agreement?'

'Our agreement, our dirty little agreement, stands.' Her eye fell on Maurice Devereux. 'God I shall be glad to be away from whores and sodomites.'

I said, 'There are plenty of both in Hove,' but I was talking to her back. I saw Jamesy, talking to Devereux. They glanced at me, then quickly away. No doubt they were discussing my public testimonial from a *bona fide* Shinner. They will not forgive nor forget.

I put my dear Jess in the passenger seat and drove back to Malpas.

Wearily, we climbed to the Temple. A spark from the over-stoked fire must have landed in some newspaper, which had blown onto the pile of kindling we keep there to start the stove. Only the balustrade remains intact, and the fireplace and log cellar. The rest is black and tumbled ruins.

Jess said, 'It's not fair. On my birthday.'

It is not the duty of a father to tell him that nothing is fair. He will learn soon enough for himself.

I sat with Dulcie tonight. Jess was in the Music Room, playing a Chopin mazurka. The music tumbled through the house, blurring in the high spaces of the ceilings. Dulcie was on her chair, making some mechanical contrivance from parts she keeps on her trolley: a wireless receiver, apparently. I said to her, 'We must think of sending Jess away.'

'He can be perfectly well educated here,' she said.

'I was not thinking about his education.'

Dulcie's face wore its pure, hard look of concentration as she bowed over the delicate machine under her fingers.

'What, then?'

'The political situation.'

She raised her eyes. They were cold as green water. She said, 'I thought you had been careful to make friends with the people you think are the right crowd.'

'The Caroes are leaving for England.'

'I don't see why your friends didn't shoot them while they were about it.'

I must say, I rocked as if she had hit me. I knew that what had been between us has cooled into something less than mere companionship. But she had never spoken with such bitterness before. I said, 'Has something happened to you?'

She said, 'Have you ever noticed, Doctor Costelloe' – she spat out my title as if it were dirt in her mouth – 'that everybody changes except you?'

I walked away, out of that light bath of music and into the lash of the rain. At the end of the colonnade, in my Laboratory, I opened this journal; unable to concentrate, though, looking about me for distraction.

And there upon the bench by the open window was a blue envelope. A new blue envelope, that had not been there before, in a place where a passer-by could have slipped it in.

Over the sound of the rain I heard the clatter of the Lanchester starting. Dulcie on her way out visiting, I supposed. Jesse would be cold and lonely in the nursery with Frau Bildt. But the wellsprings of talk are dead in me, and I have nothing to say, even to him.

The envelope had already been opened. There was a letter inside it, written in a large, childish hand.

Dear John, it said.

Here I am in the stockyards, working away; they have me counting cattle, one hundred and thirty-eight of them this last hour, three with three legs, eighty-one without horns, Hereford Poll I should think. It is lovely here. Hurry out your own self and tell the Doctor I think of him and remember the old times; and that although I am different now I remember it all. It is all thanks to him, and what he did to bring me my mind back, and made me remember . . .

There might have been another page. But this was the one Johnny wanted me to read. Mairi, cured, sending news across the ocean. News of the old time, and of the things she remembers.

I can walk away from the present. But no matter how hard I try, the things that Mairi remembers will haunt me till the day I die.

I screwed up the paper and threw it at the basket. Not that it makes any difference. I can destroy her paper, but I cannot make her unremember the things she has seen.

God help us all.

Walker Archive, Transcript, 1973 – 6
There is a man with a fiddle inside in the bar and another lad Bridie Corrigan's Jerry with the box and they are dancing the Siege of Ennis and God be praised I am above on the table all done up in a three-quarter-length gown of

*white silk with a scoop neck and charmeuse lace sleeves and when I look I can
see my feet which look little o so little in white satin shoes and white silk
stockings, I wanted to wear my good brown dress but Johnny said no, we will
have a white wedding, dear Johnny in his blue suit he is so handsome his hair
brushed just right with a lick of soap and his eye all sparked up like diamonds
and a stiff collar on him, a green tie for Ireland with a gold ring to keep it there
and the ones are all around me now Mary and Bridget and Attracta and
Dymphna and Deirdre my friends and cousins and we are talking and talking
and talking and I do not know what we are saying, not really, because I am
inside in it and outside it at the same time and I can hear the clatter of us like
birds in a tree, not a tree that you will find here in the South Side of Chicago
but maybe a tree behind the Pink House on the River, not the white heron trees,
white as this dress, but the trees south of the house where you will get the
starlings coming in the winter to clatter and natter and kick up their fuss, and
when my mind goes back there I can feel so sad, so sad, that she is not here that
coughed out her lungs into the turf box and my little Doctor, my little Doctor,
that brought me so far from the cage of bars where they kept me when I was
little, and put up another cage of bars in me where I can keep the terrible
things I have seen, and the girls are gone quiet now and are looking at me and
Dymphna is saying o gods sure you're never roaring and Bridget is saying
Happy-come-sad and Mary is giving a big wink and saying Just you wait for
later on when yer man gets you on the bed, then you will see is it happy or sad
and I'd say Happy as Larry, but Johnny's here looking out for me like he does
and laughing and saying ah sheddep youse and getting me by the hand and
away I go with him, and yer man on the box is up up and away and I am
dancing, not all quick and pretty like the other girls but moving so steady and
fine and Johnny too, and we must be happy because this is our wedding day
and Johnny must be on the Limited in the morning, and away, away to finish
the job in Ireland and God knows when he will be back but we must not talk
about it just now, I must put it in the cage room with the terrible things I have
seen, so I must store them up and be away from Malpas, far, far away, like a
press you would fill with your bad secrets and put in the river to float away
down to the broad sea, where no-one would find it at all, but now we are away
away and I have thrown my bouquet and my great Johnny is taking me off, he
is after picking me out of the turf box and putting me in Chicago and one day*

when all is quiet in that quarter and Ireland a nation once again we will go back to the Pink House, the roses are out on the door says Johnny, and now it is all quiet, and from the room here above you can still hear the box small and thin like the buzz of a fly in a window, and it is just Johnny and me and the things I know, for ever . . .

Letter to George Gale

Dear George,

I have suddenly realised that it is already summer term, and that I am nowhere near Helmstone. I hope this is okay with you. My research here is proving very interesting. Did you get my last letter? As a sample I am enclosing some more notes on Mairi D, the autistic/obsessive, in the hope that you will agree with me that this is intensely important material.

Yrs

Dave

This letter writing stemmed from a Thursday breakfast time. I had been posting toast soldiers into Hannah. Thrushes were hopping on the lawn.

Helen said, 'Hasn't your term begun?'

'What's the date?'

'Fifteenth of May. Are you going back?'

Actually, term had been going for a month.

I said, 'Do you want me to?'

She said, 'Won't you get into trouble? I mean what about your grant?'

I said, 'That should be all right.' I had no way of telling, of course; Gale had so far failed to answer four letters. Frankly, I did not care. 'I thought I'd stick around until I heard, anyway.' That was not quite true. Real life was here, now, with my child and her mother.

'That's Malpas,' said Helen, wagging a finger. 'The death of aspiration.'

I said, 'And of course you're all ready for Fermoy.'

For some reason, she blushed. 'Oh, shit, Fermoy,' she said. We went and spent a merry evening drinking slightly too much wine while we wrapped her pictures up in old newspapers. Next day I swept out the farm van and mopped it with bleach. I helped her load up the paintings, kissed her goodbye, and watched her rattle off up the avenue. Then I put Hannah in the pram and went and found Angela. That was the great thing about Angela. You always knew where to find her, and she was always good company. Good company was what there was a shortage of at Malpas.

She left her mother in the care of the cleaning lady. We went over the terraces and across the bottom lawn towards the coal quay, Hannah standing up and holding the pram sides like a small bargee. We pushed her to the screen of laurels that hid the old gasworks from the house. I spread my leather jacket on the wet grass, and took Hannah out. She immediately got busy pulling seedheads off the grass. Angela sat down with her arms wrapped around her shins and her knees under her chin.

I said, 'You had an affair with Steve.'

She gave me her broad-faced smile. It made her look a little as she had in the picture over her mother's bed. 'I did not,' she said. A cream satin strap had strayed into the neck of her T-shirt. She was one of those women for whom nakedness was only a nanometre away, no matter how many clothes she was wearing. A cynic might have said she was on the make, looking for a passport out of an intolerable situation. I was not a cynic. I really liked her. The unconscious sexiness was part of what I liked. 'You love Helen,' she said.

'Yep.'

The smile went. 'Well, that's a pity,' she said. 'Because I could really fancy you, you know that?'

'If things had been different . . .' I said, and as I heard the words come out of my mouth I realised I was only speaking half out of politeness.

'Maybe they are,' she said.

'What?'

The question did not get answered. Her eyes had gone past my shoulder. 'Dave,' she said, in an odd, cramped voice.

The space behind the laurel hedge was a green lawn. The gasworks

208

was underground, entered from a sort of trench. Between the trench and the laurels was a forty-foot disc of green that could have been a lawn, if any lawn at Malpas had been that tidy. In fact it was the moss-grown top of the gasometer, empty, descended to ground level. And standing in the geometrical centre of the disc in her going-for-a-walk outfit of pink bobble hat, blue coat and small red gumboots, was my daughter Hannah.

I stood up.

'Don't go on there,' said Angela. 'It's destroyed with rust. There's ten foot of water below.'

Hannah, having caught my eye, gave me a vast, peg-toothed grin. This was a personal best for outdoor standing, and she wished all present to note the fact.

'Hannah!' I said.

She bent her knees like a downhill racer and pogoed vigorously. 'Ba!' she cried triumphantly. The gasometer top made a dull splitting noise. Across the green disc there had appeared a long, dark line of a crack.

I croaked, 'Hannah.'

Hannah bounced again. The line broadened and narrowed as the rotten iron flexed.

'*Hannah*,' I said, over the thunder of my heart. 'Come here.'

She waved her arms and sat down, harder than she had intended. She started to cry.

'Gods,' said Angela. 'What now?'

I went to the edge of the gasometer furthest from the crack. I squatted down and pulled a biscuit out of my pocket. Hannah stopped crying, got up on her hands and feet, spreading her weight, clever girl, and began to spider-walk towards me. Five more scuttles and she would have been there. But her hand slipped and she fell on her nose and began to cry properly. I held out the biscuit. She shouted louder. I knew her well enough to be sure that this was the end. Unless someone went to fetch her she would now stay where she had fallen for the rest of history.

'Sit on my feet,' I said to Angela. I lay in the grass and wormed my way out onto the disc, waiting for the crack and split that would have us both swimming in ten feet of toxic water below. When I was lying flat out, I groped onwards with my fingers until they touched the cloth of Hannah's coat. I got a handful, and pulled.

Out by the crack, metal ground on metal. Hannah was sliding towards me. I lifted her and threw her at Angela. Then I rolled onto the edge.

There was a brief moment of silence, during which Hannah turned purple, and a sheet of cold sweat flowed over my body. The metal made a sound somewhere between a creak and a ping. The crack vanished. Hannah began to roar.

'Well,' said Angela, once Hannah was back in the pram and sucking a biscuit. 'He nearly had you killed that time.'

I sat and waited for my heart to come back to normal. The blood brought with it a warm flush of affection for Angela. If she had not been there, Hannah would have been dead. Well, both of us. But it was Hannah that mattered.

We walked back towards the house. It had started to rain. I put up an umbrella. After a while, my knees stopped shaking. I said, 'Angela, I don't know how to thank you. Can I buy you a drink tonight?'

She said, 'Of all the invitations, and I bloody can't. I've got to take the mother to stay with some cousins. Next week.' She kissed my cheek. 'Monday, though. Come to the house at six o'clock.'

I said, 'I'll be there. Take the umbrella.'

'Are you sure?' She took it, and ran.

I put Hannah to bed, and asked Margaret the daily to listen out for her. After the horrors had come a sort of euphoria. Outside the house, the River Cliff trees gave off a fresh green steam. You could almost hear the creak of leaves growing. I decided to fetch back the umbrella. I went out into this dazzle and turned up towards the Dower House. For the first time that year, there was real heat in the sun. I loved Helen, and I had a true friend in Angela. I felt ludicrously full of the joys of spring.

Which is why I went not up the drive to her front door, but through the park, where the grass was long and green and lush, and the raindrops sparkled in diamond fans when I kicked the tufts.

That was how they did not hear me.

I heard them, though.

At first I could not work out what it was that I was hearing. I heard a man's voice, grunting. There was a sort of pavilion at the bottom of the slope leading up to the Dower House garden. It was a detached part of the garden, a hundred yards into the park from the gate, a little onion-domed kiosk half-buried in a rashly planted Paul's Himalayan Musk rose. Steps ran up to the door, and the stone seat inside. To left and right of it were large, straggling rosemary bushes. The door was open. On the top step, framed with dreadful symmetry by the onion dome, the path, and the rosemary bushes, lit in razor-sharp chiaroscuro by the brilliant spring sun, was the back of a woman. The woman was facing away from me. She was wearing a cream satin slip and nothing else. She was straddling the lap of a man. The heads were in shadow. All I could see of the man was a pair of hairy shins, and a pair of hands kneading the woman's white buttocks where they appeared below the hem of the slip. Finbarr's hands. All I could see of the woman was her back, narrow-waisted, and the hips, which were churning powerfully. Finbarr put out his hand to brace himself on the door pillar. A branch of rose flopped across the woman's back. Its thorns hooked the slip and tore across the skin. Finbarr batted it away. The woman writhed harder, silent, concentrating. Three drops of blood came through the creamy fabric.

I stood there for half an hour, though I did not breathe, nor did my heart beat, so it was probably more like half a second. Then I walked back to the laboratory.

Quarrels over women, Emily had said, and I had thought she was mad. Mad like Einstein. In her ancient cynicism, she had presumed there was something between me and Angela. But she had also known that Angela was having an affair with Finbarr.

Bloody Angela, collecting men like stamps.

Well, if Emily thought I was a sucker for Angela, she was wrong. I had Helen and Hannah. I had nothing to be angry about.

But I was angry, all right.

Chapter Twenty

From the Casebooks of Peter Costelloe
Since the Slaughterbridge horror, I have told Dulcie I am turning over a new leaf. She nodded, without looking at me. I think she is relieved, but we have grown so far apart I cannot tell.

These are the resolutions that go to make up the new leaf:

I will take no strong drink or drug. I will bring up my son to think, not have prejudices. I will present to him the appearance of a happily married man. I will take an interest in the running of the estate. I will strive to make a friend of Jamesy again. And I will dismiss from my mind the horrors over which Mairi Cosgrave stands guard.

Easier said than done, you will say. Read on.

This morning I set off on my round. It started well. I noted in my book that the stags, each with his group of hinds, are healthy. The harvest is complete. The foresters are waiting the fall of the leaves to start thinning Brady's Plantation. There is no rebuilding yet in the Temple of the Graces. But Dulcie says, rightly – when was she not right? – that first things must come first, and there is not the money nor the labour to rebuild such fripperies. But that is not how it appears to Jesse or me, damn her heartlessness—

But this is supposed to be a level-headed sort of catalogue.

I took a cot from the House Creek and rowed across the river to visit old Eileen Cosgrave, Johnny's cousin. In the absence of Johnny and Mairi Dugdale she has brought some of her own family to reside with her. They have taken on the fishing, which they seem to do well enough – the tally of fish caught is if not accurate at least probable. She plied me with strong tea, and showed me a picture-postcard sent by

Johnny from Chicago. 'Look,' she said, pointing to the postmark, dated ten days ago. 'Isn't it good, so fast?'

'Very good,' I said, feeling my heart turn to lead. There had been another burning three days ago near Youghal. The word was that it was the column to which Johnny was attached. I was being shown an alibi, and would be expected to transmit it to my influential friends.

She brought tea while I went through the salmon book, and a most delicious knot of soda bread spread with honey from the bees on the banks of heather that line the river-cliff margins here. We sat on the net-mending bench, and looked across the black water at the House. The sun shone down, and curlews cried. It was easy for a moment to forget the trouble across the water. The Cosgraves have a gift for going with the current of things. We talked for a while about eels and salmon.

Then into this discourse there burst, once I was safely lulled, a harder note.

'And the Crown of Tara,' said Mrs Cosgrave, her broad face shining with purely academic interest. 'You'd have it by you still, with the troubles and all?'

I remember leaning my head upon the stone wall of the cottage, tired, feeling the sun on my face. 'There are certain things that belong in certain places,' I said. 'The Crown will be one of them.'

'You wouldn't give it up to the Government of Ireland?'

'Which Government of Ireland?' This was the time when Dail Eireann was set up in opposition to the British government. The Dail was unrecognised by some of the population, the British administration by the rest. There was plenty of law in Ireland, but no order at all.

'Right, so,' breathed Mrs Cosgrave. I could see that she was desperate to know about it: how much gold, what jewels. But I was tired of being exploited. I preferred to keep her in ignorance. Out of vanity, of course – the same vanity, perhaps, that sent me creeping up behind Tom Carruthers with my brown-paper bag.

I left with Johnny's alibi, the salmon books and the good wishes of all Cosgraves, and rowed across the river.

I was checking the young pheasants in the Kennel Wood when I heard a sort of crashing. In times like these, it is worth being circumspect when approaching strange noises, even in woods close to home. So I waited in a wet rhododendron as the crashing drew nearer, which it did in a curious, mazy fashion, as if someone was having difficulty negotiating the clear areas between the shrubs. Eventually I caught sight of something blue and white beyond the trunk of an oak. This resolved itself into a woman in pyjamas, wading through a thicket of brambles.

Her face was blotched and puffy, her pale-blonde hair awry, and she was weeping. She seemed to be having great trouble in staying upright. I came out of my bush and said, 'Can I help at all?'

She stopped. She swayed, shuffling her bramble-scratched feet as if the ground was moving. To my astonishment, she was surrounded by a sort of fog of alcohol.

'Where have you come from?' I said.

She wiped away tears, smearing dirt over her face. 'Dr Durcan's Academy and Lounge Bar,' she said, and sat down suddenly in the brambles.

I gave her my hand. She consented to being hauled to her feet. I said, 'What are you doing in your pyjamas?'

'I am preparing,' she said, 'to be psychoanananananalysed. According to the principles of Dr Freud of Vienna because of my ferocity complex. In these cases Doctor Durcan says patient becomes more receptive post exhibition of ethyl alcohol. Also forthcoming. Pie-eyed for a week. No fresh air. Came for a walk. My name is Beryl Muspratt. How do you do?'

She looked unhappy and vulnerable, her white breasts loose beneath the pyjama coat. Alcohol, forsooth! Jamesy, you quack. 'We'll get you back,' I said.

She shuddered theatrically. She was a big girl, with wide outdoor shoulders. Caught when she had not been drunk for a week, she would have seemed strong and wholesome. 'Oh dear,' she said. '*Oh* dear. Doc Durc won't like it. Psychowhatthehellisis matter of mutual consent. Unconscious hatred of father leads to slide down drainpipe. I do not want any more drink. Please. I *hate* drink. Loathe and bominate it and this is not fair.'

My resolutions dissolved in a tide of anger. It was all very well cultivating Jamesy, but this was too much. The poor girl should have been riding to hounds, not rotting in the Kennels.

A stout man in a tweed suit was sitting in the little lodge by the back door of the Kennels. He smelt of drink, but he had no therapeutic excuse. 'Sullivan, you are drunk, and I am not here,' I said, and went past him. The interior walls of the Kennels were brick, painted in gloss, slime green below, pus yellow above. 'Where's your room?' I said to the girl.

She took my hand and led me on. From behind a closed door came the sound of a man crying.

'Here,' she said.

It was not so much a room as a cell. There was a fixed bed, linoleum on the floor, a hard chair bolted down, a rubber carafe, a window heavily barred. There were no personal possessions. She sat down on the bed. I was frankly horrified. I said, 'Do you know why you are here?'

'I fell in love, you see. So unsuitable, my stepmother said. Docker Durcan says I am in love because I am jealous of my stepmother because she is hem hem you know with my father. Docker Durcan is going to psycho me and then my stepmother and me can be the best of friends. But actually if this is mad I'd rather be mad.' She started to cry again.

I found I was angry. It is medieval to send a girl to an asylum for such a reason. And it is still worse – if fashionable in America – to warp a normal brain with alcohol before setting to work with Dr Freud's home-made tool kit.

'I want to go home,' said the girl.

I gave her a drink of water from the rubber carafe. I said, 'Where are your clothes?'

'They took them away.'

The door opened. A big woman came in. Her black hair was slicked down with some sort of grease, and she carried a bottle of whiskey in her hand. She opened her mouth to tell me to go to hell. Then she realised who I was, and her expression became sickly sweet. 'Doctor,' she said, very surprised.

'We'll be needing the patient's clothes.'

She set down the whiskey bottle. 'I'll fetch 'em.'

I did not want her going off on her own, in case she met Jamesy, and felt impelled to explain herself. I said, 'I'll go with you.' As we left the room, I heard a crash of breaking glass from the yard below the window. Miss Muspratt had taken her revenge on the whiskey.

The nurse unlocked a dividing door with brown leather padding shredded at fingernail height. Beyond the door the smell changed from whiskey and sweat to polish and flowers. There was a Turkey runner on the floor and portraits of prize cattle on the walls. There was a room lined with lockers, each locker with a cardholder on its door, a card in each holder and on each card a name. The nurse went to the one bearing Miss Muspratt's name.

'All the clothes,' I said. 'And her valise.'

'All?'

I did not answer. There were voices in the house, soft and low. One of them was Jamesy's. That should have been the one that alarmed me, here in his own house, while I took it upon myself to discharge one of his patients.

But it was the other voice that froze me in my shoes.

Jamesy's voice said, 'When again?'

'Soon,' said the voice. 'When your man's away. Thursday night, I'd say.'

'The whole night?'

'All of it. Darling.'

I walked out of the roomful of lunatic's clothes with its smell of sweat and mothballs. I walked onto the landing that ran gallery-like round the hall of the private quarters of Jamesy's asylum. I looked over the edge and into the hall.

There were two people down there. One of them was Jamesy in a heather-mixture suit, trilby in hand. The other, holding his head and kissing him on the mouth while the sun made a bonfire out of her hair, was Dulcie.

217

Dulcie, to whom I had been married for ten years. The mother of my son. The mainspring of my life, without whom everything would have happened differently.

Everything.

I took the clothes to poor Miss Muspratt. I shouldered her valise and walked her to my Laboratory. There I gave her black coffee, and wrote a letter to her father. Then I called for the car and had her taken down to Dunquin Station and bought a ticket.

After that, I cancelled my plans to go away on Thursday night.

At home, Dulcie was much the same as usual. We both speak to little Jess. But we do not speak to each other directly. I am hurt. God, I am hurt. She is all I ever wanted. I gave up so much to get her and did so much to keep her. But of course I could not volunteer anything.

The chance presented itself in the drawing room at teatime.

She was pouring tea. She said, 'I couldn't find you this afternoon.'

I fixed her green eye. 'I was at the Kennels,' I said.

'So was I.' The amber stream from the pot stayed steady. 'One of Jamesy's patients got out.'

'I let her go.'

She frowned, adding milk. 'What do you mean?'

'He had subjected her to a regime of no therapeutic value. So I packed her off to her people in England, with a note explaining how she had been swindled.'

A sugar lump bounced off the table and rolled across the hearth rug. 'Explaining *what*?'

'That she had been practised on by a charlatan who sees in the afflicted a fountain of ready money, and in the bizarre torments to which he subjects them a never-failing source of self-advertisement.'

Her face was a fearsome white. 'And you are perfection itself.'

I said, 'I am your husband. And you are an adulteress, damn you, Dulcie.'

She stared at me. 'Then you will want to leave,' she said finally.

'I will not leave our son. He is mine?'

Here she lowered her eye. 'I loved you,' she said. 'Once.'

And you will again, I wanted to say. Perhaps you still do. But I had said things that cannot be unsaid. So I held my peace as she left the room. And now I sit here, hearing her voice scheming adultery with my pupil. And I know that our lives have fallen under the shadow that spreads its dark wings over my past, and the other shadow that lies inside the walls of Malpas.

Or perhaps in the end they are the same thing.

Oh, for a glass of whiskey.

Book 4

Chapter Twenty-One

By noon on the Saturday after Hannah's narrow escape, all the cars but the Zephyr had gone from Malpas, and Hannah and I were the only people on the place. It was the ideal time for finding out what was in Finbarr's house that should be in the Laboratory, and I was in the ideal frame of mind for doing things that Finbarr would not want me to do.

The little hut where Sullivan the doorkeeper had once sat was half full of wet coal ash. The back door was locked. But I ran a hand along the ledge above, and there was the key.

To the right was the kitchen, two leatherette armchairs on the engineering brick floor, and a mantelpiece with a row of books. The books were Burke's Peerage (snob!), Old Moore's Almanac (crank!) and a couple of osteopathic texts (quack!). By the books were several feet of unopened bills, stacked on edge ready for use in lighting the range. The cupboards held sardines, instant coffee, ill-washed saucepans and cracked white china. There was a squalid, out-of-control feeling about the inner Finbarr.

The ground-floor rooms were full of institutional furniture piled anyhow. There was a tiled room full of weird pipes terminating in perished and sinister hoses; Jamesy's hydrotherapy room, presumably. There was a room with a full-sized billiard table on whose ragged baize three rats scuttled each to a different pocket. There were chairs, tables, whatnots, secretaires, shelves, cheap, ragged, powdery with woodworm. It was all most encouraging, from the point of view of his having lied about burning stolen casebooks. People with anal tendencies this strong seldom get rid of anything.

The only problem was that there were no books.

The stairs were concrete, with a wire-mesh roof halfway up to stop the Nervous casting themselves down the well. Finbarr's bedroom had a window on the yard, an iron double bed and a little shelf of books on the cabbala and astrology. There was a pile of loose coppers on a chest of drawers. Beside the change was a little plastic-bound diary. I picked it up and flipped through the pages. It was full of entries in small, hieroglyphic writing. I looked up the date of the first lunch party. There was no mention of it, only *stg Riordan 6.00*. That would be the deer he had delivered to the car in the layby en route for the pub. I took out a pen and started to copy the entries into my notebook. There was game, fish, three oak trees, several loads of firewood, seven names – Windrush, I remember, and Tramore Girl – that would have been horses for doctoring. There were a lot of other indecipherable appointments. In particular, there was one the day after the lunch party, a sort of squiggle, with a telephone number.

I wrote it all down.

Further along the corridor from the bathroom, the doors had peepholes – the cells, presumably, in which poor Beryl Muspratt had been shut. At the end of the passage was the leather-padded door of which Costelloe had written. The leather looked not so much scratched as gnawed. Beyond it would be Emily's part of the house. If Emily's husband had been committing adultery with Dulcie, it was not surprising that she had called her a prostitute. Or that she had erected a fantasy of rape by the Doctor to account for the unsatisfactoriness of her own marriage.

There were no books in the cells or anywhere else. I slunk out of the back door and trudged through the rain to the laboratory. I put the kettle on and made tea. The river ran grey under the rain. Frankly, I was disappointed. The Kennels was a mess, not a maze.

I leafed through the diary pages I had transcribed, the squalid tale of stiff fish and wet-dog stags. A waste of effort, unless I could prove it was a record of embezzlement. At the telephone number, I stopped, and got out a magnifying glass. The words swam up at me. They might have said *lab bks*. There again, wishful thinking is a powerful influence on eyesight. Without hope, I picked up the telephone and dialled the number.

It rang for a long time. Then an ancient voice said, 'Surgery.'

I said, 'Who's this?'

'Moriarty,' said the voice. 'Who's that?'

My heart was suddenly walloping in my chest. 'Finbarr Durcan,' I said, in the best approximation to his voice I could manage. 'Have you the books still?'

'They're below in the museum,' he said. 'You don't sound yourself, Finbarr.'

'I have the throat gonorrhoea,' I said, and put the telephone down, trusting in Moriarty's powers of gossip.

I went out of the Laboratory at a run, and bundled Hannah into the Zephyr. I hurled her at Mary the daily, then jounced down the avenue, past the puke-green lodge and onto the road to Dunquin. At half past five I was hammering on the door of the grim villa of Dr Moriarty. Moriarty's sister's head appeared, pained and bony. Her expression softened when she saw it was me. 'No Hannah?' she said. 'Too bad.' I went past her into the noxious hall. 'Look!' cried the sister. 'Here's Mister Walker, Denis!'

The old man unfolded himself from his chair, grinning with his thousands of teeth. 'The proud father!' he said. 'You're welcome here! Nobody ill, I hope?'

'Not at all,' I said. 'Finbarr Durcan said he sent some books to the town museum. Would you know anything about that?'

'I have the honour to be the curator,' he said, ancient eyes gleaming with what I now recognised as prurient curiosity.

'I've been here a while now,' I said. 'You know how it is, you get interested in the history of a place? I was talking to Finbarr, and he said you had the books.'

'Quite so, quite so,' he said. He was frowning now. I got the idea he did not entirely believe me. Maybe he and Finbarr had discussed me, and Finbarr had given him a word picture of our relationship.

I said, 'If you'd just lend me the key, I'll pop down and have a look.'

He bridled. 'I couldn't do that,' he said. I ploughed on.

'The thing being,' I said, 'that this would be a matter between us. Confidential. Not like another matter, the matter of paternity, you know? Which I thought was to be between doctor and patient only, according to the oath governing your profession?'

His face seemed suddenly to sink, so that the teeth bulged beyond the cheekbones. His eyes shifted to and fro. 'Ah,' he said.

I said, 'As to that matter, was it Detective Rourke came asking you questions?'

He contrived to look shocked. 'I may be out of line Mr Walker but not that far, not at all. If I let slip a fact about you and the young lady it would only have been to Finbarr Durcan who is after all an old friend.'

'And nobody else?'

He pursed his lips and looked at me sideways, wondering if he should try another lie and deciding against it. 'Well your man Rourke is after coming round having heard from Finbarr now, and asking the question direct, and him being a polis I couldn't send him away now and him knowing already.'

So Moriarty had told Finbarr, and Finbarr had told the Guards. Dear Finbarr.

I loaded Moriarty into the Zephyr, and off we purred into the crapulous heart of Dunquin.

The museum was a warehouse crumbling onto the Fish Quay. Moriarty fumbled a large key into the door, and turned on a switch. A sixty-watt bulb illuminated a large room. There were a couple of glass cases in the middle, hedged around by a wall of boxes and tea-chests. 'It is in need of a little arrangement,' said Moriarty, blowing dust. We walked across the room on a road of footprints trodden into the filth on the floor.

There were cases of dirty manuscripts. 'The Town Charter,' said Moriarty. 'Signed by the great Sir Walter Raleigh. Swisser Swosser, Sweet Sir Walter, ye know.'

I was not looking at the cases. I was lifting the flaps on cardboard boxes, seeing an edge of carved stone, the butt of a narwhal horn wrapped in yellowed pages of the Cork *Examiner*. 'Kind donations,' said

Moriarty, breathing his grave-fumes past my ear. 'What you're looking for will be there beyond.'

'Tell you what,' I said. 'I'll be a while, I think. Will I find you in Riley's?'

'Ah,' said Moriarty. 'Ah-*hah*. And why not? Only you will be careful with the, eh, donations, ah, exhibits?'

'Of course.'

'Now.' He shuffled out of the yellow pool of the light. The door opened and closed.

I adopted a strategy of opening the least dusty box first. I had a false alarm about the parish papers of some dead-and-alive village in the mountains. Then I pulled open a box that still smelt faintly of horses. And there inside, looking up at me, was a row of brown leather book spines.

I crouched on the dirty floorboards, flicking through the pages. The Doctor and Jamesy must have used the same stationer. There were two dozen casebooks filled with Jamesy's clotted writing. There were some fat ledgers in a more clerkly hand, showing income and outgoings, and wads of papers in folders.

And something else. As I went through, I found a box of letters in a hand I recognised. A woman's hand, firm and neat; Dulcie. And last of all, five books labelled on the spine by the Doctor; numbers twenty to twenty-four, listed in the catalogue but missing from the Laboratory.

I crouched there transfixed. Why would Finbarr have lied?

Pathological secretiveness. Anal fixation, compensation for deep-seated feelings of inadequacy. A heritage decision, to ensure the continuing lustre of his family name. Bless his nasty little heart.

I put the boxes together, carried them to a window at the side of the building, piled them on the sill, and opened the catch. I was a burglar again. But this time I was a righteous burglar, stealing back for Malpas things that belonged to Malpas. I obliterated my passage across the floor to the window, wrecking in the process the feathers of an ambassador's hat. Then I went to the pub.

Moriarty was holding forth to the bar from behind a large Paddy. I bought him another, joined awkwardly in the conversation, and after a decent interval took him home. 'Did you find whatever it was?' he said.

'I wasn't really looking for anything special,' I said. 'Just trying to assess the material, you know?'

He winked at me, an ancient gossip's wink. He put his mouth close to my ear. 'The Crown of Tara,' he said, like a sewer whispering.

'What about it?'

'He was asking after it.'

'Who was?'

'Finbarr Durcan,' he said. 'He called to me just the other day and said did I believe there was such a thing.'

'And what did you say?'

He pursed his lips with a faint clatter of teeth. 'I told him more than likely.'

'Why was Finbarr asking after it?'

'I asked myself the same question,' said Moriarty, screwing up his eyes at this psychological conundrum. 'And I concluded, treasure is treasure, and it would be foolish to ask a man who was hunting for it, because you wouldn't get an answer. But I got the idea that someone had said he had the thing in his possession, and Finbarr wanted it.'

'Who would that have been?'

'If he had told me,' said Moriarty, 'he would as good have been letting me into the hunt.' He tried to fall off his bar stool. I caught him, helped him into the Zephyr and back into the care of his sister.

I turned the Zephyr round, drove back to the Museum, opened the window I had left unlatched, and loaded the boxes into the boot of the car. I drove sedately out of town, thinking about Finbarr, and the person who knew the whereabouts of the Crown of Tara.

In the Laboratory I lit the lamps and began to examine my loot. Reverently, I placed the Doctor's final volumes in their gaps in the shelf. Then, duster in hand, I went over Jamesy's casebooks with the excitement of a prospector making a preliminary inspection of a promising claim.

His books ran from 1917 to 1930. A brief flick through their pages confirmed that he had used just about any therapeutic method that came into his head, from hydrotherapy, via psychoanalysis with and without ethyl intoxication, to insulin shock, barbiturates, and all known measures against cerebral syphilis, including infection with malaria.

The last of the books was only half finished. It did duty as a sort of file folder. There was a wad of letters tucked into the blank pages, the earliest dated 1910. As well as the letters there was a funeral order of service for Jamesy himself, dated February 12th 1930. And there was something that appeared to be a flyer for some sort of variety theatre or music hall, bearing a photograph of a man with slicked-back dark hair and an eyebrow moustache. The eyes were huge, and looked as if they had been enlarged by the discreet use of mascara. They stared out of the picture with bullying intensity. THE GREAT MENTALINI, said the sixty-four-point type of the headline. *THE GREAT MENTALINI has studied under Ancient Masters the Control of the Human Will. His early training was in fabled Egypt with the Secret Magi, Builders of the Pyramids, famed among Initiates for their astonishing feats of Mind Power! THRILL as he demonstrates his powers of ABSOLUTE CONTROL!! GASP as he bends the STRONGEST to his DEEPEST DESIRES!!!*

Scrawled on the bottom of the flyer was a line of writing: *We're in the same business now, Da! Timsy.*

I pinned it onto the wall above the bench, and went on through the papers. The letters were from Dulcie to a friend, by the look of them. I kept them for later. I flicked through the bank books in the folders, and a name caught my eye: Caroe of Slaughterbridge. There were payments of £10 every week between 1910 and 1920 – £5,000, at a time when a shilling an hour was big wages. It was a sum of money that explained Mrs Caroe's eagerness for the Doctor to have her bank's name after the burning.

But it did not explain the reason for the payments. It was certainly very bad luck to discover that your fiancée was your half-sister, and plausible grounds for suicide if you were an aesthetic creature like Henry Costelloe, and it was revealed to you by Mrs Caroe the night before the wedding. But it seemed unlikely that the Doctor would pay Mrs Caroe such a significant pension, in return for her silence in the matter of a scandal that affected him and Dulcie hardly at all.

It was getting late. My mind was droning with unanswered questions. I put my head on my hands, and stared at the face I had bluetacked to the wall. And as I watched it, it changed.

This was Timsy, Jamesy's son. One con-man following another, as he was pointing out. But it was not the relationship between them that had me staring into those stage-hypnotic eyes.

The weird thing about the portrait of that dead mountebank was that it was changing into a face I had seen somewhere before.

But where?

Helen came back on the Sunday night, haggard and almost too tired to speak. She said she had sold a few pictures and seen a lot of people. I had dug up some spaghetti, and made a carbonara with a salad of lettuces from the garden. She ate it as if she was starving, and fell asleep in a chair. I hauled Hannah upstairs into her bedroom, and put her to bed with the bunnies and the rot spores. I left her door open and went downstairs.

Helen had woken up, and was reading by the range. I had decided what I would do. I said, 'I found a lot more stuff yesterday.'

'Stuff?'

'Diaries,' I said. 'Costelloe. Jamesy. And letters from Dulcie.'

Her finger was in her book. 'Where did you find it?'

'In the museum. Finbarr stole it.'

She frowned. 'What?'

'It belongs in the Laboratory. Here. He'd scooped it all up. He told me he'd burned it. But he'd taken it to the museum.' Pause. 'I'm telling you this. Not him.'

She was pale. In fact, she looked frightened. But she said, 'He would have done it because it was right.'

'What?'

She said, 'I know you don't like him. But he knows more about the place than anyone else, and he loves it, and he's honest. What more do you want?'

I thought of showing her the poacher's catalogue in the diary, and asking her how much of the money she had seen. I thought of telling her that he had made mischief with Moriarty and the Gardai. But Helen was Helen. If she had decided Finbarr was a good thing, it was a waste of breath to try and convince her otherwise, and I might as well change the subject. So I took the Great Mentalini flyer out of my pocket. 'By the way,' I said. 'I'm sure I've seen this man before. But it's Timsy, Finbarr's father. He died before I got here. So how—'

I had passed the paper over to her as I spoke. She had looked up again from the book, tired and a little sulky. She took the paper, looked at the photograph.

And froze. Just sat there for perhaps twenty seconds, not moving. Not even breathing, as far as I could see.

I said, 'What is it?'

She did not answer.

'Helen?' I said.

Nothing.

I put myself in her line of vision.

She blinked. She was back.

I said, 'What's wrong?'

'Wrong?'

I said, 'You switched off.'

'What do you mean?'

'Was it the picture?'

'Picture?' She looked at the Great Mentalini. 'Who's that?'

I told her. 'Oh,' she said, not interested.

'Have you ever seen him before?'

'Don't think so.' She took my hand. Her palm was cold and sweaty. 'Dave, you're so nice to come home to.'

This was a remarkable change of script, but none the less welcome for that. I said, 'Why?'

'Please,' she said. 'Hold me.'

I put my arm around her and held her for a long time. I said, 'Do you ever wonder why you went swimming off the pier that night?'

'No.'

'Not at all?'

'I never give it one tiny second's thought. Now for God's sake will you stop going on and on about it.'

I felt something wet on my neck, and realised she was crying. I said, 'What is it?'

'Nothing.'

'Something about that face?'

'What face?'

I found myself thinking about my visit to Brady's with Angela: the warm dark of the place, Finbarr's voice, soothing; and that feeling I had had then, of *switching off*. I said, 'Does Finbarr hypnotise you?'

'Does he *what*? Of course not. Stop trying to make everything not ordinary. I'm crying because of ordinary usual things and you don't need to know what. Can I have a glass of wine?'

I fetched her a glass of wine. She drank it immediately, and then two more. I said, 'I'll go back to work.'

'Don't leave me,' she said. Her face was drawn, the freckles standing out on the white skin. I was shocked. This was a Helen who wanted me not out of affection, but out of . . . well, fear of the dark, was the only explanation I could find. There was a lot of it about, at Malpas.

So there we sat while the house groaned around us like a sick mammoth. I told her about her grandfather's payments to the Caroes. She nodded, not listening. At eleven, she said, 'I'm going to bed. Could you come too? I need company.' The eyes were deep and desperate.

I could feel a darkness between us; a distance across which even love could not travel. I said, 'Of course.'

And there we lay, at opposite sides of her lumpy bed, holding hands, separated by dark miles.

We went to sleep.

By the time Helen was sixteen, her father had arranged his foreign tours to coincide with her school terms. She boarded, in England. She quite liked it; she had a lot of friends. Though of course they all had homes to go to, and all she had was a hotel room and a boat and when her friends said that sounded super, she thought of their horses and their dances and a favourite view from a bedroom window somewhere you knew really well, and was horribly envious. The envy had something (she did not know quite what) to do with the fact that she led expeditions to smoke cigarettes and drink gin on the roof. And she bought a motorbike, an in retrospect pathetic ex-Post Office BSA Bantam, off a rocker called Den in a transport café by the A24. Later that same day, after Den had taught her to ride it, he had fed her four gin and limes and six of chips, and tunnelled his way through her virginity on a tarpaulin in a small wood near Dorking. She realised even as Den puffed on top of her that she was giving her treasure to a large greaser in a manner most would hold to be squalid. But actually Den was rather sweet. And she really really liked this feeling of being in control but out of control at the same time, and not sure what was going to happen next.

The next time she saw her father, in his room with the baby grand in Claridge's, she felt completely different. She was wearing a leather jacket and tight Wranglers and a lot of mascara and pale lipstick. When she went up to the room and he got up to kiss her, what she saw getting up from the piano was a tall, slim, *old* man – he had never struck her as old before. Since she had had breasts, she had always leaned far forward to kiss him, so that they would not touch him and remind him that things were different. This time she put her arms around his neck and gave him a whole-body hug and kissed him on both cheeks *à la* Sylvie Vartan, to demonstrate to him once and for all that things had changed. He smelt faintly of sandalwood soap, as usual. In fact he was completely as usual, except for a sort of disorientated look in his eyes. She followed up her advantage quickly. She said, 'It's time I went to Malpas.'

'It wouldn't be a good idea. It's let. The tenants wouldn't like it.'

These were too many reasons for them all to be true. She said, 'I'll go anyway.'

'Please,' he said, and suddenly something truly awful was showing in his eyes. 'I beg you. It's not a good idea. Not for a landlord to go.'

'I'm not a landlord.'

He sat down. His face looked grey. 'Yes you are.'

'Huh?'

'It belongs to you. The tenant has notice to quit on your twenty-third birthday, if you get that far, which I very much hope you will.'

She stared at him, her white-lipsticked mouth hanging open.

'This will sound stupid,' he said. 'But there was a man there at the beginning of the eighteenth century, ancestor of ours, Herbert Costelloe, a bit of a bastard, actually. He'd let the place, and on gale day, rent day they call it now, his steward took the rents to him and Herbert changed it all to gold, and got into a sort of barge affair they had there then, and made his men row him up from Dunquin. He had arranged for all the tenants to be waiting so he could show them that gold, and he could give them a lecture about the alchemy of landlordism, how it was turning base labour into gold. Which was just about the last thing they wanted to hear, but Herbert didn't mind, probably drunk too. And when he stepped off that barge he missed his footing (maybe it was the drink) and went into the deep part of the House Pool. And all that gold in his pockets took him straight down, heavy as lead it is. And it was generally recognised to be his own damn fault, and everyone went looking for his body, not to bury it particularly, but because of the gold. And they never found it, and that's that.'

There was a silence. Then she said, 'So?'

'So you stay away from Malpas until you are twenty-three, and I will rent you a flat and send you to university.'

'Art school.'

'All right.'

'And I need a motorbike.'

'You look as if you've already got one.'

'A Trident.'

'You have to stay away from Malpas. Or it'll all go.'

'Okay.'

She kissed him, and they went out to dinner, and it was just about the same as always. Until later, when she had had some wine, and she had summoned up the courage to ask a question she had never asked before. Then she said, 'Why do you hate Malpas so much?'

He smiled at her. 'Darling,' he said, 'I hope you never find out.'

So of course from that moment on she could not, just simply could not *wait*.

Chapter Twenty-Two

As I went down to make tea next morning, the sun was pouring into the hall and Hannah was babbling cheerfully in her room. The darkness had blown away in the night. It was a terrific morning. Nothing could spoil it, or so I thought for about five minutes.

At breakfast, Helen gave me a bundle of letters. She said, 'Sorry. They came on Friday.' They were all harmless. Except one.

It crouched next to the toast, a long cream envelope addressed in the loopy girl's-boarding-school script that I recognised as Mara's. I glanced at Helen. She was gazing out of the window. Guiltily, I carried the letter out to the Laboratory. Mara's talent for souring atmospheres at long range would have excited the envy of a howitzer firing gas shells.

If I had known exactly how powerful her talent was, I would have burned the letter unread.

Dear Dave

Back again for the summer term, and where are you? I am sort of lonely without you, can you believe that?! I know I didn't see you for ages but absence makes the heart grow fonder, I suppose. And Finals coming up, and me saying goodbye to my old wicked ways, but no disapproving Dave to keep my nose in a book. Just some awful hoorays I met in Gstaad in the vac, fabulous skiing though of course you would not approve darling. They want me to go and have picnics on the Downs. So far I am claiming to be Vegan to get out of their salmon mayyonaise, so uncool. But I have got a feeling that unless you come back and remind me about the way things were, I will give in to my baser side. One of them is called

237

Torquil, and has a rather super moustache. I caught myself casting longing looks at a twinset in Jaeger. So you can see that I am in greater danger of seduction by the Straight and Narrow.

I think there is another reason you should come back too, and that is George Gale. George was being really sweet all last term, and I relly was coming round to the idea that we might end up getting it on. The other day he told me he had heard from you, something about a research project you are doing? He said it was a pretty good project, by the sound of it. But Dave this is so weird but for some reason he really dosent like you. He took me out to dinner and had quite a lot of wine and started talking in a rather horrific gloting way about how you thought you were onto somthing hot, but it was not nearly as good as you thought it was, and when you – he said – fucked up he was going to pick up the pieces and turn them into a nice little book. Then he told me that he is going out with a black girl from Callifornia now, but still he could come and sleep with me if I wanted. Well of course I didnt. So I am not going to see him any more particularly because I think it was her that gave him the NSU that he gave me. It is so typical of him to give me disgusting American diseases and steal your thesis or whatever it is.

So anyway, when I went round to get some of my stuff from his flat he wasn't there so naturally I had a nose round including a look at the notes in your file, the ones he had made about someone called Peter Costelloe, right? I thought you might be interested in a Xerox.

Darling dave, I think you should come back soon to save yourself from George and me from Torquil.

Lots of love xx oo

Mara

It was a typically Mara letter. There were threats (only Mara knew the exact dire truth of what was happening to my career and prospects). There was self-interest (she had a medical requirement for someone under a thumb, and I was the logical next in line). There was what she imagined to be coercion through jealousy (I did not for one moment believe in Torquil or his moustache). Finally, and much the most important, there was revenge (she would never have told me about

Gale's plagiaristic manoeuvres if she had not been furious with him).

I turned idly to the photocopied sheets she had stapled to the handwritten page.

They were grey and shiny, in the manner of photocopies then. It seemed to be a page from a newspaper. The masthead was missing, but the date was 8th January 1910.

. . .allegations too distressing to repeat, according to Dr J.B. Withers, Assistant Secretary to the General Medical Council. While the august protectors of the Profession may not wish to contemplate charges that one of their members has offended against the person of a female patient, this paper is made of sterner metal. The facts of the case are as follows, and we challenge the Doctor and his defenders to refute them:

That on or about 1st of December last, Mrs D—, a young widow of Cheyne-Walk, Chelsea, did go to the consulting rooms of James Costelloe, M.D. in Wimpole-Street, London, W., to seek treatment for a nervous complaint. This complaint took the form of a great timidity in everyday life, specially in the matter of germs. To this end Mrs D— washed her hands with great frequency – a frequency that soon overtook most of her other activities, to the extent that she was incapacitated with terror whenever she was more than fifteen feet from a washbasin. Doctor Costelloe has set himself up as a 'psychiatrist', that is to say, a doctor whose chosen speciality is nervous disorders. Mrs D— having courageously brought herself to his consulting rooms, Dr Costelloe embarked on a course of therapy. This started harmlessly enough. The Doctor threw Mrs D— into a hypnotic trance, and then joined with her in the care and maintenance of a small portable garden he had caused to be made in his office. Mrs D—'s hands were thus dirtied, a state of affairs that would normally have caused her great terror, but which under hypnosis she accepted with the greatest equanimity.

After four treatments, Mrs D— found herself much improved. She confesses that under the influence of 'post hypnotic suggestion' she enjoyed a game at mud-pies with Dr Costelloe. Indeed, she admits that she was almost entirely cured of her complaint. Imagine then her feelings when at the fifth session she emerged from her hypnotic trance to find herself partially disrobed and the Doctor likewise, in a position highly compromising to one of her strong moral leanings, and indeed to any respectable woman.

The following dialogue ensued.

Mrs D—: Sir! Doctor! What is the meaning of this outrage?

Costelloe: Madam, it is not possible for the subject of a hypnotic trance to do anything that is against her deep-seated inclinations.

Mrs D—: I beg you, doctor, recollect yourself!

Costelloe: My own recollections, dear Madam, are intact, and will remain so, thanks to the wax cylinder device I have had beside me during our pleasant exchange. To ensure that I am not tempted to share these recollections with your husband, you will do me the honour of keeping silent about our intercourse.

Mrs D—: [sobs]

After this illuminating conversation, Mrs D—, horrified, returned to her home vowing never again to seek medical help. Costelloe might have gone on to ever greater outrages, had Mrs D— not fallen into a state of complete mental collapse, and given a full account to the doctor of the Dorrien Institute, at whose hands she was receiving treatment. Upon this the whole story came out.

Happily, his case is now under investigation by the Police, who have every hope that more of his unfortunate victims, should they exist, may be persuaded pro bono publico to give an account of their horrible experiences. Perhaps the GMC will then see its way to making quite sure that Dr James Costelloe, M.D., will never again practise upon the confidence of an unsuspecting public!

There was a photograph of a dark-haired man with a large moustache. The caption beneath it said: Dr James Costelloe – Blackmailer and Libertine.

Under the moustache, the face was undoubtedly the face of Peter Costelloe.

I sat there and stared at that face. I did not believe it. The doctor, of whose tender conscience I had followed every twist and turn, using his medical arts as an aid to rape? The idea was ludicrous.

But once the idea had gained admittance to my mind, others followed. There had been his willingness to stay on in Ireland and care for Dulcie, turning his back on an apparently brilliant career. There were the hints at secrets to be covered up: secrets about that career? And there was Emily's accusation of rape, of course. There was plenty about Peter Costelloe that did not fit together. Perhaps the missing ingredient was that he was a fraud and a rapist.

In which case, why not a murderer too?

From the Casebooks of Peter Costelloe

It has been summer at Malpas: one of those summers when the trees and the ground are clotted with green, and a cloying, unbreathable vapour fills the void between the sopping ground and the blanket clouds. It is a summer like a stuck record. The rain falls, evaporates, condenses, falls again in the same place. The air smells used and rotten—

But I am talking about the weather. I am talking about the weather because I can hardly bear to talk even to myself about the things that have come to pass. I have been trying to shrink my cuckold's horns. But my attempts to improve things with Dulcie meet with failure. Worse than failure.

It is raining again.

The sun was shining yesterday evening. As we took dinner, Jess and I, the light poured in through the west window like honey. We had salmon. As usual, Dulcie took hers on a tray in her study. Jess said, 'Poor mummy, she doesn't know what she's missing,' and made Jack the terrier beg for a pink flake. He is a bright, confident boy, as yet unmarked by the approach of manhood. Until that evening – even after the Slaughterbridge horror – his world had been a simple, delightful place.

No longer.

We drank our coffee and watched a red stag in the green park. Jess was rattling on about a plan he has to breed ferrets. Suddenly he said, 'Who's that?'

I could hear nothing.

'A car,' he said. 'Two.' (His ears, like all his senses, are splendid.)

There were no visitors due. Cars are a rarity still, in these parts. I rang the bell for Bridget the maid. Nobody came. I rang again. Still nobody. I could hear the engines myself now. As we went across the hall – visitors are always an event, at Malpas – I was aware of something unusual. It took me a moment to identify what it was.

Malpas employs twenty-three servants. They do very little, on the whole. But their presence is always noise – the faraway buzz of a conversation, or a peal of laughter.

This evening, the house was quiet as a church.

By the time this had sunk in, we were outside the front door. The sun had gone behind the hill, and the light was fading into dusk. Against the darkening hillside I could see a long, low shape, and another, higher and boxier, moving down the avenue towards the house.

Their steady advance turned my heart to ice. I said to Jess, 'Get inside. Tell your mother.'

'Tell her what?'

I said, in a voice annoyingly tightened by fear, 'They're here. And Jess. Listen to me. If ever there's trouble, go up to the log cellar by the Temple of the Graces. Hide in there. Then we'll know where to look.'

'Why not in the house?'

'Certainly not in the house. Go when you have told Mummy.'

He stared at me, all eyes. Then he nodded, and scuttled in at the front door like a rabbit into its burrow.

A stink of exhaust floated down the small breeze. The shapes became a car and a lorry. The car drew up, the lorry behind it. Men jumped down from the back of the lorry. The driver climbed out of the car. The passenger remained. The men from the lorry wore baggy suits and carried rifles. The man from the car had a golfing cap and an Aran jersey. He limped slightly under the weight of the revolver strapped at his waist. As he drew nearer I saw he had a handkerchief over his face, and that he held his head turned a little away from me, to favour his single eye.

He approached slowly. The men from the lorry fell in behind him, scuffling gravel. He said, 'I am Brigadier O'Connell of the Irish Republican Army.'

I gave him the smallest of bows. The name was a *nom de guerre*. The pistol was a Webley. The ears, great pink shells pierced by the last ray of the sun, were Johnny Cosgrave's. I said with a dry mouth, 'And how may I be of service?'

Johnny said, 'In the name of the People of Ireland I must make an example of the building here.'

My knees tried to smack together. I said, 'Does that mean a burning?'

Johnny's eye shifted behind him, to the passenger in the car. The lights in his ears went out. The passenger wore a Homburg hat. The hat's brim rose an inch, returned.

'All right lads,' said Johnny. His eyes had not returned to mine. The men from the lorry started forward. Three of them were carrying big square cans of the kind used for the storage of paraffin.

'Wait,' I croaked. The avenue and the men were in darkness, but the upper storeys of Malpas were golden with sun, the windows glittering and alive. I thought of all this black, eyeless, ruined. I wanted to weep.

But the men crunched past me, rifles slung. One of them rattled a box of matches, casually, like a man checking before he lights a Sweet Afton.

'Johnny,' I said.

I saw him check; the faintest of hesitations, it was, then a glance at the Homburg hat in the passenger seat of the car. I had his ear. I said, 'You told me at Slaughterbridge this would not happen.'

'It's not you,' he said. 'It's herself, on account of Jamesy Durcan and that queer bastard Devereux.'

'So burn them, not us.'

He would not meet my eye. Jamesy and Maurice were both well guarded by heavily armed men. Malpas was easier meat. I stood silent, my ideas exhausted, my brain humming with fear. Then an idea burst upon me; an idea that might save the house, and win me back Dulcie. The blood flowed hot in my face. I said, 'The Crown. Do you want it?'

'Where is it?'

'It might be inside.'

I held his eye. In it I read violent desire, then calculation. He turned away. 'Wait a bit,' he called to the men.

They did not hear him. Already they were kicking at the front door. 'WAIT!'

They waited.

'Stand easy,' he said.

They sat on the steps under the pediment and lit cigarettes.

Johnny came closer to me. I could smell his sweat. 'Make your speech,' he said, low-voiced.

'Speech?'

He was looking anxious now. The Crown was burning in his mind. 'It's yer man in the car,' he said. 'Ye'll have to make an impression on the lads. Just the smallest bit of an impression. No need to mention the Crown, now. Then I can go inside in the house with you, to pick up the thing itself, no fuss. Go on. Do it now.'

My palms were wet, and a lavatory would have been a useful thing. But this was Jess's home, and Dulcie's. So I walked loose-kneed up the first two of the steps under the pediment. I said, 'Good evening, lads.'

Silence, thick and utter.

'You're here to burn the house,' I said. 'Well, it's a war, and you must obey orders. But there's a couple of things I must say. One, Malpas has been a place where we have played fair, anyone wanting to buy a farm of land has been given the chance, and life has been conducted in a decent and orderly fashion. Ask anyone.' Pure ham, sure, but they were listening now. I carried on.

'Two, it's a great house, and there is stuff inside in it that shouldn't be burned. Pretty soon we'll have the Saxon out of here, and Ireland will be a nation once again God willing, and there will be need of great houses as a place to show the beauty and skill of Ireland down the years. If you burn the house, you'll burn with it paintings by Irish men. Jack Butler Yeats, you'll have heard of him, AE, papers from the Parliament when Ireland was a nation the time before.' Someone

belched. These were farmboys, not intellectuals. This was a waste of
time.

'And me,' I said. 'It's my home, here. I am a doctor and I treat all
alike, rich and poor, ask if you don't believe me.' God, the unfairness of
it. Spurned by the gentry, burned by the peasantry . . . 'My wife is not
one of your Ascendancy belles. She was born in a boarding house in
Dunquin, and she is here only because she was put here by tragedy and
misfortune. What has the house or the stuff inside it or my family done
to deserve a burning?'

Still the silence. But its nature was changing like cream in the churn.

'And if you don't believe me,' I said, 'come inside, and look around;
but not the lot of you, the way I don't want Mrs Costelloe or the little
fella to be frightened.' Pause. 'Captain O'Connell,' I said. 'And a couple
of men, if you like?'

'I'll see for myself,' said Johnny. 'You men, stand easy.' And up the
steps he came, to the front door. But when I tried the handle, it was
locked from the inside.

'You can't come in,' said the voice of Dulcie, high and tight.

'We have to,' I said.

'Never.'

'Now listen, my dear,' I said. 'These are the brave soldiers of Ireland
out here, and if you don't open the door they'll break it down, and if
that takes too long, they'll come in the windows.'

Silence. She had certainly never heard me speak this way before.
Then the clash of bolts top and bottom, and the rattle of the key. And
there was Dulcie.

'Mrs Costelloe,' said Johnny, very polite.

'And what in the name of Hell,' said Dulcie out of her Fury's mask,
'are you doing at my front door, Johnny Cosgrave, instead of in the
servant's hall where you belong?'

I saw Johnny's face darken. I thought of the men rattling their vestas
in the sweep. I said, 'Brigadier O'Connell is welcome here. Hold your
peace, woman.'

This was not the way I speak to her, and she was shocked by it. But I
could feel approval from Johnny. He found it in himself to be polite. He

245

said, 'I am sorry to trouble you, Mrs Costelloe, but me and the Doctor is doing our best.'

Now she turned on me a look of green poison. 'It is a peculiar world,' she said, 'when a gurrier from the river decides what is best for the likes of Malpas. And when a man who has lived ten years in such a place turns coward.'

I said, quickly, 'Dulcie, your tongue is running away with you. Brigadier, come to my study,' and turned my back on her. Johnny hesitated, then fell into step.

'Coward!' screeched Dulcie. 'Off you go with your Shinner friends—'

I shut the study door on her noise. Johnny shook his head. I shook mine. We were linked by the ancient camaraderie of two men getting an earful from a woman. I sat Johnny down in the comfortable chair, and took out a sheet of paper and my silver pencil. I pulled my own chair close to his, and began to write. He said, 'What's that for?'

I said, 'A receipt. From the people of Ireland, for the Crown of Tara. All you have to do is sign it.'

'We will conduct this exchange without such formalities,' he said. And I knew that what had Johnny in its grip was not nationalist fervour, but greed. So I lay back in my chair and caught the light with my silver pencil, and began to speak to him quietly about the history of this crown, and its great importance. And his pupils dilated, and down he went, down and down, easy as a stone sinking.

And at the end of it I went to the safe behind the bound volumes of the *Irish Herpetologist*, brought back the box and handed it over to him. He looked inside, and shook his head in wonder. 'So there it is,' he said.

'There it is,' I said. 'You must never show it to anyone. Not till the war is over. Do I have your promise?'

He looked at me, solemn, a little dazed. 'You have my promise,' he said.

'Well, now.'

He stowed the box away in his haversack. He will tell nobody, I am sure of it. We went down the passage and into the hall.

And there was Dulcie, standing up dead straight in front of the fireplace. But now she held in her hand the revolver that lives with the gloves in the drawer of the hall table.

Johnny looked at the gun as if he did not know what it was. I said, 'My dear, Johnny and I are after having a bit of a talk, and there is no need for guns.'

'And what was this talk about?'

I said, 'There will be no burning.'

'So who did you betray this time?' she said – referring, I suppose, to Carson and the Caroes, for neither of whom I was of course responsible. The great heavy gun wavered towards Johnny.

I stepped across to put myself between her and Johnny. She pointed the gun at me, holding it with both hands. It was cocked. I remember feeling not fear, but despair. I said, 'Please.'

'What have you done?'

I was very close to her now. I said, 'It has been arranged.'

'What?' Her face was rigid, her eyes round and glassy. Whatever I told her she would not hear.

I said, 'Please.'

She said, 'You will not make your damned arrangements about my house. I will chase these damned bandits away from here. You are a bloody coward and I despise you.'

'The gun,' I said.

'Coward,' she said.

I put out my hand and grasped the pistol. I am her husband, the father of her son. I grasped it by the cylinder, so that the web between my thumb and first finger was between the hammer and the firing pin. As I did so I felt a violent pain in my hand. I realised that she had pulled the trigger.

Johnny had spent much time among armed men. He realised it too. He said, 'She would have had you there, Doctor,' and laughed. He turned and went out of the door, and I heard him talking to his people.

Dulcie looked as if she might faint. I untangled her cold fingers from the gun and took it away. I said, 'Dulcie, we must at least be friends.'

She nodded. Thank God, she nodded. It is a beginning.

I tipped the bullets from the cylinder, and put the revolver in my safe, out of harm's way. Outside, the men were climbing back into the lorry. Johnny came over to me, lips pursed in a relieved whistle. 'In view of past services,' he said, 'yer man says we need to make a token gesture only.' The passenger did not turn to us. I saw his face in profile, long-nosed, the eyes hot above deep pouches. The drivers swung the engines. They rattled away, paused for a moment by the West Pavilion, and vanished into the dark trees.

I was shaking now. My hand hurt. When I looked down, it was wet with blood where the hammer had ripped it.

'You let them go,' said Dulcie. Jesse came across the dark lawn from the rhododendrons. She put an arm round his shoulders, a stiff arm, as always. In the windows of the West Pavilion an orange light appeared – a fiery light, that blossomed and grew. I said, 'I shall be outside the Pavilion. Now you go and find some people with buckets, do you understand?'

'What?' The poor woman was shocked past the point of action. 'Why?' I let her eyes do the work. 'The West Pavilion,' she said. 'What is wrong with it?'

'They have set it on fire,' I said. 'They had to be allowed to destroy something.'

'So you gave them . . . *permission* . . . to set fire to the pavilion.'

'I negotiated the sparing of Malpas.'

I can still hear her snort as I write.

We fought the flames all night. It did not spread – the colonnade offers little food to a fire. The roof of the pavilion went, the usual firework-show of sparks. But I had not been quite frank with Johnny. What was inside it amounted to little more than the estate cricket outfit, and a punt so rotten as to be perfectly unsafe. I do not think either of them will be missed!

And there is more on the bright side of the account. We are in the grip of frightful atrocities, sure. But even in Ireland, atrocities cannot go on for ever. And at least now that we have received our visitation from the Republicans, we will be safe from the attentions of the Black and Tans.

Now I must go to luncheon and see if I can persuade Dulcie to talk to me. She is very low, poor thing; very low indeed.

And so am I, so am I. Partly because of a manly worry as to what will become of my family. But partly because of the things I have done in my life that may come back to haunt me – the giving away of the Crown, for one. There are others.

The air smells of burning from the Pavilion. Sometimes I can feel the ghosts of the past thicken around me like smoke, until there is no light, no oxygen—

And today, Dulcie pointed a revolver at me, and pulled the trigger.

I am tired. Some whiskey, some sleep. All will seem different in the morning.

Please God!

Walker Archive, Transcript, 1973 – 7

It is a time of secrets. Johnny is coming and going, now you see him, now you don't. He comes and takes me by surprise, across the ocean he says, ten days on the Olympic or the Carnatic or some such, steerage class, he says, not like the nobs, nobody ever asks questions in the steerage. Then it is the Limited and here he is, and you can see how tired he is, thin in the face and with the smell of tobacco and ship's oil sour on the clothes of him. I am in the room here and I make him his bacon and cabbage and hamburg steaks, and he tells me the news, the secrets of his life and the life of Malpas, o the secrets he knows, the fierce burden of secrets that is on him, the secrets of the men here in Chicago he meets in the bar who give him the money for the things he will not speak of. And there are the secrets of the family, the secret of the Crown of Tara now that nobody must speak of, the secret of my little Doctor, who has saved my Johnny from death and the great house from burning, Johnny says. Johnny passes into my life and out of my life. And when he is out of my life I am working, working, and when he is in my life I am feeding him until the hollows are gone from his poor face, and holding him inside in the bed. It is such a happiness to hold him inside in the bed, and he me, and I love him so.

And now I have my own secrets. I have the secret of my little Doctor that only I know and not even Johnny. And I have the other secret, that is that my bleeding has stopped and now soon there will be a little fella. But I cannot tell Johnny this the way it might make him weak and fond, if they caught him and asked him.

It is the Durcans' job to do things that will become secrets. It is the Cosgraves' job to keep them.

Chapter Twenty-Three

Two days after the Mara letter, it was still a disaster. My attempts to verify the photocopy had failed, but I was pretty sure it was genuine.

I found Helen in the morning room, dancing among the easels with Hannah, who was stumping about holding her hands, her round red face glowing like a sun in splendour. Finbarr was watching the proceedings from an armchair, blowing cigarette smoke at his muddy boots. He glanced at me, nodded coldly and turned back to Helen. 'Well,' he said, 'I'll be away.' He stood up, took Helen by the waist and kissed her on the cheek, close to the mouth. Too close. She pulled away from him, flushing. He went into the hall. I went after him. He turned. I was not frightened of him any more. I was angry. He said, 'What do you want?'

I said, 'You will not maul Helen about like that.'

He said, 'I will do what I bloody well please.'

I watched him, and thought, now, at last, I know things that you do not know. I said to him, 'You are not the tenant, you are the farm manager, and you are stealing her money and her game. So would you get out of here, please?'

His face turned suddenly thick and hostile. 'I'll see you around,' he said. 'I certainly will, so.' And he stumped out.

I waited for my heart to slow down. Then I went back into the morning room. Hannah scuttled across and hung onto my leg. Helen said, 'Was that you shouting at Finbarr?'

'Not shouting.'

'Arguing, then?'

'Yes. I've told you. You're being taken advantage of.'

'That is for me to decide. You have to make allowances.'

'I don't see why.'

She smiled at me forgivingly. 'One of the things I love about you,' she said, 'is that you are so damn English. Finbarr doesn't get paid, so he pays himself, within reason. He's having a bad day today. He'll be over it by tomorrow. Now, tell me, what's happening at the office?'

I told her about the IRA raid on the house. She sat and listened, poised in the wrecked armchair with that Gainsborough elegance. She said, 'She meant to shoot him.'

'You think so?'

'Put yourself in her boots. She's been having an affair with Jamesy for years. She's sick of Grandpa getting her into trouble, the way she sees it. She wants to get rid of him. Big revolver, IRA in the house. Who's going to say it wasn't them that shot him?'

'But they're married, with a son.'

'There's a war. As far as she's concerned, they're on different sides, now.' She picked at her lower lip. 'But if that wasn't enough, how do you know that it wasn't Grandpa who shot Desmond? Dulcie can't grass him up because that would have made her an accessory all those years. But she doesn't love him any more, she doesn't need him, so she sees a way of getting rid of him without an embarrassing murder trial.'

These were the precise thoughts I had managed to dismiss from my mind. Hearing them in Helen's mouth brought them back, bright and new and plausible.

We had lunch. The table was quieter than usual, and not only because of Finbarr. I could believe in Peter Costelloe as professionally misguided, clinically spurious, a wronged husband, an anxious father, a victim in a nasty game of civil-war politics. But I could not bring myself to concede on the basis of a tipoff from Mara that he had been a lecher and quack. Let alone a murderer.

Emily would have first-hand knowledge, of course. But Emily was the widow of Peter Costelloe's rival in science and love, the victim of his wife's adultery. You could not expect her to be objective . . .

Get the evidence, or you have nothing to test. And get it quick, before Finbarr tells Emily you threw him out of the house.

* * *

As I walked between the fuchsia hedges to the front door of the Kennels, Emily's meringue of hair rose from a flowerbed on the right. She shooed me inside. The savage Bridie brought coffee like a gale bringing leaves. She said, 'I think I was a bit off last time I saw you. Touch of flu.'

This was a most welcome display of the olive branch, and left her exactly where I wanted her. I said, 'Not at all, not at all. It sounds as if it must have been pretty horrific, though.'

'What?'

'Peter Costelloe. Attacking you, you said.'

She looked away, folding her hands. 'Quite,' she said.

'What exactly was it that happened?'

She scrabbled a cigarette out of her packet and lit it. She said, 'You're supposed to talk about these things, aren't you? Get them off your chest and all that. Well, then. It was in 1920. Jamesy had been away, and so had Dulcie, for a week or two, I don't know, and the Doctor and I were getting on with things, each of us in our own corner of Malpas. I had this bay mare, a really terrific bay mare. I was sort of in love with her really. I mean, horses are easier than people. I was in the stables, giving her a rub down. And you know how it is when someone is there, you can feel them watching you. Particularly the Doctor. He had those very black eyes on him, you'd feel you could fall into them. A lot of women found him quite attractive, I know that. But I always thought he was a bit small. So anyway there I was in the loose box and there was that little Doctor watching me. I said good afternoon to him, and I can still remember wondering could I get away with not asking him in to tea. He told me how lonely he was, and he suggested I might be lonely too, and then he put his hands in my shirt and he tried to kiss me. I told him to go away.'

'Did he go?'

'He did.'

'I thought he tried to rape you.'

'Well in those days that was really jolly nearly the same thing. And there were stories.'

'What stories?'

'From England. Someone who was staying saw him and said he had been in the papers. A sex scandal. And I thought, there but for fortune, you know?'

Not a rape, then. A presumed rape, stoked up by a story in a newspaper.

But still. The doctor who had been so clear in my mind was now a blur. From the blur a new creature was emerging, with features sketchy but visible. The beginning of a forked tail. The buds of horns. I said, 'And you never did anything to encourage him?'

'Of course not!' A pause, while she watched me, and seemed to come to some decision. 'I think he did it because of what Dulcie was up to. I think he wanted to get his revenge on Jamesy.'

'Dulcie?'

'You know she had an affair with Jamesy,' she said. 'For a long, long time.' She leaned forward to light a new Senior Service. 'I didn't really mind.' Her face was grim and grey. 'I was never all that keen on the . . . bed stuff, actually. And I had my darling boys. Well, I hope that was some help?' She smiled brightly, as if she had given me the weather forecast, not a sketch of a hollow life.

I made my way back to the house.

What I had were allegations, not evidence. But they were hard to beat. The Doctor had arrived out of nowhere, and stayed for ever. That was the behaviour of a man on the run, not a successful doctor. His anxiety to get Francis Galton to publish his work could be read as the anxiety of a man seeing his last chance to rehabilitate himself.

And of course, what I had been reading were not diaries. They were casebooks. Casebooks are scientific records, intended to be read by people other than the writer.

It boiled down to this. Did you believe a newspaper story and Dulcie, or a lifetime of casebooks?

Yesterday, I would have said the casebooks.

Today I was not sure.

Next morning I could not face the Doctor. I walked through the balmy Malpas morning with the thrushes singing round my head, and found myself in the walled garden. I had planted some lettuces, which in the heat and the wet were growing nearly as fast as the weeds. I hoed away, trying to sweat the confusion out of my head.

A voice behind me said, 'Have the rabbits not found ye?'

It was Paddy Cosgrave, grinning out of his large, dirt-seamed face. I told him the rabbits had not, and he said they would, and together we hauled out of the nettles a roll of wire, with which we fortified the lettuces. By the time we had finished, it was well past one, and we were sweaty and tired. I said, 'Do you want a pint?'

'Ah no,' he said. 'Once I start I'll never stop.'

So we sat on the stump of a walnut tree felled to raise cash in the fifties, and talked about this and that. In time, it came round to Steve.

'Poor fella,' he said. 'There's few enough to chat with here, without him.'

I said. 'You knew him well.'

His mouth opened and closed. He said, 'I did.' His eyes turned vacant. His face took on that mask-like look it had worn the first time I had met him by the Owenafisk. Then a wren fluttered across the vegetable patch and vanished into a hole in the wall. His face cleared. 'Switcharse,' he said. Switcharse was what the vanished Mairi had called wrens before Costelloe had rerouted her mind. History at Malpas was a deep well of clear water, in which you could see the dead live.

I said, 'What's wrong?'

He shook his head. I saw there were tears in his eyes.

I said, 'Is it what happened with Steve?'

'He was dead.' He shook his head, unable to speak.

I said, 'It's a hell of a shock, to find a body.'

'I don't remember.'

'Nothing?'

His eyes were locked onto mine, as if he was trying to draw something out of me. And it came into my head that this was not an ordinary locking. It was as if he expected some process to take place, a signal for him to start a routine in which he had been trained.

I said, 'Let's try this, Paddy.' I held up a finger and raised it until I could see his eyes strain; the beginning of the Braid induction, as used by Peter Costelloe himself. I started talking to him soothingly about something or other. He kept his eyes on the finger. He had done this before. I said, 'You will be asleep, but you will hear everything. You will fall asleep when I say, now, now, *now*.'

The eyes slammed shut.

I said, 'You cannot open your eyes.' I watched him try. 'Good,' I said, murmuring on, breaking up the words, disturbing the rhythm to keep him down there in his trance. 'Someone has done this with you before. Someone has told you before that you cannot open your eyes. Who is this person? You want to tell me.'

His eyes stayed closed. Muscles contracted in his forehead. I kept soothing him, but he did not respond. Someone had forbidden him to answer the question. I knew the answer anyway. Now, now, *now* was Finbarr's line, the night he had tried to persuade me I did not like Helen.

I said, 'The person who has told you this thing is Finbarr Durcan.'

'It is,' said Paddy. The muscles in his brow had become still.

'What is it then? What have you done for Finbarr?'

'Done nothing for Finbarr.'

More murmuring. I said, 'Steve, then. What have you done for Steve?'

I expected nothing. To my astonishment, his face cleared as if I had flicked a switch.

'It is wet,' he said. 'The grass is wet. I am carrying him, yer man Steve. I can feel his skin, 'tis cold, and his trousers are half down with the weight of the stones that's in them. I have the sun in my eyes when we go up the bank, so I'm falling on the stones.'

I felt the chill of the morning, saw the light picking out the horror in the weir pool. There was another chill, too. This was not everyday Paddy talking. This was Paddy a hypnotic subject, fallen into what seemed like a full-scale trance. Trance is a state that can be learned. Finbarr had taught it to him.

The day was warm and muggy, but I found myself shivering. Finbarr, brother of Timsy Durcan, the Great Mentalini. Son of Jamesy, disciple of Peter Costelloe, generator of this legacy of madness and control.

'The last morning he came to your house,' I said. 'The Monday morning, when Steve came to visit your house. What was he saying then?'

'He is inside in the house,' he said. 'He has come inside and he is at the table and Mammy is giving him tea and he is talking.'

'What is he saying?'

'Oh the usual bilge, you can't make no sense of it at all. It is all Crown of Tara Men Fought and Died for it, all that stuff, and it does belong to no one person but to the people, he is saying.'

'Did you ever see the Crown of Tara?' I said.

'Never.'

'Does it exist?'

'I don't know, I don't know, I don't know.'

'Did he talk about anything else that last morning?'

'Maybe he did and maybe he didn't.'

'Why do you say that?'

'Because I had to go off to the fishing so I wouldn't know.'

'And did he have his little book with him at the table?'

'He did.'

'When I ask you to wake up, you will remember none of this. You will wake up when I say right now, and you will feel fresh and peaceful, and none of this has happened. Right . . . *now*.'

The eyes opened. 'Christ,' he said, 'is that the time? I'm to be at the coal quay now, there's the new netting to pick up for the weir tomorrow.' He looked past me. 'There's Finbarr,' he said. 'Good luck.' He buttoned up his coat and walked off.

Finbarr's Land Rover was waiting on the avenue. I saw his face, pale, with dark eye sockets. The car rattled after Paddy and stopped next to him. Paddy was hanging his head. Then I saw it rise, and he was looking at Finbarr, with a strange steadiness. I knew what that steadiness meant. I went after them. 'How's it going?' I cried, with much cheeriness.

Finbarr's head swung towards me. He exuded a casual authority, like a man with a tame animal. The eyes had a dangerous glow. Paddy was standing beside him, looking dazed.

'Keep away from my mother,' he said. 'Keep away from me, or I'll send you swimming. Third and last public warning.' Then he was gone, roaring towards the Park gates.

Paddy was looking after the Land Rover with his mouth open. 'That's torn it,' he said. 'That's torn it, all right.' He walked away, shaking his head, and climbed into a cot tied up at the quay. The last I saw of him, he was pulling away across the broad black ribbon of the water, towards the pink house under the white heronry.

And Finbarr had right out loud threatened me with death by drowning.

I went to the Laboratory. I tried to convince myself it had been his idea of a joke. No luck. At Brady's, it might or might not have been a threat. This time, there was no doubt.

The memory of those hot, ferocious eyes made it hard to concentrate. I wrote two letters: one to the Director of the Dorrien Institute about the patients of Doctor James Costelloe, and another to George Gale, copy to the Dean of Studies at Helmstone, outlining my thesis plans. Wriggle out of that, George, I thought. Then I climbed into the Zephyr, took the letter to the post, came back, arranged my notes, and went back into the house to peel potatoes for dinner.

Halfway through the operation, Helen came in. She looked at the saucepanful of potatoes, and said, 'Does the Army be coming to dine?'

While reflecting that there was soon going to be room for me or Finbarr at Malpas, but not both, I had peeled the best part of a stone. I put them on to boil. She said, 'Is something wrong?'

'Finbarr.'

'Again?'

'I was talking to Paddy Cosgrave about Steve's notebook. Finbarr threatened to drown me.'

She said, 'You've really got it in for him, haven't you?'

The ground was shifting under my feet. 'When I arrived, you said you didn't trust him. All I'm saying is that you were right. He's having an affair with Angela, did you know that?'

Her cheeks suddenly flushed. She said, 'Who Angela has affairs with is her business. When I said all that stuff to you you weren't making any . . . demands, you know. But now you're Hannah's father, I think you're jealous.'

'What the hell are you talking about?'

She said, 'It is very flattering of course, all that. But it is deeply childish. Finbarr and I are friends, you know. We talk.' She paused, took a deep breath. 'It is nice having you here, Dave. But you're just staying. Finbarr lives here, and so do I.'

I felt as if she had walloped me in the stomach. 'You told me you were frightened.'

'I'm not frightened any more. I was going through a bad patch. It's better now.'

I could feel a wind blowing me out of here. I did not understand where it was coming from. I said, 'And I've been here. And we love each other. And there's Hannah. Let's get married.'

There was a silence then. She stared at me. She was still angry. That had been my big throw, and I had wasted it, because it was no use saying anything to Helen when she was angry.

'Well?' I said. The word fell hollow in the room.

'Absolutely *not*,' she said. 'And if this is how you feel, you'll just be making yourself miserable and maybe you should be thinking about leaving.' She glared at me. She looked like a stranger. Hannah started howling. 'Come to Mummy,' said Helen, swinging her up, interposing her body between Hannah and me. 'Tell you what,' she said over her shoulder, 'maybe it would be a good idea if you found somewhere else to sleep tonight.'

She was right, of course. I was jealous, for no reason. I was trying to tie her down because I was lonely and needy and all the rest of it. When one of the reasons I loved her was her wildness, her refusal to be tied down. She was wrong about Finbarr, of course. But I should have worked quietly away at that, not made a lot of petulant fuss.

Too late. And there went the family I had found at last, sliding away to hell.

That night I stared at the ceiling of a bedroom a hundred yards from Helen's, kept awake (despite my excellent resolutions) by a ferocious sense of injustice. Helen wanted me gone. Finbarr wanted me dead. Angela was having an affair with my enemy. What was keeping me here?

Hannah, of course. And Peter Costelloe, and all the questions without answers. And Helen.

I closed my eyes. I would find a way to make up with her in the morning. Things would get back to normal.

But I would have to do something about Finbarr.

And of course at the thought of bloody Finbarr I was awake, staring at the moonlight on the ceiling, going over it all again and coming to a single conclusion.

He could not have drowned Steve. But I was just about sure he had.

Paddy Cosgrave would have more to tell me.

Next morning, there was no sign of Helen or Hannah. It was streaming rain. I pulled on a yellow oilskin coat that hung by the front door, and made for the Herring Weir.

As I came out of the rhododendrons and onto the inch I saw Finbarr's Land Rover parked on the avenue where it ran close to the Herring Weir. I waited.

I watched Finbarr trudge back across the inch from the weir. The Land Rover drew away. Paddy Cosgrave was on the weir, working. I pulled up the hood of the coat against the rain, and walked down the side of the river.

For five minutes, the weir was hidden from view by reedbeds. Beyond the reedbeds, I could see the fence and the pier. It was about an hour after low water. At the end of the snaking brown path the wheelbarrow was standing on the bank, dripping water through the holes in its rust-eaten bottom. Paddy was gone; having a cup of tea under a tree, presumably, like a sensible person. As I drew near, a couple of crows flapped up from the barrow. One of them dropped something as it went. I could hear its irate cawing over the drum of the rain on the hood of the oilskin. As I walked closer, I saw that the thing it had dropped was a white trout, perhaps a pound in weight.

I walked up to the barrow. There were two decent-sized grilse in it. One of them had its eyes pecked out. It was not like Paddy to leave good fish uncovered and unguarded. I called his name. There was no reply. His cot was tied up to the outside weir post. He had definitely been on the weir ten minutes ago.

'Paddy!' I shouted.

There was only the hiss of the rain in the disc of water inside the weir, and the heavy cawing of the crows.

'Paddy!' I roared. The roar coincided with a little lull in the rain. I heard the echo of it come back from the sandstone cliffs on the far bank of the river. There was still no sign of life.

The rain swept up the river again on a wind that flattened the grass and bowed the willows horizontal. An evil morning. No wonder Paddy was not in it. He had probably got a lift home with a passing friend while I was behind the reeds. He would be drinking tea in the Pink House on the far side of the water.

My eye snagged on something out there in the river. A log, perhaps, a dark ridge on the sheet of frosted grey. Part of it, a branch perhaps, came above the water and flopped back in.

Not a branch. An arm. A hand.

I shuffled down the bank and onto the stone pier in which the weir's upright stood. I slithered across the muddy stones to the cot – easy to slip, easy to slip – and fumbled at the length of frayed string Paddy used for a painter. After what seemed like hours, the knot came undone.

The cot slid into the eddy. The bank and the river whirled about me. The oars had loops of string instead of rowlocks. I prodded at the water, caught a crab. A gust of wind lashed up from the south, raising a dirty grey chop. Suddenly I was in the middle of the River, between the Cosgraves and the House. Must be careful, or I would blow past him.

Wherever he was.

Chapter Twenty-Four

The rain whipped at my eyeballs. The cot spun again. There was only grey water, grey-black banks. Something black in the water. A branch, a real one this time. Then to the left and beyond it that rise and flop again, the dark arm with the pale hand at its end. God knew what was keeping him afloat.

While I was thinking this, I was rowing. Malpas cots were primeval, long-keeled, unsteerable. Another broom of rain swept over the water. In the middle of its stinging greyness the boat hit something with a wet thump. I went to the side in time to see a face staring up at me, and a great bulge of black, shiny material below it. Paddy's oilskin smock, holding enough air to keep him near the surface, if not actually afloat. I reached over. Paddy made no move to assist. He lay face down, his arms and legs limp. Bubbles poured from the oilskins as I grabbed a handful. Suddenly he was heavy, sinking away into the black water. I found myself stretched over the side of the boat, swearing, fingers slipping, near as dammit losing my hold. With my free hand I fumbled for the painter. Water came slopping in over the side. The rain was harder again. I could not get the painter round him, his body being too thick, and my arms too short, and my hands (by now) too cold.

In the end, I did the first thing that came into my head. I wrapped the painter round the first part of him I could, which turned out to be his neck, and finished it with what I hoped was a bowline. Then I rowed as best I could to the fish weir, hoping I could get there before he strangled, assuming he was not already drowned.

I remember the rain lashing my face as I rowed. There was salt in it, not from the water – the estuary here is almost fresh – but because I was quite definitely crying. And behind it all was something else. Paddy had lived forty years on this river. God knew how many times he had patched the weir. It was not like him just to step off and start drowning.

I pulled past the eddy at the weir head. The cot and its tow surged into the lee of the structure. One more pull and I was at the bank, hauling the boat's nose up, slithering waist-deep to take the noose from around Paddy's neck. I caught the collar of his oilskin. I hauled him up on the mud-slimed pebbles. He lay on his back. Silence. No crows. The hiss of the rain. No breathing.

I rolled him onto his back. His face was bluish-white. The eyes were half-open, red-rimmed. I remember thinking, if they are red-rimmed there is still oxygen in the blood. Naturally I had never done first aid, but I had read a Reader's Digest book about it when the Zephyr had blown off its radiator cap and I was waiting (on a day as rainy as this, in a layby off the A24, far away and long ago in England, wherever that was) for the temperature to sink out of the red.

So I stuck my finger in his mouth and fished around for his tongue, which was not down his throat. Then I pinched his nose and gave him the mouth-to-mouth and thumped away at his black oilskin chest where his heart must surely be.

It was no bloody good. Ten minutes ago I had been walking over the inch, my head full of a sort of soup of Helen, Finbarr, Steve. And here I was trying to blow life into (breathe twice. Bang heel of hand on chest) a dead body. And what they did not tell you about in the Reader's Digest was that casualties did not shave and had breath that smelt of onions—

Breath?

The figure on the pebbles coughed. It coughed until it was sick. I rolled it into the recovery position. It kept coughing, but it carried on breathing. Paddy Cosgrave, I should say, carried on breathing. I sat down with my knees up and my head down, and concentrated on not fainting. After a little while some things came into my mind that I dimly recognised as ideas.

I left him in the recovery position, ran up the bank to the house, and called the ambulance, watching Paddy out of the window as I talked into the telephone. I grabbed a handful of mothy picnic rugs from the hall chest and covered him up and sat beside him for a wet hour till the ambulance arrived. I arranged for a message to be taken to Mrs Cosgrave, who seemed to be out. Then I walked away down the avenue.

It was still raining. The Kennels crouched dirty and dark-windowed under the downpour. Finbarr's Land Rover was in the yard. In the stables a horseshoe rang on stone, and a voice cursed. Lamplight shone in the stable ahead. I kicked open the door and went in.

A hurricane lamp hissed over a closed loosebox door. There was a horse behind the door, a great brown thing – bay, I suppose I should call it – tied by the head to a ring in the wall. Up in the roof, something white and gangling dangled by its arms from a purlin, trampling the horse's back. It was Finbarr, dressed in a pair of yellowish knee-length underpants and a pair of big rubber-soled army boots. Finbarr the horse osteopath, in mid treatment. The air stank of his sweat. I hated the bastard.

'Finbarr!' I shouted.

I heard him grunt as he brought his boots down. I saw the heels sink into the big muscles behind where the saddle would go. The horse squealed and hopped sideways. Finbarr turned his head, still hanging, and looked at me. He swung down from the rafters onto the straw.

I said, 'What did you do to Paddy?'

'What are you talking about?'

'You've just tried to drown him to stop him telling me things you don't want me to hear.'

He laughed. He turned to go away. I caught his arm. He whirled on me and said, 'Don't touch me, you little English maggot.'

I could hear my heart in my head. I said, 'So tell me what it is Paddy's not allowed to tell me.'

He stood there, and said, 'Let go of my arm.'

'Something about Steve,' I said. 'Something about the way you want this place back and the ride you're taking Helen for. Well, make sure you're in later in the day, because the Gardai are going to be here with a list of questions about theft, embezzlement and murder.'

He laughed again. He was seeing Guard Rourke's face as I told him about hypnosis as a murder weapon. Then, suddenly, he yanked the loosebox door open. I found myself looking at the horse's hind-quarters. He clapped his hands sharply and stepped back, all in the same movement. The horse kicked out at me with both hind feet. I was not used to horses, or violence. One hoof whacked chips out of the gatepost by my right ear. The other landed on the round muscle of my upper right arm. It hurt like hell. Finbarr was coming at me from the side. There was something in his hand that I recognised as a pitchfork. I stumbled backwards, fell, and scuttled away down the stables walkway on all fours, and the pitchfork, badly flung, whacked into a post beside me.

Then I was in the cold rain, running for the shelter of a rhododendron thicket. Here I waited, panting. I touched the muscle of my arm, moved the fingers, flexed the elbow. Not broken. Somewhere on the other side of the stables, a Land Rover clashed gears and faded into the woods.

I went back to the house. I could not stop shaking. Helen came in, dripping, pushing the pram. She stared at me. 'What's the matter?' she said.

I told her. She made me explain it twice. She had gone very pale. 'And Paddy's in hospital?'

'The Mercy, they said. In Cork.'

'Let's go and see him,' she said. She took my hand, and squeezed it. It was about as close as I was going to get to an apology.

We put Hannah into the Zephyr. As we turned onto the main road, Helen said, 'You're sure Finbarr tried to kill you.'

'And Paddy.'

'Couldn't it have been that Paddy fell in, and you got kicked?'

'Paddy's a true somnambulist. Finbarr's been hypnotising him. Finbarr put him in the river.'

At the Mercy we sat outside Paddy's door in a corridor furnished with pattering nuns and altars of grey stone. I could feel Helen fuming. A young nun stuck her head out of the door and said, 'You can see him if you want. Only a minute, now. He's had dirty water inside in his lungs.'

Paddy was wearing an oxygen mask. There was a bandage on his neck where the cot's string had been.

'How did you come to be in the river?' said Helen, straight out. Checking my story.

'I was fixing up the fish weir,' he croaked. 'What the feck was it happened?'

I said, 'You damn near drowned yourself.'

'And Dave came just in time.'

I said, 'Were you alone at the weir?'

'I was.'

'Nobody else?'

Paddy closed his eyes. 'Nobody,' he said.

'You see?' said Helen.

'I saw Finbarr there,' I said. 'He's told Paddy to forget.'

There was the sound of a large person coming through a small door, a deep, musty smell, and Mrs Cosgrave was in our midst. 'God bless all here,' she said. 'Patrick, what in the name of hell are you after doing to yourself?'

'Dunno, Mammy,' he whispered.

'Not too clever, is it?' she said. 'And me getting a spin fifty seven and a half miles and the same to go back—'

'Right so, Mammy,' said Paddy, very weak. He closed his eyes again.

Helen and I got up. I said, 'It might be best if he has someone with him.'

Mrs Cosgrave turned her black eyes on me, took my hand and squeezed it in a powerful bony grip. 'We'll make sure no harm comes to him,' she said. 'You saved him, the silly boy,' she said. 'By God we will not forget it.'

In the car, Helen said, 'You are seriously telling me that he needs protecting against Finbarr?'

My arm was throbbing angrily where the horse had kicked me. It did not seem worth answering. I said, 'Ask him. If you can find him. But you won't, because he's on the run.'

And for the first time, thank God, Helen looked frightened.

When we got back to Malpas, I called the Kennels. The telephone rang on and on. He was not at Brady's, either. When I called Emily, she said, 'He's gone away.' Her voice was thin and strained. 'Staying with people.'

'What people?'

'He didn't say.'

'Did he say when he'd be back?'

'No.' She put the phone down.

I rang Angela. She said, 'I'm having a drink with him this evening.'

I said, 'Ask him to call, would you?'

'Is something wrong?' The excitement was warming her voice. Something was happening, and she would want to be part of it.

'Just trying to find him,' I said.

She rang back at seven thirty. 'He didn't turn up,' she said. 'What's going on?'

'No idea,' I said. 'If you do see him, give me a ring, would you?'

At eight o'clock I was sitting in the Laboratory when a dogged beating came on the door. I walked across the red stripes of sun that lay on the floorboards. Mrs Cosgrave was standing on the step. I said, 'Good evening,' to her. She did not answer. She just stood, a massive black silence against the rosy light. 'Come in,' I said.

She came in. I took books and papers off a chair. She sat down. Still she did not say anything. 'How's Paddy?' I said.

'Not great.' The voice low and gravelly, the words lying across the silence the way her body had bulked against the light. 'We have some cousins inside with him now. How did ye find him, this morning?'

I told her. I did not mention Finbarr.

'The crows,' she said. She sat there, massive in her smell and her silence. Then she said, 'Finbarr Durcan.'

'What about him?'

Silence. Then, suddenly, she said, 'Paddy said he was after telling you about the two stones he took from Stephen's pockets there.' Her joints cracked like branches as she stood up. She strode out of the Laboratory, led me through a couple of gaps in the terrace balustrades, and out to the inch. The sun was slopping streaks of blood into the Herring Weir.

'There beyond,' she said, and pointed at a grove of scrubby willows on the bank downstream of the weir. 'Four along.' I found myself in the trees, brushing away reeds, nettles stinging my hands.

'Under the root,' she said. 'He put them under the root below.'

I burrowed my hands through the slime and the freshwater mussel shells, into the dark.

'There,' she said.

My hands found something hard and cold. I pulled one out. There was another in there. Two stones.

I hauled them out into the light. They were rectangular, about the size of bricks, but slimmer. Not very heavy. But together, they would add up to fifteen pounds. One in each pocket would increase your specific gravity plenty enough to sink you, if you were a thin man. Like Steve.

I lifted the stones gingerly and took them onto the inch, one in each hand. He had selected his stones. Walked in. And that had been that.

Well-organised. Cold-blooded.

Not qualities normally associated with Steve.

Mrs Cosgrave reached out and took a stone, hefting its weight in her great bony hand. Then she said, 'And where would he find that class of a rock around here?'

The river stones were round, water-smoothed. The stones in her hand were brick-shaped, items of masonry. There was no masonry down here at the weir, only mud and pebbles.

Mrs Cosgrave waited, patiently, it seemed to me. Waiting for me to get the point.

I let my mind walk round Malpas.

And suddenly I was two miles away, on the slope of Dulcie's dam, at a place where the turf had come away and water wept from the chinks of a substrate of squared-off stones.

Stones like these.

Three miles is a long way to carry the stones with which you plan to drown yourself, even if you are a tidy person.

Steve had not been a tidy person at all.

'Mrs Cosgrave,' I said. 'When Paddy's better, we'll have a little chat, him and me.'

'Sure you will,' she said. 'Sure, sure, sure, sure, sure, sure.' She put out her hand. There was something in it; a key. There was a label on the key. It said, in Steve's writing: *Engine house.*

Then she strode into the night, and was gone.

Chapter Twenty-Five

Walker Archive, Transcript, 1973 – 8

It is a little room, I said. A small little room, hot in the summer, steamy in the winter, with the lines of washing hung above by the ceiling, and the traffic all roaring in the road below. Our room. After a while there is a lot more of Johnny, and he gets some work too, delivering beer old Johnny, and he says it is a great game pretty like what he was doing at home, now, and did I ever think of going back there? Well the room is small and it smells bad and there is the coughing that comes from next door all the time where Mrs Coughlan is dying with the blood on her chin. The little fella is sometimes not so good him being two years old now, and all the time I think of the river and the clean air that is in it. And one day Johnny comes in with a fella who is a class of a parson, who had fierce drink taken, and there is a lot of talk I do not understand. And Johnny tells me that we are to go back to Ireland to the Pink House that is empty now, and the parson says that Miss Dulcie will make no objection, none at all, because of something the parson has told her and the Doctor, and we can be there quiet as mice. So I am on the boat now and you can hear the propeller under your ear in the night grinding like the great stone that grinds the salt into the sea, and coming on the train to Dunquin and my cousin Declan on the ass-cart and home, sweet home, with the roses on the door and the place of my cage just a hole with shelves in it, now, and there will never be bars on it again.

I have arranged the fishing. The nets are bad but my two cousins are after mending them on the long bench on the stones, and I have made them mend the boat, and we are off and away now, nice and quiet, catching fish. The garden is bad now, there are fierce weeds and some dirty gurriers have smashed in a couple of the glasshouses. But we are all working there, and the little fella

271

playing in the potatoes and pulling up the carrots the way he can gnaw them. And one day here is the Doctor!

'You're looking grand, Mairi, look at yourself,' says the Doctor.

He is not so good. He is little and where he was rosy he is grey and the underneath of his eyes is pot-of-ink black.

'And this will be the little fella!' he says.

But I can hear that his voice is hollow, and his mind, that great mind he has on him, is somewhere else and it full of trouble. I say to him: 'Don't you worry at all, we're safe now.'

He looks at me, sad and weary, not saying anything. And I can see that he knows. Her that should love him has been talking to them that hate him. They have it planned out between them. My little Doctor has seen what he has seen, and she cannot let him hide it.

The only one not safe here at Malpas is the Doctor himself.

From the Last Casebook of Peter Costelloe, M.D.

Something will happen soon. Something must happen. My life is become a thundercloud swollen with death, ready to release bolts of a dreadful energy that will destroy everything—

Calm.

I am in the Laboratory now. The lamp glows yellow and steady. The paper before me is white, the ink black, flowing smoothly from the pen. The thoughts themselves are not smooth. A turmoil of thought, a hurricane, a whirlwind, a volcano of terror and fury—

Calm, I say.

Pick up the pen again. Dip it in the ink. Let the nib move; let it explain what has brought me to this, now. Perhaps explaining will make things better.

After the burning of the Pavilion, Dulcie did not talk to me for thirteen days. Every night I would sit here and look at the healing wound on the web of skin between my thumb and forefinger – the web that saved my life, but left me alive to wonder whether my life was worth saving.

I think (incurable optimist) that she has come to recognise that what I did that night was for the best. We have been civil to each other;

distant, but united over the care of dear Jess.

Until today.

Today, I came in from my morning work in the Laboratory to find Jamesy drinking coffee with her by the fire in the hall. As I came in, they stopped talking and looked at me, so I knew that I had been the subject of their conversation. Jamesy has a thick, boiled look that makes me wonder about his blood pressure. I said good morning to them. They both looked at me, cold as ice, not replying. As I walked away I heard their talk start up again, low, as if they were making plans, and I knew that I was the subject of their discourse.

I took myself into the library with the Cork *Examiner*. The news of the burning of the Pavilion was three weeks ago. The Mayor of Cork was on hunger strike in prison. The country was in an uproar. I looked at the paper again. The words made no sense.

My life makes no sense.

I think there is nothing left that I can do.

This morning Bridie the maid, whisking past with a pair of boots for cleaning, hissed that there was one wanted to see me at Cosgraves'.

I walked down to the House Creek and put myself on the seat of the cot. They have been cutting spires for thatch, and the bottom of the boat was covered with a pale, tubular straw, like the pen of an animal. I shoved the boat onto the river, pulled into midstream, and rested for a moment on my oars. Suspended, I felt, on that shining path, between the trouble that lowered from the ponderous mass of Malpas, and the other trouble winking pink from between the autumn russets of the Cosgraves' bank. I should have liked to hang on this silver ribbon for ever. But I am a husband in name, and a father in fact. I must land on one bank or the other, even if I like neither. Were it not for Jess I could rest here, surrender to the current, allow myself to be washed into the great dark dissolution of the sea . . .

I brought the cot alongside the little quay with the salmon boat moored off it. I went up the steps. If it was Johnny I must tell him to get away, of course. The Black and Tans are active in the district, under an officer of peculiar ferocity they call the Twitcher. They will come looking for Johnny, and if they find him—

'Hello,' said a voice from the quay.

I looked up, and found myself gazing upon a woman. A huge woman, tall and wide, well-shaped in her gigantic way, with a face like an Indian and great legs planted sturdily in enormous black boots. My heart seemed to roll in my chest. 'By the living God,' I said. 'Mairi.' She kept her eyes on me, bright and dark and steady where once they had been dull and blank and flickering. 'How have you been?'

'Five years forty days three hours and a couple of minutes ago, you cured me, I suppose,' she said, and still her eyes did not waver. 'So I'm better now and thank God I have a little fella of my own. But I am a bit muddled up about things, Doctor.' She did not shift her gaze.

'Well, Mairi,' I said, very hearty. 'Splendid to see you, but I must go up and have a word with your Johnny.'

'He's away to Kilmacthomas,' she said, in a voice like a door closing. 'Somewhere like that, annyways, you can't be sure, can you? Come up to the house.'

For all her weight, she went up the steps like a gazelle. We sat on the elm bench where I had sliced away the wreck of Johnny's eye, resting our feet on a pile of nets and looking back towards Malpas. She said, 'I have six and a half gills of buttermilk and the half of a loaf, if you'd like a feed.'

I accepted only a small cup of buttermilk, as was my duty as a guest. (How can I write so calmly, knowing what I now know, and where it may lead?) 'Well, Mairi,' I said. 'How have you been?'

'Grand,' she said. 'But I lost the most of my power, you know. You'd have to say cured, really.' I nodded, a bedside nod. Mairi is the great success of my professional life, and she will live for ever in the literature. 'I get lonely without the patterns,' she said. 'It leaves all these loose ends, and no way of tidying up. I hate a loose end. But I try to keep it tidy and in count. I have an end now that I must tidy, so.'

I felt something of a chill here. I said, 'How so?'

'There was a fella called Munslow,' she said. 'A class of a minister, would you call him, a Protestant priest, an old man. In Chicago? He was a fierce drinker. He said he was once a curate in Dunquin, knew the river very well and loved it, by Christ he loved it, wanted to hear all about it. He came looking for us on the South Side in Chicago, hunted us up, you might say, there's more people from the County Waterford below in Chicago than there is in the County Waterford, and we all know each other still. So I told him, four talks we had, good long ones, each half an hour by the clock above in the bar where we did the talking, and him drinking his poor head off.'

I said, 'Ah.' I could smell whatever it was she was about to say like coming rain.

'Fierce keen on the river, he was. He said he had a friend who had a great house down here, oh, a long time ago. There had been something bad happened. And I could see he was hinting at something and I said, did he mean Malpas and he stared at me like and said, yes, certainly, that was it, Malpas. Doctor?'

'Yes,' I said. 'And then?'

'He was an old fella. He drank a lot. He went to sleep, and Johnny took him to where he was staying.'

I felt myself relax for a moment.

'But we gave him our addresses, and he wanted to hear all about it, that was including all about Mrs Costelloe, he had a great interest in her. And the funny thing is,' here she paused, 'that yer man is after writing me a letter from America, with a letter to Mrs Costelloe inside in the envelope.'

I said, 'He did.'

'He's very well,' said Mairi. 'He has a lot of trouble in the hips, and his heart's rotten, and his chest is destroyed with the bronchitis, he says. It was a nice letter altogether, and his regards to Malpas with it.'

I said, 'And you want me to take the letter to my wife.'

'Oh, no,' she said. 'Bridie is after putting it in with the post this morning. All I wanted to know was, did I do right?'

I do not remember what I did after that. I have a dim recollection of a frantic row across the river, the oars jumping out of the thole-pins.

The letter was waiting on Dulcie's desk at that very moment.

She was not in the house. I walked through to her office. The lawns were smooth and green. Little gold coins of sun came through the red needles of the metasequoia beyond the window. The desk was an eighteenth-century bureau by Reisener, with cabriole legs and ormolu satyrs that grinned at me and said, too late, too late. The plaster ceiling writhed at me, the Turkey carpet shifted its patterns into a sneer. This is the final moment, it all said. The culmination of years of deception, you dirty thing of a Doctor. There were papers on the desk, many papers, as always. Dulcie's habit is to open her mail as it arrives, glance, and examine it in more detail at tea. I sorted through seed catalogues, electrical fittings lists, invitations (to her, nowadays, of course. Not to me. Oh, dear no). Then there was her personal correspondence, half-a-dozen envelopes from her friends. She has many friends. I used to be one myself. And finally, there at the bottom of the pile, an envelope of a coarse greyish paper, addressed in an ancient and wavering hand to Miss Dulcie White at Malpas House. Opened, of course. But undestroyed. And so unread.

I slipped it into the breast pocket of my coat (it took me two tries, my hand shook so) and carried it away to my Laboratory. Here, I smoothed it onto the bench.

It was as I had thought. God be praised that I have drawn it away from Dulcie before she could destroy it! Perhaps I may yet be able to use it in my defence. Yes, defence. For suddenly, the urge to live runs strongly in me again, and I know that Johnny was right, and she does not care if I live or die. Perhaps would even prefer me to die . . .

Now Jess is at the door with Jack yapping, both of them are half-mad with excitement. They want to be taken fishing. Of course we will go! My darling son and I, heading to the river, singing. The clouds I felt when I began to write have rolled away. The brooding feeling of electricity is gone from the air.

But I fear there will be no fishing; for there is the sound of a motor on the avenue. We have callers, who must be entertained.

Here the casebooks of Peter Costelloe cease, except for a letter, scorched at one edge and bearing signs of having been crumpled, that is pasted into the book.

Chicago

Dear, dear Miss White,

    This is a hard letter for me to write, and will I think be a hard letter for you to receive. All I can say to you now by way of apology is that the events the Lord has set me to describe below have made my life a torment; have first forced me to live a lie, and then driven me out into the strange places of the world, where I have sought expiation by bringing the Lord's word to the heathen. Here and there – in Africa and latterly in America – news of that blessed valley in which you reside has come to me, washed up like messages in bottles on the shores of the great sea of humanity. As has happened with Mairi Dugdale, whose acquaintance I have had the pleasure of making, and whose conversation has come as a sign powerful as any spouting rock or burning bush.

    So it has been revealed unto me that I must tell you of the sin that has burdened me this many and many a year.

    My first curacy after I left Wycliffe Hall was in Limehouse, part of the docks of London. There I was sorely tried by the lusts of the flesh, and thence, at the suggestion of my Bishop, I withdrew myself, lest my soul fall into fire eternal. I attached myself to the Church of Ireland, and became curate to the Reverend Archibald Hamilton, Vicar of Dunquin.

    My duties were to conduct services at Dunquin, and to visit in the parish – a large one as regards area, but a small one as regards souls, the great majority of the flock being of the Papist tendency – but you will know this, and I can see I am expending words to put off the thing that must be said.

    In the course of my parish rounds I visited Malpas House, that great and glorious establishment, then owned by the kind and chaste Henry Costelloe, a pillar of the Church – one of life's bachelors, his base urges entirely sublimated into a zest for culture, improvement, and love for his fellow man. I say entirely; but once, when we were walking together in the back woods so he could show me a new planting of (I believe) rhododendrons, I admit that he clasped me to his manly bosom and sought my lips with his. But this I attribute only to a rush of fellowship and goodwill, and not to any unnatural urge.

———————————

Though as you will see, there were others less charitably disposed.

We were sitting at tea one day, watching the hymnodist's 'purple-headed mountain, the river running by', when old Diplock the butler announced a Miss White. And into the room there glided the dearest little thing! Auburn curls peeping from under a straw bonnet and the neatest little foot you ever saw; the whole set off by a rosy mouth and a sparkling eye. It chanced that as she entered, Henry was holding my hand, making some emphatic point or other, as was his way. And by the first glitter and dart of her eye, I saw that she had formed a certain conclusion about the nature of my friendship with Henry – justified, I am sure, by neither of our natures – God forbid!

Henry introduced us, and told me that she was a milliner in Dunquin, and trimmed the sweetest things in hats, à la mode de Paris. (He loves to concern himself with the furbelows of the Sex). He tried to talk about hats. But Miss White directed her attention entirely at me – rather I think to his disgust – and perhaps misinterpreted my natural shyness as an actual fear of women. For as we parted on the doorstep, to drive en convoi to Dunquin, she leaned towards me and said, 'Well, Reverend, but I'll be the converting of you yet!' Then she was gone, leaving only a breath of perfume. And I must confess a very powerful impression.

How strangely pride creeps on the soul! That perfume stayed with me through a week of visiting the sick and strained politeness with Father Heenan, one of the Devil's sharpest instruments in the parish (forgive such detail, but it comes back now fresh as if it was yesterday; and it was the last happy time in my sinful life, so I relive it! I relive it!) Often and often I fell into a reverie as to how I could best prove to Miss White that I was not of the aesthetic persuasion, but was on the contrary a mad enthusiast for the company of women.

A solution was not long in presenting itself.

On the Thursday, after evensong, I went to call on Miss White at the milliner's, feigning an interest in having a hat trimmed for my Mother. She was sweetly kind, lowering her eyes and mantling, but letting (I noticed) her fingers tangle with mine as we both reached for an errant cotton reel. I called on her the next day, and the day after that. Then,

God forgive me, I visited her at home, and found (the minx!) that her mother was not there, having gone to visit relatives in Cork. I know now that I should there and then have remembered my cloth, and shaken the dust of that place from my sandals.

But Satan tempted me, and I fell. Oh, how I fell!

I must say that Miss White and her mother made it very easy for me; suspiciously easy, I should perhaps in retrospect say. Perhaps – certainly – I should impute to them a dishonourable motive. But let us admit that it was no more dishonourable than my own. In short, with full mutual consent we had carnal knowledge one of the other. On the first occasion, Miss White did me the honour of yielding up to me her maidenhead. All that May of 1880 we were scarcely out of each other's sight, God forgive me. I found an abandoned cottage at Malpas. Henry Costelloe was away in Egypt, and we lived like Adam and Eve in that Eden of Munster, hidden from the eyes of all.

But not the eye of God, who sees everything!

Matters changed. Henry Costelloe came back from Egypt, the Vicar put me in charge of the Luttrellstown school, and my mother wrote from England. It was while I was pondering this letter that there was a sharp knock at the door of my digs, and Mrs Slevin the landlady showed up Mrs White, cold as steel and somewhat harder. I had dealt shamefully with her daughter. I had abused the trust of God and man. The Vicar, the Police, Henry Costelloe, my family in England, all would certainly know. Unless, of course, I consented to an immediate wedding, which would give her daughter back her honour, and provide a father for the child who would arrive in six months.

The child, my poor Mrs Costelloe, who was to be christened Dulcibella, and grow to become you.

So it was, my dearest Dulcibella, that your unworthy father went immediately to Queenstown and boarded an emigrant ship. Cowardly, you may say. But how would I have explained my marriage to an Irish milliner to the Vicar, the Bishop, and my Mother? Not to mention my second cousin Emily, whom I had married a year previously in Southampton?

I have since then devoted my life to good works, my daughter. I hope

and pray that this will make it possible for you to forgive one who has the honour to be
   Your father
   Nathanael Slater.

I read the letter to Helen in the morning. She was pale and abstracted, bouncing Hannah on her knee in one of the wrecked chairs by the hall fire. When I had finished, the bouncing stopped. Then she said, 'So no-one told Desmond that Dulcie was his half sister. No Victorian orgy.'

'Your grandfather invented it to cover up something else.'

'How do you know?'

'He talked to Mrs Caroe. Then he paid her off, ten pounds a week, all those years. Big money. Big secret.'

She put Hannah on the carpet. Hannah beetled towards me, walking on her fingers and her toes. She said, 'Grandpa had the motive. He had the opportunity. He found the body.'

'Mairi Dugdale found the body.'

'And had a special relationship with Grandpa ever after. Grandpa had to do what the Cosgraves told him, even when it destroyed his life.' I picked up Hannah, small, warm and clean-smelling. She hauled at my ear with her sticky hands. It would have been nice and homely, if it had not been for ancient deaths, and my arm feeling as if it wanted to come off, and Finbarr out there somewhere.

The telephone rang. I gave Hannah to Helen and walked across the hall and picked up the receiver with my good hand. Angela's voice said, 'Have you seen him?'

'No.'

'Listen,' said Angela. 'I think something's happened. He didn't turn up last night and now his clothes have gone. So's his car. Emily's in a state.'

'Do you want to talk to Helen?'

'No.' She put the phone down.

When I went back in, Helen said, 'What is it?'

'It's time I called the Guards.'

Her freckles looked like grey mud on white paper. 'I'll do it,' she said. 'I'll try Emily first.' She gave me Hannah, and went out of the room to the telephone. I heard her ask for Emily's number, then a murmured conversation. When she came back, she looked pale. No, distraught; and frightened. She said, 'She's in a hell of a state. He told her he had to sort things out. Then he left. She doesn't know what he meant. I'll ring the Guards now.'

I had never heard her sound like this before.

'I've got to go out,' I said.

'Where?'

'Work.' I had Mrs Cosgrave's key in my pocket.

'Don't leave us alone too long.' She took my hand, a little shame-faced. She had got the message, at last.

I pulled on an old tweed coat from the hall. I was on my way out of the door when I had another thought. I went to the gun room and took from the rack a shotgun and a pocketful of cartridges. It was a dirty grey day. The thickets pressing onto the lawn could have held hundreds of Finbarrs. What was I doing here?

Looking after my family.

The Owenafisk was ugly and turbid with rain. I walked through the reedbeds and onto the path that rose towards the dam. The generator shed stood bland and boxy on its flat patch of ground, the empty poles marching into the black woods.

The door was padlocked shut. I took out the key Mrs Cosgrave had given me.

It turned in the lock.

The generators stood side by side, hunchbacked in the light sneaking through the cobwebby window. My feet crunched on the usual Malpas filth. I held my breath.

On top of the housing of the first generator the paint was scratched, the scratches rusty but not ancient. I raised my eyes to the rafters.

On the tie-beam of the truss over the generator was a square-sided thickening. I climbed onto the machine housing, put up my hand and gave it a push. A gritty dust fell in my face. Something smacked onto the floor. I scrambled down, blinking and spitting.

There was a bundle on the concrete: a bundle of drawing books. The cartridge paper pages were full of small, precise drawings, each framed in a little square of pencil. Near the beginning, a page caught my eye.

There we were, the day after we had met.

There was Helen, serene, the way she had looked during our time together in England, without the shadow of anxiety she had acquired since Malpas. There was a date, early October the year before last. There was me, dark, closed, threatening. This was the page I had tried to buy off Steve in Helen's room in the safe, clean streets of Helmstone. And Steve had refused to sell it. 'Come to my retrospective,' he said. 'In, what, fifty years?'

It had been more like eighteen months.

I put the bundle into my coat pocket. I locked up the shed. Putting the shotgun on my good shoulder, I made my way home.

Chapter Twenty-Six

Some of what follows I have had to reconstruct from the small evidence at my disposal. I am sure it is true, though. The signs are all there, buried in the minds of witnesses, and visible in the fabric of Malpas itself.

There had been the rumble of engines on the drive, a sharp whiff of petrol blown down from the hill. It said so on the last page of the last of Peter Costelloe's casebooks.

The Doctor would have stepped out of his Laboratory. Not the confident doctor of old, this, his black eyes gleaming with professional confidence and secrets comfortably stored. This was a pale doctor, his heather-mixture suit hanging off him, black rings under his eyes. A doctor who stood behind one of the pillars in the colonnade, and watched Jesse's terrier Jack gallop out to bark at the shapes of the vehicles emerging from the rain.

There were three lorries, painted drab Army green. The men in them wore khaki uniforms and dark-green RIC bonnets soaked black by the rain. Some carried rifles whose bayonets shone pale in the grey light from the clouds. They formed up in a double line. Someone shouted an order. The shouter was a smallish man, with a high, cracked voice and brown boots below his breeches.

The Doctor recognised the pale face, once boyish, but now with the flesh gone from it so it was all tics and angles. A sharp, driven face. The face of Carruthers, whom they called the Twitcher.

The Doctor would have drawn in a breath, held it. Dulcie came out of the house. Carruthers snapped a salute at her. She flushed. He said something to her – it would have been too far away for the Doctor to hear what. She started to raise an arm. Jack the terrier yapped, his black ears dancing on his white head. A small figure ran down the steps: Jess, pursued by Frau Bildt in a flurry of skirts. Carruthers looked down at the boy. His hand went to the gun on his belt. Dulcie's arm continued its arrested motion. She pointed towards the Laboratory, outside whose door the Doctor was standing.

Had been standing.

The colonnade was empty. The Doctor had gone.

From the Letters of D.W.

It happened very quickly. Too quickly, almost. Last night I called on dear Jamesy, Emily being away. He comforted me for an hour – what strength I draw from him! Then he motored me to Kiltane, and we talked at length to Maurice Devereux about what must be done.

A simple police action was proposed. I came back much easier in my mind. Frau Bildt brought Jess down. Everything seems to worry the boy. I know that part of him that is mine will be resolute. But there is another half to him, and on that he will need God's pity and forbearance.

So an early dinner in my study, and to bed. A calm night – calmer than for many months, years, even. The boil I have sensed this long, long time is coming to a head. Soon it will be lanced, uncertainty banished, good order re-established, justice done, a curtain drawn on the shame of the past.

This morning I was up early, still calm, and took toast and tea in the morning room. I told Frau Bildt to look after Jess, not to let him out of her sight. The appointed hour was nine o'clock. But the engines sounded on the hill at half past eight, and by five-and-twenty to, they were in the drive, and I was upon the steps to greet them.

'Good morning, ma'am,' said Lieutenant Carruthers.

He was pale and greasy under his bonnet. His eyes have a way of looking not at one but beside one. He chews his lips constantly, and the skin under his right eye gathers and releases, gathers and releases. As he stood there in front of his forty young men, I thought what a responsibility it was for one yet so young, and how smart they were compared with the Fenian rabble that burned the Pavilion at the suggestion of that man.

'My dear Mrs Costelloe,' said Lieutenant Carruthers. 'I think you know why we're here.' He chewed his lips some more. Really, he does look awfully tired. 'Now, then. Where's the bugger hiding? Shun, damn you!' This to one of his men, a fat fellow with a great scar on his face, who had broken wind.

There was a snigger in the ranks. Well, boys will be boys, I suppose, and these Black and Tans are irregulars, so I suppose they must be forgiven a little vulgarity. I began to point towards the East Pavilion, where at this time of day he would usually be skulking in the Laboratory. But at that moment, there was the noise of Frau Bildt shouting in the house, and the door burst open, and Jess was suddenly standing at my side, white and (to a mother's eye) trembling.

'Who are these men?' he said, in a high, strained voice.

'Auxiliary police,' I said, for the name 'black and tan' is not one that he would properly have understood.

But he said it himself. 'Black and Tans,' he said. 'Murdering vermin. Go away!'

I was *so* cross. How dare he! But dear Lieutenant Carruthers was soldier enough to know what to do. He pulled his great revolver from his belt, and tugged back the hammer, and presented it at Jess's white, obstinate little face. 'Manners, sonny Jim,' he said, and pulled the trigger.

Well, of course the cylinder was empty, but Jess did not know that. I saw the dark wet spread down the leg of his shorts, heard the terrier Jack whimper. I felt a strong motherly urge to pick him up and protect him from these men. But one must be firm. Spare the rod, spoil the child; the boy was learning a lesson he would not soon forget.

I pointed to the pavilion. I said, 'He will be over there.'

'What do you want?' said Jess.

'Word with him,' said Carruthers.

'What sort of a word?'

'Shut your — mouth,' said Carruthers. 'Stand easy, lads.'

I said, 'There is no need to use that kind of language.'

'You too, old girl,' said Carruthers.

I stared at him. For a moment I saw not brave Tom Carruthers, but a vicious little officer and forty bravoes, grinning and smoking and spitting now, no better than the dirty Shinners. Then I reflected on the way the Doctor had taken me in, his falsity, the way he had abused his friends. If there is anyone to blame for this ugliness, it is him. I looked at Lieutenant Carruthers, worn to a frazzle in the cause of Right. And a voice inside me said, *The hour produces the man.*

'Oi!' cried a voice from the ranks. I heard feet pounding on stone. And there was Jess, naughty boy, sprinting down the colonnade as fast as his little legs would carry him (Frau Bildt, needless to say, had fled indoors). I turned back to Carruthers to apologise for his behaviour – Jess is a strange child, highly strung, his father's influence of course – to see half a dozen of the troop with their guns up, pointing at him! I think I screamed. I am sure I did. 'Hold your fire,' roared Lieutenant Carruthers. To me, he said, 'Shut your — yap, woman!'

Bang, went one of the guns, and the stone pineapple on top of the pavilion rolled smash into the gutter.

I was about to protest. But Lieutenant Carruthers spoke before I could. 'If you do not hold your row,' he said, 'Jenkins here will put your little boy's brains up the roof. Do you understand?'

The shock was terrible. I thought I was going to faint. But I kept my countenance. I said, 'Do not hurt the boy. Please.'

Carruthers' face moved as if there were insects under the skin. 'All right, then. Jenkins, Miles, come here.'

'And me?' I said.

'Get lost, you old tart,' he said, and turned away. Then he looked back. 'By the way,' he said. 'We've been talking to your pal Jamesy and his pal Maurice, and they've told us some nasty little stories about things here. So we're going to arrange something a bit special for hubby. *Pour encourager les autres*, all that. Do you want to watch?'

He was grinning. His eyes were mad. But Jamesy respects him. He says that Maurice has sent him to free us of this burden. And once he is done, Malpas will be itself again.

But still. I did not want to watch.

* * *

Again, I have no direct evidence for what follows. I never met Helen Costelloe's father. But I know the facts are true in outline, and from there to what follows is a small leap of the imagination.

More's the pity.

Jess, running.

He could still feel the cold round press of the gun barrel on his head. He had played with guns, toy guns, and next birthday Daddy was going to give him a 28-bore and start him off shooting a bit. But that twitching man in the dark-green bonnet had had a different sort of gun, big and heavy and stinking of oil and probably gunpowder. A gun meant for shooting people, not ducks.

At first he had been jolly excited. Uniforms were thrilling – guns, marching, army men, all that. But just now they had stopped being exciting and become frightening. So frightening that he was crying. He could not help it.

Out of the colonnade and into the trees.

Oh, crikey, Mummy. But Mummy had just stood there as if she trusted that man. Who had had an awful, wriggling, twitching sort of face and beastly eyes that would not look at you properly. And a laugh that was not at anything except what was inside his own head. A really really cruel frightening man, but Mummy seemed not to mind.

Keep running, keep running, bend low through the cinnamon trunks of the rhododendrons, run, run where nobody big could follow . . .

Frau Bildt would not talk about it but Bridie would, and she said the Lads were everywhere, they were only great, and there were these murdering torturing animals of Tans, God save us, and the Twitcher the worst of them. And when he had said what kind of Tans, she had said Black and Tans, in a whisper, because everyone knew that Naming Calls.

His breath was coming hard now. There was a feeling like nails in his chest. But he kept going, through the Bamboozery, out over the Avenue Bridge and along the path until the ground started to rise.

They were after Daddy. They could not be allowed to get him.

Mummy seemed to think it was all right but she did not understand. She did not talk to Bridie anyway, or to Daddy. She just talked to fat smelly red Jamesy, who was probably too stupid to know about Black and Tans.

Up the hill, up the hill. Twenty more steps running and he would let himself walk for a bit. Except that it was important to go quick so even though his heart was going whack whack whack and his lungs hurt and his legs were tired he must keep on—

Whoops. Over a root he went, knee lots of blood brave soldiers don't cry, except he did cry because it hurt awfully and he was crying already anyway, but he did not stop running because he had to warn Daddy and help him get away, he did not know how, but Daddy would think of something, he always thought of everything.

On top of the River Cliff now. Stop, hands on knees, panting. Blink the tears away, let the gallop of the heart slow to a canter. Thread through the rubble of the Temple of the Graces. The marble table burnt to powder, the pillars fallen down. The only place that had not burned in the fire was the log cellar. Always go to the log cellar if you were in trouble. Down the path to the iron door. The leaf-litter scuffed with feet. Bend down. 'Daddy?'

Silence. A pigeon cooing in the trees.

'Daddy, it's me.'

The black iron door of the cellar opening a crack. A voice. 'Go away.' Daddy's voice.

'They're after you.'

'I know. Go away, quick, somewhere else.'

'But Daddy—'

'Now.'

A dog, barking. Jack. Dear Jack.

'Quite right,' said a voice. 'You go away.' The voice of the man in a khaki uniform with a dark-green bonnet, who had just stepped into the clearing. The man was carrying a sort of gun with a round thing under it. A Tommy gun. Jess had seen them in the papers. 'You're a hell of a runner, young fellow-me-lad. But so's your little dog, and so am I. Now you come out of there, Costelloe, before I mince you up tidy.' He stuck a cigarette between his thin, grinning lips. The machine gun did not waver.

And the black iron door opened, and Daddy came out, all dirty and a horrible white colour about the face, and the man with the gun kicked him.

Jack the terrier tried to bite the man, but he was wearing thick boots and all he did was give a big kick of his foot and Jack cartwheeled away, and landed on his back, and then the man put up his gun and shot him.

At first Jesse could not believe it. He went to pick up poor Jack but he was all blood with his eyes open and his tongue out a bit. Tears burned his eyes. He ran at the man with the gun. The man with the gun clouted him on the side of the head so the world went dim and red and he could not stand up any more. And the one thing he knew, then and for ever afterwards, was this.

It was all his fault.

Chapter Twenty-Seven

My original idea had been to take the sketchbooks in to Helen. Not immediately, though. They would be painful for her. Forewarned would be forearmed.

Or so I told myself. But I know there was also an element of academic greed here. I had earned first look by my persistence, and I would have it.

So I took the books and the gun to the Laboratory, and locked myself in, and settled by a window that overlooked the sweep in front of the house, in case Finbarr decided to pay a visit. Then I lit the lamp, cleared a space on the bench, and laid out the sketchbooks.

I flicked backwards to the page on which I had first met Helen. There she was. There I was, closed and hostile. Over a page, I was walking out of a door, slump-shouldered, defeated. The date was the date of my last tryst with Mara. Then Steve and Helen were in a car, and Fishguard sat above its bay. There were two people outside a building that must have been the registry office, the woman – Helen, solemn – holding out to the man – Steve, grinning – the palm of her hand, on which there sat a child. Then there was a train passing over a bridge; and a sheet of water that was the river, and at the top of it Malpas. A Malpas brilliantly lit and smiling, with in the foreground Helen, her hands on her great belly, quiet and proud as a Madonna.

Then something happened. There was a picture of mother and child: Hannah close up, smiling at the painter, her eyes shining, hands reaching out. But Helen was further away, eyes lowered, unreachable. Then she had moved further, down a colonnade into a world lit from elsewhere.

On the next page there was Steve, hair lank, eyes haunted, staring straight out at me. Round him, the world darkened into a wild scribble of ink, into which appeared to have been rubbed soil, leaves, river mud: a dark, oppressive mess surrounding the terrified figure in the middle. A portrait of a man buried alive.

Early in the books, the dates of the drawings had been continuous. Now they appeared at monthly intervals. After the drawing of himself in the darkness, they were replaced by shopping lists, paint and drink mostly, and draft letters to God and Rembrandt. Then there was a blank page marked in rotten, dripping letters THREE MONTHS. On the page after that, in the middle, was another oddity. It looked like a pen. It was not a pen, though. It was a silver propelling pencil, held between a thumb and forefinger drawn in the style of Dürer's *Praying Hands*. And behind the pencil, a tiny, brilliantly drawn face. The foxy, horribly intense face of Finbarr Durcan.

After the silver pencil, the pages changed. The desperate irony had gone. The drawings were bigger, bolder. Helen scarcely featured. Instead, there was Angela. There was a full-page drawing of her, demure, eyes down, arms folded, in a black polo-neck and pearls. On the next page was the same drawing, but nude, the breasts heavy over the folded arms, still demure, but the demureness now erotic and enticing. And after that there was Angela sprawled on her back, fingers sunk in her breasts, moaning in orgasm. And a dreadful little cartoon of naked Angela on hands and knees, naked Steve kneeling up behind her like a dog, both of them looking out of the page, winking with the right eye, the tongues hanging out.

There were pages of this stuff, minute, pornographic, executed with the pen strokes of a knife murderer, each more manic than the last. They were dated hours, sometimes minutes apart. And at the end of the pages, a picture of Finbarr, arms folded, frowning. In his right hand he held the silver pencil, which he seemed to be tapping irritably on the table at which he sat. There was a glass on the table, and a whiskey bottle, lying on its side to show it was empty. And finally there was another self-portrait, this time of Steve in a stupid Edwardian bathing costume, jumping up and down. There was a medal hung round his neck, and he was giving someone the finger.

The last page of the last book was covered in writing.

to Eamon de Valera
Dáil Eireann
A Chara
  I have the pleasure to inform you that I have discovered one of Ireland's great treasures, namely the Crown of Tara. This priceless jewel has been for many years at Malpas, having been put here for safe keeping long ago in 1801, and had been thought lost. I have discovered its whereabouts, and propose that you send an armoured truck to collect it to the above address, at a time to suit your convenience. It is the property of the nation, and the nation must have it back without delay.
  Mise, le meas
  Stephen Brennan

I read it twice. My body was glazed with cold sweat. I did not know what to do. I really did not know. It was not the manic fantasy – I was used to that. Or even the fact that he might be telling the truth, that he had known the whereabouts of this treasure. The horror of this letter was that it had directly caused his death.

Finbarr had told me. He wanted the Crown of Tara to sell, to revive Malpas' wrecked fortunes, or his own. Finbarr had been unable to find the Crown, but he had told Moriarty he knew a man who knew where it was.

Steve had found it. He had drafted this letter. He would have shown it to Finbarr, because he knew Finbarr wanted the Crown the way he had wanted the Trident. Steve would have enjoyed tormenting him with it. And three days later, he had committed suicide.

Curious coincidence.

I moistened my dry lips. I rang the house. Helen answered. She said. 'I called the Guards. They can't arrest him. He hasn't done anything. But they have him under their eye.' She sounded nervous. 'What now?'

'Lock the door,' I said. 'Don't open it for anyone except me.'

I put the sketchbook in the cupboard, locked the Laboratory door and pocketed the key. Then I shouldered the gun, walked up to the Dower House and hammered on the door.

It opened a crack. Angela's face was haloed gold by the light behind her hair. She said, 'Why the gun?'

'Pigeons. I want to talk.'

'Can't it wait?'

'About you and Steve.' I walked forward. She kept her hand on the door, but offered no resistance.

For a moment, all the sexy plumpness had gone out of her face. Then she said, 'Won't be a minute, now. There's whiskey in the kitchen.'

When she came back, she had put her face straight. She reached across the table and poured herself some whiskey. She said, 'I gave her a pill. You don't look so great.'

I said, 'I was kicked by a horse.'

'Oh.'

'Tell me about Steve.'

Her glass stopped halfway to her mouth.

'You and the landlady's husband, was the way you put it last time. I've got evidence.'

She drank from her glass. She said, with a twist to her mouth, 'What evidence would that be?'

I said, 'You don't need to know. But if you don't tell the truth, I think the landlady might be interested in it.'

A dull tide of blood spread up her neck. 'You are a creepy bastard,' she said. 'The truth about what?'

'About Steve,' I said. 'From the beginning.'

'One is not a sodding desk diary.'

'He arrived,' I said. 'With his wife. How did they strike you?'

'What do you think?' she said. 'I mean frankly one had been getting on perfectly well without them one's whole life. And all of a sudden there we are on our best behaviour, me, Finbarr as well. Helen was all right. Made herself at home, nice girl, easy to get on with, understanding, kept self to self, all that. Wasn't so sure about Steve. But at least he could paint, and nobody ever minds having someone around who can actually do something. And time went on, and she got more and more pregnant, and I don't think she was talking to him much. He drank more and more and worked less and less. I used to look at him stumbling about the place, and think, how long can that man go on like this?' She reached for the bottle. 'And that's it.'

'No,' I said. 'There's more. He stopped drawing.'

Her eyebrows went up. 'Ah,' she said. 'The sketchbook.' Then she blushed, properly this time, as if a pink sheet was being drawn slowly up her face. The blush was rather endearing.

'He stopped,' I said. 'And then he started again. What happened?'

She said, 'You know, don't you. You've got the book.'

I did not answer.

'All right,' she said. 'What happened was that silly Steve lost it. He disappeared right up his own arsehole and sort of sat there sucking his thumb. He didn't even get to the pub. Just sat up on the dam all day, every day, rain or shine, painting, burning the paintings. I tried to get him out of it. He said, oh, no, couldn't paint, what was the point? Blocked, he said he was.'

'Blocked.'

'No point in painting. Might as well give up. He said it was all too big, too beautiful, too real. Plus a lot of hot air about Ireland, must be undivided, land of saints and scholars, you know. And poor Helen had enough to do with the baby. And I'd been no good, and the doctors were bloody useless. So Finbarr took over.'

'Him and his silver pencil.'

She had been looking down at the table. Now she looked up, one eyebrow in the air. 'How did you know that?'

'Steve drew it. It is what you would call an heirloom, that pencil.'

'Finbarr said that he, Steve that is, was blocked in with shadows, you know how he talks. He made him turn those shadows into shading on a paper. He made him rub them out, blow them away. It was incredible. Six goes, was all it took. And he was cured. Too cured.'

'What do you mean?'

Angela waved the whiskey bottle at her glass. 'One minute he was squatting there on that dam, not painting, not talking, even. Then

Finbarr got hold of him, and you couldn't stop him at all.'

'Couldn't stop him what?'

'Anything. I mean I remember he was in the woods painting, and I ran into him and said good morning, and took a look at the picture he was painting, and said it looked great, because it did. He was a really lovely painter. He had a way of sort of getting inside a thing and painting what it was made of. I began to think he was like that as a person. I mean, he had fewer layers than other people, which meant that he felt things more deeply.'

'You were in the woods.'

'He started just sort of explaining everything, as if someone had uncorked him, which they had, I mean Finbarr had. He told me about Helen and him, and how he loved her and got amazed when she married him, but how since they'd come here she didn't pay any attention to him, and he was in bits. All the time he was talking he was doing this incredible stuff with his brush, just splashes of colours coming alive, amazing. It was one of the most beautiful things I'd ever seen, and he was laughing about it too, and saying it was all Finbarr that had released him so he could do it again, bloody marvellous, you know how English people talk, while this picture just poured out of him natural as rain.' She fell silent.

Perhaps Finbarr had effected a magical cure. Or perhaps he had climbed on the upswing of Steve's bipolar disorder, and it was nothing to do with him at all.

I said, 'And then?'

'I kissed him,' she said.

'And then?'

'And all that.'

'You had an affair?'

She shrugged and made a face. 'You've seen the drawings. They are taken from life.'

'And were you still having one when he was killed?'

'No.'

'What stopped you?'

'It just stopped.'

'Nothing to do with Finbarr, then.'

She put her elbow on the table and laid her head in the crook of her arm. 'It is very lonely here,' she said. 'I don't think you've got any idea just how lonely it is. A person will do almost anything for a bit of warmth.' Pause. 'All right. I stopped it. It was getting out of control.'

'He wanted to run off with you?'

'Of course. But that wasn't it.' She blushed again, that endearing blush.

'Go on.'

'You've seen the painting over Mummy's bed,' she said. 'Mummy likes it. Finbarr didn't.'

'You showed it to him?'

'That is not the way it was,' she said. 'I told you, Steve had like a firework up his behind. Once Finbarr set him going there was no stopping him till he was in orbit. So he painted that picture of me, and just to show Finbarr how cured he was, he made him a present of it.'

'Or maybe to show he was grateful for being cured.'

'Steve was not a grateful person. He had rights, not duties. You know he only gave pictures away when he wanted to beat the shite out of someone. He didn't like Finbarr. Not many people do.'

'You like him.'

'We're neighbours.'

I thought of Finbarr's hands kneading her buttocks. In a neighbourly manner.

'So he gave Finbarr the picture to rub his nose in it. And Finbarr passed it on to me, so I would know he knew. Three days later, we broke up.' She smiled at me, a tight, false smile. 'He was telling everyone he'd found the Crown of Tara. I brought him back to the house and told him not to be so silly. He started screaming at me and walked out, and I told him not to come back.'

'You didn't believe him?'

She sighed. 'He also said he knew where the Apostle Paul had his lunch, that there were Russian submarines coming up the river with supplies of vodka for him and him alone, and that if he wanted he could make the night last for ever. Everyone is always talking about the

Crown of Tara and I have to tell you I do not believe in it or any other miracle that is going to save this place.'

'What exactly did he say?'

'I honestly can't remember. And since you've been asking all these questions,' she said, 'let me ask you one. What happened to you Monday afternoon?'

'I thought you might be busy with Finbarr.'

'Finbarr?'

'I came to see you after we walked down to the gasometer. Finbarr was sitting on the doorstep of the pavilion in the park. You were sitting on Finbarr.'

She stared at me. She opened her mouth to say something. Then she began to laugh. She laughed like a hyena. I felt the sulky blood rise to my face. I got up and left her to it.

The Laboratory was cool and quiet, full of balmy yellow light. I sat at the bench and leafed through the early pages of the sketchbook, the ones I had not bothered with yesterday. There was a lot of Helmstone. You could see people working and playing, getting on a footing with life. Not like Malpas.

I turned the page.

There was a picture of an old man against a dark background. The background was full of the glints of water, and pillars that might have been the supports of a pier. The caption said 'Old man on Beach – Helmstone'. The date was the date of my first meeting with Helen, the date of her almost fatal swim.

The face in the drawing was ancient and haggard. It had a family resemblance to Finbarr. Except that the eyes were bigger and darker, the bags under them deep and dreadful and cardiac.

I held the drawing next to the handbill I had tacked to the laboratory wall. The two faces were the same. They were both the face of the late Timsy Durcan, alias the Great Mentalini.

Chapter Twenty-Eight

This is another passage based on thin records. I have pieced the action together from conversations, and atmospheres, and of course the archeological evidence in the great dank rooms of Malpas itself.

The house was full of smoke: blue smoke, perfumed with myrrh and other essences, or as close as anyone could get in the County Waterford, which meant a bit of incense swiped by Bridie's brother Declan from Cappoquin Church, where he was the altar boy. The reason for the smoke was that Jamesy was in Egypt, far away from Emily, his wife, and Dulcie, who for all the pleasure in her these days might as well have been his other wife.

Not literally in Egypt, of course. The farming was gone to hell and the patients did not come and all in all funds were none too plentiful, these last five years since the Doctor was not around any more. The grass on the lawns was longer, the laurel and ponticum growing unlopped over the rides in the shrubberies. When a window in the stables broke, someone banged a bit of an old cardboard box into it, instead of worrying the bank with the expense of a glazier.

So when Jamesy wished to go to Egypt, he no longer sent a telegram to Thomas Cook. He merely shut himself up in the Big Drawing Room with whatever books on that old pyramid pancake he could find in the library, latched the shutters, and raised the temperature to Nile Valley levels with the aid of paraffin heaters. Meals were as Egyptian as spaghetti and sultanas could make them. They were served by Jerry the boots, temporarily promoted to majordomo by the assumption of bedroom slippers and a fez, in the atmosphere of spice and mystery provided by the holy myrrh.

The boy Jesse stood in the cold hall hating the stink and wondering what he was doing here. He was away at school now. He had gone five years ago, to England, after . . . what had happened. The first holidays he had returned, he had walked around the park for the first few days vacant and distraught, as if looking for something or someone. Then he had gone missing, and had been found two days later, after a general search, in the Pink House over the river, being cared for by the Cosgraves. He had been taken back to the House, and (on his mother's instructions) soundly whipped by beef-red Jamesy.

After that, Jesse had refused to return to Malpas in the holidays. He had stayed with friends in England – away from Malpas, he was a bright, good-natured boy – or even remained at school.

But at the end of last term, Dulcie had written to him in such affectionate terms that he had assumed she must be fatally ill. He loved her only in the formal sense of the word – she was not one to give love the opportunity to develop, and besides, he had hardly seen her since he had been nine. But he was a boy who combined with his other good qualities a powerful sense of duty.

Or so his school reports said. To meet, he was now a lanky youth with a big Adam's apple and a long, narrow face crowded with freckles. His eyes were brown and guarded. His nose, currently wrinkled against Jamesy's ersatz myrrh, was long and high-bridged.

His mother swept into the hall. In her hand was a clipboard bearing a thick wad of lists. Her hair was a grey frizz. Her green eye was large and imperious. 'What do you want?' she said.

The boy said, 'You asked me to come.'

Something like confusion showed in her face. Then she recalled that this was indeed her son, whom she had borne and watched grow. Who had according to his school reports proved himself worthy . . . But that was all arranged.

Her mind floated away to the reorganisation of the dairy. A new milking parlour would make all the difference, if the money could be found, as it might be, given an acceleration of the felling in the Nier woods. She must talk to Jamesy about that.

She rustled her lists at Jesse with a short, oil-stained finger. 'Yes, yes.

There is some legal business to be done. Come here.' She swept across the hall to her study – a bright room, free of incense, unfeminine except for a gigantic vase of dried hydrangeas that stood among rolled-up blueprints on the mulberry-wood table in the window. She sat at her desk and leafed through a rack of files hanging in a drawer. 'Here,' she said, and placed a folder on the leather in front of her.

The boy made to come round the table and look over her shoulder. 'No,' she said. 'No, no, no. Stay there.' He stood awkwardly in front of her. She said, 'Dear Jess.' The words sounded foreign as Egypt in her mouth.

Jesse did not know what you said when people went on like this. Harry Fortescue had asked him to shoot in Northumberland. It would have been good fun and much, much less *odd*. Jesse hated oddness more than anything.

'Look at it,' she said, and pushed a paper across the table. He picked it up. His hands were damp, the writing strange and loopy, full of hereinunders and wheretofores. Even if he had not felt so nervous and embarrassed he would not have been able to make head nor tail of it. 'Well?' she said, frowning.

He said, 'I don't . . . I mean, what is it?'

'Oh, God.' She had no patience with misunderstanding. She was always wanting to get on to the next thing. He began to feel rushed and flustered. 'A will. A new one. It means that when I die, this place will be yours. Malpas. Look.' She snatched the paper out of his hands. 'It'll all be yours.'

He said, 'Why?'

'You're my son.'

'Yes.' She was not like other mothers. Malpas was not like other places. Malpas had been a thing he sensed dimly, hanging in his future like a thunderstorm not yet arrived. Now he could feel the storm almost upon him, dimming the light.

'But don't tell anyone,' she said.

'What?'

'There are those who think they have it already. They think they've got round me.' She was grinning. It was a frightening grin, with a fox in its ancestry. Jesse absolutely hated it. It brought back everything about Malpas that was chaotic, and cold, and nightmarish.

'Aren't you pleased?' she said. Then, without waiting for an answer, 'Well, you will be.' She snatched the paper out of his hand, put it and her own copy back in the file. 'And Probus has got one,' she said. 'Now what are you going to do?'

He stood for a moment gazing vaguely past her and out of the window. There were brambles in the ha-ha, he noticed, and the lawn was hairy round the balustrades where once it had been clipped neat. Memories too dreadful for actual recall rolled in the cellars of his mind. He took a decision. He said, 'I think I'll go.'

'Where?'

He knew she was not interested; it was merely that she liked to know things. 'Harry Fortescue. In Northumberland.'

'England.' She sounded surprised.

'Yes.' Of course, you silly old idiot, he shouted in his head. Why would he want to stay in Ireland, where there was nothing but being bored and lonely and worse?

But she was not going to argue. She was already leaving the room, bent on . . . something or other, that had nothing to do with him. Her life had nothing to do with him, nor his with her.

God, he hated this beastly place.

He left on the four o'clock from Dunquin. His mother would have said goodbye, but she was really exceptionally busy, the way she was every afternoon, so she simply did not get the chance.

Then, or (as it turned out) ever.

Jamesy left Egypt that night and popped around for a chat the next morning, as usual. He was fat now, Jamesy, and getting bigger by the week, so that the waistcoat of his new thornproof suit was already under pressure, and the expanse between his shoulders was a great meaty curve, like a small piece of downland. He had two chins, and his blue eyes gleamed brilliantly in his broad red face. Dangerously red, the face, with hints of purple. But while James was strict with his own patients in the matter of diet, he gave himself great latitude, attributing the pains that racked his lower ribs after meals to a dyspepsia, and quieting them with great creamy draughts of milk from his prize Jerseys.

He was proud of his cattle. He spent much time leaning on a stick in the pasture, admiring their dark, lustrous eyes and the thickness of their lashes. He was proud of Malpas. It was (he told himself) an ideal sort of an estate, considering the times. Now that all the politics was out of the way, he was running the Refuge for the Nervous as it should be run, and the farm as that should be run. The house was going on well, too. It would be better when it belonged to him. And all that stood between him and it was the woman problem.

Not sex, of course; Jamesy was not really interested in sex. Emily had always been a cold fish in that respect. And even Dulcie, who had been pretty hot about the britches a while ago, was less than she used to be, which was good, because doing his duty nowadays left Jamesy badly winded, and with a disconcertingly loud pulse banging in his head.

No, the trouble about the woman problem was that it was intractable. Emily was out of the way, of course, happy as anything as long as she had her Timsy. It had been easy to keep Dulcie in line when that damn Doctor had infested the place. But Jamesy had not become Munster's best hand at nervous diseases by ignoring signals from people around him. Since the Doctor's departure, things had been out of balance. Dulcie, never biddable, had developed a fierce independent cast of mind that took all his skill to counter. And this morning, Mr Probus the solicitor had come to visit him, a confidential visit, one member of the Lodge to another, and one bringing bad tidings.

Yes, thought Jamesy. Matters were indeed at a critical point. But after his sojourn by the Nile, he felt refreshed and able for anything. It was time for action.

From a Statement by James Durcan, 1925, brought in evidence to Dunquin Coroner's Court

On arriving at Malpas House today, I was unable to find Mrs Costelloe, with whom I had made an appointment, her heart presenting certain symptoms I did not altogether like (palpitations, amounting in some cases to actual fibrillation, accompanied by shortness of breath, dropsy and feelings of lassitude).

I had arranged to examine the patient in her study, as was my custom of many years' standing. But I found that she was not there. When I enquired of a servant as to her whereabouts, I was informed that she was above in the Battery House. This came as no surprise, as the patient was an intensely practical lady, who took as much pleasure in her mechanical contrivances as others of the Sex in their clothes or their horses. So to the Battery House I repaired.

At first, I thought it was empty. The atmosphere of the place was somewhat submarine, I found: the long rows of green-glass batteries, the polished brass switches, the whole illuminated by a bluish glow from the bulb, waxing and waning, that indicated how much power was coming down the wires from the Dam. This is fanciful, of course. I mention it only because I, a man of science, found myself, for reasons I could not identify, oddly worried. And when I asked myself why, I realised that the *smell* was wrong.

Normally, the place had a brisk whiff of ozone, and a faint, vinegary suspicion of acid. This morning, the balance was out. The smell of acid was too strong.

I made haste down the alley between the glass battery cases. It was as I had feared.

Mrs Costelloe lay in front of the switching gear. Closer examination pointed to the fact that she had died of a myocardial infarction – a diagnosis confirmed by the later post-mortem examination (melancholy task!) that I conducted at the behest of the Coroner. It seems, therefore, that my poor friend, while cleaning the switches that were her pride and joy, was seized by the heart-pang; or possibly by electrocution, the bus-bars being close at hand. It is an established fact that an ill-timed shock can aggravate a cardiac arrhythmia, with fatal consequences.

I myself am not well. I am afflicted with terrible indigestion, now almost constant. Tomorrow I am to meet with Mr Probus the solicitor on the question of poor Mrs Costelloe's Will, which he says will be of great interest to me and mine.

Letter from Jeremiah Probus to Mrs Emily Durcan

Strictly personal & Without Prejudice
Dear Mrs Durcan,

It is indeed with a heavy heart that I write this letter. I am so sorry about what has happened – and sorrier, I must say, that it was in my own office that the blow fell. I felt I should write to you and tell you the precise circumstances. Painful it may be, but I always feel that things are better said than unsaid.

Well, I wrote to your Husband apprising him that there were matters we should discuss and inviting him to call to my offices. He and I had long worked together on the disposition of the Estate, and I think we understood each other well. So well, indeed, that I took a great interest in the drawing up of Mrs Costelloe's will, of which your late husband was the beneficiary – the whole estate passing to him, with a mere legacy for Master Jesse Costelloe. This disposition of Malpas always seemed fair to me – for who understands the place like a Durcan?

But the day I wrote to your late Husband I had received most surprising news, in the form of a communication from England. There was a while ago – at the time young Costelloe left for England – the idea in Mrs Costelloe's head, impelled by maternal feelings blooming late in life, that she would make a new Will. I duly drew this up according to her desires, which were that the Estate *in toto* should pass to Mr Jesse Costelloe and thereafter to the heirs of his body. I sent it to her to read. As seemed only prudent, I revealed its contents to your late Husband, who I think pointed out to her the folly of such a course: to place Malpas, I mean, in the hands of an inexperienced child rather than of a Durcan.

The new Will was never, to my knowledge, signed. And never would be, for Mrs Costelloe tragically passed away before the formalities could be completed. So on that fatal morning, your late Husband entered my office, accepted a glass of Madeira, and asked me 'what was up?' All glowing, he was, in the anticipation of his family's at last coming into what I know he had come to regard as its rightful fortune.

And I was forced to narrate to him the following shocking events.

On the very morning of Mrs Costelloe's funeral, there had arrived from England an envelope addressed in a fair legal hand. Inside in the envelope was a copy of the Will, duly signed by Mrs Costelloe and witnessed by Sullivan's, a firm of solicitors in Cork renowned for their litigation and inheritance work, as I expect you will know.

'Well?' said your late Husband.

I pushed the Will towards him. I did not trust myself to speak. He read it. The smile congealed on his lips. He turned pale. He rose to his feet. He clapped his hands to his chest. That great face of his turned white, then blue. He fell.

'I love her,' he said, as he lay on the floor. 'All that, and I love her.' These were his exact words, Mrs Durcan. I knew that at this sad time you would want to hear them.

Your friend
Jeremiah Probus

'Of course,' said Emily, 'I knew as soon as I got the letter that it wasn't me he was talking about at all, the fat pig. It was Dulcie.' Her meringue of hair stood dynamited into lacquer-matted strands. The makeup was only half on, the mouth a bright red smear against the sagging grey background.

'Mr Walker, you must go,' hissed the dragon Bridie. 'Can't you see she's upset?'

'Go away,' said Emily. The room was full of stale smoke. 'Now what is it you want, Dave?' Her smile was a stressed-out caricature of the old roguish grin.

I had come to see her and strayed into Jamesy's death because I did not know how to come to the point. Which was that, judging by Steve's drawing, her son Timsy had sent Helen swimming round Helmstone pier with the reasonable certainty that she would not survive.

But she was past telling. 'Finbarr's gone,' she said. Her voice had a hard, digging sound. She was frightened. 'You think you chased him away. He knows this place, you know. We all know it, better than any Costelloe idiots that come and go and fly by night. We're the family here. And I'd say that he's not the one that's going to get hurt. He'll be above in the woods somewhere, watching, never you fear. And he'll be around when you're gone.'

I said, 'The Guards are looking for him. The charge will be attempted murder.'

'Oh,' she said, 'and only attempted, was it? In my day we knew how to fight, you poor feeble thing. But maybe you'd like to lash on the murder anyway, while you're dreaming, and maybe make out that he killed that Stephen Brennan into the bargain.'

I should not have come. I was getting angry. 'I'll pass that on to Helen,' I said. 'And we'll see how long you last here then, you eternal Durcans.'

She narrowed her eyes to black slits. 'My boys are worth forty of you, you wet thing,' she said. 'So you go back and tout about what a bad lot we are and see who listens to you. And you go and talk to your lunatics, your Dugdales or Cosgraves or whatever they call themselves, and believe what they say if you want.'

'Dugdales?' I said.

'Bridie!' she screeched. 'Bridie! BRIDIE!'

Then I was outside, shaking, in the rain.

As I walked down the drive, I saw the diesel-cloud from the Cork bus floating blue above the trees. I sat down on a tree-stump. Soon a huge, rangy figure came loping out of the thicket and down the hill.

I waited for her to come near. 'Mrs Cosgrave,' I said. 'How's Paddy?'

'Out of danger,' she said. 'For the moment, annyway, thank God, and him with someone inside with him all the time. Did you see Finbarr Durcan?'

'He's gone,' I said. I looked into her black eyes, and had one of those moments of quiet, when the present untangles and turns into something you can read.

I said, 'Come and have a cup of tea in the Laboratory.'

So to the Laboratory we went. I made tea, and sat her by the window in the good chair, and picked up a chrome paperweight, and put it where she had to strain her eyes to look at it, and counted her down. And she slipped into trance like a pair of old shoes.

I said, 'Your name is Mrs Cosgrave.'

'It is.'

'Mairi Cosgrave.'

'It is.'

'And before that?'

'Mairi Dugdale,' she said, and sighed a deep, gusting sigh of perfect relief. 'And oh, Doctor!' she said. 'The things I've seen, the things I've seen!'

So I took out a silver florin and a tape recorder, and I started a Braid induction. And very soon, Mairi was telling me the story of her life as she was living it, and the spools of tape were turning.

In his late fifties, Jesse Costelloe had embarked on a tour of Northern Europe, playing the complete Beethoven piano sonatas. This project took him the spring and summer. By September, he was in need of rest.

His invariable technique of resting was to take *St Cecilia* to sea. He sent Helen the usual postcard, but she was occupied with her foundation year and an exciting but very unsafe affair she was having with an armed robber from Lewisham. So she had not got round to answering, and her father had set off singlehanded from Milford Haven, bound for Scilly.

The wind at first blew westerly, as is not unusual at that time of year. *St Cecilia* was sighted by a tanker heading southwest, some fifty miles southwest of St Anne's Head, with Jesse at the wheel. It is hard to be precise about subsequent events. All that the investigation concluded for sure is that the wind went southerly, then southeasterly, and blew between force nine and ten for two days. The wreck of the *St Cecilia* was found in the rocks west of Ardmore on the southern Irish coast. There was no sign of her owner. It was never satisfactorily explained, at least in public, why a well-found vessel like *St Cecilia* would not have run for cover in Waterford, or, had she found herself too far west, in

Youghal or Dunquin. The conclusion of the investigation was that poor Mr Costelloe must have had a heart attack, brought on by exhaustion, and fallen overboard.

There was another view, held by his daughter and perhaps a couple of other people. That was that, gale or no gale, he would have done everything in his power to beat away from the agonising land of Ireland. And when it had been evident that any other landfall was impossible, he had preferred the impossible, and paid the price.

Chapter Twenty-Nine

Walker Archive, Transcript, 1973 – 9
The Doctor, my poor little Doctor. I was inside in the rhodies the day those devils came. I thought they were coming for my Johnny and him away on the mountain. But those Tans they didn't mind who they killed, and that was the way of it, so I thought I should hide, and I hid in the Abbey and then above in the crow oak, as soon as I saw the lorries of them on the river road from Kiltane.

But they did not come near the Pink House. What they had in their dirty minds was different. Which I saw when I was above in the oak: the poor child Jess first, him coming back down the hill bawling and crying as if his heart was broken and him carrying the small little dog he had, and it bleeding all down his shirt. Jesus, it was so terrible to see!

[Q: And what was it that you saw?]

The door is open. The iron door of the log cellar in the Temple place. He is creeping out, my little Doctor, brushing at his knees, poor man, he's all messed up with kipplings and wood dust. The Tan has the gun pointed at him. They're walking down the path from the river cliff, onto the lawns now. The fella with the gun takes the Doctor up to Mrs Costelloe. Mrs Costelloe is with yer man James Durcan and the little Tan with the sharp face that wriggles like it's got worms under it. Jesus, I hate that man, and Mrs Costelloe no better. But I'm inside in the rhododendrons and only for them killing the little dog they'd find me, but they're after killing the dog, so I'm safe, more fool them.

The Doctor is white as a sheet of paper. He says to Mrs Costelloe, 'Don't leave me with these people.' Mrs Costelloe looks at the Doctor with those eyes of hers like cold green water, and she looks away again and Jamesy Durcan the great pig takes her by the arm and leads her into the house like he owns it and her too.

311

The boy was going to his mother, but she turned away from him, and then he goes to the Doctor but the Doctor says in a strange voice, 'Run away! Run away!' And the boy just gives a lep and he is gone, down the ha-ha, still with the little dog, and all those devils laughing at him. And there is the Doctor, all alone, standing in front of the house with all those dirty Tans. His wife has gone and his boy has gone and I can see the knees of him shaking inside in his trousers, dirty trousers, poor man. And the Twitcher says to him in his scratchy voice, 'Now then, old liver-and-lights, what about this Crown of Tara, then?'

'What about it?' says the Doctor, with a sort of a flap to his jaw.

'Where is it, where is it?' says the Twitcher.

'Stolen by the IRA,' says the Doctor.

'Not stolen,' says the Twitcher. 'You gave it to them. And do you know, I think you know where it is. And we'd like it back.'

'I do not know,' said the Doctor. 'I give you my word, I do not.'

'Yes,' says the Twitcher, and he pulls his chin so the bottom teeth show long like a rabbit's. 'That's just the kind of thing he would say, ain't it?'

I am inside in the bushes still. There is a silence now, a thick class of a silence, thick and cold, with all those fellas in the dark-green bonnets looking in at the poor Doctor, and the jaws of them working like dogs the way you can hear the spit wash round in their heads.

'Take him to the stables,' says the Twitcher in a quiet sort of voice, but you can hear the death in it.

Then the Doctor starts a class of a quiet deadly struggle, with a sort of a whimper to it, the way he knew there would be no point crying out. But they are big men those men, big as cattle, and they just laugh at him and they pick him up, my poor little Doctor, and they are taking him round to the stables yard, and him struggling, struggling, and the grit and squinch of their boot-nails on the stones. The bushes are hot and tight and I am hellish frightened but I mustn't lose sight of my dear little Doctor. So I go after them, a way I know, which is back through the bamboos and in at the tack-room door, and I hear a noise from the yard.

[Silence. A long silence.]

A noise from the yard. A terrible bawling and shrieking from the yard. I am crying before I even look out of the window because the noise is the Doctor's, but a noise I never expect to hear out of him. And when I look out of the window very carefully, there in front of me is the window with the webs of spiders on it, and beyond there the stable yard and the stone paving of it in a pattern like the rays of the sun, leading up to the great double doors of the coach house, that are painted greeny blue. The Tans are all round that door laughing, and the smoke of the cigarettes coming off them in clouds, and for a moment I can't see, because of the backs. Then they fall away, like men who are stepping back from their work, and there is a bit of a silence except for that awful roaring and screaming. I can see the whole door now. What there is halfway up the doors is the Doctor, my little Doctor, with his arms spread out, like to say Go away, Go away, and at first I thought he wanted to hunt everybody out of it. But his hands are all red, and so are the fronts of his boots, sweet Jesus. And he is moaning and crying and his face is the colour of silver, my God, and they are after nailing him to the door, and the grins on the faces of them, Jesus, the grins. And the little Twitcher is standing in front of him saying to him, where is the Crown of Tara? And my poor little Doctor is saying he doesn't know, he doesn't know. And that devil of a Twitcher laughs and lights a cigarette and says, well then, we've made a mistake, we'll wait until your wife comes out and saves you. Won't we? And my poor little Doctor just hangs his head. For I know and the Twitcher knows that Mrs Costelloe will never come out to him. Because she knows, she knows she will be safe now. And nothing that happens to the Doctor will worry her.

And I am standing there with a hive of bees in my head, watching the red blood run down the Doctor's arms and his legs and off the toes of his neat little boots drip, drip on the sunray paving. But I cannot move, because the Twitcher is a devil and a murderer, but he is right, I have seen with my own eyes he is right. And that is no affair of mine, or of anyone but God, or perhaps the devil.

[Q: I don't understand. How can it be right, to crucify a man on his own stable door? What is it that Mrs Costelloe knows?]

What? What? [here the subject shows signs of distress] The tackroom window is dirty, there are three spiders, three, and they will cross the pane, so I look at them, the way I will not have to look at my poor little Doctor. And there is something pale above in the window the other side of the yard, and I see: Jesus! It's Master Jess, and him watching his own father smashed and tormented, and his own mother not coming to help him!

[Q: Jesus Christ.]

He's gone. Thanks God, Jess is after going, the way he won't have to look at the agony in the yard, poor man. They're back at the questions now, where's the crown, where's the crown, yanking my poor little Doctor about the way the nails will tear at him. But I will not stay here to watch this. I will go out of there, round the back to where the stable stairs come out, and there he is, Jess, sitting on the step, with his hands over his ears. I go and sit with him. He is shaking high and quick like a fiddle string. Go on back, I said to him, go to your mammy, she'll look after you. He looks at me with those huge mad eyes, and he says, what about Daddy? Why aren't they helping Daddy? And the only thing I can say then is that we will do what we can. But the words are not out of my mouth when there is a fierce bang that echoes all round the yard. And poor Jess falls down in a dead faint, and I pick him up, poor child, and him a poor small thing.

The boots are at it again. I stay where I am, very quiet, until the lorry engines get going. Then I leave Jess and I go round to the yard.

And there is my poor little Doctor, nailed to the carriage house door. And at first I think that because his head is on one side and he is calm and his eyes are open, he is fit and well, give or take a few nails. But close up, you can see there is a bit of a hole under his chin, and the top of his head is not really there at all.

[Q: Jesus. You can stop now.]

And all in front of that poor child. She never came. That hellish woman never came. She could have stopped them.

[Q: You can stop. Please stop.]

So I sat there with my poor little Doctor. I could hear the crows.

[Q: I'm going to—]

And I could have told them fellas where the stupid Crown of Tara was hid, but did I? I did not. But I'll tell you, Mr Walker, and we'll be shot of the thing all right.

[Q: . . . count to three. On the count of three you will wake up. One, two, three.]

I could not tell Helen. I could not tell her that the reason her father would not touch Ireland even on pain of death was what he had watched from the stable window while his mother, who could have intervened, had stayed in the House with her lover. Having tea. They would have been having tea.

It was not the kind of thing anyone needed to know about their grandparents.

I watched Mairi row across the river. Then I walked to the stables. There were nettles among the sunray stones. I stood among the beams of the collapsed tack-room ceiling, and looked across at the window where Helen's father had watched the Tans crucify her grandfather. I walked across to the coach-house door, its remnants of grey-green paint pale in the moonlight. There were the holes the nails had made. And another hole, starting as a groove, deepening, passing through the door and into the dark beyond. The track of the bullet that had ended the Doctor's pain, and started years of silence.

When I went into the house, Helen was playing a form of pat-a-cake with Hannah. She raised a sarcastic eyebrow at me. 'Here's Daddy,' she said. 'And us alone all this time, God have mercy. Where have you been, where have you been?'

'Talking to Emily and Mairi Cosgrave.'

'Mairi now, is it, the old madwoman?' She looked at me more closely. 'Is there something wrong?'

I was going to tell her what I had heard about her grandfather and grandmother. But the facts hung in my head so dark and revolting that I could not bring myself to describe them in front of Hannah, though of course she would have understood nothing at all.

I said, 'I'll put Hannah to bed.' I picked her up, milky-smelling, bouncy, a chunk of the future. A great antidote to all that vileness in the past.

She battered the bath water, and afterwards, having been dried, she gave one of her demonstrations of assisted walking. But even this could not still the echo of the shot in the stable yard or fill the years of silence that had followed.

I plugged in the intercom and walked down the ill-lit corridor and onto the stairs. The hall stretched away below, a huge chessboard illuminated by a forty-watt bulb. A figure was walking across it, carrying a box and a bundle. At first I thought it was Helen, dressed in an overcoat against the house's evening dankness. I said, 'Let's have a drink.' The figure looked up.

It was Finbarr.

I ran down the remaining flight of stairs. He had been heading for the door that led to the butler's pantry and the kitchen. There was something in his hand. I said, 'What the hell are you doing here? The Guards are looking for you—'

At this point I slipped on something on one of the tiles. At the same time he took a swipe at me with the bundle in his hand. He caught me on the shoulder, the same one the horse had kicked, and knocked me over. I had time to conclude that what was in the bundle was probably an iron bar. Then the pain hit, and I lost interest. By the time I could think again, it was to reflect that the bloody shotgun was locked in the Laboratory. But it was too late, too late, because the Land Rover was whinnying, then grinding out of the sweep onto the avenue.

I went through to the kitchen. Helen was opening a bottle of wine. 'What was all that noise?' she said.

'Finbarr was here.'

'Finbarr?'

'He's gone. He had an iron bar. I'm calling the Guards once and for all, tell them we want them right here.'

She stared at me. 'What for?'

'He's violent. Dangerous.'

'He wouldn't hurt us, surely.'

I said, 'I found Steve's sketchbooks.'

She stared at me. She was very pale.

'I'll show you,' I said. The glass of wine helped the shoulder. Helen and I walked gingerly down the colonnade to the Laboratory.

I knew something was wrong before I got there. The door looked wrong. That was because someone had got a sledgehammer and battered it off its lock. 'What the hell?' she said.

'Finbarr,' I said, and walked in, just about ready to weep.

Devastation. There was paper everywhere. The books were out of the cases, piled on the floor. The bottles of chemicals were smashed, the sink with plug in, taps on, overflowing into Peter Costelloe's *Fish*. Weirdly, though, my notes were only bent, not destroyed, and the Casebooks were intact. Of course, that was the first thing I looked at.

Helen had her priorities right. She said, 'Where are these sketchbooks?'

The sketchbooks were gone. So was the shotgun. I sat down on a chair and told Helen instead. 'The night we met,' I said. 'Timsy Durcan persuaded you to go swimming. He was the brother of Finbarr. If you had drowned, Finbarr would have had Malpas back. And they told you not to remember, so you didn't. You didn't even wonder why you'd gone swimming. That's the kind of harmless they are.'

She gazed at the face of the Great Mentalini tacked to the wall. Finally she sighed. She said, 'Come back to the house while I call the Guards again.' She helped me back. That night I slept in her bed, just like before. Nobody mentioned Finbarr's name, but I had another shotgun under the bed, and the doors and windows locked up tight. Up here in our warm space, with Hannah sleeping next door, she mocked me gently for being one-armed and just about useless. I could not bring myself to tell her about her grandfather's death. We were happy again, and for the moment that was good enough.

Next morning dawned bright and clear and Finbarrless. I made a start on clearing up the mess in the laboratory. Then I dropped everyone off with Angela, climbed into the Zephyr, and went to Cork.

Paddy did not appear to have moved since the last time I had seen him. His oxygen mask was off, though, and beside his bed sat Mairi, her hands on her knees, big as a house. She went off on some errand. Paddy was hellish weak, but the pneumonia was getting better, very nice of me to call by, very nice grapes, they used to grow a fierce Muscat in the glass houses but now they were destroyed entirely.

After a little bit of this, I said, 'Did you ever hear of the Crown of Tara?'

'Feck,' said Paddy, and rolled his head away from me.

The door opened. Mairi came back in. I had the idea she might have been listening outside the door. 'Tell him,' she said.

'I never saw it,' said Paddy. 'But Daddy was always on about it. Yer man Steve was always on about it, too, but I never knew where it was, because Finbarr would have had it out of me. We hold the secret between us, my mother and I.' He sounded as if he was reciting from Holy Writ. 'It is the High Crown of Tara,' said Paddy. 'It was took from the house at Malpas the day the Brigade burned the wing, where there is no roof and the camellia tree below. It come into the possession of my Daddy, Lord knows how.' We all nodded, not because any of us did not know how, but in acknowledgement of the correct spirit of tact with which he had phrased the admission. 'And Daddy hid it, and Mammy knows where, and I told this much to yer man Steve, but Mammy wouldn't tell him the last of it. But now we both agree it is time it was out of there, and you're the man pulled me out of the river.'

I said, 'If I take the Crown, it is on the understanding that this said Crown was taken in the name of the People of Ireland and should be returned to them.'

'Right, so,' said Mairi. And she told me.

'Much good may it do you,' said Paddy. 'It killed yer man Steve, and the Doctor.'

'Killed him?'

'He had a letter written, to Eamon de Valera. He said he would give it to the Government, like you. He showed it to them all at lunch in the big house on the Sunday. He gave them the idea that he had the Crown by him already, but of course he never would have. And we knew they wouldn't like it, so we took the books off him and hid them out of harm's way, above where you found them. We would have given them back again, after. But we never got the chance. When I took the books was the last time I saw him. The last . . .' He stopped. His eyes looked dazed. 'What was it, now?'

'Ye'll have to do him,' said Mairi.

I stared at her great hollow face. Far away in the hospital, doors slammed, and the shoes of nuns went clip, clop on stone.

'You know,' she said, impatient, waving her hand in front of her face as if swinging a silver propelling pencil.

'Now?'

'No time like the present,' she said, and heaved herself to her feet. 'I'll get a cup of tea, now.'

So I moved my chair to the side of the bed. I told Paddy to look at my pen. I counted him down. And down he went.

I said, 'Tell me the things that happened to you at the weir.'

Something took place in the eyes, now. They were not hanging on mine, but looking inwards, at things they were recognising for the first time. 'I was mending the fence,' he said. 'Yer man came up behind me and said, step over there, on the stone. And I did as he said. But there was no stone, nothing underneath the water but more water. So I went in.'

I was holding my breath. 'That was Finbarr?' I said.

'It was.'

'And the other time at the weir, when Steve died?'

Silence.

I said, 'You told me once. You had the sun in your eyes. You were carrying a body up the bank.' Something extraordinary happened to his face, as if it was unknotting itself. 'Yes,' he said. 'Oh, Christ, yes, sure.' A silence. 'That's how it works,' he said. 'You'll get a bit sleepy. Then he'll ask you to do something small, like you'd take an extra step, only the result would be big, and you'd find yourself in deep water and you not a great swimmer. And there was a body, sure. Of course, the body, poor Steve. I found him, and I carried him out, and that's that.' It was a great confident burst, and it left him transfigured with happiness. It also left him coughing horribly. Halfway through the coughing, his mother came in, and a nun who had heard the racket through the open door, pushed me out of the room. So I climbed aboard the Zephyr, and drove across the river and east along the coast road, heading for Malpas.

Midleton came up, a slew of grey cement houses and a factory of sorts. I thought of Paddy in the dawn with Steve's body in his arms, staggering up from the river, eyes screwed against the sun.

The sun?

A lorry horn went off like a bomb dead ahead. I yanked the Zephyr onto the strip of old newspaper and broken bottles beside the road and slammed on the brakes. I sat there, not taking my hands off the wheel.

Paddy had found Steve's body at dawn, in the Herring Weir, two miles away from the nearest human being. He had waded into the water, and come up the bank and onto the grass with the sun in his eyes.

Not in the Herring Weir, he hadn't. The bank of the Herring Weir was the right bank of the river, which at that point ran north and south. If he had been wading out of the Herring Weir at dawn, holding up a body with stones in its trouser pockets, the sun would have been on the back of his head. Nobody needed to persuade Paddy to pull a body out of the weir. But they might have needed to persuade him that he was in a place where he had not actually been.

I put the Zephyr in gear and moved out into the road. I drove on, steady and careful, as befitted a man with a lot on his mind and plenty to do. By one o'clock, I was back at Malpas. There was no sign of Finbarr. The Guards would be looking out for him, though there was no sign of them either.

By two thirty, I was walking up to the ruins of the church. I say ruins; but actually by Malpas standards they were in quite good repair. True, the graves were choked with brambles. But half the roof was more or less intact, and the nail-studded doors still met in the middle.

A cloud of jackdaws chacked in the tower as I rattled the latch. The door opened grudgingly. I crunched over heaving red-and-yellow tiles towards what had once been the altar.

The vestry was still watertight. There was a wardrobe with mouldy vestments, an open safe, gone red and furry with rust. Above the safe was a board into which someone had screwed half a dozen square brass hooks. On each hook hung a rusty key. Once, the keys had been labelled. The labels were gone. All that remained were loops of string.

I took them all down. I walked out of the church and closed the doors. Hannah was making cheerful noises twenty-five yards away, in another world. The keys were cold in my hand, and my mouth was dry. The vault was a long, squat shape in the brambles. I trod over the brambles and went down the steps. At the bottom was a litter of twigs and a dead jackdaw. The doors were made of bronze, with trefoil piercings that exuded darkness. I took the oilcan out of my pocket and dropped a little in the lock. Then I tried the keys.

The third one turned a little, then stuck. I pulled it out, re-oiled it, and put it back in. This time it turned all the way. The tumblers clashed. Echoes bounced unpleasantly in the vault's interior. I really did not want to go in.

But there was nothing in there that could hurt anyone. Only the real Malpas legacy, that was handed down to everyone, whether they lived at Malpas or not.

I swallowed. My mouth felt like sandpaper. I pushed the doors. With a conventional but nonetheless deeply alarming moan of hinges, the right-hand one opened. I pulled the bag with the two candles out of my pocket, lit them with a match from the box I had stolen from the kitchen – the warm, friendly kitchen, full of daylight, a million miles away. I walked in.

Chapter Thirty

The vault was amazingly tidy; probably the tidiest place inside the Malpas demesne wall. The floor was made of flagstones. You could have eaten your lunch off them, always providing you had been the sort of person who visits vaults at lunchtime and you had brought your food with you. (I found I had a tendency to giggle nervously. My feet rang loud on the stones. There was a damp, musty chill in the air, but I was sweating.) On either side were stone shelves, three high. Naturally, there were coffins on the shelves. On twelve of the shelves, to be precise. The rest were empty, to the number of thirty-two.

I held the candle up to the lines of coffins. There was the mighty oak sarcophagus of Desmond Perceval Costelloe, at a convenient height for climbing out in the event of premature burial. The famous whiskey bottle was gone. On top of the next rank was Dulcibella Maria Costelloe, also in a coffin of tremendous grandeur. A little apart, on the ground, was a coffin of less glorious construction. It was deal, with wooden handles. There was no outer casket. It was a plain, ordinary thing, with a cut-steel plate on which was engraved simply Peter Costelloe, without dates. Dulcie had done the minimum. Still, as father of Jesse, the heir, he was in the family vault, and that was what counted.

Actually, that was not what counted. Faced with this quiet, horrible place, and the horrible thing I had to do, my mind was gibbering nonsense at me.

I bent down to the coffin.

It was crooked.

The others were laid on their shelves with mathematical exactness.

But the coffin of Dr Peter Costelloe looked as if it had been slung on the ground, shoved aside so as not to trip people up, and abandoned.

I bent, and took the handle, and hauled the coffin from under the shelf above. At least, I hauled it halfway out. At that point the handle came away. Well, not exactly the handle. The handle and half the left-hand side of the coffin, which (it turned out) was made not so much of deal as of sawdust and woodworm. I fell over. There was a lot of noise. I did not know where it was coming from until I realised it was me, shouting. The candle rolled towards the coffin, still burning.

There was a face looking at me. It was a grey face, with ragged holes where the eyes should have been and a toothy grin inside something that might once have been cheeks. Where the top of the head should have been was nothingness. I was at last eye to eye with the real Doctor Peter Costelloe.

The candle went out. I rolled away, still shouting, hit my head on something. Next thing I knew I was at the vault door in the brilliant grey daylight, breathing in great gasps that came nowhere near satisfying my blood's demand for oxygen.

The vault was quiet. Obviously it was quiet. It was populated by dead people. Not people at all. Dust.

Dust I knew. Dust in whose spatial envelopes I had bent over casebooks and letters. Dust that had harboured and transacted the Crown of Tara.

I lit a match. I went back into the vault. When the match went out, I lit another, with which I found the candle on the floor, which I lit. I held the second candle so it illuminated the interior of the coffin. I looked steadily at the dreadful skull, the bones draped in a coating of mingled cloth and leather, the barrel of the ribs, the rest gone away.

And where the stomach should have been, a box of French-polished mahogany.

I took the box from its resting place. It was the size of a biscuit tin, but heavier. I placed it on the floor beside the coffin. Then I turned poor Doctor Costelloe's coffin around. His head was no longer facing Jerusalem, but he would not have been a man to worry about that.

More importantly, anyone who came into the vault would not notice that someone had torn his coffin apart in search of the Crown of Tara. I brushed away the splinters, picked up the candles, the tool box (a tidy vault is a happy vault) and the mahogany box. And a moment later, there I was, outside the bronze doors, trying to steady my hand to the point where I could get the key into the keyhole.

I did it eventually, using two hands. I climbed the steps. I wiped off the box in the nettles. Then I crunched through the church and hung up the keys, and put what I was carrying into a sack, and went under the lych-gate and back to the wreckage of the Laboratory. There I put the box on the workbench and unlatched it. Then I turned on the radio, and poured myself a glass of whiskey.

A little later, I went to visit Angela. She was feeding tea to her mother, who was making ghastly sucking noises. 'Sit down,' she said. She looked tired and desperate.

I stood, leaning on the mantelpiece. I was past tact and discretion. I said, 'Where were you the morning Steve was found dead?'

'What—'

'Tell me,' I said. 'Or tell the Guards, and tell Helen.'

She turned to look at me. Her mother made turtle-mouthed hunting movements after the spoon. 'What are you talking about?' she said.

'You weren't in bed with Steve.'

'Of course not!'

'Who were you in bed with?'

She summoned up a maidenly blush. 'Nobody,' she said. I gave her a long, unbelieving silence. She stuck her chin up. 'Actually,' she said, 'it's true. Sad but true.'

'I saw them in the bathroom,' said Alice. 'Maurice and Desmond. Awful, awful.'

'For God's sake, mummy,' said Angela. And for the first time ever I realised the desperation of her. She was not just an ironic, self-contained woman with nobody to please but herself and her ancient mother. She was someone growing out of her best years, not knowing where she was headed. Desperate, was the word. Kind. Wanting fun. And security, or at least company and warmth. 'Where was Steve?' I said.

'In Finbarr's house.'

'What was he doing there?'

'Being a bloody idiot.'

'What does that mean?'

She sighed. She said, 'You already know.'

I held my peace.

'Steve had something that Finbarr wanted.'

'What?'

'That bloody crown or something. Steve was baiting him about it all the time, and Finbarr was laughing his head off, but you could see he really hated it. Finbarr hates being on the losing side.' She paused. 'He's always been on it, too. Always having to watch a lot of Costelloes making a mess of things. And then being the tenant, and making a mess of it yourself.'

I said, 'And you definitely slept alone that night.'

'Yes, damn you,' she said. 'He had Steve staying. He went to bed early, I should think, and got up early, and went swimming, like he always does. In the lake.' She stopped. There was a fearsome silence.

I said, 'Alone?'

She said, 'I wasn't there.'

'Bastard,' said Alice.

My heart was wrapped in a deep chill. I said, 'Did he take Steve swimming?'

'I think you should go. I've got to bath Mummy.'

I said, 'Angela, you've told me before, if I tell Helen you were sleeping with Steve it's not going to make life very easy, is it? And the other thing is that it sounds as if you're covering up for Finbarr, and the Guards are onto him and they'd be very interested. So really please tell me the truth, or your life will be such a mess.'

'Couldn't be worse,' said Alice, *à propos* of nothing. 'No, no, no, no, no, no, no.'

'Well?'

'I need to think about this,' said Angela.

'Think aloud.'

'You are an utter utter shit and you don't understand.'

'Try me.'

'I told you. This silly crown thing,' she said. 'Finbarr wanted it. It was worth a lot of money. Steve said he knew where it was. He wanted to give it to the Government. He was weird, you know, all laughing and gabbling, you couldn't stop him. Helen had had enough. So eventually after he'd been in the pub all day Finbarr found him and took him home and locked him in a bedroom. Finbarr went swimming the next morning like he always did, and when he got back Steve had got himself let out. And next thing they knew, they found him in the weir.'

'How did he get out?'

'Emily heard him kicking the door and roaring. She went up to see he was all right – she didn't know him very well – and he went out of the door, nearly flattened her on the way, and off he goes, and an hour later there he is, dead in the weir.'

'With stones in his pockets.'

'So they say.'

I leaned back on the sofa. I said, 'That's not right.'

I could see Steve, wild, manic, rushing after Finbarr. The lake, dark and musty-smelling as the vault. The sun a mere glow on the horizon still. Finbarr and Steve on the dam. Steve jabbering: showing his cleverness, telling Finbarr about the crown. Claiming he knew where it was. Lying. Finbarr taking Steve by the arm. In a rage. Overpowering him with those osteopath's hands of his. Shoving the stones into his pockets, rolling him into the water. Waiting for the bubbles to stop. Diving for him. The body blue-white, Finbarr realising what he had done. Desperate to separate himself from this horrible thing. And here comes Paddy Cosgrave, fishing for white trout at dawn. A couple of words to Paddy: now, now, *now*, this is the weir, there is the body. Paddy carting poor Steve up the dam with the eastern sun in his eyes. Lugging him down to the Herring Weir. Finding himself at the weir, with the body on the ground. Far away from Finbarr, who was swimming peacefully to and fro, alone in the lake, the way he did every morning.

Why, though?

It was still not right.

I got up. Angela said, 'What are you going to do?'

'Tell the Guards.'

'Everything?'

'As much as is necessary.'

'Shit.'

'Shit!' said Alice. 'Shit, shit!'

It was dark when I got back to the House. Helen was in her usual spot at the kitchen table, glass of wine in front of her, drawing pad open. The page was blank. The wine bottle was three-quarters empty. Her eyes took me in, then slithered off to one side. She said, 'Where have you been?'

I sat down and hooked the bottle. 'Took Hannah for a walk,' I said. 'Went into the family vault. Broke open the Doctor's coffin. Found the Crown of Tara.'

The eyes stayed on mine this time. They blinked. She said, in a weird, shaky voice, 'Have you got it with you?'

I shook my head. I said, 'I have evidence that it was Finbarr who drowned Steve.'

She said, 'Where's the crown?'

I said, 'Never mind the crown.' She looked at me properly then. She put out her hand for the wine bottle. She did not look shocked so much as very, very sad.

I thought I knew what was going on in her head. There had been a moment when Malpas had been strange and wild and beautiful, a little group of people living harmonious lives, minding their own business, being good friends. It had been warm and cosy. Then I had turned up. She had thought I was a good idea. But I was the outside, the cold wind.

It had been a dream. And I had woken her up.

I said, 'I'm sorry.'

She nodded, head down. She was crying.

I said, 'Finbarr drowned Steve in the lake above the dam.'

Silence.

'Did you know?'

She looked up at me. She said, 'Steve drowned himself.'

'I don't think so.'

'I know,' she said.

'How?'

'I was there.'

Silence. The creak of the house, the flap of an unshut door.

'I was talking to Finbarr,' she said. 'All night. He was worrying like hell. He'd been doing hypnotherapy on Steve. It was going wrong or it wasn't working, he couldn't tell. Steve was totally manic, totally. So Finbarr had shut him up for the night. A nice night,' she said. 'Warm. Stars everywhere. Then at about five we went out on the dam. The moon was setting, the sun was going to come up, all wonderful. We let Steve out of his room. He seemed okay. Belting about with his shirt off, you know? But sort of all right.' Pause. 'Then he did a fecking stupid thing.'

'Being?'

'He had these army trousers on. He challenged Finbarr to a swimming race. Finbarr said, all right, wanting to humour him, I suppose. But Steve won't do a simple race. He says he can beat anybody there with one hand behind his back. In particular, he can beat Finbarr with his trousers on. I remember seeing him in that morning half-light, white as wax, with goose-pimples, waving his arms and screaming, and Finbarr beside him. Out round an old bit of wood and back, it was, the race. I was watching Steve, screwy old Steve with his trousers hanging down, and I remember thinking, they're a bit low, they'll come right off and leave his arse in the breeze. Then they both dive in. Finbarr goes off like a porpoise, miles ahead. And Steve comes back up, flaps twice, and sinks like a brick. I thought he was playing games. By the time I realised he wasn't, Finbarr was too far away to hear. I got in there, but I couldn't find him. We got him eventually. There was something in his pockets. Stones, they turned out to be. He'd put them in to show Finbarr he could beat him even . . . with . . . stones.' She was crying again.

I put an arm around her.

'Finbarr said we should clean it all up,' she said. 'He got Paddy to take him down to the weir, miles away from where we were, you know.

You can always count on Irish people to hush up a suicide.'

'But if it was an accident, why did you tell all these lies?'

'Because Finbarr was frightened people would think he had killed him.'

'Why would Finbarr want to kill him?'

She said, 'It was five in the morning. I was drunk. Finbarr said it. I didn't ask him why, you don't, when there's a body on the grass in front of you. By the time I was thinking straight it was all too late, the lies were all told and you couldn't untell them. Imagine that Rourke, what he'd say.'

I said, 'Steve went in of his own free will?'

'If you can call it that, the state he was in.'

I thought of what Paddy had told me at the Mercy: *He'll ask you do something small, like you'd take an extra step, only you'd find yourself in deep water and you not a great swimmer.*

'I think Finbarr has designs on you. I think Finbarr put those stones in Steve's pockets, and buttoned up the pockets and persuaded poor bloody manic Steve to go swimming. To give himself a clear go at you.'

'At *me*?'

'Finbarr's brighter than Timsy. He'd want to marry you, not kill you.'

'Don't be silly.' But I could hear the doubt in her voice.

I said, 'Where are those Guards?'

Her eyes were luminous with tears. I had never seen her look so beautiful. She said, 'Around, somewhere.' She did not care any more. She needed taking away. Now was my moment, if ever.

I said, 'I think you should marry me instead.'

Her face did not change. Her hand came across the table and rested dry and light on mine. She said, 'I don't want to think about anything, not one tiny thing. Let's go to bed now and do all that stuff in the morning.'

'Will you marry me?'

She smiled at me, the old wild smile. 'I'll tell you in the morning,' she said, and took off her T-shirt so that her breasts swung free, and came and sat on my lap and put her arms around my neck and brought her mouth down to mine.

Never do today what you can do tomorrow, I thought, with my last coherent thought for quite a while. Very Malpas.

I did not know exactly how Malpas until the next day.

Soon after that I carried her upstairs and put her on her bed, the bed where Dulcie had lain, from which the Doctor had seen Mrs Caroe pouring her poison into Desmond's ear, the night before the wedding, sixty-five years ago.

'Come here,' said Helen.

Neither of us had any clothes on by then. I forgot that the Doctor had been inventing Mrs Caroe's speech to Desmond. I forgot just about everything except that there on the pillow was Helen, sleepy-eyed, heavy-mouthed, with her arm stretched out towards me.

Perhaps I should have remembered.

Chapter Thirty-One

It was a weirdly peaceful night, at least the first part of it. We made love. Then we talked, quietly, forehead to forehead in the dark. Then she fell silent. I felt her tears on my face. I said, 'What is it?'

'Nothing.'

'It must be something.'

'You. Here. Now.' She put her arms round my neck and wound me down to her mouth.

At some point, we must have gone to sleep. Because I remember waking up, and seeing the curve of her hip in the moonlight, and lying there thinking that it was all over, all the living in the past, and we would be a family and have all the closeness and togetherness in the world.

But even as I thought it, I could feel the great void out there, Finbarr stalking the night, the mahogany box I had hidden after I had taken it from the vault. I could smell the house, hear it, a great creaking bladder of rot and time: feel the pressure of history in it . . .

And I was back in that history, like falling down a well, head over shoes through diaries and casebooks and letters. Hearing in particular one voice. The voice of Mad Alice, coming from under her dreadful empty eyes. *I saw him in the bathroom.* Maurice Devereux and Desmond Costelloe, in the bathroom. As the window lightened with the dawn, I climbed quietly out of bed. Helen murmured something.

I said, 'Back later.'

'How much later?'

I wanted the morning to myself. 'Lunchtime.' She put out her hand. I squeezed it, pulled on some clothes and went for the stairs. I made coffee in the kitchen and went outside.

The dawn was a canary-yellow smudge in the eastern sky, and the river smelt dank and muddy. I hoped Finbarr was cold and wet, wherever he was, far from the new life Helen and I were beginning. The cot was in the House Creek. I climbed in and pushed off, hopping the black eddies towards the pale smudge in the trees that was the Cosgraves' house. I came alongside and waited a minute in the boat; waiting in that pre-dawn chill for God knew what – the crack of a twig, perhaps, the sound of Finbarr stalking through the dark woods. But there was only the suck and gurgle of the river in the pilings. I got out, and went up the steps.

There was a light in the house, two cars outside. A dog started a frenzied cursing, yanking painfully at its chain. A light went on indoors. There were voices. I said, 'It's me. Dave.'

The door opened. A man stood gigantic against the light. 'Who?' he said.

''Tis all right,' said Mairi's voice inside. The giant growled and went away. 'Cousin Dinny,' she said, by way of explanation. She was well protected.

The kitchen was long and low-ceilinged and frowsy, Mairi vast in a dirty pink dressing gown. I said, 'Sorry to be so early.'

'Sure I was up.'

'I had an idea.'

'You did?'

'I spent a lot of time with the Doctor. So did you. Do you believe he would have killed Desmond?'

She did not answer. Her head was moving, side to side, dazed.

'Could we go through it?'

'Sure.' She brought me a cup of tea. Then she sat herself down under the light and, for the last time in all my recession episodes with Mairi Dugdale, I started the Braid induction.

Walker Archive, Transcript, 1973 – 10

It is the evening, a warm one, a bit softish, and I am in the House Creek and there is little balls of rain in the grass of the lawn, and what I must do today is go round and see that it is all in order, that the numbers are right and it all adds up. And there ahead is Miss Dulcibella herself, and I am so pleased I melt inside and I would like to overflow, for she is to be the bride, the lovely bride, and live in the House of golden sugar and be happy ever after with kind Mr Desmond. She is walking slowly, along the lawn and across the bridge, the small bridge not the big one, and up into the woods. They are lovely these woods, the stalks of them like cinnamon sticks, the sound falling dead in them, so I can hear the breath inside in my ears, and I am dancing with it, light as a feather as if I had bubbles fizzing inside in my blood. And there is a spotter and an orangeman, all flapping and winding through the trunks far into the halls of the wood to sing like angels. There is the wedding tomorrow, and we are all excited, because it is going to be Mr Desmond and Miss Dulcibella living happy ever after, like God's angels in the great golden House.

And up I climb after Miss Dulcibella, one and a third steps to every breath, up, up like a bird, through the cinnamon tunnel to the Temple where I will stop and sing and count what needs counting.

Then I hear a noise, an odd class of a noise, a sort of a grunting and a groaning, and I go up more slowly, because I do not know what it is.

So I walk slower at the top. And what I see is a peculiar thing altogether. I see two fellas without their clothes on, great white hairy chaps they were, and they were having a sort of wrestling match or so I thought at the beginning of it, and then I saw that they were not wrestling but holding onto each other, and what they were doing was what a man should do with a woman or a bull to a cow, and here they were both bulls. One of them I did not know so well, he being Mr Maurice who came in a black car for dinner before the wedding and other times. But the other fella, all licking and kissing Mr Maurice, that fella was Mr Desmond.

Just then I heard a sort of a whirl and a rustle, and Miss Dulcie comes past where I was standing, and her with a face fire-red and the tears pouring out of her the way she did not see me at all. Well I was destroyed with it, destroyed altogether, and I went after her away from those grunting devils above and I wanted to be close to her and protect her and deliver her from evil. I heard her stop her walking, and shout this way: 'Horrible!' she bellowed. 'Oh, horrible!'

I could see that she would need looking after, because things are not right. It was not right what those fellas were doing above, because love is love and there is only one of it at the one time, and what Mr Desmond was doing to your man above is what Miss Dulcibella should be doing with him as his lawfully wedded wife. So I am in the rhodies, waiting. And I see her coming past me, and it getting dark. So I go up to her and I say, 'Is there anything I can do Miss Dulcibella?'

And she is looking at me with those great green eyes on her, and she says, 'No, no, Mairi. Nothing.' Then she says, 'Wait, though.' And she gives me a bit of a grin, and whips out a pencil, and writes two notes. And she gives them to me, and says, 'Hand this to Mr Desmond, would you?' So of course I take them, and off she goes. And then I am standing there, hoping it will all be well, and suddenly I am looking at another lady, and her with a great meaty face on her, and it is Mrs Caroe from Slaughterbridge. And she whips the notes out of my hand and before I can pull it back she has them open and is reading. And she says An assignation is it? And I say even if that is what it is what is it to you what a man and wife choose to do on their wedding day? And she turns red as raw beef and runs away, and I take the note to Mr Desmond, and go back to my place in the trees by the house where I can watch the window of her room, and wait and see.

So at four o'clock in the morning and it getting light I am there, very tired, and there is a spotter singing inside in the wood. And out comes Miss Dulcibella, and away she goes up the park, and on her back she is carrying a class of a satchel. And then by another path here comes Mister Desmond. I am in the rhodies, with the light coming up grey. And I see the two of them talking together, Miss Dulcie not moving. And I see yer man Desmond sit down on the bench above, as if somebody took the bone from his leg. And I see Miss Dulcie hand him something from her bag, and then go back to the house. And I went back myself: except that on the way I met my little Doctor, and he saw me. And as we stood together a moment with the sun not up there was a great bang of all bangs. So I went up to see what it was, above, and then I fetched the Doctor.

There came into my mind the Doctor's account of the Slaughterbridge fire: Mrs Caroe, spitting venom, thanking God she would be away from sodomites. That had not been invective. By her lights, it had been a precise description of Maurice Devereux. The half-sister business had been a fabrication, invented by the Doctor to protect Dulcie. What vindictive Mrs Caroe had been saying to Desmond on the terrace at midnight was that she knew about Desmond's affair with Maurice; perhaps that she would blackmail him with it. What could a man like Desmond do, in such a case, in 1910? Not come out, that was for sure.

Take him a revolver in a class of a satchel, and he would know what to do with it. And if he would not do the decent thing, Dulcie would have been the woman to help him along. There was only the Doctor's word as to whose fingerprints he had found on the gun.

I thanked Mairi, and rowed back across the river. I moored the cot in the House Creek and walked up the overgrown path to the House. There had been enough history.

Helen was playing with Hannah in the morning room. Hannah sounded fractious and squally. 'You're tired, you wee creep,' she said. She looked up. There were dark circles under her eyes. 'Dave, would you ever get me a new nappy for her? They're in the washing room.'

I went to the washing room. The clean nappies were in a basket, mixed up with a lot of other laundry. I went through, folding it up while I was there, to earn a few points. I was thinking about the wickedness of Dulcie, arranging the Doctor's murder after he had protected her from enquiries about Desmond's death all those years, ruined his own career, earned general odium, come by his death—

I was folding a cream satin slip. There was a stain on the top right-hand side. It looked like blood; three little drops of blood, cooked into the cloth by the hot wash. Helen was vague on the chemistry of washing.

But that was not what stopped me.

In the middle of each spot of blood was a little tear. As if Helen had been wearing it when, say, the branch of a Paul's Himalayan Musk rose had dropped on her shoulder and dug its spines into her flesh as she writhed on Finbarr's dick . . .

I heard Angela shrieking with laughter when I accused her of having an affair with Finbarr. Now I knew why. And I knew why the Guards had not arrived after Helen said she would call them.

I threw the nappy into the morning room. I could have stayed to talk to Helen. But there were people at Malpas who knew more than

Helen, if they were asked the right questions. I walked under a skyful of dirty water to the Dower House. Angela was in the garden, grubbing for couch roots with a fork, her knees round her ears. She looked up when she heard me coming. When she saw my face, she did not move.

I felt flat and blank with shock. I said, 'You knew.'

She looked down at her filthy gloves. She said, 'She tried. She asked you over from England, remember? She was trying to make a life of her own. With you. It's not easy here. You get taken over.' The tears were sliding down her face. 'The romance,' she said. 'The history. Fucking Finbarr Durcan. She gave it a try with you, she really did. But she likes all that wild stuff and Dave I knew as soon as I saw you you are not it, not for her. She didn't believe you'd ever find out anything about Steve. She just wanted to keep you happy. Make you feel useful.'

I had been happy, all right. I said, 'Why didn't you tell me?'

She got up, stiffly, as if she was growing old. 'She was my landlady,' she said. 'And my friend.' She brushed her gloves against her thighs. I could smell the sweat under her perfume. 'Anyway, I did tell you. Not in words. But you didn't understand. Or you wouldn't be persuaded.' She laughed, a false, self-hating laugh. 'And now you think I've been a liar all along and you hate me and it's too late.'

I stood there. My heart was pushing cold mud round my body. I did not hate her. I did not feel anything, really. It was too late for just about everything.

'It's this place,' she said. 'This nasty wicked fucking place.'

It was nothing to do with the place. But the place had been where it had happened, and that was bad enough.

I said, 'You should have told me.' She had been wrong. But I had been wrong, too. In our respective ways, we had betrayed each other. I turned and walked away.

All Finbarr's visits on farm business. Not only farm business. A weekend in Fermoy, for Helen's exhibition? No, Dave, would you ever stay and look after Hannah? When Finbarr had been in the hall last night, he had not been breaking in. He had been visiting his girlfriend. I had been the interloper.

I went on out, over the balustrades and across the terraces, towards the gasworks hedge. I was probably crying. I pushed open the gas house door and went through the stinking forest of pipes. I picked up the mahogany box that had come out of the Doctor's coffin, and turned back towards the bright oblong of the door.

A figure suddenly cut the light. 'Morning,' said the voice of Finbarr Durcan.

He was wearing a ragged brown raincoat and leaning on a stick. He was part of the past, insignificant. There was nothing here any more. I was trying to work out how to get back into another world. As I pushed past him into the daylight I caught a whiff of drink and cigarettes and earth, as if he had slept in a cellar.

'What have you there?' he said.

'Mind your own business,' I said. It was only then that I looked at him properly, and saw that what I had taken for a stick was the shotgun he had stolen from the Laboratory.

'I tell you what,' he said. 'I tell you what it is. I think that what you have got inside in that box is the Crown of fecking Ireland, which you have no fecking business with.'

I stopped. The shotgun had come up, and was looking at me with its close-set black eyes. It was a pretty disgusting sensation, but no more disgusting than the rest of my life. I said, 'What makes you think that?'

'I have my sources,' he said darkly.

'Like what?'

His face took on an evil sort of grin. 'I went to see an old friend for breakfast,' he said. 'Before breakfast, actually. The usual time.'

'What the hell are you talking about?' I knew, though.

'She's so sweet in the morning, our Helen.'

I stared at him, sweating. He was saying it to hurt. It was working.

He said, 'Now give me the box, there's a good little English fella.' His eyes had a truly wild look above the gun. We were standing beside the mossy top of the old gasometer. I swung the box, and threw it onto the green disc. It landed with a dull booming sound, just about in the middle.

'Go and fetch it,' said Finbarr.

'Fetch it yourself.' The Crown was what he wanted. I started for the house. I was going to call the Guards, and tell them to come and get Finbarr. For all I cared they could take Helen with them.

Someone came running round the screen of trees. It was Helen. I loved her. And she loved me. There was a perfectly reasonable explanation for all this. I put my arms out to stop her. Finbarr was saying his things out of pure malice. Angela's washing had somehow got mixed up with hers . . .

She dodged round me. As I turned to go after her I slipped and fell. By the time I was up, Finbarr was halfway out onto the mossy disc.

And Helen was with him.

I said, 'Wait!'

They turned. The muzzle of the gun came up. Helen's eyes narrowed a little, the way they might have narrowed when she saw Finbarr stuff stones into the pockets of poor mad Steve.

I said, 'He killed Steve to get at you. And now he's got you, Helen.'

She said, 'And I've got him.'

'But you asked me to stay.'

She looked away.

'Playing hard to get?' I said. 'Using me to encourage the boyfriend?'

'No!' she cried, and I took satisfaction from the real pain in her voice. She had loved me. She had truly thought I had been her last chance to join the human race.

But Steve had been dead, and the chance had already been gone.

She said, 'I'm sorry, Dave. I was so pleased to see you, but this is my life. So go away.'

'And Hannah?'

'I'm getting tired now,' said Finbarr. I saw Helen's face turn to him, horrified. Then the shotgun in his hand boomed.

But I had already started running, and slipped again on the wet ground, and immediately fallen over with my cheek in the grass. So the shot (as I later found out) failed to blow my guts out through my spine. Instead, it removed the point of my left shoulder.

And along the ground I saw Finbarr and Helen and the mahogany box all together, on that mossy disc, Finbarr taking a step back, aiming the second barrel.

Then they were not there.

I thought my eyes had gone, something to do with the shock of being shot. I lay there with my ears ringing and waited for my sight to return.

Nothing happened. But over the tinnitus of the explosion I could hear screams. They were terrible screams. I was very weak. I got to my hands and knees: hand, rather, because my sleeve was soaking with blood, and there was no strength in my arm. I made my way slowly towards where I had last seen them. My head was turning round, and everything was going dark. From then on, I remember only isolated glimpses. Frames from the movie, you might say.

I remember that the mossy iron disc of the gasometer was not a disc any more. A great triangle of darkness now lay across it. I remember putting my face to the triangle. I remember the reek of ancient chemicals that came up to me. I remember the hollow boom of water. And I remember an arm, a hand, a face turned up to me. The same face I had seen on Helmstone pier, all that time ago. But not coming into my life, this time. Leaving it.

I should have run for a rope, of course. I should have climbed down the side, arm or no arm, and pulled her out of that sump of poisoned water, smooth-walled, fifteen feet deep.

But her lover had shot my arm half off, and the blood was coming out of me like water from a hose.

So I did not save her. I fainted instead.

Mairi found me, or so Angela said. She had heard the shot, and rowed across the river, and fetched Angela. I told them that it had all been an accident. I did not tell them what I had seen after I brought the mahogany box from the Costelloe vault and put it on my workbench.

I had knocked the hook off the nail, and opened the lid.

There was a red-spotted handkerchief. Something was wrapped in it, something round and heavy. I unwrapped it.

I looked at it for perhaps a minute. Then I began to laugh. I laughed so hard I had to sit down, and the thing I had unwrapped sat on the workbench, its sheen making starbursts in the tears that filled my eyes.

Because it was not a crown, of Tara or anywhere else. It was a horseshoe; a huge bronze horseshoe. The plaque on the horseshoe said *First Prize – All Ireland Ploughing Match, Cashel Co. Tipperary awarded to James Kerrigan and Malpas Hero – 1905.*

It did not say that the Crown of Tara was an invention of the Doctor. And that when Johnny Cosgrave had gone in to discuss the Crown of Tara with the Doctor, the Doctor had taken out his silver pencil, and persuaded Johnny that this was not a silly ploughing match trophy, but one of his country's great treasures.

Of course it did not say that. That was something known only to the Doctor and me.

A week after the horror on the gasometer, I was well enough to load Hannah into the Zephyr, and drive away from Malpas for ever. We were leaving for Helmstone. I had talked to George Gale on the telephone, and read him a letter I had received from the Dorrien Institute.

Dear Mr Walker,

Thank you for your letter about Mrs Davidson and the unfortunate Dr Costelloe. I can inform you that while Mrs Davidson did indeed foment a great scandal with regard to the accusations she made, these were later found to be part of a delusional scheme affecting her at the time, and held by the General Medical Council to be groundless and mischievous. Indeed, I have myself listened to the wax cylinder, and can assure you that it contains no sounds except those associated with the culture of a window box.

I hope this is some help

Yours sincerely

Martin Stephens

Archivist

Angela watched us go, standing by her mother. She waved. She would have liked to be coming too. Churlishly, I did not wave back. I did not want to leave any part of us in that place: though of course it was too late for such scruples. Malpas belonged to Hannah now, and in her ten-month-old mercy she had assented to my proposal that Angela and Alice should remain for as long as they wished. So with our carload of books and papers and nappies and pictures, we drove under the crows to Rosslare, and did not return.

Epilogue

Until now, twenty-six years later.

We sat on the boat's deck and listened to the current gurgle in the anchor chain and watched the one dim light in the trees. Angela, perhaps, fifty-five now. Emily must be dead, and Alice, and Mairi. All swept away by the river. So that only the house remained, that great chilly block, filthy with the history that was inside it. My house. But not my history.

I told Jerry and Dave we were leaving. Then I went and put my toe on the windlass button. The anchor came out of the mud. The boat's nose fell away, pointing at the open sea. The house began to fall astern.

Out of the trees on the opposite bank came a low black boat, the shape of a pea-pod. It sat on the water lightly, leaving no wake. The man in it stared. For a moment, house and boat and man and we were in conjunction, outside time, self-contained. Then the headland passed between us and them, and they vanished from our lives for ever.

Hannah Costelloe
Menton, 2001